BRING
HER
HOME

DAVID BELL

BERKLEY
NEW YORK

BERKLEY
An imprint of Penguin Random House LLC
375 Hudson Street, New York, New York 10014

Copyright © 2017 by David J. Bell
Readers Guide copyright © 2017 by Penguin Random House LLC
Penguin Random House supports copyright. Copyright fuels creativity, encourages diverse voices,
promotes free speech, and creates a vibrant culture. Thank you for buying an authorized edition
of this book and for complying with copyright laws by not reproducing, scanning, or distributing
any part of it in any form without permission. You are supporting writers and allowing
Penguin Random House to continue to publish books for every reader.

BERKLEY is a registered trademark and the B colophon is a trademark of
Penguin Random House LLC.

Library of Congress Cataloging-in-Publication Data

Names: Bell, David, 1969 November 17– author.
Title: Bring her home/David Bell.
Description: First edition. | New York: Berkley, 2017.
Identifiers: LCCN 2016053301 (print) | LCCN 2017000021 (ebook) |
ISBN 9780399584442 (softcover) | ISBN 9780399584459 (ebook)
Subjects: LCSH: Fathers and daughters—Fiction. | Teenage girls—Fiction.
| BISAC: FICTION/Suspense. | GSAFD: Suspense fiction. | Mystery fiction.
Classification: LCC PS3602.E64544 B75 2017 (print) | LCC PS3602.E64544 (ebook) |
DDC 813/.6—dc23
LC record available at https://lccn.loc.gov/2016053301

First Edition: July 2017

Printed in the United States of America
1 3 5 7 9 10 8 6 4 2

Cover photos: forest by Danielle D. Hughson/Moment/Getty Images; hair by Sven Krobot/
EyeEm/Getty Images; leaves by OJO Images/Robert Daly/Iconica/Getty Images
Cover design by Colleen Reinhart
Title page photos: leaves by vnlit/Shutterstock Images

In memory of Ed Gorman and Jim Reiss

BRING
HER
HOME

PART
ONE

CHAPTER ONE

Bill Price stepped into the whirling chaos of the emergency room.

To the left, he saw a woman holding a red-faced, crying baby. The child's eyes were pools of tears, its mouth contorted into a wailing "O." The mother made shushing noises, but the baby didn't seem to hear them. Ahead of Bill, a teenage girl with a nose ring and a neck tattoo tried to calm a man holding a bloody rag against his shaven head. The man appeared agitated, waving his free hand around as though orating.

Bill looked to his right. He saw a small crowd gathered but no one he recognized.

He felt overwhelmed. Alone.

A nurse sat behind the admitting desk. She held a metal clipboard and wore half-moon glasses perched on the end of her nose. The glasses aged her, made her look ten years older than she probably was.

Bill approached her, a knot of tension growing in his chest.

"Excuse me," Bill said.

"Just a minute." The woman turned and stood up, walking away from Bill and going through a door behind her.

"Hello?" Bill said, his voice low.

He tapped his finger on the Formica desk.

She's here. Somewhere. She's here.

Should I just go find her?

"Hey," he said, his voice louder.

But the nurse didn't return. And no one else came out of the room to help him.

It felt like one of those dreams, the kind he'd been having too often lately. In the dreams, he'd open his mouth to scream but could make no sound. And the very act of trying to force words out made his throat feel as if he'd swallowed broken glass.

Bill looked around, hoping to see a familiar face. He saw only misery. The people in the room—the bleeders and the criers and the scared—were all his companions in misery.

She is here. She too is one of them. . . .

The admitting nurse appeared again. She still carried the clipboard. She went out of her way not to make eye contact with Bill. She focused on the desktop, coming over and reaching for a piece of paper.

"Excuse me," Bill said. "I'm here because—"

"One second, hon," she said.

The nurse lifted the paper, studying it through her glasses. Her hair was streaked with gray, her pink smock decorated with a small mustard stain.

"My daughter—," Bill said.

The woman raised her index finger in the air, requesting silence. She turned again, disappearing back behind the door through which she'd just emerged.

"Wait," Bill said.

But she was gone.

Bill craned his neck, rising up on tiptoes to try to see into the room through the window in the door. He couldn't.

"Hello?"

No response.

"Hey!" he said, his voice rising.

The nurse stuck her head out the door, her face creased with agitation. "Sir, we're backed up now. I'll be right there."

"No, no."

"Excuse me?"

"No!"

Echoing off the walls and the tiled floor, the single word cut through the room, bringing everyone to a halt. Bill sensed their anticipation, their fear, and, yes, their glee. They might get to witness a scene.

Some guy went apeshit in the ER. . . .

The nurse looked angry as she walked toward him.

"My daughter is here," Bill said. "Summer Price. Summer Price is my daughter."

And then the nurse's features softened. She understood.

She recognized the name. Everyone in the room probably did.

"Oh," she said, removing her glasses. "I know who to call."

A minute passed, maybe less, and then someone came through another door and into the emergency room, a familiar face above a coat and tie.

"Mr. Price?"

Bill felt the smallest measure of relief. "Detective Hawkins," he said. "Where is she? Where's Summer? Someone called. They said you were here—"

Hawkins wiggled his fingers, his hand in the air. "This way, okay? This way."

Bill followed the detective as Hawkins stepped over to a plain brown door and turned the knob. It looked like a janitor's closet, and Bill wondered why he was being led where mops and buckets were stored.

But then he saw it was a consultation room, one of those places where doctors took families to give them bad news. Bill had been in one of them before, almost a year and a half earlier. Nothing good ever happened in one of those rooms.

He stopped in his tracks even as Hawkins reached for him, trying to guide Bill along.

"Where is she?" Bill asked. "Just tell me something."

"Inside, Bill. Please? We can talk in there."

"Is she alive?" Bill felt anger laced with fear building in his chest, the heat and pressure at his core like lava waiting to burst forth. He gritted his teeth. "Just tell me the truth. On the phone they said she's alive. Is Summer alive?"

Hawkins stared directly into Bill's eyes. "She's alive, Bill. Summer *is* alive."

Bill closed his eyes, as though bracing for a blow. He felt a slight cooling in his body, a tiny sliver of relief. *Okay,* he thought. *Alive. She's alive.*

"When can I see her?" he asked, opening his eyes.

"She's alive, Bill," Hawkins said. "But—we should talk inside."

CHAPTER TWO

Bill's hands shook as he sat in the consultation room.

The space was small, confining. The papered walls were brown, earth tones, something meant to be soothing. The furniture felt stiff and unforgiving. Some well-meaning soul had placed a vase full of artificial flowers on the coffee table, an attempt to cheer the uncheerable. Bill stared at them, wishing his eyes were lasers that could destroy.

Hawkins sat down across from him. He looked to be in his early fifties, about ten years older than Bill. His salt-and-pepper hair was messy, as if he'd just come inside out of a stiff wind. He wore a sport coat and no tie, his graying chest hair reaching up from the open-neck shirt like spiders' legs.

Bill tried to keep his voice steady, to not shout at or berate the public servant before him. "Tell me what's going on, Detective. Tell me when I can see Summer. I want to see her."

The room felt too familiar. Hell, it might have been the same one he sat in when Julia died. He feared he would be getting horrible news from Detective Hawkins.

"Summer is alive, but she's critically injured. She's been stabilized, and they're moving her to Intensive Care. You can see her in a moment, once they have her settled in up there."

"What happened to her? How was she injured? Wait a minute—where the hell was she? She's been gone for almost two days. Where? Tell me something."

"They were found in Dunlap Park." Hawkins spoke with a soothing Kentucky accent, his words rolling out like a gentle stream. Bill tried to reconcile the awful message with the sweet sound of the messenger. "Early this morning, we received an anonymous call at the station. Not a nine-one-one call—just the general line. The caller told the officer who answered that two girls could be found in Dunlap Park."

"Dunlap Park?" Bill looked down and saw the flowers again. He lifted his head.

"Did Summer hang out there?" Hawkins asked.

"No," Bill said before the question was even finished. "I told her to stay away from that park. You know what it's like there."

"I do."

When Bill and Julia moved to town eight years earlier, brought there by Bill's job, the park was a notorious gay cruising ground. A math teacher from Jakesville High, a meek man with a wife and two children, was arrested in a park restroom after soliciting a male undercover cop. Just a few years earlier, a Jakesville town councilman was caught there having sex with a county auditor, a woman who was not his wife.

"All I hear about these days are the drugs out there. Heroin even," Bill said. "Right?"

"There have been some problems with that, yes. Also a homeless issue. People living in tents and other makeshift shelters. I'm not saying they are responsible for all of the crime, but it doesn't help."

"Some problems? No, I told Summer to never go there. Never."

Bill shifted forward in his uncomfortable chair, moving his body closer to the edge so that he almost slid onto the floor. He felt control slipping away as the angry part of him asserted itself, almost like another man who lived inside of him and jumped out in situations like the one in the hospital. "Who made this call? Do you know?"

"We don't. It was a man, speaking with a deep voice, possibly disguised. The call was too short to trace, and we don't record the calls that come in on that line. But the tip proved to be accurate, so we're going to do what we can to find out who called."

"You haven't told me what happened to her. What are her injuries? Hold it—are we talking about . . . Did somebody . . ."

"She's being checked for everything, including sexual assault. There's no obvious sign of sexual trauma, but some of her clothes were torn when she was found. We're lucky it's above freezing today, or exposure could have been an issue. She might have been out there for a number of hours."

Bill folded his hands and lowered his head. He wanted to close his eyes and make the whole situation go away. And he understood he was one of a long line of people to sit in a room like this and wish more than anything they could be somewhere else.

"The problem right now is that Summer has been severely beaten. She has extensive wounds to her head and torso. And a lot of swelling. They're doing X-rays and CAT scans and all of that to see how bad it is inside. But her injuries are quite severe, and you need to brace yourself for the likelihood that she'll need surgery and possibly extensive rehabilitation. Whoever did this wanted to hurt her, and they did. Very badly."

"I just want to see her. I don't want her lying somewhere alone while she goes through this. Can you do that for me, please?"

Hawkins said, "Of course. I just wanted you to understand where we stood before you saw her."

"She's my daughter," Bill said. "I can handle anything that has to do with her."

He hoped he could. He had to do it alone.

The two men stood up. Hawkins was larger than Bill, barrel-chested, but with a gentle manner that seemed in contrast with the probing intensity of his blue-gray eyes. Bill wondered if the police assigned Hawkins to Summer's case for a reason, if they believed that the detective's soothing tones and intimidating size would somehow placate, or, short of that, corral Bill and keep him calm.

Before Hawkins opened the door, Bill grabbed the detective's arm. It felt like taking hold of a tree trunk.

"Wait a minute," Bill said. "Them. You said *they* were found. You mean Summer and Haley. I didn't think to ask, but how is Haley doing?"

Hawkins hesitated for the briefest of seconds. Then he said, "I'm sorry, Bill, but Haley was deceased at the scene. She'd been beaten more severely than Summer. Her injuries were too extensive for any-one to survive."

The room tilted. Bill reached out and braced himself against the wall. Hawkins placed his rocklike hand on Bill's shoulder, steadying him.

"Are you going to pass out?" he asked. "Do you want some water?"

Bill stood still for a moment. Images of the ever-inseparable Haley and Summer flashed across his mind. The two skinny, blond girls running through a sprinkler on a summer day when they were ten. The two girls giggling over a silly movie when they were twelve. The two girls leaving his house together on Saturday afternoon . . .

"Her mother? She lives with her mother," Bill said.

"She's been informed." Hawkins's voice conveyed the pain of that conversation, the necessary but awful duty he probably performed himself. "Would you like to sit down?"

He felt sick. Physically sick. His body seemed to have turned to ice.

But he shook his head. He needed to go on.

His daughter needed him. Desperately.

But before he left the room, he needed to do one thing. He took two steps to the coffee table, took hold of the offending vase, and hurled it against the wall—screaming as he did so—where it shattered into hundreds of fragments.

Bill's breathing was fast, his heart thumping.

He really didn't feel any better. He turned to Hawkins, who wore an impassive look on his face.

"I'm okay," Bill said. "I want to see Summer. Now."

CHAPTER THREE

A doctor waited outside the door to Summer's room.

She looked young, not much older than Summer to Bill's eyes. She wore blue scrubs and a white lab coat. At some point in the day she'd put a pencil in her hair to hold it up in a messy bun.

"I'm Dr. Renee Davis," she said, cutting to the chase. "Summer's injuries are severe. She has two broken ribs. She also has a hairline fracture of the skull as well as a fracture of her eye socket. And a number of cuts and abrasions, some of which required stitches. She doesn't need surgery right now, but we can't rule that out. It's too early to tell whether she'll have any long-term damage from these injuries."

An annoying beeping sound came from Dr. Davis's pocket. She reached in and pressed a button, making it stop. But she didn't say anything else. She looked at Bill as though she expected him to say something. He felt like an actor on a stage who didn't know his lines.

"I don't understand," he said. "Long-term damage. What does that mean?"

He looked from the doctor to the detective and back again, unsure who would provide the answer.

"It means we don't know if her vision will be affected," Davis said. "Or if there is any brain damage. We're encouraged because there doesn't appear to be any bleeding or swelling in the brain. But we'll have to watch her closely for the next forty-eight hours."

Brain damage. Vision loss.

The nightmare might never end. It might continue on and on for the rest of Summer's life. The very essence of who she was could be shattered. Her laugh. Her intelligence. Her sarcastic humor.

But she was alive. Bill reminded himself of that.

Life. That mattered.

"I just want to see her," he said. "Even if she's not awake, I don't want her to be alone."

"Her injuries are quite severe," Davis said. "I'm not going to sugar-coat this, Mr. Price, but we have to watch her very carefully. She's gravely injured."

"I heard that already."

"Because of the swelling in her face, she looks . . ."

"Bad?" Bill said. "Is seeing that worse than not knowing where she was all weekend?"

"She's not going to look like the girl who left your house two days ago," Davis said.

Bill stepped past the doctor.

"Bill?" It was Detective Hawkins's voice.

Bill stopped and looked at the two professionals.

Hawkins turned to Davis as though they both knew something, and then Hawkins said, "Her hands are bandaged. She had a number of injuries to them."

"Are her hands permanently damaged?" Bill asked.

"It means she resisted, Bill," Hawkins said, his voice tinged with a paternal pride he seemed to want Bill to experience as well. "They're injuries consistent with putting up a very good fight."

Bill knew the detective was trying to make him feel better, but the information came as no surprise. Bill already knew Summer would resist. He knew she'd fight. He'd fought with Summer enough since Julia died.

But even as a child, she'd fought. Resisting bedtimes. Resisting foods.

Stubbornly independent. Bill quickly learned one of parenting's hardest lessons—you're going to see yourself, warts and all, in your kid.

"I hope she kicked his nuts up into his throat," Bill said.

The detective and the doctor just nodded, indicating agreement with the statement.

Bill said, "Doctor, the detective mentioned something about . . . checking for sexual assault. I was just . . . How long does that take to know?"

"Given her condition, we didn't conduct a full examination. Much of it is invasive. . . . But we'll hand everything over to the police."

"She didn't ever say anything, did she?" Bill asked. "Anything at all?"

Davis looked disappointed that she couldn't deliver better news to Bill. "No, she didn't. But please let me know if you have any questions. We'll all be keeping a close eye on her."

"Thanks," Bill said.

"When you come out, Bill, I'll have some more questions for you," Hawkins said. "I know you need to be in there now, but we have some more work to do out here."

Bill took a deep breath, one he seemed to hold at the center of his being, and pushed open the door to Summer's room.

CHAPTER FOUR

T he lights above were so bright.

Staring at the indistinct lump beneath the covers on the bed, Bill stood with his back to the door as it eased shut.

A monitor beeped a steady rhythm. His daughter's heartbeat. When Summer was a baby, Bill used to slip into the nursery and stand over the crib, just making sure her tiny heart continued to beat. She was so small then, so helpless, the life inside her seemed nearly impossible to sustain. A flickering candle in a strong wind.

Bill stepped over to the bed.

Her hands were wrapped in gauze. The blankets neatly tucked under her arms.

Her face, though, the left side . . . Swollen like a balloon and badly bruised. Her eyes swollen as well. A gauze wrap of some kind covered the top of her head, obscuring most of Summer's blond hair.

Bill knew he was biased—but she was a naturally beautiful girl. When she smiled, which wasn't as often since Julia died, she lit up so much, she could probably be used as a power source. Just like her mother. Whenever Bill looked at Summer's face, he saw Julia. Bill occasionally compared snapshots of Julia and Summer at the same age, and they were like twins. The bright blue of their eyes, the freckles that appeared when the weather turned warm.

Bill felt somewhat relieved to see there were no tubes down her throat or up her nose. She breathed on her own. An IV line dripped a clear fluid into the crook of her elbow.

Bill wanted to climb into the bed with her, to pull her close and keep her warm and safe. But he feared that placing any weight on or near her body would disturb her or cause her pain. He dragged a stool over to the side of the bed and sat down, and then placed his hand gently, ever so gently, on Summer's left forearm, the only area of her body not covered by injuries or blankets or bandages.

He stroked the soft, downy hair, felt the smoothness of her skin. Like a baby still. She looked as vulnerable and weak as that tiny infant in her crib fifteen years ago. Her arm looked even smaller than he remembered, bony like a child's.

"Oh, honey, what have they done to you?" he whispered. "Who did this to you?"

No response came. Summer's lips looked parched and cracked. Painfully so. Bill checked for a pitcher of water, for a rag he could dab against her lips, but there was none. He wanted to do something. To act.

But there was nothing for him to do.

"Are you okay, Summer? I'm here. It's Dad, and I'm going to be right here the whole time you get better."

Bill irrationally hoped for something. A grunt. A moan. A movement. But nothing came.

He continued to stroke her arm. "I'm torn, honey. Part of me wishes your mom were here to help us through this. And part of me is glad she isn't here to see you in this condition."

Bill's lower lip quivered, and he swallowed, biting back the tears. He took several deep breaths and tried to make sense of how his life had gone from being so normal a few days earlier to utterly out of control and disastrous in the hospital. He looked back over the chain of events. Summer asked if she could go out with Haley on Saturday afternoon. Bill said yes, because why wouldn't he? The girls did everything together. Except for the accident of being born into different families, they might very well have been siblings. And then by late Saturday evening, the girls were nowhere to be found. No responses to calls or texts. No sign of either one of them.

And nothing until that morning when the police called, waking Bill out of a restless, paper-thin sleep to say Summer had been found and to get to the hospital as soon as possible.

Bill hated the helplessness he felt, the sense of being paralyzed and impotent in the face of his daughter's injuries. In the face of what had been done to her. By someone.

Someone out there had committed this atrocity.

The door clicked open behind him. Bill didn't turn or acknowledge whoever it was. He kept his eyes trained on Summer, the gentle rising and falling of her chest as she breathed. The horrible swelling in her face. He replayed the doctor's words about long-term damage and wondered how anyone could recover from wounds like these. Would it be possible for her young body to heal?

And then what about the psychological scars? What if the tests they were doing for rape came back positive?

What if . . . ?

He refused to let every "what if" into his mind. One would lead to another, and then a tidal wave would roar through his brain.

"Bill?" The detective eased over and gently placed his hand on Bill's shoulder. "I think you and I need to talk a little more."

"Can't we do it here?" Bill asked. "I don't want to leave her."

"I think it's best if we talk in private," Hawkins said, his homey whisper allowing no room for discussion. He knew what was best, and he intended to see it done. "A nurse is on her way in to check on Summer. We should get out of the way."

"I want to stay close."

"You can, bud. But let's go find a private spot. The sooner you answer the questions I have, the better our chances of finding out who did this to Summer."

Bill continued to stare at Summer. His only child. His baby. That vibrant, bright life.

"It won't take long?" he asked.

"Not too long," Hawkins said.

Bill bent down and kissed her arm. "I love you, Summer. I'll be right back. It's Dad."

When he spoke those words, his daughter's cracked lips twitched, and she made a very low, very slight groaning sound deep in her throat.

She's in there, Bill thought. *She's in there, and she heard me.*

CHAPTER FIVE

Hawkins led Bill out to a small leather couch in the hallway. Nurses and technicians streamed past them, and Bill couldn't stop turning his head to look back at the door to Summer's room. He wanted to know whether anyone was coming or going from there, whether there were any hints of an emergency or a deepening crisis.

"Is there someone you want to call?" Hawkins asked, his big hands resting on his knees. "Family or friends?"

"My sister's coming tomorrow. She lives in Ohio."

"Good. You don't have other family in Jakesville, right?"

"You know neither Julia nor I was born here."

Hawkins got down to business by changing the direction of the conversation. "I wanted to bring you up-to-date on the investigation."

"I've been wondering about something," Bill said. "Has this ever happened here? I can't remember any crimes like this in Jakesville."

Hawkins pursed his lips thoughtfully. "Not recently, no. Nothing like a kidnapping. You know what it's like here, Bill. We don't have crimes like this. It's a safe community." He brought out a small notebook. "Bill, we're trying our best to piece together where those girls were and what they were doing on Saturday. You said you didn't know where they were going when they left your house."

"I assumed they were going to Haley's house."

"Right." Hawkins didn't say more, but Bill knew what he was thinking. What everyone would be thinking.

"Yeah, yeah. I didn't ask. I'm the clueless dad. They're both fifteen, Detective. They're going to be driving soon. Some of their friends already drive. I can't know everything they do. And, like you said, what could happen to them in Jakesville? It was daylight when they left."

"Sure." Hawkins nodded, his face encouraging and calm. His demeanor said, *No judgment here.* He cleared his throat. "The problem is only a couple of people saw them walking together that afternoon. Someone saw them heading down Anderson Road, right by your house and on the way to Haley's. So they could have been going that way." Hawkins frowned. "And then another witness claims to have seen Summer walking in the opposite direction on Anderson Road. Back toward your house."

"What does that mean?"

"We don't know." He held his hands out, pleading for patience. "This witness was an eighty-eight-year-old man who was driving by. And he had his license taken away by his kids because his eyesight is so bad. He saw a girl walking there. She may not have been Summer. And according to Haley's mother, they never came to her house. We're assuming they disappeared somewhere during that walk, but since we don't know exactly where they were going . . ."

"So someone just took them," Bill said. "A maniac pulled over and grabbed them. That happens, doesn't it?"

"It happens, yes," Hawkins said. "But it's rare. We're not ruling anything out at this point."

Bill closed his eyes. He told himself it was foolish to keep hoping for a break, but he couldn't turn his mind off. It worked to make him believe, to dangle possibilities, if only as a means of keeping his spirits up and his will strong. *Don't forget,* he told himself, *you just got the biggest break of all. She's here. She's alive.*

"That has to be it," Bill said. "Someone just grabbed them, threw them in the back of a van or something."

"I wanted to follow up on some of Summer's other friends," Hawkins said. "You told me that there were a few boys in her extended social circle. Maybe two or three of them."

"Yeah, sure."

Hawkins checked the notebook again, holding the pad at arm's length so he could read the writing. "We're talking about Clinton Fields, Todd Stone, and Brandon Cooke. Right?"

"Yeah, that's them. I guess. You have to understand that Julia knew more about Summer's friends than I did. She talked to Summer more, you know? Mother-and-daughter stuff."

"So how was your relationship with Summer? You said on Saturday that things could be tense between the two of you, but you never really told me why. Have you thought about that more?"

Bill lifted his hands, then let them fall back into his lap. He knew he seemed exasperated. He couldn't hide it. "Look, she's a teenage girl. I'm her middle-aged dad. I just didn't always know if I was teaching her the things she needed to be taught. You know how teenagers are."

"My kids are grown now, so it's been a while. Enlighten me."

"Okay, they're a little contemptuous of their parents. Summer seemed that way with me." Bill hoped that was the end, but the detective seemed to expect more. "We had tensions between us. Normal stuff, I guess. Shit, try being a man raising a woman. Her mother died a year and a half ago. It was just—" Something caught in his throat, and he paused, taking a deep breath. "It was Julia's birthday a couple of weeks ago. Would have been her birthday. Still is, I guess. But . . ."

"It's been hard for Summer," Hawkins said, prompting Bill. "Losing her mother."

"Yeah. It's hard enough just being a teenager. Ever since Julia died, Summer's been more rebellious, more mouthy. Standoffish to me. I thought we'd get closer because Julia died, and in some ways we have. We've cried together. Reminisced. But Summer is really hurting—I know that. She's like me. When she hurts, she gets angry. Defensive. And she's had a wall up since her mom died."

A nurse walked past, her pace quicker than anyone else's, and Bill turned his head to follow her. But she passed Summer's room, her white shoes squeaking against the tile floor.

"I understand. A young girl needs and wants her mother." Hawkins's voice pulled Bill back. "You never really answered the question of whether Summer was sexually active."

Bill turned all the way around, his eyes fixing on the detective, his teeth grinding together again at the back of his mouth. "I did answer that."

Hawkins sounded more assertive, more determined. Some of the Kentucky charm dropped from his voice. "You actually said you didn't want to talk about it. But now I think it's imperative that we know everything there is to know about Summer."

"She's fifteen. She's not sexually active. Why are you asking me this?"

Hawkins kept his blue-gray eyes trained on Bill, the scrutiny slicing in like sleet. "We have to understand every aspect of Summer's life if we're going to figure out who did this to her." He pointed theatrically at the door of Summer's room, conjuring the picture of the battered girl into Bill's mind. "We're looking into everything in this town. Her online communications. Her friends and teachers at school. Local sex offenders. You're our best resource about Summer."

Bill felt unnerved by where Hawkins was going. The conversation was causing a small pain to grow in the pit of his stomach. "Is there something I need to know?"

"Was she sexually active?" Hawkins asked. "Did she spend a lot of time with these boys from school? Or any boys that you know of?"

"Sure, they were friends." Bill chewed on a piece of loose skin near his thumbnail. "They've been to the house. Hell, Summer's known some of them since they were in grade school, so I've seen those kids the whole time they were growing up." Bill shifted in his seat, trying to articulate his thoughts about the boys Hawkins had mentioned. "They seemed like pretty normal kids. I know what boys want from girls. I know how pretty Summer and Haley both are. I thought I'd be dealing with this a little later. And I always thought I'd be dealing with it with Julia's help. Not on my own."

"And that's it about them?"

"She went to a dance with the Stone kid, but she told me they were just friends. Hanging out, I think she said. He and Summer went to junior high together. The other one, Cooke? Isn't he on the cross-country team at school?"

"He's a good runner, yes. He might go to state this year as a sophomore."

"And so the other one is Clinton Fields, right?" Bill asked. "Yeah, he's in their extended social circle. Kind of a jerky kid."

"Why do you say that?" Hawkins asked.

"I don't know. He's arrogant, snotty. Sure, he's polite to my face when he comes around, and he's a smart kid, a good student. But there's a hint of aggression and disrespect beneath everything he says. I can imagine him walking out the door and badmouthing me. High schools are full of those kinds of guys."

"Was he dating Summer?" Hawkins asked.

"They'd all been spending time together the past few months.

They were always with a group of kids, but I guess that's how they date now. Groups of kids."

"Is that it?"

"Is there something else I need to know about any of them?" Bill asked. "Did I miss something?"

"Remember, I'm investigating. Everything is on the table. And everyone."

"Where were they when Summer and Haley disappeared?"

"We're checking their alibis. We're checking everyone's alibis. They're kids. They weren't punching a clock at work or anything like that, but they say they were at the Fields house, playing video games. The parents weren't there."

Bill felt a jagged pressure growing behind his right eye, a pulsing sensation that made him squirm in his seat. "Just arrest them," he said. "Bring them in and get them to talk."

"It doesn't work quite that way, Bill."

"Do you think I care about their fucking civil liberties? You shouldn't either. Not when my daughter is in a coma and another girl is dead."

"Has Summer been in trouble lately?" Hawkins asked. "Anything? You said the two of you weren't getting along, that it's been tough since your wife died."

Bill thought back over the past year and a half, the series of ups and downs, arguments, and strained silences between Summer and him. "I told you already. It's been hard on her. And she's been pushing my buttons a little. Missing some curfews, not answering my texts when she's out, that kind of thing."

"I wanted to ask you about—"

"Wait," Bill said. "That Fields kid. Wasn't he into something a couple of years ago?"

An alarm started ringing overhead. An insistent beeping that probed at the headache growing behind Bill's right eye.

Two nurses rushed by, and Bill watched them.

They dashed into Summer's room.

"Jesus," Bill said. "No."

He followed in their wake and was cut off by Dr. Davis, who went in ahead of him. When Bill entered the room, he heard one phrase that stuck in his mind like a driven nail.

Her oxygen level's dropping.

CHAPTER SIX

Bill watched the medical team swarm around Summer.

They called out terms and numbers Bill didn't understand. It was like hearing another language.

Her voice calm and steady, Dr. Davis said, "We're going to have to put in a chest tube."

Bill stepped forward as Dr. Davis pulled on a pair of surgical gloves. They snapped into place against her wrists. She reached toward a silver tray and lifted a shining scalpel, something that looked sharp enough to cut through a tree trunk.

"You have to go, Mr. Price," Davis said.

A nurse started removing Summer's gown, exposing her breast. Another nurse used alcohol to sterilize the skin where the doctor intended to cut. Bill didn't like the way they manhandled her, strangers treating her body as if it were a piece of meat.

Someone stepped in front of him, a pudgy young man in scrubs, his thinning hair a stringy mess. "Why don't you just step outside, sir?"

"I want to stay."

"You can't be in here, sir."

The man placed his hand on Bill's chest and appli[...]
firm pressure, moving him backward and toward the d[...]
along, but he said, "You can't be in there either. I don't want [...]
strange man—"

But he was out the door and into the hallway, and the man in the
scrubs disappeared inside the room again. Bill took a step forward,
intending to go back in, but he stopped himself.

The doctor was right. He didn't want to see that.

When Summer was little and receiving a new vaccine every other
month, it was Julia who went with her. Julia held her hand and told
her to look the other way. Bill either didn't make trips to the doctor,
or stayed in the waiting room reading out-of-date magazines while
Julia took their daughter back.

He saw that shining, brutally sharp scalpel in his mind again. A
device made to puncture and slice and penetrate. He'd watched
enough TV shows to know they'd be slipping a rubber tube through
the incision. The images nauseated him.

He stepped back from the door and turned around.

Detective Hawkins waited. He placed one of his ham-hock hands
on Bill's shoulder and made a gesture with his head, indicating that
Bill should return to his seat on the couch where they had been talking. Bill happily obliged. It felt good to sit, and the nausea subsided
once he was on the couch.

Hawkins wandered off for a moment and came back with a paper
cup full of water. "Drink this," he said.

Bill swallowed the cool water and smacked his lips. "Thank you."

"You're sure there's no one you want to call?" Hawkins asked.
"What about your neighbor? Mr. Fleetwood?"

"Adam."

"Right. You're good friends with him. Do you want to call him to
come sit with you?"

"I'll talk to him soon. He might be working." Bill used a shaking hand to reach into his pants pocket. He pulled out his phone and checked the screen. A text. "My sister. Paige. She's coming. Tomorrow, I think."

Bill struggled to type a response, his hands shaking like a ninety-year-old man's. He marveled at the way Summer and Haley composed texts at lightning speed, almost like machines trained to do so.

"How about work? Do you need to check in there?"

"I'm an IT guy at a small college," Bill said. "They can live without me for a while. They'll probably miss me the most when I can't go to Trivia Tuesday at the Tenth Inning."

Hawkins stared at him blankly.

"The sports bar. A group of us from work plays trivia there."

"Right, I hear you," Hawkins said. He looked at the closed door to Summer's room and then back at Bill. The detective's hands rested on his hips, the skin of his thick ring finger swallowing the gold band.

"What about that stuff you were asking me?" Bill asked, his voice shaky. "Summer's behavior. I'm confused by all of this right now. I don't know what to think."

"I understand completely," Hawkins said. "I'll come back and check on you later."

"That Fields kid, Clinton," Bill said. "There was something about him, something that happened a year or two ago. What was it?"

Hawkins took a moment before he answered. "He got in a fight at school with another kid."

Bill waited. "That's it? I thought there was more—" Then it came back to Bill. The story made the local news for a couple of days. Everybody with kids at the high school heard about it and talked about it. "Oh, I remember. Not just a fight, Detective." Bill felt sweat forming at his hairline, a sticky, cloying liquid. "He hurt that kid. Put him in the hospital, right?"

"He did, Bill. Clinton Fields got in a fight at the bus stop almost two years ago, when he was fourteen. Broke the other boy's jaw."

"Oh, no." Bill's hand went to his face involuntarily to rub his own jaw. "He's a thug—that's what you're telling me. A true menace. And you don't want to arrest him yet?"

"Did Summer ever mention him being violent? Or threatening violence?"

"No. But what does that matter? You've got to talk to him. Arrest him."

"I will, Bill. We're well aware of all of this. In fact, I'm on my way to check into it more right now."

"Will you tell me what you find?"

"Of course. Will you call me if you need anything? And let me know how Summer is." He started to walk away and stopped, his big body showing surprising grace. "I had a collapsed lung once. When I was in college. I collided with another guy during a basketball game. That was enough to do it. I had to have the whole chest-tube thing in to relieve the pressure. The worst part was in the beginning. They said I'd feel a little discomfort, and then they put that tube in." Hawkins winced, and the exaggerated face looked comical on the big man. "But then I could breathe again."

Bill didn't know what to say, so he said, "Thanks."

"My point is, a collapsed lung isn't as scary as it looks."

"That's one thing that isn't, I guess," Bill said.

CHAPTER SEVEN

Bill jumped off the couch when Dr. Davis came out of Summer's room.

She looked slightly winded, like a jogger after a good, solid run. She told Bill that everything had gone according to plan. "We reinflated the lung, and her oxygen levels are returning to normal. We'll continue to keep an eye on everything else. Our goal here is to make sure she's stable. When she is, we'll transfer her to our rehab wing."

"I'm going to go back in and sit with her."

"Give them a few minutes to get everything cleaned up."

Bill imagined a room swimming in his daughter's blood, the stained scalpel tossed on the floor amid soiled bandages. They needed to put her gown back on the proper way, to cover Summer up so everyone in the world couldn't just walk in and see her breast exposed. His daughter had been handed over to strangers for the past two days. First when she was kidnapped and beaten and who knew what else. And again in the hospital where her body had been probed and prodded and sliced.

"I can contact the hospital social worker if you'd like," Davis said.

"Or the chaplain. I imagine people will want to come by and see Summer. Friends from school. Family. It might get complicated."

"No, thanks," Bill said. "I'm good."

Davis considered him for a moment, then said, "The nurses will let you know when you can go back in."

Bill returned to the couch and waited. The headache that had started forming when he was speaking with Hawkins seemed to have eased. He heard back from Paige. She told him, via text, that she intended to come directly to the hospital when she reached Jakesville the next day.

He hadn't seen his younger sister in six months. They spoke on the phone from time to time, but mostly they communicated through texts and Facebook messages. They shared an irreverent sense of humor, and each tried to top the other by sending the most bizarre news stories or links to weird Web sites. On more than one occasion, Bill ended up chuckling to himself at work or at home over one of Paige's messages.

Bill found himself looking forward to her arrival. He and Paige grew close the summer before he left for college when they spent a week driving around the country seeing R.E.M. in concert five times. Bill had never said it out loud, but he wished they'd grown closer sooner instead of right before he moved away. He always seemed to figure things out when it was too late. It was like a curse.

Someone said his name just then, and he looked up.

"There he is."

Bill saw two figures approaching him from down the hallway. It took a moment, but then he saw who one of them was. Candy Rodgers, Haley's mom. An older man with steel gray hair walked by her side. He wore a polo shirt and khaki pants with a cell phone clipped to the belt.

Bill stood up. Candy came directly toward Bill, her arms open for a hug. She wore black pants and a pink shirt, and a gold bracelet jangled from her wrist as she and Bill embraced. He caught a whiff of something floral, a shampoo or perfume.

"I'm so sorry, Candy."

"I'm sorry too."

They held each other longer than Bill was expecting. He'd never hugged Candy Rodgers before, didn't even know her very well. He did know Haley's parents were divorced—apparently a nasty split—and her father lived out west and had little contact with the family. Bill wondered if the man with Candy was a relative or a new love interest.

"This is our pastor," Candy said, nodding at the man in the khaki pants. "Caleb Blankenship."

The minister, who looked to be about sixty, gave Bill a firm handshake and a sympathetic look. Candy dabbed at her eyes with a balled-up tissue. She looked older than Bill remembered, but that may have been because she wasn't wearing makeup. Her unnaturally blond hair hung limp and loose around her shoulders.

"I don't know what to say, Candy," Bill said. "I'm just so sorry about Haley. My God. She was such a wonderful, beautiful young girl."

"I asked where you were, where Summer was, and they told us. I couldn't leave the hospital without coming up here and seeing her." She gestured widely. "The police have been asking a lot of questions, of course, and Caleb was kind enough to come with me while I . . . It turns out I couldn't really make an identification. I mean, Haley, her body . . . It's in bad shape." Her voice sounded on the edge of breaking, but she held it together, impressing Bill with her poise. "We're going to the funeral home next."

"Oh, my God," Bill said. "I can't imagine."

"How is Summer?" Candy asked. "They didn't say much to us except that she was critically injured."

Bill tried to explain what he knew of Summer's condition. He managed to talk about the collapsed lung, but the rest of the words jumbled in his brain, and he found himself verbally flailing until Candy placed her hand on his elbow.

"It's okay," she said. "It's all too complicated."

Bill felt calmed by seeing Candy's familiar face. He had little in common with Haley's family and didn't really travel in the same circles they did, with the exception of attending the same events at the school and picking up and dropping the girls off at each other's house. If it hadn't been for the kids' friendship—which started when they were in the first grade and never stopped—he wouldn't know much about Candy at all. But Candy's was the first friendly face he'd seen all morning, and he found the tension in his chest, the grinding of his back molars against each other, easing in her presence.

"Do you know anything about this, Candy?" Bill asked. "Do you know what the girls were doing or how they ended up out in that park? Or who might have tipped off the police?"

"I don't know anything," Candy said. "The police don't sound like they know very much either. Nobody does. They said you thought they were coming to our house, but they never showed up. I was home. I would have seen them. Haley told me she was going to your house."

"We have a lot of unanswered questions now," Caleb, the pastor, said.

Bill gave him a quick look. "The police are hinting at all kinds of things."

"Let's not delve into these complicated matters in a time of grief," Caleb said. "Candy has to go—"

"Candy, do you know something about these boys? Do you think they're involved? Detective Hawkins was asking me about them."

"It's okay, Caleb," she said. Her lip quivered for a long moment, and she lifted her hand to her chest while she suppressed a deep sob.

Collected again, she turned to Bill. "The police have been asking me about everything, but I don't know what I can tell them. Haley's sex life." She shivered. "All kinds of things. I mean, I'm no dummy. I know what kids do. But I can't imagine who would do this." She made a vague gesture in the direction of Summer's room.

"I don't know anything either," Bill said, studying Candy's face. He wanted her to say something, anything, to convince him none of it was real. Candy was a mother. She must know more than he did. "He was asking me about Clinton Fields and those other kids. Remember he beat that kid up a couple of years ago? Beat him up bad—"

But then Bill remembered himself. The woman standing before him had just lost her daughter. Lost. Gone forever. He dialed back on his own zealousness. He knew Candy was experiencing the same things he was experiencing. But multiplied to an infinite degree.

"I'm sorry, Candy," he said. "I shouldn't be pushing about these things. Haley was a wonderful girl. She and Summer . . . They were such good friends. My God . . . since first grade. All those trips to the mall, the sleepovers. Girl Scouts . . ."

"They were great friends, yes."

"Maybe . . ." He didn't know if completing the thought would bring any comfort to anyone. But Candy gave him an expectant look, so he finished by saying, "Well, at least they weren't alone. They were together when this happened."

Candy considered the statement for a moment, her face distant, her eyes red with grief. "That is a good thought."

A young nurse with long red hair tied in a ponytail emerged from Summer's room and approached Bill. She told him that he could go back in and sit with his daughter whenever he wanted, that she was resting comfortably and breathing normally.

"I should get back inside there," Bill said. "I don't want her to be alone."

"Of course." She looked at Caleb. "I think I have to be the one to call Rich." Bill knew Rich was Haley's father. Candy's voice held steady. "He's going to be shocked. I don't know what other word to use."

Bill looked to the pastor for help and, finding none, said, "Can you tell Rich . . . tell him how sorry I am? I don't know what else to say right now."

But Candy's eyes drifted past Bill in the direction of Summer's room. Bill looked back, expecting to see something, but there was nothing going on. Nothing he could see.

"What is it?" he asked.

"We were wondering about something," Candy said, looking over at Caleb.

"We were wondering if we could step inside and pray for Summer," Caleb said.

"I don't . . ."

Candy reached out and took Bill's hand. Her skin felt hot, almost feverish. "I know you haven't been attending a church, not since Julia died." She looked over at Caleb as though seeking encouragement. "We thought maybe prayers would help right now as Summer heals."

Bill looked down to where their hands were joined, felt the pressure she exerted against his skin. It seemed like a form of pleading, a way of begging Bill to let them into Summer's room. And while he wasn't entirely comfortable with the religious display, he also couldn't say no to a mother who had just lost her daughter in such a horrible way.

"Okay," Bill said. "Sure."

Candy squeezed even harder. "Good. I think you'll see God can do a lot of good in Summer's life. It's never too late for that to happen."

CHAPTER EIGHT

The three of them entered Summer's room. Bill made sure he went in first, and he checked her left side where the chest tube had been inserted. The tube remained in place, its rubber length snaking out from under her hospital gown and reaching a portable machine by the side of the bed. Summer's gown was mostly back in place over her chest, so Bill waved Candy and the pastor forward.

Candy gasped when she saw Summer. Bill remembered Candy's comment from moments before about not being able to identify Haley's body due to the damage inflicted. He shuddered.

The pastor moved to the left side of the bed, his face solemn, and Candy moved next to him. Bill stayed on the other side—across Summer's body and opposite them—and watched as they both bowed their heads and closed their eyes.

Bill and Julia had been married in the Catholic Church. They'd both attended their whole lives, and when Summer was born, they raised her in the church as well. Baptism, First Communion, Sunday school. They did it all. He could summon the feel of the heavy wooden pews, the sickeningly sweet aroma of incense. Bill never would have described himself as a man of great faith or a true believer, but he liked the structure the church provided in his life, the sense that there were boundaries and end lines and a promise of order amid the chaos.

Candy leaned close. "Oh, Summer, you sweet girl. I'm so sorry, baby."

Summer's lips moved. One side of her mouth turned down in an agitated frown.

"It's okay, Summer. I know you're in there."

She made the face again, even more agitated. Candy smiled without showing her teeth.

"Father above," Caleb said. "We come to you today . . ."

Bill kept his eyes open, watching his daughter. When Julia died suddenly and unexpectedly, Bill couldn't summon any desire to set foot inside a church again. Something disappeared inside of him that day, like dry ground sucking down a puddle of water. He bristled at the cruelty of some unseen being who ruled the universe and randomly struck down his wife at such a young age. But Julia's death also led to an intense questioning of himself. Bill couldn't see a path forward—not through any church, at least—that would allow him to forgive himself for not being there when Julia died. Instead, he lived with the image of Julia falling off the ladder to the kitchen floor— alone, scared, and in pain as she suffered her fatal injury. And Bill wasn't even the first to find her. Summer came home from school and found her dead mother on the cold linoleum like a beached fish.

"We ask this all in the name of Jesus, who saves us. Amen."

"Amen," Candy said.

A silence settled over the room, the gentle hisses and beeps of the machines the only noises as both of them looked at Bill. He ignored their appraisal and kept his mouth shut, refusing to join in the amen chorus.

Candy looked wounded by Bill's silence, and he wished he'd gone along, wished he'd done whatever he could for the grieving woman in the room. She stepped forward and bent down, placing her hand on Summer's arm and giving it a gentle squeeze.

"We're praying for you, Summer. We're all behind you, honey."

A moment passed, and rather than making the frowning face, Summer's lips parted and smacked together a few times. Bill moved closer, watching, fearing that something was wrong, but the girl continued to work her lips that way for about ten seconds as though trying to form a word. An "M" sound or an "O." When that effort failed, she simply emitted a very low and brief groan. And then silence.

Candy smiled, her body still bent toward the bed. "We know you're in there," she said. "We hear you."

"She did that earlier when I was talking to her," Bill said, fully aware that the movement of Summer's lips as Candy spoke outpaced anything she had done at the sound of Bill's voice. But maybe she felt better, more energetic, with a reinflated lung.

The same red-haired nurse slipped through the door, her shoes making no sound, as though she walked on air. "We might want to limit our visits," she said. "Immediate family only and not too long."

"We were just going," Caleb said, offering the calming, pastoral smile.

"We'll come back and see you, Summer," Candy said.

And again the same movement of Summer's lips, although briefer and with less energy.

When the three of them were out in the hall, Bill kept his distance as Candy started to lean in for a hug.

"I felt something in there, Bill," she said. "I felt . . . I don't know."

"What did you mean by saying it's not too late for God to come into Summer's life?" he asked.

Candy didn't answer, so Caleb said, "It's been an extremely long morning for everyone." He placed his hand on the small of Candy's back and tried to gently guide her away from Bill and the entrance to Summer's room.

"Are you saying if Summer went to church on a regular basis, this wouldn't have happened to her?" Bill asked, stopping them. "Both of our daughters were out there. They both were hurt."

Candy moved away from Caleb's touch and faced Bill. Her eyes were filled with tears, and Bill saw deep lines etched at the corners of her mouth. "You know as well as I do that Haley worshipped Summer. She did everything Summer did. The clothes, the hair, the music. Summer was the leader, the dominant one."

"Summer is strong-willed," Bill said. "That's a good quality."

"I remember the time they stole that tube of lipstick from Walgreens. Haley came home, and she told me, 'Mom, Summer pushed me into doing it.'"

"You're talking about the lipstick they stole when they were twelve?"

"And the missed curfews lately. The back talk. That's not my daughter. Summer strolls into my house and talks to me like I'm her peer, like we're both adults. She's fifteen going on thirty-five."

"She's mature," Bill said. "She's an only child."

"Haley was just so . . . good-natured." Candy's face crumpled with grief. "Who do you think followed who . . . whatever they were doing?"

Bill wanted to say more, but he didn't as Caleb led Candy away.

When Bill turned around, the red-haired nurse stood in his way. She held a small bottle, something Bill didn't recognize. She seemed to want to say something to him but didn't. He couldn't identify the source of the expectant look on her face.

"Were we talking too loud?" Bill asked. He realized his hands were clenched into fists in the aftermath of his exchange with Candy, and it required a conscious effort to relax them. His heart thumped, and he knew if he'd been at home, he would have thrown something in frustration.

"No," the nurse said. "Not at all. I just wanted to tell you I'm going in to take care of something with Summer. Something quick."

"She's okay?"

"There's no problem." The nurse again looked like she wanted to say more. Her eyes almost appeared mischievous, like she possessed a secret. "Why don't you come in and I'll show you?"

Bill followed her through the door and watched as she gently moved the covers down Summer's body. Bill held his hand out. "Wait. What is this?"

"It's okay," she said, and continued on. The covers now down, she took great care lifting Summer's gown. Bill felt like he shouldn't be looking, but the nurse nodded to Summer's stomach.

First he saw the bruise. About the size of an orange, or someone's fist, it sat just above her belly button. And his daughter looked even thinner than he remembered. Had she been losing weight? Dieting? Or just getting taller and losing her baby fat?

Then he saw what the nurse must have wanted him to notice.

"What's that?" he asked, although he knew. A half-inch-wide hoop was stuck into the soft flesh, the skin around the post red and tender. "Who did that to her?"

"Somebody who didn't know to sterilize first," the nurse said. "We're pumping her full of antibiotics through the IV, but I thought I'd give it a cleaning as well."

"She didn't have that—" But Bill stopped himself. How did he know what she'd done to her body? He hadn't seen his daughter naked since she was three. And the piercing fit with her recent defiant, rebellious attitude. She probably would have loved to see the look on Bill's face when he discovered it.

He also remembered Hawkins's questions about her sex life. She was fifteen, living on the border between girl and woman.

"I guess I don't know much of anything," Bill said, somewhat defeated.

The nurse nodded as she worked, applying a solution to a piece of gauze. She carefully wiped the red skin around the piercing, her thin fingers as gentle and steady as a surgeon's.

"I figure I just did Summer a favor," she said while she worked. "When she wakes up, you'll be so happy to see her, you won't care about a little thing like a piercing she got without your permission. It's not a big deal to have one. Some of us got them in college." She chuckled softly.

Bill sensed that he was being manipulated, that just like Hawkins saying the collapsed lung wasn't as bad as it seemed, the nurse was not so subtly reminding him of his priorities.

He didn't need to be reminded, even though the sight of the piercing made his skin crawl. Not knowing how much Summer could hear or understand, he moved to the head of the bed and leaned down close.

"I don't care about the piercing," he said. "All I care about is your getting better."

Summer started moving her lips, again as if she wanted to form a word. Bill looked to the nurse, who shrugged lightly, the bottle of alcohol and the swab still in her hand.

"Do you want to say something, Summer? It's Dad."

And the puckering grew more rapid, accompanied by a low clucking sound in her mouth, the intensity of the movement increasing. Her head twitched once, to the left and then back to the right.

"Did you want to say something to me?" Bill asked. "Do you want something from me?"

Bill leaned in even closer. And he heard the word she seemed to be saying.

"No. No. No. No. No. No."

CHAPTER NINE

Near noon the next day, a gentle touch on his shoulder brought him awake.

He lurched forward in the seat, having dozed off.

"Summer?"

Reality landed on him again. He saw the hospital bed before him, the tubes, and heard the beeping. His daughter's body under the covers, little changed in the past day.

"I'm sorry," a voice said.

He looked up, his head foggy with sleep. A familiar and welcome face smiled down at him. Paige.

"You're here," he said, standing up.

"I thought about not waking you."

"I'm glad you did." He reached out and took his sister into his arms, pulling her close and gripping her as tightly as he would a life preserver. "You're a sight for sore eyes."

They stepped back, taking each other in. "I'm sorry I couldn't come sooner."

"It's okay. You have a family, a life." He gestured at the room, the bed. Summer's unconscious form. "I'm glad to have the support."

"I'm here." Paige wiped tears from her cheeks. "I'm sorry for all of this. I can't believe . . ." She left the thought unfinished, but Bill understood.

"It looks terrible," he said. "She looks terrible." Bill remembered Summer's slight reactions from the day before, both when he spoke to her and when Candy did. He reminded himself to lower his voice so she didn't hear him talking about her condition in such bleak terms, even if the terms were perfectly appropriate. "Let's talk in the hallway."

He followed his sister out. He noticed paint splatters on her scuffed boots, evidence of the art she created in the spare time she stole from raising her two teenagers, Summer's cousins. She looked like she'd gained a little weight since the last time they'd seen each other, but she wore it well. Their mother, dead more than ten years, always said Paige had a big appetite for everything—life, food, drink, fun. The comment made Paige fume when she was an awkward teenager, two years younger than Bill, but he always saw it as a compliment. His sister was open to the world, one of those people who lived with her arms thrown open wide. He envied her easygoing nature, her enthusiastic acceptance of whatever came her way.

When they made their trip together, the one following R.E.M., it was Paige whose energy never flagged. It was Paige who pushed for them to do more and more. He felt the whole time like he was swimming in her wake.

And he had one of the best times of his life.

When they were out in the hallway, Paige pointed at the middle-aged security guard and said loudly enough for the man to hear, "That guy tried to tell me immediate family only when I got here, but I told them I was Summer's aunt. And your sister. And if they tried to keep me out, I'd knock somebody down."

Bill shrugged at the guard, who showed no reaction to Paige's words. "I told him you were coming today." Bill felt stuck. What did he want to say to his sister? "Really, Paige, thanks for coming. I know you have the kids, and it's a long drive."

"Of course. Mom and Dad are dead, so you're stuck with me."

The comment struck Bill as oddly funny, and he almost laughed. And almost laughing felt good.

He quickly told her where they found Summer and Haley and about Summer's condition, including the collapsed lung. When he said that Haley was dead, Paige raised her hand to her mouth, stifling her own cry of grief over Summer's friend.

"She was a sweet girl, wasn't she?" she asked. "An easygoing kid. I remember meeting her at your house. Those two were together all the time, joined at the hip."

"Yeah," Bill said. "They were just like that. They were going somewhere together on Saturday when they disappeared. We're just not sure where."

"Ugh."

"I didn't ask," Bill said. "I just let them go out the door to . . . wherever. Why did I do that? Why didn't I ask? Just ask one question, that's all I needed to do."

"Bill, it's okay. This isn't your fault."

"Every other parent asks these questions. Why didn't I? You know Summer's heart was broken by Julia's death and I'm trying not to be another drag on her life."

"I get it," Paige said. "I do."

A bundle of words jammed up in Bill's throat. "Come here," he said, and led Paige farther away from the nurses' station and over to the couch where he had sat with Hawkins. When they were seated Bill said, "Get a load of what the cops are saying."

"Do they have a suspect?"

Every atom in Bill's body quivered as he spoke. He told her that the police had been questioning him about Summer's sex life and the boys she knew at school, including Clinton's history of violence. All the words that had been jumbled in his throat fell out of his mouth like heavy stones.

When he was finished, he looked back at his sister. Paige's lips were parted, her cheeks flushed red. She'd flushed the same way when she was angry or upset ever since she was a little kid throwing tantrums over their parents' rules and edicts, and he saw the shadow of that child in her face, even though a few more lines were apparent and her once-brown hair was streaked with a little gray. He saw Summer there as well, in the shape of her nose.

"You're thinking maybe a kid at school did something to Summer," she said, the fury simmering below her words. "That maybe they hurt her."

"What else can I think?" he said. "What else am I supposed to conclude when the cops show that kind of interest in these kids? I know what it's like to be a boy. I was as horny as any of them when I was a teen. You know, the cops told me she fought back, that her hands and fingers are a mess because she fought off her attacker. Maybe those boys tried to do something to her, and she let them have it. Summer was spending time with them, especially the one named Todd Stone. If his friend, this Clinton Fields, has beat up other kids, who's to say he didn't do it to Summer?"

"If Summer has your temper, yes, I can imagine she'd fight back."

"I'm trying not to think of calling my neighbor, Adam, and asking to borrow his gun. Or going to a pawnshop and buying one myself."

"I'm sorry, Bill, but you have to let the police handle this. You can't fly off the handle or confront anybody about this. You need to be here for Summer. Let the cops do their jobs."

"That's so rational of you."

"Has Summer said anything or shown any significant signs?"

Bill remembered that one word, that one syllable repeated over and over as he leaned in close to Summer's face.

No. No. No. No. No.

Was she remembering the attack? Did she not want him so close when she was in such pain?

"Not really. Just some groans. She barely moved all night or this morning."

"Maybe she'll talk soon."

He'd reached a point of exasperation. "And she has a fucking belly button ring, Paige. A belly button ring. I didn't even know. The nurse showed me. Am I the most clueless dad on earth? Did I simply have no idea about anything my daughter was doing in her life? I'm thinking maybe I don't really understand what fifteen-year-olds do."

"Nobody does, Bill."

Something sounded off in the tone of Paige's voice. He'd heard her give pep talks before, had even on occasion been on the receiving end of one. When she dished out her advice or pick-me-ups, Paige's voice achieved a buoyancy, a sense that her words and maybe even her body were about to lift off into the air.

In the Intensive Care hallway, her tone became muted, the look on her face apprehensive. Bill wanted to ascribe the changes to the circumstances, to know that his sister looked and sounded different because of the gravity of the situation. But he didn't buy it. That wasn't Paige's style at all. It would be more likely for her tone to rise, for her energy level to swell as the situation grew more dire. At their father's funeral, when they were both in their twenties, Paige became giggly at the viewing, responding to every offer of sympathy with a high-pitched laugh. At the end of the evening, he pulled her aside and told her to knock it off, that they were at a funeral. That was when Paige cried, broke down sobbing in his arms, making him feel—justifiably—like the biggest jerk alive.

"What's going on, Paige?" he asked. "What are you holding back?"

"I want you to keep your perspective here," she said. "I know you're probably on the brink of losing your cool and getting frustrated."

"Paige." But she was right. His hands were clenched into fists. He'd already spotted a stack of magazines on a side table, objects ripe for throwing. "What are you talking about?"

"I know something that might be related to all of this," she said. "Shit, I didn't want to dump it on you right away, but it might shed some light on these things you're talking about with these boys."

CHAPTER TEN

Bill waited for Paige to go on.

For the first time he noticed that some kind of low, tinny Muzak bled out of speakers set into the ceiling tiles over his head, the notes so faint and distant as to barely be heard. And he recognized his sister's ploy. At various times, both his parents and Paige had used it on him. They mentioned his temper before they told him something, suggesting that any display of anger was unnecessary and even unreasonable.

But he didn't dwell on his sister's psychological manipulations. He stopped looking for something to throw and zeroed in on her, waiting to hear what she knew.

"What, Paige?" he asked, the words emerging from his mouth like pellets of ice.

"Summer called me. About six months ago."

"I didn't know she called you."

"She never had before. But she wanted my advice about something. Remember, Bill, she doesn't have a mom she can go to anymore. This is the kind of thing I would have tried to talk to Mom about when I was fifteen. She wouldn't have listened, but I would have wanted her to. And we'd just visited, remember? We'd driven through and spent some time with both of you, so I was, I don't know, fresh in her mind."

"What are we talking about here?" Bill asked.

"She wanted to know about birth control. About the best kind to use and where to get it. She was worried about going on the pill because she'd heard that it affects your body and your moods."

"She was on the pill?"

"I don't know," Paige said. "She never called back. And I . . . To be honest, she seemed kind of freaked out by the conversation, so I assumed maybe she dropped the whole thing."

"You didn't follow up with her to see what she decided to do?"

Paige gave him a withering look. "How stupid do you think I am? Of course I followed up. I texted her and asked her how things were going. She told me she had everything under control, that she didn't think she needed any birth control after all. She seemed certain. Maybe she got cold feet. That's what I hoped. I hoped she got cold feet and decided to wait before taking such a big step."

In the swirl of emotions that tumbled through his chest, sadness quickly overcame anger as his response to Paige's information. How lonely and scared Summer must have been, reaching out to an aunt who lived in another state. How much she must have craved and longed for the presence of her mother over the past year.

"Why didn't you tell me?" he asked.

"Bill, I was in an almost impossible situation," Paige said. "If I told you, I'd betray her trust forever. She'd never open up to either one of us again."

"She asked you not to tell me?"

"Of course. She didn't want her dad to know about these things."

"I'd have told you if it was your kid."

"My kids wouldn't call you."

"You know what? Fuck you, Paige."

"Bill." She placed her hand on his arm, even though he'd made no move to stand up. "None of this is helping Summer, okay? If you're pissed at me, fine. You can be pissed at me. Maybe I was wrong—I don't know. I'm telling you this so you know what to make of what the police are telling you."

Bill took a few deep breaths. He scratched at the back of his head where his hair stood up. He hadn't taken a shower or shaven or anything before running out the door the previous morning when the police called.

"So she might have been having sex with one of those boys," he said. "Probably that little shit Todd Stone who she went to that dance with. And he or his friends turned on her for some reason, beat the crap out of her." He wrung his hands together. "But she's only fifteen."

"Fifteen-year-olds have sex," Paige said. "I did."

"I know."

"It's not a problem that I had sex when I was fifteen, Bill. You and Mom and Dad acted like it was, but it wasn't. It was normal. *I* was normal."

"And here I was worried about some pudgy male orderly seeing her with her clothes off."

"Bill, you need to make this about Summer's well-being, about catching the person who hurt her. And killed Haley." Paige looked distracted for a moment, her brow furrowing. "Why did she go to a dance with one of these boys if they're such shits?"

"Good question. Todd's smart, I guess. Gets good grades. He's a good-looking kid. They're both involved in student council, and they worked on this group project for their history class last semester. His friend Clinton, I don't know quite as well. I guess as long as you're on his good side, he won't break your jaw."

Paige reached up and touched her face. "I don't even want to think about that."

"You're going to tell the police all about this," Bill said, pointing at her. "Then the detective can stare at me and shake his head and secretly wonder why I knew so little about my own child. He'll call me 'bud' in his syrupy Southern voice, but inside he'll think I had no control over my kid."

"They just want to catch the bad guy." Paige studied Bill as he pulled out his phone and prepared to call Hawkins. "Have you been sitting here this whole time? When's the last time you took a shower?"

"I don't even know. Over the last few days . . . I've barely eaten."

"Do you want to go home and take a shower? Change clothes?"

"No."

"I can sit with Summer," she said. "You live five minutes away. You'll feel better. And smell better. You're a little ripe. If anything happens, I'll call you. Right away." She held up her hand as though taking an oath. "I promise."

"Would you leave the bedside of one of your kids?" he asked.

"I know, Bill. I know. But you have to take care of yourself. And you're going to have people coming to the hospital. Kids and adults who will want to visit or talk to you. And see Summer as she gets better."

"Being in the house has felt weird with Summer gone. Missing."

"Lonely?"

"Sure, that. To be honest, I've been a little uneasy. Someone assaulted her. I've been lying in bed, trying to sleep, just wishing she'd come in the door. Everything feels off, in the whole town. It said on the news people are calling security companies to buy alarm systems. Lord knows how many guns and canisters of pepper spray have been sold. I slept with all the lights on in the house. Like a scared kid. And I use the term 'sleep' lightly. I couldn't do it. Dreams. And hearing noises."

"Okay, you're not alone here. You do have help." She pointed to her own chest, her index finger sinking into the material of her heavy sweater. "Me."

"Right." He scratched his stubbled cheek. "But I'm calling Detective Hawkins first. You can fill him in on my daughter's sex life. Then I'll think about bathing."

As he started to press the SEND button on his phone, Paige reached out and placed her hand over his. "Bill? First tell me how you and Summer were really getting along."

"Fine."

"Bill. Were you there for her? Really there? I know it's tough—"

"Because her mother and my wife died a year and a half ago? Yeah, it is tough. Summer's been pushing boundaries ever since then. I'm sure it's teenage rebellion, but also a form of anger and grieving. Maybe that's why she ran into the arms of a teenage sociopath. To act out or rebel. So I didn't ask where she was going on Saturday. I'm trying to let her live her life. We've had some dustups, but we seemed to be turning a corner." Bill still held the phone in the air, his finger poised but not pushing any buttons. "It was Julia's birthday two weeks ago."

Paige lifted her hand to her chest. "Oh, shit. Right."

"You know, last year on her birthday, the first one since . . . Summer and I were so friggin' sad. We both cried all day. We just locked ourselves up in the house and cried."

"I'm sorry, Bill. I meant to call you that day."

"It's fine." He patted his sister's hand. "This year, with everybody feeling a little better, I tried not to make too big of a deal out of it. You know, just act like it was any other day. But she was down—I could tell." Bill remembered Summer leaving for school that day, her shoulders slumped, her eyes downcast. When Bill came home from work, he insisted on ordering a pizza, and the two of them found a cheesy movie on the Syfy network, something about giant flying roaches. "I should have talked to her more. I shouldn't have assumed she was fine."

"Bill—"

He held up his index finger, asking for quiet.

"I have to call the detective."

CHAPTER ELEVEN

The stinging hot water washed over Bill. He stood beneath the showerhead, after soaping his entire body, until the steam billowed, obscuring his feet. He didn't want to turn off the water and step out. He wanted to remain lost in the soothing fog.

But he knew he couldn't.

The longer he dawdled in the house, the longer Summer lay in the hospital without him nearby. He shut the water off, felt the slight chill in the air as he stepped outside the stall. He listened. The furnace made its usual loud clicking noise as it cycled on. He remained still, waiting to see if there were any other noises, anything out of the ordinary. He wanted to hear only one thing—the sound of Summer at home and healthy.

He knew he'd feel better if he shaved, so he cleared a circle in the condensation on the mirror and lathered his face.

The house was crammed full of memories. Everywhere he turned, he thought of an association with Julia or Summer. He saw the swing set in the backyard, where he parked the car. He saw Summer's heights marked on the doorjamb when he entered the house. He repeatedly walked across the kitchen floor where Julia died.

Just a month before, at the end of January, he and Summer had bonded during three snowy days when school was canceled and Bill took a couple of personal days off work. They watched two full seasons of *Game of Thrones*, sharing frozen pizza and cookies and making insane predictions about who would ultimately reign at the end of the series. Bill had even convinced Summer to watch at least one season of the original *Star Trek* with him, and he looked forward to it as though he were a kid again. At times like those, parenting felt so easy, so natural. If only every problem could be solved with binge watching and junk food . . .

Bill fought back against the tears welling in his eyes. *Focus,* he told himself, scraping the stubble off his face. *Summer's health is all that matters.* But even the mundane act of shaving was fraught with memories. He could picture Summer standing in the bathroom doorway, age three or so, watching him shave as if it were the most fascinating thing in the world. He always bent down and smeared a dollop of shaving cream on the end of her nose, causing her to squeal with delight. He almost sold the house when Julia died, thinking he couldn't stand to walk through that kitchen every day, to eat meals and drink coffee over the exact spot where his wife had died alone. But Summer talked him out of it. She said the house had the opposite effect on her. She liked being in the place where her mother had both lived and died. She didn't want to forget anything.

Bill set the razor aside, then rinsed his face with warm water. It felt good, bracing and cleansing. He'd given in to Summer's wishes back then and didn't sell, saying he understood. He wanted to give his daughter the most normal life possible, even if she didn't have a mother anymore, and if staying in the house helped that along, so be it.

He studied his face in the mirror. Dark, baggy circles under his eyes. Slightly thinning hair. Julia's death made him feel tired and worn in a way nothing ever had, a power drain he wasn't sure he'd recovered from.

And now Summer was in the hospital.

If the worst happened, if she didn't come home, no way he'd stay in the house. He'd burn it to the ground along with everything in it. . . .

"Stop," he said out loud. "Just stop."

He left the bathroom for the bedroom. Once dressed, Bill wanted to get out of the house as quickly as possible. It felt painfully empty and lonely, its quiet an oppressive force that seemed to be pushing against him. Every footstep echoed, and every movement sounded loud and lonely.

But he did make one stop on his way out. He went into Summer's bedroom. Just a couple of years earlier, she'd insisted on a change— the pink walls, the ruffled bedspread, and the American Girl dolls went away in favor of a sleeker, more modern look she chose with Julia's help. Her room looked clean and crisp, white and gray and modern like the Apple Store at the mall in Nashville. Bill considered the space off-limits. He never entered without knocking, and even then he usually talked to her from the doorway as though an invisible force field kept him from venturing farther inside.

But the police had been through the room more than once during the past few days. They went through every drawer, dug through the closet, shone flashlights under the bed and into every corner. They took her computer and turned it inside out.

And found nothing.

Bill wandered over to her dresser. On top, he saw a picture of Summer and Julia at the beach. They'd driven to Destin, Florida, three years earlier and spent a week on the white sand, Summer spastically running in and out of the tide and all of them acquiring stinging sunburns. She and Julia posed for the photo on the last day, one of many shots taken, but the one on the dresser was the best. Their smiles so big and natural, the love between them burning through the two-dimensional image. The sun-bleached, radiant joy made them look more like sisters than mother and daughter. How could any of them contemplate the accident on the horizon, the one that would kill Julia in the kitchen just a year and a half later?

Bill pulled open the top drawer of the dresser and peered inside. He saw a jumble of colored panties and white socks. Looking into his daughter's underwear drawer seemed particularly invasive. The items looked forlorn and small, things most of the world never glimpsed. After his conversation with Paige, he expected to find a stash of birth control pills or condoms, but if the police had found anything of that nature, they hadn't told him. And even with Summer in the hospital fighting for her life, it seemed like a violation of her privacy to dig around.

He closed the drawer and looked at her bed. About the only thing that survived the decorating purge that marked his daughter's transition from child to adolescent was a stuffed Winnie the Pooh Julia had bought when Summer was still a baby. Winnie rested on top of the white pillows, his chubby stomach and coal black eyes pointed toward the ceiling. The bear's fur had lost some of its luster over the years, growing stained and dirty from years of being dragged around the house. Bill reached out and grabbed the bear by one of its legs, hoping to bring a piece of home to the hospital for Summer.

CHAPTER TWELVE

On his way down the hallway toward the front of the house, Bill stopped one more time, hesitating in the doorway of the spare bedroom he used as a home office. Bill rarely brought his job home, preferring to do as much as possible on-site at the college, where he worked as a network engineer in the IT division. The job rarely required late hours, and Bill made a point of being home as much as possible when Summer was.

Julia had used the office more than he did. When Summer turned ten, Julia went back to school, working part-time on a master's degree in counseling, with the goal of working in the school system or for a social welfare agency in the county. The dream never materialized. She was two-thirds of the way through the program when she died. Sometimes Bill considered quitting his own job and going back for a degree like the one Julia was pursuing, an act that would complete her dream in her absence. But he couldn't justify it financially. With no one else helping out, he needed to hang on to his job in order to pay for everything he and Summer needed—a car, health insurance, clothes, college.

A state budget crunch had frozen his salary for the previous few years, and Bill wondered how long they'd have such a precarious stability. And that was before he had to worry about the possibility of Summer's medical bills and long-term care. Therapy, nurses, modifications to the home if Summer was disabled . . .

He stopped running through the list. *Summer's health,* he reminded himself. *Right now.* Nothing else mattered. Nothing else was promised or certain.

Bill wanted to resist going inside the office at all, but his mind and heart knew better. He wanted and needed to do it today more than ever.

He set Winnie the Pooh on the desk and sat down, lifting the lid on the aging Dell laptop he still kept there. While the machine booted up, making a low grinding sound, he looked around the somewhat disordered room. There was one filing cabinet with a messy stack of papers and manuals on top. A futon sat against the far wall, converted for the moment into its position as a couch. More papers littered its surface, and Bill knew he'd have to clear it off for Paige to sleep on. He'd been promising himself to clean and organize the place for about six months.

The laptop had belonged to Julia, and she'd used it for her schoolwork. Bill knew the computer wasn't worth much. It wasn't even good enough for Summer to use at school, but he held on to it for a variety of reasons, all of them sentimental. He just couldn't bear to get rid of something that contained so much of who Julia was.

Just before Julia suffered her fatal accident in the kitchen—before she mounted a ladder to scrape wallpaper off the walls and lost her balance, tumbling to her death from a head injury—she made three phone calls. Two to Bill that he didn't answer. And one to their neighbor in back, Adam Fleetwood, a call he told Bill later he didn't answer because he was in a meeting at work. Messages stayed on voice mail for only thirty days, so before that time was up, Bill converted Julia's last words to an MP3 file and kept them on the laptop.

He bent down and reached behind the plastic garbage can in the corner of the room, fumbling for a moment until he found what he was looking for. Julia's ancient flip phone, the one she refused to trade in for an upgrade and the one she carried at the time she died. The one she called him from. It was attached to the wall by its black charging cord, and when he picked it up, he held it in his hand like a large black jewel, a sleek, obsidian talisman. Bill hadn't brought himself to disconnect the line. He'd kept it active for the past year for the same reason he kept Julia's laptop in the office—it was a part of her. He lifted the phone to his face and took a quick sniff. He liked to think it carried a remnant of her, a reminder of her essence that was transferred to the phone on the day she died. He smelled her familiar scent—the lavender shampoo she used, the lotion she spread on her hands. Did the phone really hold it? Bill doubted it. He didn't care. He liked having the object around, even if it cost him money to keep it going.

He set the phone on the desk and turned to the laptop. Even though he'd performed the ritual many times before, his hands trembled slightly as he pressed the proper keys and increased the volume. A longer than usual pause ensued, and a quaking panic passed through Bill as he wondered if the file had become corrupt or had been accidentally deleted when the cops went through the house searching everything and anything.

But then he heard the familiar sound of Julia's voice.

"It's me. . . . Look, I'm sorry we fought that way. You know I hate it." She laughed a little. "We both hate it, of course. I'm going to go ahead and paint the kitchen. It needs it. You don't have to be involved."

The recording beeped. Winnie the Pooh's dead black eyes watched him from the desk. And then the next message began.

And Julia sounded more serious.

"I'm sorry that you feel the way you feel, that you'd ever think I'd do what you suggested. I . . . I wish you'd answer. I know you're giving me the silent treatment, so I guess we'll talk about this when you get home. We can settle it all, and I'll tell you what's been going on with me lately. It's time."

Bill wanted to listen again but didn't have time. He snapped the laptop shut and pushed it back away from the edge of the desk. Holding the phone in his hands for a long moment, he applied pressure from both sides, cupping it like a baby bird.

He didn't care what Julia had done. He really didn't care.

"I wish you were here, babe. I really wish you were here."

CHAPTER THIRTEEN

Before he stood up, Bill heard something at the back door. He listened, his head cocked, and then he understood. Someone was there, knocking and knocking.

Bill's stomach turned to ice. Was it the police? Had something happened to Summer at the hospital?

He dismissed that possibility. If something had gone wrong, if a crisis had developed, someone would have called. A doctor. Or Paige.

The knocking came again.

Bill grabbed the stuffed bear, sighing loudly. Someone selling something, or a religious freak trying to convert him. He didn't have the time or the patience for it. But when he stomped into the family room, he saw a familiar figure standing at the back door, trying to see inside, his face pressed against the glass. Relief surged through his body like a flood. A truly friendly face.

"Adam." Bill undid the lock, then pulled the door open, letting in a cool gust of air. "How long have you been out there? I was in the shower."

"Not long. I saw your car." Adam stepped inside, rubbing his hands together. "I was going to call, but I decided to come over instead." He wore a heavy coat over a white button-down shirt and black pants.

Adam stood a few inches taller than Bill and was five years younger. His sales job kept him on the road during the week, and on weekends, he spent his time in the yard that backed up to Bill's. Tending a garden in the spring and summer and digging and raking in the fall and winter gave him the aura of an outdoorsman, a strong and ruggedly fit man who looked like he belonged in a catalog selling camping gear. More than once, Julia had commented on Adam's good looks, paying special attention to his broad shoulders and bulging muscles. But some of the color was drained from his face. His movements seemed jerky, uncertain, lacking his usual athletic grace. "I've been hearing more things on the radio, Bill, as I drove back into town. I was over in Hughes County for work, or I would have run by the hospital today. None of it makes sense."

"The cops don't have everything straight yet."

"What is the story, Bill? Is there anything new?"

Bill had never heard Adam's voice so insistent, so pleading. But none of them had ever been through anything like Summer's disappearance before. Bill gave Adam an update, and running through everything again made Bill feel better. Unburdened a little.

Adam listened with his lips slightly parted, his face still pale. He'd been in the house a few times since Summer disappeared, keeping Bill company and trying to lift his spirits. He'd been Bill's main support system. Bill had always felt a pull toward Adam and couldn't help but think it was a vestigial desire, something left over from junior high and high school when he and others like him gravitated toward the better-looking kids, the stronger kids, the more capable kids. Adam once told Bill he'd been a star baseball player growing up, and that piece of news didn't surprise Bill at all.

Adam's hands rested on his hips, his coat still on. "I'm sorry," he said. "On the radio, it sounded bleak."

"I'm on my way back to the hospital now. I just came home to shower. And I thought I'd bring this guy back for Summer." He lifted the bear, Winnie's pudgy legs dangling. "You know, to make her feel more at home or whatever."

Images of the ICU tumbled through his mind. The scalpel, the rubber tube inserted into Summer's chest. Her small body exposed to all those strangers. Bill felt weak, his joints loose and rubbery. He took a seat on the couch, the bear in his lap. "She's bad, Adam. Really bad." Bill struggled to keep his thoughts and emotions together. "They beat her within an inch of her life." As he spoke, he found it hard to believe his words applied to his own daughter. That they came out of his mouth at all made him think his own mind was playing a trick, convincing itself that he spoke about another child, one not related to him in any way. "She might have brain damage. Or vision damage." He swallowed. "She might not even wake up."

"Is she moving at all?" Adam asked.

"She makes noises." Bill looked down at his fingernails. He'd forgotten to clip them. "She acts all agitated sometimes. If I try to talk to her or comfort her. It scares me. I don't know what she's thinking, if she's thinking anything at all."

Adam looked frozen in place. He'd known Summer as long as he'd lived behind them—seven years—and had watched her grow from a child to a teenager. Adam had been married once, with a son, but he and his wife had split up shortly after Bill and Julia moved in. His ex-wife and child moved away, back to Oklahoma where Adam had grown up. Somewhere along the way, Julia had invited Adam to spend Thanksgiving with the three of them when he didn't have the time to travel home, and they'd spent every Thanksgiving together since, including the past two after Julia's death. Bill had friends from work, friends from a film club he occasionally attended, but it was safe to say Adam was his closest friend in town, the person he talked to the most outside of his family.

Something seemed to click into place in Adam's mind just then. He took a couple of steps forward and slumped into a chair across the room, exhaling a deep breath.

"I'm sorry," he said. "You probably want to get back."

"I do. My sister's there. She's sitting with Summer so I could come home and shower."

"That's good." Some certainty returned to Adam's face, some sense of equilibrium being restored. "Do you want me to go with you? Or I can keep an eye on things here, or . . . Hell, maybe you'd like a drink. Some of that Tennessee you've got?"

Adam didn't wait for an answer. He was out of the chair and into the kitchen, opening the corner cabinet where Bill kept his liquor. Adam brought down the bottle of George Dickel, then reached into another cabinet and pulled out two glasses. He carried all of it over to the coffee table and poured two healthy shots. His hands shook as he screwed the cap onto the bottle.

"Maybe I shouldn't," Bill said. "I need a clear head."

"You've had a hell of a shock. This will steady you." He pushed one glass toward Bill and lifted the other one for himself. "I know I could use a drink after hearing about this."

Bill took the glass and tossed the shot down. The burn spread through his throat and into his nasal passages, but then a wave of calm swept through him. The liquor served its purpose, and he wondered why he hadn't thrown down more shots in the past couple days. Maybe because Adam hadn't suggested it.

"That's good," Bill said. "Thanks."

"More?"

"No, no. One will do."

Adam came over and clapped Bill on the shoulder. The gesture felt oddly calming and appropriate. Adam always knew what to do or say. The right word, the right joke. "Want me to drive you? You look a little wrung out."

"I need to ask you something. And, no, you don't have to drive me." Adam stayed standing, forcing Bill to crane his neck up from where he remained on the couch. "I'm going to try to keep this simple, but have you ever seen any boys coming or going over here? With Summer?"

"You mean the day she disappeared? No. The cops went over all this with me. More than once."

"Not just then. Anytime. The last six months, I guess. Did you see anything?"

"I'm here less than you are, buddy. And even when I'm working in the yard, I guess I'm in my own head."

"You didn't see any boys or any parties? After school, you know?"

Adam's face grew more serious, and his voice dropped lower. "That's who they think did this? Boys at school?"

"It's a theory. Summer has a few of them in her social circle, including one she went to a dance with at Christmas. Do you remember that kid at the high school who broke another kid's jaw at the bus stop? About two years ago."

Adam scratched his head. "I don't. But I'm not plugged in to the high school scene. You think he did it?"

Bill jumped when his cell phone rang, the noise slicing through the room. "It's the police." He scrambled to take the call. "What is it?" he asked before Hawkins could say anything.

"Are you at home, Bill?" Hawkins asked.

"I am. Is she all right?"

"I'm not calling because there's anything wrong. In fact, I just finished speaking with your sister at the hospital, and Summer's condition is unchanged."

"Jesus." Bill's hands felt sweaty. He wiped one on his pant leg. "What is it, then?"

"I'm on my way to your house now. You're still there, right? I wanted to ask you about something."

"Can we talk at the hospital?"

"I'd rather talk at the house. I'm coming right by there if you sit tight."

Bill detected something beneath Hawkins's voice, an edge that seemed out of step with the cop's usual practiced detachment. "I wish you'd hurry. I've already been gone too long."

Hawkins hung up without saying anything else.

"What's that?" Adam asked. "Trouble?"

"The cops. They want to talk to me. Here."

"But . . ."

"He says Summer is fine. Unchanged."

"Good," Adam said.

"But I'm going to call Paige just to make sure."

"You don't need me to stay?" Adam asked. "I can."

"No, thanks, Adam. I'll keep you up-to-date."

"If you need anything, call. Or come by for another Dickel when you're home."

"I think I'm going to be at the hospital a lot."

"And, look, when all of this is over, when Summer is better, we'll go fishing again or something. All of us. We'll do something normal."

"Thanks. That sounds, well, it sounds normal."

Bill dialed Paige while Adam showed himself out of the house.

CHAPTER FOURTEEN

―――――

"She's doing fine," Paige said. "I mean, her condition hasn't changed since you left."

"Is something wrong?" Bill asked.

He couldn't tell if Paige's voice sounded subdued due to her location in the hospital, or if, as he feared, it was something else, something worse.

"You have to tell me, Paige. If I need to come down there now . . ."

"You don't." There was a pause, and then a shuffling as Paige moved around, perhaps to a different location where she could speak more freely. "Hawkins just left."

"And you told him everything you knew? About the phone call Summer made to you?"

"Of course."

"Did she mention those kids to you on the phone? Clinton or Todd?"

"No, Bill." She sounded frazzled, on edge.

"So what's wrong?" he asked.

"It's the police, that detective. They're going to be asking *you* questions."

Bill looked out the front window where at that moment Hawkins's dark blue Impala was pulling into the driveway. He watched the detective step out of the car, hitching up his pants a little as he started up the walk to the front of the house.

"What kind of questions, Paige? About Summer's sex life?"

"No, not that," she said. "Something else."

"What?"

But then Hawkins was ringing the doorbell and peering through the window, his face pressed against the glass until it grew dark.

"Call me if anything changes," Bill said. "And I mean anything."

He hung up and went to let the detective in.

Hawkins came in, walking with a more purposeful stride than Bill had seen him use before. His shoulders were thrown back, and he passed by Bill without making eye contact.

Bill shut the door and followed the detective into the living room. "What is this, Detective? I'm trying to get back to the hospital."

"Sit down, Bill. We need to talk about something." But Hawkins remained standing.

Bill stopped a few feet away from the detective and didn't sit down either. "I know my sister told you about that birth control stuff. But it's not fair if you start to look at Summer differently because of that. She's too young to know what she's doing. And even if she did consent to sex with Todd Stone or any other boy, he still might have hurt her. In fact, that makes it more likely, right? Aren't people usually hurt by someone close to them?"

"This isn't about your sister. Or the birth control."

"Then what is it?" Bill asked. "Did you catch somebody?"

"Have a seat, Bill."

Bill understood. The detective wanted to push him around a little, assert his authority over Bill and control the situation. The urge to resist, to push back, tried to take over Bill's mind, but he knew he couldn't get anywhere that way. As though the effort pained him, Bill eased down into a chair. Once he was settled, the detective took his time following suit, adjusting his pant legs and then reaching into his coat pocket to take out a small spiral notebook, one that almost disappeared in his big hand. It seemed to take another twenty minutes for Hawkins to find his glasses and perch them on the end of his nose, changing his demeanor from gentle good old boy to no-nonsense inquisitor.

"Is there anything you've been meaning to tell us, Bill?" he asked, his voice cold.

Bill's eyes rolled of their own accord. He felt like he had no control over their coordinated motion. "This again? Haven't we been through all this—"

"I'm thinking of something that occurred in the early-morning hours of November first last year."

"You want me to remember that far back. I don't know—" Bill stopped as he remembered the events of that night a few months earlier. Through the window behind Hawkins's head, Bill saw the bare trees moving in the wind, the branches jerky and awkward. "You're not going to bring that up."

Hawkins studied the tiny, low-tech notebook. "At one thirty-five in the morning on November first, the police received a nine-one-one call from this residence." He looked at Bill over his glasses. "Summer placed the call." He let that hang in the air a moment, then turned back to the notebook. "She said her father had grabbed her and shaken her, causing an injury to her arm. She wanted the police to come and help her."

A burning sensation grew on Bill's scalp, the kind a person felt from sitting out in the sun too long without a hat. "I don't have to listen to this."

"I think you do," Hawkins said. "Now, just tell me what happened that night, and we'll see what we do with the information."

"I'm going to the hospital."

"Bill." Hawkins removed the glasses, his blue-gray eyes boring in. "This is going to be a huge distraction. Secrets are a killer when a case like this is going on."

"The killer is the killer, not this so-called secret."

"What happened that night?"

Bill saw no way out, but he said, "You've turned my life upside down already. You've been through the whole house, my financial records, and my computer. I handed all that over to you voluntarily. I want you to look at everything there is to look at."

"But you didn't mention this. And I need to know what happened."

CHAPTER FIFTEEN

"How did you find out?" Bill asked.

"The officer who responded that night came forward," Hawkins said, his voice a little warmer. "He filled me in. He still had detailed notes in a logbook, even though no charges were filed."

Bill squirmed on the couch. As if seeing Summer in the condition she was in at the hospital, her body on display to be poked and prodded by strangers, her every action and flaw examined by the police and the media weren't bad enough, now Bill found himself forced to relive one of the worst nights of his life. He tried not to feel sorry for himself, not to indulge in an unproductive round of self-pity, but he had to admit his days hadn't been so golden recently. Julia's death. Summer's disappearance. Summer's injuries. Haley's death.

And the autumn night the police came to his house.

Summer went out that night with Haley. It was Halloween, but he knew the girls weren't going trick-or-treating. Without probing for too many details, Bill learned they were going over to someone's house to watch movies. Unprompted, Summer said to him, "It's just girls."

At the time, the comment raised a red flag. Why point that out when he hadn't asked any questions about anyone's gender? But Bill tried hard not to be *that* dad, the guy who stood on the porch with his loaded and racked shotgun, the one who followed his child's movements through her cell phone. He felt like he faced enough challenges raising a daughter on his own without adding to them. And Halloween fell just a month past the one-year anniversary of Julia's death. He wanted to think Summer was moving on, having fun like any other kid.

Bill refused to give out Halloween candy. Every year, he turned out the lights and retreated to the back of the house where he watched an NBA game or a documentary on the Civil War while the neighborhood kids passed by. He enjoyed the holiday when Summer was little, when a sense of wonder filled her eyes as she dressed up and then returned home with a bag full of candy. But for several years, Bill had lacked patience for the whole thing. The kids who came to the door often seemed rude, and he dreaded the inevitable small talk with neighbors and acquaintances who, even a year and a half later, continued to speak to him in a pitying voice as though Julia had died just a few days ago.

Bill fell asleep that night as the Spurs and the Warriors went into overtime. When he woke on the couch, the clock across the room reading one thirty-five a.m., he assumed Summer was already in. He'd told her to be home by midnight, and even before Julia died, she always pushed it to the last minute. In the year since Julia's death, Summer had started coming in later and later. Never all night and never so late that Bill grew really worried, but she was pushing and pushing at the boundaries he had set for her.

And that night when he woke up, she wasn't in her room.

Bill walked by the open doorway, the hair on the back of his head mussed from the couch, his unlaced shoes in his hand, and saw no sign of Summer. Her bed was empty, the Ikea lamp glowing. Bill walked through the rest of the house, checking every room. Nothing. And then he checked his phone. Also nothing.

He put his tennis shoes on and walked out back, making sure Summer and her friends weren't sitting on the patio, gabbing away beneath the stars while the night grew chilly. But all was silent there.

Every few minutes Bill sent texts to Summer, but she answered none of them.

"I look back on that night now," Bill said, his voice expansive, "and I realize it was kind of a sneak preview of what I've gone through the last couple of days."

"She was running around with her friends and didn't call," Hawkins said, clearly using information he'd gleaned from the responding officer.

"I don't know which friends now," Bill said. "Paige told me Summer called her about six months ago, asking about birth control. This night I'm talking about was about four months ago. Maybe the two are related."

"But you don't know if she was with the boys I mentioned that night," Hawkins said. "You don't know if Clinton Fields or any of his friends were there."

"I never found out." Bill squirmed again, his scalp burning not with anger but embarrassment. "First I went out the front door—you know, checking to see if she was out there or on her way in. Some little assholes had smeared dog shit on the window, that window right behind your head. Probably because I didn't give out candy or something. So I'm doubly pissed then, you know? I don't know where my daughter is. I've got dog shit to wash off the window. . . . I'm just about to start calling her friends' parents when she comes strolling in the front door almost two hours late."

"Had she been drinking?" Hawkins asked.

"I don't know." Bill shrugged. "Not obviously, but I didn't smell her breath."

"Did she say where she was or who she was with?"

"She said she was with her friends and that she lost track of time." Bill's laugh sounded brittle, like cracking ice. "The thing is, that's the most normal, believable explanation in the world. Nothing dramatic. Nothing crazy. No excuses. She lost track of time."

"From what I've heard about Summer, she was usually in control of her own destiny. Kids and teachers from school say she was the one who made plans. She was the one who made decisions. Probably nobody led her astray that night. No one else made her late." He watched Bill, almost like a therapist, waiting for him to go on and finish the story.

"All of a sudden it's a problem that my daughter was confident," he said.

But Summer's explanation didn't set Bill off that night. Her attitude did. For the first time ever, she was openly disdainful of her father, as though she considered him simply a peripheral figure in her life, no more important than a neighbor down the street or the guy who came once a month to read the gas meter.

They'd stood near each other in the living room, the glow from the streetlight distorted by the smeared dog shit on the window, and Summer waved her hand at Bill as she started to walk away, a gesture of complete and total dismissal.

Bill surprised himself. He reached out and grabbed her by the forearm, and when Summer gasped and tried to pull loose from his grip, Bill tugged even harder, causing her to lose her balance and slip to the floor.

The whole thing took two seconds, and it unfolded with a dream-like quality, as though Bill were watching someone else, some crazy man, take hold of his daughter and shove her down.

When Summer hit the floor, Bill let go, stepping back. Her eyes filled with tears—not of hurt but of anger—and she called Bill an asshole as she stormed down the hall to her room.

CHAPTER SIXTEEN

B ill closed his eyes, unable to look at the detective sitting across from him. He couldn't bear for those all-seeing, all-judging eyes to rake him like searchlights. He doubted a man like Hawkins ever lost his cool, even with his own children.

"I snapped out of it," Bill said. "I was back inside myself once she stormed off. And I told myself to let it go. To let her cool down overnight while I simmered down as well. We'd lost Julia just a year earlier. I felt shitty. Totally shitty, like I wanted to chop off my offending hand. But I was still mad at her too. Summer could be so, so defiant. So stubborn. That dismissive attitude. The same attitude that told those kids they could smear dog shit on my window because I didn't give out candy on Halloween." He looked to Hawkins for understanding. "She's a teenager, you know? You give one a stern look, and they lose their minds. We tried to raise Summer not to be an entitled brat, but I guess she couldn't help acting the way kids sometimes act."

"So she called the police," Hawkins said, prodding.

"From her room. Next thing I know, there's a cop at the door. I honestly thought maybe he'd seen the dog shit and stopped by to take a report. Instead, he wanted to talk to me. An abuse allegation, he called it. I didn't know what the fuck he was talking about."

Bill nearly fell through the floor when Summer emerged from her bedroom, cell phone in hand, and told the officer she was the one who called the police, that she'd reported Bill for grabbing her by the arm.

But she backpedaled right away. Seeing the cop in the house—gun at his side, badge gleaming in the light—and understanding what it meant to report her father for abuse caused her to reconsider. She answered a bunch of questions the officer asked, and then Bill answered a bunch more, and in the end the officer left without filing a report or contacting the child welfare agency.

"We never talked about it," Bill said. "She went to bed, and I went to bed. The next day, things were a little tense, but neither of us brought it up. I guess my enduring punishment was a bit of the cold shoulder and standing out in the sun cleaning crusty dog shit off my window. It's like that with a teenager. Hot and cold. A week later, we watched a football game together. We were fine. I wanted to tell her not to be as whiny as everyone else her age, but I didn't. I left well enough alone."

"And it never—"

Bill sighed and looked over at the detective. "I'm sure every guy who's ever abused his wife or children says it's the only time it ever happened, but that's the only time it ever happened. She got spanked on rare occasions when she was a kid, more by Julia than by me. And we're talking a handful of times, if that. No, I never touched her again. Never."

"You're lucky they didn't press charges," Hawkins said. "If she'd insisted, if she'd made a bigger stink about the injuries or requested medical attention, they would have taken her away from you and investigated further. It could have been ugly. The responding officer is supposed to file a report, even if he doesn't make an arrest. They don't always do it, so you caught a break."

"I don't need you to lecture me on close calls. I'm living in one, remember? Can I go to the hospital now?"

Hawkins held up his meaty hand, telling Bill to slow down. "Do you think something happened that night to set her off? Something with her friends?"

"I don't know. Summer has other girlfriends. That Teena Everett I told you about. She's kind of the third wheel to Summer and Haley. They were better friends in junior high, and I get the feeling they don't always want her around."

"They have a fight or something?"

"No. Teena's just a little squirrely. Haley and Summer kind of left her behind the way kids do. They outgrew her. But maybe she knows something about that night. For some reason, Teena's been hanging around a little more lately. Have you talked to her?"

"We did."

"And?"

"She wasn't with them the day they disappeared. She's mostly been giving us background on the kids at the school, especially Summer and Haley's friends. It's kind of scary for a kid to talk to the police this way. She's dealing with a lot of complicated emotions."

"We all are."

"Do you think Summer's mood, her defiance, was affected by the proximity of her mother's death anniversary? You said this Halloween thing was a month later."

"Maybe. I mean, sure."

"And you told me on the day the girls disappeared that your wife's birthday had just passed. I believe . . ." He flipped through the notebook. "Was that two weeks earlier?"

"It was," Bill said, his heart sinking. "She lost her mother. She was in a lot of pain."

"Of course. And so were you."

"Sure. I'd like to think I wouldn't have grabbed her if I hadn't lost my wife a year earlier. Sure."

Hawkins gave Bill a paternal nod, a recognition they'd reached some mutual understanding. "I know we discussed you giving a DNA sample when Summer disappeared, and I think now would be a good time for you to provide one. Like I said back at the hospital, there could very well be evidence from the attacker on Summer's body, and we'd pretty quickly want to exclude you."

Bill's mouth felt dry. "I thought you wanted DNA for . . . to help identify her if you found her in some condition where she couldn't be . . ."

The look on Hawkins's face didn't change. And he didn't say anything.

"My God, do you really think I might have done that to my own daughter? Beating her and almost killing her?"

"We need your DNA to exclude you from anything found on the girls' bodies. You're heading back to the hospital now, right? We can arrange for the DNA sample to be taken there. One of our technicians can come by."

"But you're also checking up on me."

"Bill, I have to. Everybody has to be cleared."

"Are you talking to that shithead Clinton Fields? What about him and his friends? They're probably a bunch of little date rapists. He put a boy in the hospital."

"I told you, we're talking to him as well."

"Are you checking their DNA? Isn't that a good idea?"

"Bill, you can't just take a DNA sample from a juvenile unless you have a strong reason to suspect him. We're not there yet."

"Maybe Clinton and I are in cahoots? You know what, get out. Just get out."

But Hawkins was already lifting his bulky body up from the

chair, adjusting his sport coat, and moving toward the door. He turned his back on Bill as he walked to the front of the house, and Bill watched the back of the man's head, his fist clenching and unclenching. He reached down for the coffee table, his hand almost touching a small ceramic bowl that sat there.

But he pulled his hand back.

He wants you to do that, Bill thought. *That's what they want. To rattle my cage so much—*

Instead, Bill spoke. "I wish they had pressed charges that night."

Hawkins stood framed by the doorway, and he turned his big head to look at Bill. "Why?" he asked.

"Maybe it would have changed something. Maybe it would have forced me to understand something about Summer that I clearly missed."

Hawkins walked out and said nothing, pulling the door shut behind him and leaving Bill seething alone in the house.

CHAPTER SEVENTEEN

Bill called Paige as he walked to his car. It was late afternoon, just past four, and the winter sun was already slipping away.

"Hey," he said when she answered. "Is everything okay there?"

"Yes, she's fine. The same."

"Hawkins just left here."

"Okay. Are you coming back?" Paige asked.

Bill clicked the key fob, unlocking his Civic. He held the phone with one hand while he pulled the door open with the other. "Paige, did Summer talk about anything else when she called you that time?"

"I told you everything."

"Did she talk about Julia?"

"I asked how she was doing. The usual stuff. But we didn't get deep into it."

Bill started the car and backed up, angling and heading down the driveway. "I have to make a stop."

"Where? Bill, what happened with the police?"

"I'll see you soon."

The halls of Jakesville High School were almost empty when Bill walked in. Bill felt a little like an intruder, a tired, frazzled, middle-aged man wandering a building meant mostly for teenagers. He passed lockers and brightly colored bulletin boards. He saw a banner advertising an upcoming basketball game and another about taking the ACT. He didn't know where he was going.

Two kids, a boy and a girl who looked to be about Summer's age, came toward Bill. Their bodies nearly touched as they walked, and their heads were inclined toward each other, their voices low, conspiratorial in the echoing hall. They didn't notice Bill until he said, "Excuse me," and then they looked up.

"Do you know where Ms. Halstrom's office is?" he asked.

The girl turned halfway around and pointed behind her, her over-stuffed backpack shifting as she moved. "Down there," she said. "I think it's, like, room one oh one?"

"Thanks."

Bill started to go, but the boy was staring at him, his mouth slightly open. "You're that girl's dad. Summer."

"Yes." Bill stopped his forward motion and turned back to the boy. "Do you know her? Are you friends with her?"

They both shook their heads, a paired set of bobbleheads. "We're freshmen," the girl said. "But we heard about it. We heard she almost died."

"Shhh, Rachel—"

"Well, I'm sorry."

"It's okay," Bill said. "She's hurt bad. But we'll see."

He was walking away, his shoes loud in the hallway, when the girl, Rachel, said, "We're both sorry."

Bill looked back one more time. "Thank you."

He meant it.

Ms. Halstrom's door stood open. Her desk was covered with books and papers, and a well-known Bob Dylan song Bill hadn't heard in years, "It Ain't Me, Babe," played over her laptop.

She looked up, brushing her long salt-and-pepper hair out of her face. She appeared to be at least ten years older than Bill, maybe even closing in on sixty.

"Mr. Price," she said. She used her index finger to lower the volume, and then she scrambled to her feet, her long, flowy skirt billowing around her like a sail. She held out her hand, and they shook. "Sit down, please. If you have the time."

"I came to see you," Bill said, sitting. He'd met Summer's guidance counselor on a couple of occasions—once at a school open house and again at Julia's funeral. Both Summer and Haley raved about Ms. Halstrom, speaking about her in the same reverent tones they normally reserved for the cast of *Pretty Little Liars* or Daniel Radcliffe. "You don't mind me just showing up like this, do you, Ms. Halstrom?"

"Of course not," she said. "And call me Anna. I was going to talk to Principal Reynolds to try to find more information out about Summer's condition. And then I was going to stop by the hospital if she's up for visitors."

"She will be soon. I hope." Bill spotted a box of tissues on the edge of the desk next to a stack of brochures about the stages of grief. "Rough time around here, I guess."

Anna nodded, her lips pressed into a tight line. "Lots of kids coming by. Lots of parents calling. Everyone is sad and scared—I can tell you that. If it's any comfort, and it has been some to me, the kids coming by have spoken very highly of Summer and Haley. They're so upset because they love those girls so much."

"That does help to know," Bill said. "Thank you. And thank you for all you've done for Summer over the last two years, especially when Julia died."

"That girl." Tears formed in Anna's eyes. "Such a good kid. You know, last year, when the school board was contemplating changes to the dress code, changes that I thought were sexist, quite frankly, Summer spoke before the student council."

"I remember that."

"She was so articulate. So polished. Just a natural. I could see her running for student body president when she's a senior. I know she's been given a heavy load. You have too. I've tried to share hers, and if I can share yours, I will. You must have a lot on your mind right now."

"Summer's on my mind right now. Haley too." Bill looked around the small office. The shelves of more books, the framed diplomas, the posters of Gandhi and Einstein. The low twang of Dylan's voice. "I know she talks to you a lot. I'm trying to figure out what might have happened, and I thought you could help me."

Anna nodded, her head moving as though she were bopping along to the music. "Yes, we always had good talks, Summer and I. She's a beautiful girl, inside and out. And I can only imagine how this is tearing you up."

"The police are saying . . . They're asking about everything."

"I know what the police are saying," Anna said. "They came to my house on Sunday morning." Anna leaned back in her chair, the springs squeaking as she moved. She considered Bill a long moment. "Ordinarily I wouldn't share the details of our counseling sessions, but since this is so serious, since lives are potentially in danger, I'm okay with it."

"I'm okay with it too," Bill said, sounding to his own ears like an eager kid. "What did Summer say to you? What did you tell the police?"

"I'm not sure the police understood everything I was telling them, but maybe you will." She leaned forward again. "Summer and I rarely talked about boys. We really didn't. I was much more concerned about something else Summer seemed to be obsessing over lately. Something she started talking about again and again."

"What was it?" Bill asked.

"Her mom's death."

CHAPTER EIGHTEEN

B ill shifted in his seat. He suddenly felt like almost thirty years had fallen away, transforming him back into a nervous high schooler, one who'd forgotten a key assignment or been caught smoking behind the football field.

"What about that?" he asked.

Anna steepled her fingers, resting the tips against the underside of her chin. "I only bring it up because I noticed that Summer's thoughts about her mother's death seemed to have changed over the past couple of months. As I'm sure you know, I spent a great deal of time talking with her—listening, really—when your wife died."

"I know," Bill said. "I'm grateful for that. Really."

Anna smiled. "Thank you for saying that." She lowered her hands. A bracelet on her wrist jangled as she moved. Another Dylan song played, one Bill was less familiar with. He tried to conjure the name. "Caribbean Wind"? Was that it?

Anna said, "Can I be honest with you, Mr. Price?"

"Bill. And, yes, I wish you would be."

"When I heard on Saturday that Summer was missing, I worried, just for a split second, that maybe she had run away."

Bill's hands tightened their grip on the arms of his chair. "Why would you say that? Had she talked about that?"

Anna was shaking her head. She seemed to be choosing her words carefully. A line from the Dylan song stood out, reaching Bill through the pause in the conversation: "I hear a voice crying, 'Daddy,' I always think it's for me. . . ."

"I'm speaking from my gut here," Anna said. "It had been months since Summer spoke about her mother in any meaningful way. I took that as a good sign. She was healing, not that anyone can ever get over losing a mother, especially so young. But a couple of weeks ago, Summer came by and brought her up again. She seemed agitated, more upset than I'd seen her in a long time."

"It was Julia's birthday a couple of weeks ago," Bill said, hoping Summer was merely upset about that and not something deeper and darker.

"I knew that." Anna waved her hands in the air, a gesture of uncertainty that made the bracelets jangle again. "There seemed to be something more at play there, something I couldn't get her to talk about. She said she felt her mother's death weighing on her again, that everywhere she turned, she was reminded of it. She talked about looking forward to college so she could move away. She kept returning to that thought. A desire to leave, to get away. It seemed like an intense feeling."

"She wanted me to stay in the house," Bill said, his voice defensive. "I would have moved or sold it. I don't care."

Anna held up a hand, a signal she understood. "Kids are fragile. They can turn on a dime. I made an appointment to follow up with her, to talk through more of it, but we never got back to it. I saw her in the hallway the week before she disappeared, and she seemed perfectly fine. The same old Summer. But it seemed to me that something had happened, something had triggered those feelings. It could have been the birthday, which is a fact of life. Birthdays come around for people, even when they're gone. But I also wondered if it was something more." Anna let out a deep, yogalike breath. "That's why I worried she'd run away. I worried something had happened, something she couldn't deal with."

Bill scrambled through his memories, searching for something that might have occurred in the last few weeks to upset Summer, something besides Julia's birthday. He'd answered the same kind of questions for the police on the day Summer disappeared, but Anna's words cast everything in a new light. "I can't think of anything. And obviously she didn't run away. We know where she is now."

"Right," Anna said. "And that's a tiny piece of good news." She clenched her hand into a fist, holding it above her desk. She looked like she was taking hold of hope and never letting go. "That's the best thing right now."

Bill nodded, hoping the affirmative gesture would make him feel better inside, make him feel as positive as Anna wanted him to feel. But he was faking it, and even as he nodded, he knew he wasn't going to be able to stop thinking about what Anna had just told him.

Bill walked through the mostly empty parking lot. The buses were gone, the cars belonging to students and faculty mostly cleared out. He replayed the talk with Anna. Julia's death? What could be bothering Summer about Julia's death so much that she'd want to run away? Hadn't they been through the worst? Why on earth weren't they emerging onto the other side?

He pressed the key fob, unlocking his doors, and as he reached for the handle, he looked up. Two kids—two boys—were walking to a car, looking back over their shoulders at him and hurrying away.

"Hey!" Bill said, recognizing them. He rushed around the back of his car, jogging lightly to make up the fifty or so feet between him and the boys. Clinton and Todd. "Hold it!"

But the boys had already stopped. They stood side by side next to a white Kia Rio each wearing light jackets and carrying backpacks. They blinked in the winter sun as Bill approached. Clinton wore his hair longer, so it brushed the tops of his shoulders, and his cheeks looked rosy at any time of year. His eyes were small brown pearls set deep in his face. Todd looked younger, a little smaller, his hands and face pale. His eyes were slightly bloodshot, and Bill wondered if they'd been drinking or getting high during the school day.

"Hi, Mr. Price," Clinton said. His voice was low, less confident and more unctuous than when he showed up at the house and laid it on thick for Bill. Todd looked even more uncertain. He shuffled from one foot to the other, his eyes cast to the ground.

Bill felt his body moving faster and faster, as though some internal engine were driving him forward like a car without brakes. He raised his index finger, the boys' faces growing larger in his vision. And then Clinton took a couple of steps back, his body bumping against the car.

"What are you doing here?" Bill asked. And, indeed, he couldn't stop himself in time. He lost his balance, falling forward and making contact with Clinton, who put his hands up so Bill didn't tumble over.

"Watch it," Clinton said. "Jesus."

Bill pulled away from the boy, straightening up. "Did you talk to the police? The police are looking for you."

"We have to go, Mr. Price," Todd said. He slung his backpack onto his shoulder and reached for the passenger door. "We have to get home."

"The police," Bill said. "What happened? Did you see Summer that day? Do you know what happened to her?" Bill still stood too close to Clinton, saw a fleck of spittle fly out of his mouth and land in the boy's hair. "Was one of you having sex with her? Is that it? Todd? You went to that dance with her. Were you dating? I don't care. Just tell me."

Clinton's hands were still out in front of him, warding Bill off. "You can't say these things to us." His voice was defiant again, laced with open contempt for Bill, as though he were speaking to a peasant. "This is rude. And inappropriate."

"Rude? What about what happened to Summer? And Haley?"

"We talked to the cops," Todd said, his door open. "More than once. Look, we're sorry, but we have to leave. We're not supposed to talk about it."

"With anybody," Clinton said. He scooted back, reaching for the door on his side.

Bill knew he needed to back away, to turn and go to the hospital or anywhere else so he wouldn't be in the faces of the two kids. But the internal engine kept pushing him. He stepped forward into the space vacated by Clinton. "Just tell me what you know. Why did you hit her? Why did you do that to those girls?"

Clinton took a moment to respond, his eyes boring in on Bill, who would have sworn one side of the boy's mouth tilted up into a smirk. "Why did I hit her? I didn't hit her. None of us did. Why did you hit her? Why did you grab her and shake her on Halloween?"

"You don't know what you're talking about."

Bill lunged forward, reaching for the boy, but he slipped back, sliding into the driver's seat of the car and pulling the door shut in one fluid motion. It flashed across Bill's brain to grab the handle, to lash out with the keys in his hand and cut into the pristine white paint.

But he stopped himself. He huffed and puffed, but he stopped himself.

The car started and drove off, the driver's side window sliding down as it pulled away.

Bill heard one word, almost obscured by the wind and the distance.

"Asshole."

CHAPTER NINETEEN

Bill's heart thudded as he drove back to the hospital, his encounter with those kids playing in his mind. He wished he'd forced them to say more, or gone after them, followed them wherever they were going. He couldn't believe any kid would speak to an adult that way. Curse at him. Defy him. Who did they think they were? Who did they think he was?

And again he asked himself: *How can I know so little about the world?*

His phone rang. Hawkins. Bill scrambled to pick it up.

"Where are you, Bill?" the detective asked.

"I'm driving."

"I thought you were going back to the hospital. We have a tech there to take the DNA sample."

Bill felt deflated. He thought he might be getting news. Important news of some kind.

"The guidance counselor at school says Summer was upset about her mom's death right before she disappeared. Have you looked into that?"

Hawkins sighed. "We're looking into everything. But you said nothing unusual had happened with Summer before the disappearance. No red flags. Nothing, right?"

Bill eased to a stop at a light, two blocks from the hospital. He saw the building looming in the distance. It was his turn to sigh. "No. Nothing."

"You know I spoke to the investigator from the coroner's office, the one who responded to your wife's death. She said there was nothing out of the ordinary about it. An accident in the home."

The light changed, and Bill rolled forward. "That's right."

"There's no reason to think anything else, is there?" Hawkins asked.

"God, no. No."

There was a pause as Bill turned into the hospital lot.

Then Hawkins said, "Get that DNA test taken care of, Bill. And then check on your daughter. I'll talk to you later."

The technician met Bill in the hallway and swabbed the inside of his mouth with a giant Q-tip. Then he went into Summer's room where Paige sat. She held a wrinkled, well-thumbed magazine, her glasses pushed on top of her head and into her thick hair.

"Did that weird little cop technician find you?" she asked, then licked her finger and turned a page.

"She swabbed so hard, I doubt I have any DNA left."

Paige looked up, her face stony. She didn't smile, didn't exude any warmth toward him. Bill recognized the look, one that made her resemble their mother. He knew she was pissed about him grabbing Summer on Halloween. His sister, champion of the oppressed and defender of the downtrodden.

"Are you ready to lay into me?" he asked. "I see your face."

Paige turned her attention back to the magazine, although he suspected she wasn't really reading any of it. She licked her finger and turned another page, this time trying to make the paper snap a little.

"I'm thinking about Summer, really," Paige said, nodding toward her bed. "She doesn't look well."

"Obviously."

"She seems thin. Had she lost weight recently?"

"Maybe. She's taller. She's growing up. What are you suggesting?"

"Teenage girls sometimes don't eat."

"An eating disorder? Look, Paige, you always come up with crazy theories. You've always been a conspiracy nut. Remember all those JFK assassination books you read in high school? The ones that said the Mafia or the Cubans or LBJ pulled the trigger? She eats fine."

"Okay, not that. And I'm not a conspiracy nut just because I try to think about things and look at them from different angles." Paige frowned with concentration. "I haven't seen her for a while, but I've seen pictures on Instagram. She just looks thinner. But I don't know. . . ."

"And that's it? That's all you want to ask me? What else have you cooked up? Mom's dead, so you're the only one who can get up my ass this way."

Paige started to object, but the look of disappointment returned in full force. "I want to hear it from your own mouth. About what happened with her when she called the police."

Bill found himself remembering something from their childhood. When he was seven and she was five, Paige borrowed Bill's new Schwinn—midnight blue with a banana seat—and started riding it around the cul-de-sac at the end of their suburban street. Around and around Paige went, laughing and pedaling, her hair billowing behind her in the wind.

Bill stepped out into the road and ordered her to stop, but she refused. She kept riding and laughing, circling closer and closer to her brother but never getting off the bike. Every circuit she made raised the temperature on Bill's anger, so he bent down and found a small stick in the gutter. When his idiot sister made her next pass, Bill brought the stick down on her knuckles, bashing them against the solid handlebar grip. When Bill saw the hysterics the blow brought his sister to—and knowing the trouble he faced—he ran into the house, hiding in his bedroom.

For a moment, a foolish moment, he thought he'd get away with it, that Paige would wipe her tears, suck it up, and refuse to tell their mother what had happened.

But, of course, it all came out. Mom heard Paige crying. Paige showed off her bloody knuckles. And their mother appeared in his bedroom doorway, that look of crumbling disappointment one of the worst things Bill could ever see. He preferred anger or yelling or punishment to that maternal disappointment.

And that day in Summer's hospital room, Paige wore a similar look.

She pushed her sweatshirt sleeves up past her elbows and stared straight at him.

"Is it true?" she asked. "What that cop said you did to her?"

"You don't even want to discuss this outside?"

"Did you?"

"You know, Paige, it's really easy to sit there and judge when you have two parents in the house."

"I think of all the stupid stuff when we were kids. The way you tried to hurt me."

"Really, Paige? Now? Are you talking about the bike? We were babies. Didn't you ever spank your kids?"

"Never. And grabbing them that way isn't the same as spanking."

"Sometimes I think the whole generation should be spanked, whether they deserve it or not."

Paige played with her sleeves, tugging one down and then pushing it up again. "I'm just surprised, Bill. Did you apologize to her?"

Bill took a couple of deep, steadying breaths. "Do you know what happened the night I hit you with that stick? You and Mom went out that night. I don't know where. And I was home alone with Dad. He was watching TV, probably a Reds game, and I was sitting on the floor. I told him what I'd done to you. I guess Mom hadn't even told him."

"Figures. If I'd hit you, Dad would have known. And he would have chewed me out."

"The point is, Paige, I told him I felt bad about what I'd done, that I made you cry by hitting you with that stupid stick. And you know what he said?"

"I guarantee you he didn't tell you to apologize, because you never did," she said. "And Dad never apologized to anyone his whole life."

No, he didn't, Bill thought. *And I'd never, ever call him an asshole.*

"Exactly," Bill said. "He told me to forget about it. He didn't even take his eyes off the TV screen. He just told me to forget about it, as though even talking about it was trivial and unimportant."

"Why are you telling me this?" Paige asked, some of the anger out of her voice.

"Because you asked me if I ever apologized to Summer for what I did." Bill looked over at her unconscious form, the gentle rising and falling of her breaths. Those words she repeated came back to him like a chant. *No. No. No. No. No.* Was she remembering the night he grabbed her? Dreaming of it?

Was she afraid of him?

"No, I never did apologize to Summer."

CHAPTER TWENTY

T he next day, when Bill returned home for his afternoon shower and shave, he saw Adam Fleetwood sitting on the back patio, a bottle of Jack Daniel's and two glasses on the table next to him.

It was late February, almost spring but still cool, and the sky above was robin's egg blue, not a cloud in sight. Adam wore sunglasses and lifted his left arm in greeting as Bill came closer.

"What are you doing here?" Bill asked.

"Checking in on you." He nodded toward the bottle and glasses. "I figure you probably don't get a chance for a pick-me-up at the hospital."

Bill's scalp itched, and he felt dirty. But he sat down in the vacant chair and said, "Sure. I'll take one."

Adam poured two shots, and then both men lifted their glasses. For a long moment, they locked eyes as Bill waited for Adam to say something before they drank. He was a guy's guy, the kind of man other men liked to have around.

But he offered no words of wisdom. He waited on Bill.

So Bill said, "Here's to better days."

Adam clinked his shot glass against Bill's, gently, not spilling a drop, and the two men drank.

Bill felt good, sitting in the sun, the gentle, warming buzz of the whiskey working its way through his body. In that moment, he tried to pretend nothing else was wrong, that Summer would soon enough come breezing home from school, sending the evening into its predictable cycle of homework and dinner and television.

Bill remembered a poem he once read in college. He couldn't remember who wrote it, but it said something like "The world is too much with us." He understood that line better than ever. The world was too much with him. There was nowhere to hide, even on a pretty day with a bottle of good whiskey and a good friend nearby.

A silence settled over the two men. A blue jay fluttered from one tree to another, its bright feathers catching Bill's eye until the bird disappeared into the branches.

"I know you must really miss Julia," Adam said. "I mean, at a time like this."

"I do." Bill stared into his own glass, and then glanced at Adam. "She was a fan of yours."

"Who?"

"Julia. She always said what a nice guy you were, what a good neighbor." The liquor loosened his tongue. "How handsome. Remember, I used to joke with her that if anything ever happened to me, she could just walk over to your house."

"I remember you saying that." Adam smiled without showing his teeth. "That's flattering."

Bill swirled the amber-colored liquid in his glass. "Yeah, I guess it was."

"You're a good dad, though," Adam said, nodding. "You're here for Summer. Every day you were here for her. I haven't seen my son in months."

Bill looked over, surprised at the mention of his son. He waited because it seemed like Adam had more to say.

"Kid doesn't know me that well, living down in Tulsa," Adam said. "But you, you're right here. Every day. And you're sitting next to that hospital bed."

"I'm here at home now."

"You have to take a break, right? That's why your sister is here."

"Yeah. In fact, I came home for a quick shower, and then I want to get back."

"How is she?" Adam asked. "Summer."

"About the same. It's hard to see much progress. I'm hoping they'll take that chest tube out soon."

"That would be a good step." Adam poured himself another shot, but when he went to fill the other glass, Bill waved his hand in the air, declining. "You sure?"

"I don't think I can go back to the hospital and sit at her bedside smelling like whiskey." Before Adam could drink, Bill asked, "Why aren't you at work? Are you off the road this week or just taking a midday break to check on me?"

"Well, I did want to check on you." Adam nodded, his upper teeth resting on his lower lip, which gave him a slightly canine appearance. "I did want to see you about something else. Maybe we should talk another time, though. You're wanting to get back."

"I am, but you have me curious. If it's something happy, like you won the lottery or bought me tickets to next year's Super Bowl, I'd like to know. I could use the boost."

Adam smiled and looked away. He tapped his fingers against the armrest of the chair. "I wish it were that. I do. But I was going to tell you I'm moving."

"Moving?"

"Yeah, I thought about not telling you, what with everything you have going on. This has been a possibility for a while, but it all came to a head pretty quickly over the last week."

"Where are you moving?" Bill asked.

"Down to Tulsa. My son and my ex are down in Texas. Dallas. She's remarried and everything, but it's a lot closer than here. I can see the kid on weekends. I've been thinking for a while that maybe I need a change in my life. You know, a realignment of my priorities."

A light breeze kicked up, scattering the remaining dead leaves across the patio, a tumbling race. "Oh." A strange twinge jabbed Bill in the chest. "You're happy about this?"

"I think so. A different place. A new adventure. I've been here almost ten years. That's a long, long time for me." Adam considered Bill, his eyes probing. "Think of all the times we sat outside on a warm night, drinking and shooting the shit. We're always saying we want to do something different with our lives, make a new plan and follow it. Try some new venture."

"Sure. I've had the same thoughts. The budget cuts at work are squeezing me. Maybe all the way out."

"Exactly. We always say we want a change, so I'm making it happen." Adam was trying not to smile too much or look too satisfied with his plan. "Should I not have told you? I mean now, with everything on your mind."

"No, it's fine," Bill said, waving his hand at Adam. "I'll miss having you as a neighbor. And a friend. And I am a little envious. A new start sounds . . . intriguing. Hell, we'd talked about that investment opportunity. Going in on it together."

"Right. Yeah."

"I guess that's out. You haven't mentioned it for the last month or two."

"Yeah, I think it is over. I haven't talked to the guy for a while. It's tied up in bankruptcy. People are suing other people. It's kind of messy."

About eight months earlier, Adam came to Bill with the chance to invest in a self-storage facility south of town. A friend of Adam's was buying in, taking over the failing business, and he needed partners to put up some money. Bill was intrigued but uncertain about the risk. Adam showed no fear at all about putting in his money, and his confidence spilled over to Bill and nudged him along, enough so that Bill started checking his bank accounts and seriously considering it. But with Adam leaving and everything more up in the air than ever . . .

"Well, maybe I shouldn't be risking my money anyway," Bill said. "Everything is so uncertain these days. And that was before this happened to Summer." Bill pointed to the bottle between them, forcing a smile. "I will say I doubt anyone who moves in behind me will bring me whiskey."

"This is bad timing, isn't it? I mean, you're devastated. Crushed. I was going to come by the hospital and talk to you, but I figured that's not a good place. The news said Summer's still in the ICU. I'm sorry."

"No, it's okay. She's a fighter. She'll get better. I have to believe that." Bill tried again to put on something close to a real smile. He held his hand out to shake Adam's, felt the bigger man's strong grip, saw his hand swallowed up by his friend's. "I'm happy for you. It sounds like this will be a good change."

"I think so."

"And I guess it won't happen right away. You have to sell the house and pack, so there'll be time for a few more of these visits. Hell, maybe we'll have something good to celebrate, something like Summer coming home."

"I'd love to do that." But Adam looked sheepish. "It might be quicker than normal. The company's going to help me sell the house and put me up in a place down there. They need me pretty soon."

"Wow. Okay." Bill eyed the bottle and the empty glass but pushed the urge away. He put his hands on the armrests and rose from the chair. "Well, I think I need to get back."

"I'm sorry, bud. I should have waited."

"No, you're cool," he said. "Heck, maybe we'll take a trip down and visit you when Summer's better. I've never been to Oklahoma."

Adam nodded. "You bet. It's still touch and go, though?" Adam asked.

"Yeah, it is. It might be for a while."

"She's not even awake? Or talking?"

"Not awake." *No. No. No. No. No.* "She kind of forms words. Maybe just sounds. She makes a weird face when you say her name. Like she wants to react in some real way but can't. It's hard to tell what she's trying to do."

"I haven't heard much in the news about suspects or anything. Maybe the cops are playing it cool."

"I don't know," Bill said, remembering his encounter with Clinton and Todd. "That school is full of snotty kids. And they're also looking into every creep in the town. I'm not very patient, I guess."

Adam nodded, his face full of sympathy. "If you need anything before I go, holler. And let me know when Summer can have visitors. Or if you want me to bring you some food or something down at the hospital."

"I will."

Adam threw back the shot as Bill went inside.

CHAPTER TWENTY-ONE

When Bill returned to the hospital, he went into Summer's room and saw no sign of Paige. He took quiet, cautious steps to the side of the bed and bent down, kissing his daughter on the top of the head. She smelled clean, freshly washed by a nurse or orderly.

He took a step back and studied her, trying to see whether her injuries looked any better than they had earlier that morning. He thought the swelling was down, the kaleidoscopic bruises losing some of their vividness. But he couldn't be certain he was really seeing that progress and not just allowing his wishful thinking to take over. He wasn't sure he cared. Wishful thinking was better than nothing.

"Summer? Honey?"

No reaction, none at all. Bill wished she'd make that scrunched-up face again. He would be happy to see anything.

He leaned down again and stroked her arm. *Patience,* he reminded himself. *Patience.*

He checked Summer's other arm and noticed something missing. The silver bracelet she always wore, one Julia had given to her on Summer's thirteenth birthday. Bill hadn't had the sense Summer loved the bracelet, but after Julia died, she never took it off. Summer's name was engraved on the inside.

Did whoever did this to her also steal that bracelet? Its only real value was sentimental. And it stabbed Bill in the heart to think something from Julia that meant so much to Summer was missing.

He sat down, expecting Paige to return at any moment. But fifteen minutes passed and then twenty. A nurse came in to check Summer's vital signs, and Bill asked if she'd seen his sister.

"She was out in the hallway last I saw her."

"Just now?" Bill asked.

"She's been out there for a while, talking to a friend of your daughter's." The nurse finished her work and smiled at Bill. "They seemed to be having a pretty intense conversation."

When the nurse was gone, Bill went out into the hallway and looked around. The ICU seemed quiet. An orderly mopped the floor to the left, his steady motions and the sloshing of the dirty water sounding almost soothing. Bill went to the right to where the hall made a turn toward the elevators and a lounge for family members to sit and decompress. The door to the sparsely furnished room stood open, and Bill saw Paige sitting on the small, dingy couch. She was nodding her head while a tiny, mousy teenage girl talked and talked. Bill recognized Teena Everett, Summer's and Haley's friend whom he had described to Detective Hawkins as their unofficial third wheel. From the time Teena had spent at their house, Bill knew her teeth were crooked and in need of braces that her mother either couldn't afford or chose not to spring for. Her eyes were baby blue, her body slender and bony. For her sake, Bill hoped she blossomed someday.

Neither of them saw Bill. He waited just outside the door, listening as best he could through the low plinking of the Muzak from overhead. He caught a few snippets in between the notes of an ear-piercingly bad rendition of the Beatles' "The Fool on the Hill."

"Summer and Haley wouldn't invite me. . . . They didn't always call me. . . . They were so much alike, and I . . ."

Bill felt a stab of sympathy for the girl. No one liked being left behind, and everyone got left behind at some point. He suspected insecure, undersize Teena got left behind more than others.

Bill was turning away when Teena said, "Those boys were there, so I didn't want . . ."

He spun back and went through the door into the lounge. When he came in, both Paige and Teena jumped a little. "What's this?" he asked. "What about the boys?"

Teena flinched as if Bill had threatened to hit her. Her shoulders hunched, and her head lowered between them so she looked like a turtle retracting into its shell. Paige seemed disappointed, and Bill understood why. He'd broken the spell. Whatever rapport the two of them had going had been temporarily severed, but he didn't care. He needed to know.

"Well?" he said. "What is it?"

Teena tried to sink farther into the couch cushions.

Paige said, "It's okay, Bill. I'll tell you about it."

"I'm here now."

Paige gave him a "What gives?" look, one that managed to communicate her low opinion of his behavior in delicate situations. She turned and spoke to Teena as though the girl were a frightened baby bird. "Teena, why don't you go on home? You said you needed to."

Teena nodded and stood up.

"Do you need a ride?" Paige asked.

"I rode my new bike," she said. "It's not far."

"Okay," Paige said. "You call me or text me if you want to talk more."

Teena started to leave, and for a fraction of a moment, Bill wanted to reach out and stop her by placing his hand on her arm. But he knew he couldn't do that, so he remained stock-still as the girl walked past him and out of the room. Bill turned and watched her walk down the hall, her shoulders still hunched, her steps shuffling and knock-kneed.

He turned to his sister. "What was that all about?"

Paige patted the couch. "Sit down. I'll tell you."

CHAPTER TWENTY-TWO

"Why isn't she at school?" Bill asked as he sat.

"Her mom started homeschooling her this semester," Paige said. "I guess Teena learns better at home. Fewer distractions."

"Why was she even here?"

"She's worried about Summer, Bill," Paige answered as though he should understand without explanation. "She thought she could visit her. She's scared. I bet every kid in that school is scared. Wouldn't you be?" Paige's face grew serious. "The girl needs someone to talk to. Do you know her mom?"

"Not really. Julia handled most of the parental socializing and PTA meetings."

"I get the feeling her mom's not the best listener," Paige said. "Teena seemed lonely. Lost."

"You can't ride in on your white horse and save everybody."

"It's so terrible that I talked to a scared teenage girl. That I offered her a sympathetic ear." Paige's eyes glistened. "You know Haley's visitation is tonight, and the burial's tomorrow."

"Ugh," Bill said. "Right. I need to go."

"You should. I'm sure it will be crowded. They're having it in the gym at the high school. That's what Teena told me."

"What else was she telling you?" Bill asked. The room felt cramped and small. A coffeemaker and foam cups sat on one side of the room, a bookshelf with a row of tattered paperbacks on the other. An enterprising hospital employee had hung a framed motivational poster, an image of a tree and a rainbow with the message, *Keep looking for the colors. They're all around.*

Paige lifted her hands and ran both of them back through her hair. She shook her head as she did it. "I feel like I need a shower because of what she said."

Bill waited. He knew it was coming.

"Those kids from school, the ones the cops were asking you about—they were having some kind of a contest," Paige said. "Something to do with girls and sex. Apparently they tried to hook up with as many girls as possible, and each one of them received a certain number of points for each thing they did."

"Points?" Bill said, his brain trying to process what he was being told. "For what kind of things?"

Paige gave him a warning look. "You know, points for kissing, points for petting, points for sex—"

"Oh, God," Bill said. "I get it." He shifted in the unforgiving seat, his body unable to get comfortable. "And Summer and Haley . . ."

Paige nodded. "The boys kept a chart. I guess this Clinton kid was the ringleader. He had the chart at his house, and Summer saw it, saw her name on it. Haley's too. According to Teena, a number of their friends knew about it, whether they were on it or not. You thought she might have been dating one of these kids, the one she went to the dance with. Right? Todd? Maybe that's why."

Bill felt nauseated. The shot he'd had with Adam came partway up his throat, leaving a burning taste in his mouth. "That means . . . If she was on there, Summer . . ."

"She could have been on there for any number of things."

Bill gave Paige a quick look. "Is that supposed to make me feel better?"

"I'm just saying . . . you were worried about her having sex because of the birth control, so maybe she . . . They're teenagers, Bill. They do things."

Bill perked up in his seat, the nausea and bad taste diminishing. "Oh, my God. That's it. That's it."

"Slow down, Bill—"

"No, no." Bill jumped off the couch. He walked to the far end of the room, his heart thudding against his rib cage. "That's it. Maybe Summer and Haley said something about the chart, so they hurt them. Maybe they threatened to tell. Those boys didn't want to get caught. They didn't want to get in trouble. They silenced them. Summer could be so outspoken, so ballsy. She scared them. Hell, I just saw them at the school. You should have seen and heard them." His hands shook. The tremor spread through his body. "That's it. Jesus."

"We don't know much, Bill. I don't think it's as cut-and-dried as you're making it. But . . ."

"But what?"

"Teena thinks—she's not sure, but she thinks—those boys were blaming Summer and Haley for people finding out. That maybe the girls talked too much to their friends, like Teena, and now the boys are worried they're going to get in big trouble."

"Right. Maybe they decided to tell," Bill said. "Maybe something got out of hand."

"Maybe, Bill. All maybes. But Teena didn't tell any teachers. She doesn't think anyone in authority at the school knows." She paused. "Now Teena just feels terrible about the whole thing. I guess she was simultaneously interested in these boys and a little afraid of them."

"They might beat the daylights out of her too." Bill stared at the sludgy black coffee, catching a whiff of it as it burned in the pot. "Did she tell the police?"

"She's been talking to them," Paige said. "Slowly but surely."

"Why didn't Hawkins tell me about it?"

"I'm sure he will in good time," Paige said. "He probably doesn't want to give you too much half-baked information. Especially stuff that's inflammatory."

Bill fumbled in his pocket, searching for his phone. His hands continued to shake. "I'm calling Hawkins to make sure he's on this. They can arrest them right now." He got a grip on the phone and pressed the right buttons. "I hope they do it in front of the entire school."

"Bill?"

He looked at her while the phone rang and then switched to voice mail.

"What?"

"Just remember. Don't fixate on what Summer may or may not have done. Let's fixate on her getting better, okay?"

CHAPTER TWENTY-THREE

As the afternoon wore on, Bill's body felt stiff sitting in the chair in Summer's room. His knees and back ached, so he stood periodically and stretched. Paige brought him coffee and a sad-looking turkey sandwich from the cafeteria. Stale bread and wilted lettuce.

Bill also called Hawkins a few more times, but Hawkins still didn't get back to him. Bill floated the idea to Paige of going to the police station in person, but she told him to sit tight, to wait to hear from the detective in his own time.

"He's busy, Bill," she said. "Don't you want him devoting his energies to the investigation instead of talking to you?"

She made sense. Good, hard, logical sense. But the words didn't extinguish his flaming desire to be out in the world, doing something to find out what happened to his daughter. To find those boys. To talk to them and hold them accountable.

Distractions came in the form of visitors. A couple of teachers came by to talk to Bill and express their concern. Even the principal showed up, an older man named Cole Reynolds who wore a pencil-thin mustache and Italian loafers that looked too small for his stout body. Bill started to tell Reynolds about the boys from the school and the contest he'd learned about.

The principal raised his hand. "I've already heard from the police about this."

"So what are you doing?"

Reynolds reached out, placing his hand gently on Bill's forearm. Bill looked down at the dark hairs and pale skin, a pair of age spots. "A lot of people are hurting now, Bill. Including you. There's time for us to deal with these kids after we've helped them start to heal."

Bill tried but could summon no arguments back. He shook Reynolds's hand and even accepted a partial hug from the man. Everybody seemed to care. It felt good to be part of a web of understanding, to know others noticed pain and tried to ease the burden, even a little. Bouquets of flowers filled the room. Balloons and stuffed animals. A fruit basket and a box of chocolates that Bill and Paige couldn't keep their hands off.

A group from work came by, bringing an assortment of Bill's favorite snacks and an update on office gossip. Bill welcomed the distraction, happy to laugh a little about something trivial and small. He told his supervisor he'd be back as soon as he could, and they all rushed to tell Bill not to hurry, to take as much time as he needed.

Bill was feeling drowsy when Dr. Davis came by and studied Summer's chart as if it contained the solutions to life's eternal mysteries. Bill stood and waited, his foot half-asleep, the pins-and-needles feeling making him shift his weight like a nervous toddler.

Dr. Davis finally turned to him, her lab coat so blindingly white, it looked fresh out of the package. She wore running shoes, and Bill pictured her sprinting through the hospital, dashing from one awful crisis to the next and not growing winded. "We're going to move her to our rehab wing. She's stable now. No breathing difficulties. She can get the best care for her needs there instead of in ICU."

Bill waited for the doctor to say more, and when she didn't, he asked, "This is a good thing, right? Moving to rehab?"

"It's a step toward a more complete recovery."

"Is she going to wake up soon?" he asked, a sliver of a plea in his voice. He knew the doctor wasn't a magician or a god—she couldn't conjure a full recovery out of thin air—but he couldn't not ask. He needed to know.

"Her body's going to decide that," Davis said. "They may be able to move her tonight."

"Can I ask you something else?" Bill said. "She makes faces. She looks agitated, maybe in pain. Is that normal?"

"She may be in pain. We're controlling it as much as we can."

"But she looks like she wants to say something, like she wants to get something out but can't."

"She may be trying to speak. That's a good sign."

When she left, her running shoes squeaking, Bill looked at Paige. "You know what, Paige? I'm counting this move to rehab as a small victory. I just have to see it that way. And the faces and the trying to talk. The doctor's right—it's a good sign."

Paige nodded, her face earnest.

Bill said, "Compared to a family about to bury a daughter, we're looking pretty good."

CHAPTER TWENTY-FOUR

Bill stepped into his darkened, quiet house at six thirty that evening. He flipped lights on as he moved back to the bedroom, his footsteps the only sound. He felt like a stranger inside the space, someone who had walked into a place once inhabited by other people, people who had left fragments of their life behind.

He tried not to stop, but he did. He froze in the doorway to Summer's room. He left the light off, but enough filtered through from the streetlights outside that he saw the vague shape of the bed and the desk, the glint against the picture frames. It was a dark hole to go down, and he didn't have the time. He tore himself away.

Bill fumbled in his closet, grabbing a sport coat and a tie he hadn't worn since an awards dinner at work six months earlier. He put on clean pants and a white shirt, then stepped into black shoes that had sat untouched for so long, they'd acquired a layer of dust. After knotting the tie under his chin, he studied himself in the mirror. More of his scalp showed through his hair, and he used a comb to part it one way and then the other, finally giving up. He decided age, the inexorable march of time, was winning the battle. Some days the march seemed to be going right over him, leaving him dusty and dazed.

He didn't want to go to the funeral. The visitation started at the school at five o'clock, and it would be more than halfway over by the time Bill arrived. And because of Julia's death—and Summer's injuries—he understood what Haley's family members were going through. They were contemplating the thousands and thousands of days they'd been robbed of, the glittering path of dreams and aspirations that no longer stretched hopefully before them. Yes, memories brought comfort, but looking backward proved only so satisfying. Parents were hardwired to look ahead, to plan and dream. Haley's family couldn't do that anymore. Bill felt it like an ice pick in his guts. Haley's family was feeling it worse. Much, much worse.

He took a deep breath, psyching himself up for what lay ahead. Hundreds of scared, grief-stricken kids. Hundreds of shell-shocked parents. People would talk to him. They'd offer him comforting words, or they'd look at him askance, wondering how or why he let his daughter walk out the door of his house without knowing where she was going. Those things weren't the worst. The worst was how easily he could picture himself in Candy Rodgers's place, burying his daughter instead of waiting out a long, slow recovery.

But he had to go. He had to be part of it.

So many people had gone to Julia's funeral. So many people were sending cards and gifts and food while Summer was in the hospital.

He *was* part of it. A rather large piece.

He started for the door, opting to leave as many lights on as possible. He tried to remind himself to buy some timers, but he knew mundane thoughts like that entered and left his brain like water through a downspout.

He stepped outside, heading to the car. The sky was darkening, turning a deep purple. His phone rang, a call from Paige.

"What's wrong?" he asked.

A pause. "Bill? Have you left yet?"

"No. What's wrong? Is Summer okay?"

"She's the same," Paige said, a little breathless.

"Asleep or whatever?"

"Yes, of course."

Bill still didn't feel relief. That meant there was something else going on. "What?" he asked.

"I just got a call from Teena," Paige said. "She needs my help. Our help."

"What's happened?"

"Something's going on at Clinton Fields's house. Something happened to another girl."

CHAPTER TWENTY-FIVE

Bill knew the way.

He didn't bother picking Paige up. He cut through side streets, daylight fully gone, and entered the subdivision where Clinton Fields lived with his parents. Bill had been there a few times, dropping off Summer and even Haley. He remembered the girls' excitement as he took them to meet their friends, their voices chattering, their energy not entirely concealing the teenage nervousness and insecurity underneath. He'd talked to the parents a few times. Clinton's father was a florid-faced insurance agent, his mother a dietitian at a clinic one town away. Once when Bill dropped the girls off they shared a drink and chatted about the kids and basketball and town gossip. They went out of their way to offer sympathy over Julia's death.

What had gone so horribly wrong in their house?

Bill turned onto their street. As soon as he did, he saw the blue strobing police lights, the spastic glow bouncing off the facing of every house. Three cop cars and, parked among them, an ambulance, a hulking beast topped with red lights.

"No, no," Bill said. "No."

He parked as close as he could, three doors away. Neighbors stood

grouped in small clusters, their arms crossed, curiosity more prominent than worry on their faces.

Bill jumped out and headed right for a stocky, uniformed cop
who stood with his thumbs hooked in his belt, a human wall.

"Is Detective Hawkins here?" Bill asked. He was breathless, his
heart thudding. Only when he stood still for a moment, in the street
with the flashing lights and confronted by the stoic face of a twenty-
something police officer, did Bill realize how fully worked up he was.
He looked at the front of the Fields house. The door was open, and
glowing yellow light spilled out onto the lawn. Another cop was in
the doorway, speaking into the radio fastened to his lapel.

Something happened to another girl.

Another. And couldn't it have been prevented if the police had
done something to Clinton and his friends sooner?

"Are you a family member?" the cop asked.

"My daughter . . . I'm Summer Price's father."

The cop's eyebrows lifted almost imperceptibly. Bill wondered
where they found these fresh-faced but passionless young cops. Were
they born? Or made?

"You should just wait here, sir."

"Tell Hawkins I'm here. What did they do? What went wrong in
there?"

"Did Detective Hawkins call you?" the cop asked.

"No. One of those kids called my sister. Teena Everett. Is she in
there? Is she hurt?"

The cop's brow wrinkled. He tilted his head to the right. "Just
hold on one minute, sir." He raised his hand, shooing Bill back, and
then spoke in a low voice into his own radio.

A couple of neighbors stood close by, a young couple in running
clothes with an aging mutt on a leash at their feet. "Do you know
what happened?" Bill asked.

The couple shook their heads. "We just moved in." Then the couple started craning their heads, trying to see around Bill.

Bill spun. He saw the paramedics in the doorway, bringing out a stretcher.

As the paramedics came closer, Bill saw the shape of a body under a white sheet. He felt immediate relief when he saw the sheet wasn't covering the girl's face. She wore an oxygen mask, and her eyes were closed. Her brown hair was a loose tangle. Bill didn't recognize her, but she looked young. Very young and very vulnerable.

Like Summer in that hospital bed.

Bill watched from a few feet away as the paramedics lifted the girl inside the ambulance. One stayed in the back with her while the other jumped out and closed the heavy metal doors.

"Is she okay?" Bill asked. "What happened to her?"

But the paramedic ignored him and walked to the front of the vehicle.

Bill looked around, saw the cop he'd first spoken to.

"Jesus, what happened to her?" he asked. "Did they beat her up?"

Bill again received no answer. The cop made the shooing gesture again.

"You can't do that," Bill said to him. "You can't just brush me aside. My daughter is in the hospital. Another girl is dead. Those animals did it. They hurt that girl."

"Sir?" the cop said, raising both of his hands chest high. "Just move back."

"Wait—"

A familiar figure emerged from the house. Even from a distance, Bill recognized Hawkins. His broad belly, his smooth movements on the uneven grass. "Bill?"

Bill took the chance to move past the cop and started across the lawn, meeting the detective halfway. "What the hell's going on?"

"What the hell are you doing here?" Hawkins asked. "Who told you about this?"

"Teena Everett. She called my sister, and I came right over."

Hawkins turned and looked at the house. Then he faced Bill again. "I see. . . ."

"What happened?"

"Bill, I think the best thing is for you to go home. You can't be in the middle of an investigation like this. Go home. I'll talk to you later, I promise."

"You haven't returned a single one of my calls all day."

Hawkins looked exasperated, the muscles in his jaw clenching. "Bill, I've been working all day. And I got called out of Haley's visitation to come here."

"Just tell me—"

"Go. You need to go. I'll call later."

Hawkins placed a not-so-gentle hand on Bill's back and applied pressure, moving Bill toward the street. Bill took two steps back and looked to the house again.

He saw two cops emerging from the doorway. Clinton Fields was in between them. When he saw Bill, the corner of his mouth lifted again, just as it had in the school parking lot. Bill moved quickly, lurching past Hawkins.

"What did you do? What did you do?"

The boy raised his hands defensively, shrinking back between the cops like a scared child. Bill swung his fist wildly, a haymaker that Clinton managed to duck away from. When he missed, Bill lost his balance. He straightened up, intending to swing again, but someone grabbed him across the chest, a thick forearm restraining and pulling him back. Bill fell to the ground, felt the damp cold through his dress pants.

"Okay, okay," Hawkins said. "Get the kid out of here. His parents are pulling up right now. Let them take him to the station."

Bill remained seated in the grass. He wiped his palms on his pant legs.

Hawkins bent down, his large face filling Bill's vision like the rising moon. "Are you calmed down now?" he asked. "Do you want to have a quick chat?"

Bill nodded his head, the blades of grass tickling his fingers.

Hawkins stood up, held out a big hand.

"Behave yourself, Bill."

He pulled Bill to his feet.

CHAPTER TWENTY-SIX

The police car smelled like fried food and vomit. The metal grate between the front and back seats obscured Bill's view of the street, preventing him from seeing what became of Clinton Fields and his parents. Bill's hands were free, and he reached out only to find there was no door handle. Just a smooth, black surface.

He waited. His pants still felt a little wet from when he fell onto the ground.

After ten more minutes, Hawkins pulled the door open and sat down, the seat groaning under his bulk. He left the door open, allowing a cool gust of wind to come into the backseat.

"I know what you're going to say," Bill said. "You're going to say I shouldn't have done that."

Hawkins held up his hand, requesting silence. For a long moment, he just sat in the seat next to Bill, staring straight ahead, his hands resting in his lap.

Bill's face flushed. He felt embarrassed but not sorry. He refused to apologize for trying to protect his daughter. He only regretted that his return to her bedside would be delayed by sitting in the back of the stinking cruiser while waiting for a lecture.

"If you had hit that boy . . . someone could have pressed charges," Hawkins said finally, his voice as cold and flat as the night wind. He reached up and scratched the area where his shirt collar touched his skin. "You shouldn't even be here."

"I got a call that something happened to a girl. Another girl just like my daughter. Of course I came."

"To do what? Take a swing at a kid?"

"A kid who is some kind of monster. Did you see the look on his face? He was taunting me, egging me on."

"I'm glad you didn't take the bait." Hawkins looked at his watch. The skin of his forearm was pale and freckled. "I have to go, but I'll tell you what I know. Not because I think you deserve it, but just to keep you off my ass as long as possible. And because I need to know more about Teena Everett." He cleared his throat and pointed at the house, his thick finger moving just in front of Bill's nose. "About six kids went to Haley's visitation tonight, but then they took the opportunity to slip out and come back here. The parents were still at the school, but the kids left. There's no school tomorrow because of the burial."

Hawkins put his hand down, but Bill looked at the house. Bright lights glowed in every window. Even in late winter, the yard looked neat and orderly, every shrub trimmed, every leaf blown. "What happened in there?" Bill asked, turning back to the detective.

"They were drinking. One of the girls had too much. Alicia Frank. Do you know her?"

"I've heard the name."

"She must have been drinking earlier to get as intoxicated as she was."

"That's the girl on the stretcher?"

Grim-faced, Hawkins nodded, the bearer of bad news. "She was unconscious. She and Clinton had gone off alone, into the laundry room. Alicia must have passed out in there. It looks like Clinton came out and got his friend Todd. They took some photos of her in that condition and shared them on Snapchat. Typical teen stuff. They drew on her. Posed her with her finger stuck up her nose. Teena was there with them. She saw the photos, and, well, that's when she called the police. And she called your sister."

Bill turned away, looking back at the house. A lone cop came out the front door, his dark shape silhouetted for a moment. "Did they . . ."

"We'll check for that. All of that. Alicia had some bruising on her legs. Clinton says it happened when she fell, that she stumbled over some laundry baskets."

"Liar."

"Why did Teena call your sister?" Hawkins asked.

Bill explained about their meeting at the hospital, the connection they seemed to have formed. "My sister is a sucker for hard-luck cases. She wants to help the girl. I guess I'm surprised Teena was there. I thought she was on the outs with those kids."

"Who knows? Maybe she's gained some status by being friends with Summer and Haley."

"I want you to nail their hides to the wall," Bill said, emphasizing his point by jabbing his finger in the air. "You've got it now. They screwed with another girl. They left Haley's funeral and attacked another girl."

"No one is using the word 'attacked' but you, Bill. You should go home. I'll forget about tonight's escapades if you just go home." Hawkins left the car. He came around to Bill's side and pulled the door open, stepping back while Bill stood up. "I've got to go to the station."

"They're so stupid," Bill said. "All of this going on and they attack someone again. And take pictures."

"Were you smart when you were young?" Hawkins asked.

CHAPTER TWENTY-SEVEN

They buried Haley the next day. Sleet fell from the sky, pinging off windows and car roofs, glazing the streets and sidewalks with a thin layer of ice. For a good reason, Bill skipped the service. The morning was given over to waiting for a brawny orderly to arrive and roll Summer's bed through the hospital's labyrinthine hallways to the new room.

Once the process of moving her began, Bill and Paige walked ahead and sat in chairs near Summer's new room. The rehab wing was newer. The modern furniture made it feel less like a hospital and more like an upscale doctor's office. The walls were painted a metallic gray; the light fixtures gave off soft light. Even the magazines looked newer and nicer.

Bill needed to say something to his sister. He tapped his fingers against the armrest.

"You should go home, Paige. She's out of danger, and we don't know how long she'll be here. You have a family to get back to."

Paige was already shaking her head, a loose strand of hair bouncing around her face. "They're fine. They're probably glad I'm gone. I'm going to stick around a while longer."

"I just don't want you to put your life on hold for me. For us."

"This is my life," she said. "We're family, remember?"

Bill stopped tapping the armrest. He reached over and squeezed her knee. "Okay."

"I got a quick text from Teena this morning," Paige said.

A woman came into the waiting area with three small children. She looked haggard and older than her years. Bill wondered if some tragedy had befallen her husband, the father of the three children, and now she was spending her days in a rehab center waiting room, hoping for the best and preparing for the worst.

"What did she say?" Bill asked.

"She's scared. She thinks those boys might be lying about what happened to Alicia. But she didn't say much more. I'm going to reach out to her later."

"I haven't heard from Hawkins, but I'm trying to be patient like you said."

"What are you doing about work?" she asked.

Bill shrugged. One benefit of not traveling much was that he had accumulated a fair amount of sick and vacation time. They needed him on the job, but the world managed to turn without him there to oversee the upgrade of Internet coverage in the residence halls or to take an occasional phone call from a befuddled history professor who simply needed to learn how to attach a Word document to an e-mail.

"They're covering for me," he said. "It's a good group."

"I read about the state budget cuts," she said.

"It's mostly on the academic side. Not in our office."

Bill wanted to convince his sister not to worry about him, but he struggled to convince himself. He was caught in a vise—he needed to be away and tend to Summer, but the longer he was away, the more his department might realize they functioned just fine without him.

As one of the more senior members of the team, he knew he'd be the first to get axed if the budget cuts grew worse. And then without health insurance or a steady income, how would he manage Summer's recovery? How much time would it take to find another job? And what if he had to relocate or commute?

"You sure?" Paige asked. "You could go in for a half day. I could sit here with Summer—"

"No, no," Bill said. "No, I can't leave her alone."

"She wouldn't be alone."

Bill just kept shaking his head. "My place is here, no matter what happens." He pointed at the floor. "A husband can't walk away. . . ."

"A dad, you mean?"

"What's that?"

"You said 'a husband.' I think you mean a dad can't walk away."

A nurse and the orderly emerged from Summer's room and indicated they could go in.

"Neither one should," he said, going back. "Neither one."

Paige followed Bill into the room. It too was a vast improvement. The walls and curtains were warmer, the bed less industrial. A large window looked out on a copse of trees, and despite the bleak weather, it felt good to be able to see something natural. If it hadn't been for the awful circumstances of Summer being severely injured, it would be a pleasant space to rest or relax in.

Bill went to Summer's bedside, leaning down close to his daughter and giving her a gentle kiss on the top of her head. She looked frail, a fragile collection of bones and flesh, one that could collapse at any moment. Paige walked to the other side of the bed and bent down, disappearing for a moment and then reemerging with Winnie the Pooh in her hand.

"He keeps ending up on the floor," Paige said.

"Probably hard to hold with her hands bandaged."

"Yeah, maybe. Are you sure she really likes to sleep with it? Maybe she doesn't anymore."

"It's been on her bed every day and night at home for twelve years."

"Okay. It just seems like . . . Never mind." Paige tucked the bear against Summer's side, securing it among the folds of the blankets.

"How would she even know the bear is there?" Bill asked. "She can't see it."

"She can feel it. If she doesn't like the sensation, she might try to push it away."

"This room is nicer, but I still just want it to feel more like home."

"She keeps doing that thing with her mouth. You know, almost like she's trying to form a word? Bill, it looks like she keeps trying to make an 'M.' She presses her lips together like she wants to say a word that begins with 'M.'" She lowered her voice. "Do you think she wants Julia? In her state, maybe she doesn't remember or know. Or it's a primal thing. Or maybe she hears my voice and thinks—"

"Paige, we just don't know."

"Did she do that when Haley's mom was here? Maybe a woman's voice throws her off."

"You know what, you should just go back to the house. Take a break. I'm here. Remember, the doctor said it's all good."

Paige studied him from across the bed, her forehead creased. She came around and reached out for Bill, taking him by the hand and guiding him away from Summer's bed.

"What are you doing?"

"I want to ask you something."

His sister led him to the two modern, leather chairs that sat in the corner. Bill's body sank into the soft material, such a change from the other room. He felt like dozing off.

Paige scooted closer. Bill looked away, his eyes on Summer where she slept in the bed.

"What was going on with you and Julia when she died?"

Bill turned back but didn't say anything. He hoped the look on his face was enough to silence his sister.

But it wasn't. Nothing ever silenced her.

"Out there in the hall you said 'husband' instead of 'father'—"

"I don't want every slip of the tongue analyzed."

"Come on, Bill. You guys visited us about a year before Julia died. I could see the strain then. I said something about it to Kyle when you left, and he agreed. It was not a happy marriage we witnessed that weekend."

"I don't even remember what happened that far back. But you know I hate to travel. I was probably just in a bad mood because of that."

"Gee, thanks. In a bad mood because you traveled to see your sister."

"Can we just drop this, please?" But his voice sounded unconvincing. He stared straight ahead, watching the steady rise and fall of Summer's chest. "That was a long time ago."

"Two and a half years?"

She reached out, resting her hand on his shoulder. But Bill jerked away, an act that felt childish even as he performed it.

"Okay," she said. "I'll let it go."

Bill felt like his father in that moment. Cold. Distant. His father's advice about hitting Paige with the stick echoed in his brain: *"Just forget it."*

But nothing was ever forgotten. Was it?

"I don't know if we would have made it, Paige. Julia and I. If she'd lived, I don't know if our marriage would have survived." He rubbed his hands together and kind of wished his sister's hand still rested on his shoulder. But he couldn't ask for her to place it there again, could he? Not after he snapped at her like an angry dog. "I thought she was cheating on me. I really did."

Paige's jaw dropped open. Bill saw her tongue and a silver filling near the back of her mouth. "No. No way."

"I was working a lot. She was at school a lot. We were like two ships that passed each other sometimes, trading off keeping an eye on Summer but not really being together." Bill tapped both of his feet, a rat-a-tat sound in the quiet room. "She made a lot of friends at school. People who shared an interest in the things she studied. We were losing the thread, losing a sense of ourselves as a couple. And then she died. She died alone on our kitchen floor because of me."

"Oh, Bill." And Paige rested her hand on his shoulder again. And he let it stay there, feeling the slight pressure and the warmth of his sister through his shirt. "She died because of an accident, the kind of thing that could have happened to anyone. It happens every day to someone, and it's awful, but no one could have stopped it."

"You don't understand, Paige. The very last thing I ever said to her, the very last words we exchanged were me accusing her of having an affair. I did that, and I left, and then she died."

CHAPTER TWENTY-EIGHT

"Do you want to go into the hallway?" Paige asked, sensing some larger revelation coming.

"No." Bill looked to the bed, to Summer's gentle sleep. Maybe he wished she could hear what he had to say as well. . . .

Maybe. Someday, if not right then.

Bill had come home for lunch the day Julia died, something he did from time to time as a cost-saving measure. With Julia in school part-time and with Summer growing out of her clothes and shoes seemingly every five minutes, they needed to spend as little as possible.

Bill brought in the mail, including the latest credit card statement. He promised himself he wouldn't open it. Opening the credit card statement only made him unhappy, and he'd made a rule in his own mind that he wouldn't open any bill until the due date grew closer. Why torture himself so far in advance? Maybe he'd win the lottery and not have to sweat it so much.

But he did open that one. And saw a $475 charge for registration for an academic conference. They'd talked about Julia attending, thinking that it could help her career when she graduated, but the cost was so high and it didn't seem the time was right. They needed to do other things—get the furnace fixed, possibly buy a new car. And Bill hated the thought of her going away with the people from school, hated the thought that her academic life might be taking her away from him. From their marriage.

That maybe there was someone there. Another man.

But Julia had signed up and charged it without revisiting the subject.

"I was furious," he told Paige. "I threw the bill across the room. And I yelled. And I'm sure I stormed around, looking and sounding a lot like Mussolini."

"I've seen that act before."

"Right," Bill said. "Thank God for family. They remember all the stuff we want to forget. You know, it's funny. You remember me whacking you with a stick. Do you remember all the times I drove you places? The times I helped with your homework? The times I let you sleep in my room when you were scared?"

"I remember those too," she said. "And, thanks."

"But you don't bring them up."

"The stick is much more dramatic." She smiled. "I bled."

"Anyway." Bill looked down at his folded hands and the gold band he still wore on his ring finger. "I accused her of having someone else, of being involved with another man, and being distracted from me and Summer and our life together."

"My God. If Kyle ever did that to me—"

"Yeah, sure, she ended up denying it. But when the words first came out of my mouth, she looked guilty. Her face just froze for a second like she'd been caught. And then she denied it. I saw it, Paige. I saw that look. So I left the house. I didn't eat. We didn't talk. I just left and went back to work. I sat at my desk, eating those stupid orange peanut butter crackers you get out of the vending machine."

"You remember that?" Paige asked.

Bill did. Peanut butter crackers and a Sprite. He remembered because—

"The wrapper was sitting on my desk the first time Julia called. That was at one thirteen."

"She called to apologize? Or to ask you to apologize?"

"First she called to say she was going ahead and painting the kitchen. She'd been planning that project for a while, but we were going to do it that weekend. Instead, she started right then, without me."

"I see." Paige lifted her hand to her mouth. "So if you hadn't fought, you might have done it together that weekend. And maybe she wouldn't have—"

"I didn't answer her calls." He played with the ring, sliding it up and down his finger. "I didn't answer that first call, and I didn't answer the second. And she said when I got home she'd tell me something, something that would clear up everything we'd been going through. I guess about the affair. Or the possible affair. See, here's the weird thing. There was an open bottle of wine in the kitchen. And a half-full glass on the counter. She never drank during the day. Never. It made her sleepy, lethargic. If she drank wine, she did it at night."

"Maybe that's why she fell."

"Right. Maybe. Hell, maybe the wine combined with being up on the ladder. Maybe fumes from the primer. Or maybe she was drinking for another reason, like someone was coming over. Or she was going somewhere. It was a mess. Paint everywhere. Spilled wine. When she fell, everything went with her. Hell, it doesn't matter. What matters is she fell, and maybe she wouldn't have been on that ladder if we hadn't fought. If I'd just picked up the phone instead of freezing her out. I ignored her. You know that's what I do, right?"

"I lived with you. I just let you cool down and then you come around."

"Well, I did it to my wife on the day she died. Instead of talking to her more about my accusation, or offering to help that weekend, I ignored her. I sat at my desk at my stupid job while she fell to the floor in our kitchen, banged her head, and died. Alone." Bill continued to play with the ring, but he stopped and looked over at his sister. "What do you think of that?"

Paige had tears in her eyes. Her face radiated pity for her big brother. She scooted her chair even closer and placed her arm around Bill's back. "But you can't think that made a difference. With an accident like that . . . she could have just as easily fallen with you there. Or if you hadn't had a fight."

"Summer found her, you know. She came home from school, and there was Julia on the floor. Stone dead. Bleeding. Summer called me at work." Bill shrugged. Helpless. A fool. "None of it had to happen. At least not that way. You see, even if Julia had to die, at least if I'd picked up the call, I could have spared Summer the experience of seeing her mom that way. Of finding her mother's body when she was just fourteen years old."

Something went by in the hallway, a cart with squeaking wheels. The noise seemed to find a nerve in Bill's inner ear, and he shivered.

"Did you ever—"

"No, I never told Summer about why I missed the phone calls. She saw a shrink right after Julia's funeral, someone the school recommended. I went a few times, but the focus was on her. And she has a guidance counselor at school. She had some bad dreams, I know. She slept with the light on for a few months. But since then, nothing I could see. I'm sure she thinks about it every day. I know I do. If I could wish for one thing besides her getting better right now, it would be that I could erase that memory from her brain. Forever."

"I'm sorry, Bill. Really, I am. I wish I could make you forget it as well."

"About a week after Julia died, after the funeral and everything, I was picking up the house. Trying to be normal, I guess. I found this balled-up piece of paper behind the trash can. A note, or the start of one, in Julia's handwriting. It just said, *I can't do this anymore.* But then it stopped. Like she started writing and then changed her mind and threw it away. Maybe she was going to leave me. Maybe when I came home that night, if she hadn't died, she was going to tell me she was leaving."

"Or maybe she wasn't," Paige said. "More likely she wasn't."

"I guess I'll never know."

Across the room, Summer stirred under her covers, a quick jostling. It was the most movement they'd seen from her since she'd been in the hospital.

They both stood up, watching.

Summer jerked her right arm and knocked Winnie the Pooh back onto the floor.

CHAPTER TWENTY-NINE

Paige walked over and picked up the stuffed bear. When she straightened, she looked back at Bill.

"She really doesn't seem to like the bear," he said. "But that's a good sign. She's moving. She's expressing something."

"I know she's been doing that thing with her mouth. Is that all you've seen from her like that?"

Bill hesitated, his eyes fixing on the stuffed animal in his sister's hand. "Why are you asking me this?"

"I'm just—I'm wondering about something."

"What?"

"Can you just answer the question? Has she tried to say anything else?"

No. No. No. No. No.

"She made some sounds, something that sounded like 'no' the other day," he said, the words emerging from his mouth as though they were covered with glue. He relented. "In fact, there've been a couple of times when I've been close to her or talked to her when she's acted that way. Like she wanted me to go away." Bill moved closer to the bed. "I figured she was having some kind of flashback to the attack. You said she might be saying 'mom' because she hears a woman's voice. Maybe the sound of a man's voice, even mine, sends her back to the attack. You have to figure it was a man who did this to her."

Paige stared down at her niece, but her face was just a cover for the swirl of thoughts racing through her mind. "Maybe," she said. "Maybe."

"Paige, you seem to be implying something. I know you. I know when you have something on your mind, so what is it?"

Paige took a deep breath. She touched her hair even though nothing appeared to be out of place. "Okay, you're going to think I'm nuts. But Summer doesn't like the bear, which you say she sleeps with every night. And when Haley's mom was here, she started doing that 'M' thing, kind of like she wanted to say the word 'mom.'"

"She did that to you too."

"I've noticed something else over the last day. When I say her name, when I call her Summer, she . . . reacts. But she reacts negatively. She scrunches up her face like she smells something bad."

"She's in pain. You heard the doctor."

"From hearing her own name?" Paige held up her hand, asking for patience. "Okay. What's the deal with Haley's dad? Where is he? I read something in the paper. He doesn't live here, does he?"

"Arizona. But he came for the funeral. He's here today."

"But Haley hadn't seen him in a few years. It sounds like he's not on the scene. At all. Reading between the lines, the guy seems like a total dick, does he not?"

"I had that impression of him, yes. A lot of people have that impression of me because I grabbed my daughter."

Paige came around the end of the bed. She tossed the stuffed bear onto one of the chairs, where it bounced once and then tumbled onto the floor. She came up to Bill, her face full of sympathy, and reached out, placing both of her hands on his. She took them in a firm grip and stared into his eyes.

"You've got to listen to me, Bill," she said. "You've got to listen, and you can't get mad at me for what I'm about to say. I could be wrong. I hope I am wrong."

"Don't start the 'Don't get mad' crap again, Paige."

"Listen."

"You're acting crazy." He pulled his hands out of her grip.

"She hates the bear and throws it on the floor. She tries to say 'mom' when Candy is here. She makes a face."

"I thought she moved her mouth that way when you spoke to her? You're not her mother."

Paige ignored him. "She's skinnier, Bill. She is. And she has that piercing. And it sounds like Haley's dad is a turd, and when you get close, she acts like she doesn't want you there."

Bill shook his head and backed away more. "She can't see me. She doesn't know who I am."

"She hears a male voice. And I've heard you. A few times you've said to her, 'It's Dad. I'm here.' If she hates her dad, she might react that way."

"Who might?"

Paige pointed at the bed. "Haley. I've seen the pictures, Bill. Hell, the girls said it themselves. They're like twins. Like sisters. Haley's a little thinner, sure, but they have the same hair, the same clothes. They're the same height. And if you can't see their faces, how could you really tell them apart?"

"Summer's ID. They found Summer's ID on that girl's body. Right there. That girl. Summer. My daughter. She had her school ID with her name on it. Okay? What do you say to that?"

Paige looked stumped, but only for a second. "Girls trade clothes all the time. Friends carry each other's IDs sometimes. Remember our trip to see R.E.M? You carried my ID the whole time because you thought I would get drunk and lose it. Remember?"

Bill had backed away so far that he was almost to the wall. He let his body go a little slack, slumping so that the wall held some of his weight.

He felt tired. Just tired.

And he didn't want to hear anything else that Paige had to say.

"Just go back to the house, Paige. You're worn out. You're cooking up another crazy theory."

"Look, look." Paige went over to the bed and stood close to Summer. She leaned down, her voice a whisper. "Summer? It's Aunt Paige. Can you hear me?"

Summer's face contorted. The left side of her lip curled, and she turned her head, slowly, first one way and then the other.

Paige looked up. "You see, Bill."

"You're torturing her. She can't speak."

"Do me one favor," she said. "Walk over here and let's look at one part of her—a part of Summer's body that we can really identify as being hers."

Bill thought of her exposed breast, her body on display for all those strangers to see. Her body exposed to the elements in skeevy Dunlap Park. "What part of her body are you talking about?"

"You tell me. Pick something."

Right then he wished he had the stick again, the one he used to bash Paige's hand when they were little kids. He wanted to lash out at her, to say or do something that would hurt her. And the very act of hurting her would allow them to not face the subject that hovered in the air between them like a noxious cloud.

But they weren't kids anymore. And he could push her away as hard as he wanted, but the substance of what she was saying wouldn't change.

Why did Summer react that way every time he came close?

Why was she so animated when Candy came nearby?

Why shake her head and make a sour face when she heard her own name?

Bill brushed past his sister, heading for the bed.

CHAPTER THIRTY

Bill reached the girl's side. He studied his daughter's form.

She had to be wrong. Paige had to be wrong.

The police, the doctors, the paramedics. Everyone looked at the two girls and reached a conclusion. Sure, they looked alike and dressed alike. Go out into the streets of Jakesville or any other town in America and see thousands upon thousands of fifteen-year-old blond girls, all wearing the same clothes and listening to the same music and carrying the same phones and talking the same way.

But people didn't mix them up.

They didn't mix them up when they died.

"I don't want to do this, Paige."

"I know. I don't want you to do it either. If you just do it now, we don't ever have to talk about it again. I'll apologize. I'll say it was a silly conspiracy theory or whatever you want to call it."

Bill felt a hitch and tremble in his legs. If a strong gust of wind came through the room, it would have sent him reeling, making him tumble end over end until he crashed into some obstacle.

He might even welcome that wind. Something—anything—to take him out of that room.

"Her hands," he said. "Summer has Julia's hands—you know that. Long, thin fingers. I know I'm biased, of course, but she has beautiful hands. When I came here to the hospital that first day and they were bandaged, I actually thought about them being damaged. It's silly and vain—"

"They are nice hands. I noticed them when you came to visit. Right before . . ." She left the thought unfinished.

And Bill stood in the hospital room, facing another moment of "right before." If he went ahead and acted on Paige's hunch, things might never be the same again.

Never.

"I'd know my boys' hands anywhere," Paige said. "And Kyle's. Hell, I'd recognize your hands anywhere. Yours look just like Dad's."

"Okay, so you want me to just . . . just look at her hands and see if they're Summer's? Fine."

He reached down and started unwrapping the gauze on Summer's hand. A silly thought entered his head, one that made him think of monster movies on late-night television. A mummy. Some dumb archaeologist sticking his nose where it didn't belong and unleashing the worst terrors imaginable on the unsuspecting victims in the way.

"Let me call a nurse," Paige said. "Be careful."

"I'm being careful."

But he didn't stop unwrapping.

And he was in the line of whatever would be revealed.

When he'd peeled the wad of gauze off the hand, he threw it onto the floor.

At first, he only saw the healing scrapes and bruises. The hand looked like it had been through a war.

But it was a smaller hand, the fingers shorter than he knew Summer's were. Nothing at all like Julia's. Nothing at all like his daughter's.

Or had Paige's crazy notion so infected his mind that he couldn't see reality right before his eyes?

No. He was right. And Paige saw it too.

"Oh, Bill."

He wished for the wind to blow him away.

PART
TWO

CHAPTER THIRTY-ONE

The man from the funeral home arrived at the house in the afternoon. He wore a dark suit, his black hair slicked back from his forehead, and he looked surprisingly young. As he came inside, shaking hands with Detective Hawkins and Paige, Bill wondered why he assumed all funeral directors would be older. After all, weren't all old funeral directors once young funeral directors?

The man gave Bill a sincere and lengthy handshake, introducing himself as Todd Winter of Winter and Sons. Bill assumed Todd's father had handled Julia's funeral, since he didn't remember meeting him then. "I'm sorry for your loss," he said, and then looked around for a place to sit, a slim black briefcase clutched in his left hand.

"We can sit at the kitchen table," Paige said, stepping in when Bill didn't speak up.

The four of them trudged out to the kitchen. In the twenty-four hours since the discovery at the hospital, a number of neighbors and coworkers had come by, bringing casseroles and desserts, more than Bill and Paige alone could eat. The food was stuffed in the refrigerator, and several cakes and pies sat on the counters untouched. Bill had leaned somewhat heavily on the Tennessee whiskey the night before, and the fog of his grief was amplified by the lingering cloud of a hangover. He vaguely remembered Adam coming by, offering support, and then Paige taking the bottle away sometime just after midnight. He thought he'd cried like a child as Paige led him back to the bedroom, slipped off his shoes and pants, and tucked him under the covers.

He knew for certain she'd left a bucket by the side of the bed, because he stumbled over it in the morning when he woke up, an inch of fuzz covering his tongue and an eyeball-melting headache roaring through his brain.

Paige offered everyone something to drink or eat.

The undertaker declined, and Bill said nothing, but Paige still went over and brought him a steaming mug of coffee, something clearly designed to keep him awake and sharp while the conversation took place.

When they were all settled, Hawkins nodded to Todd Winter, who nodded back and slid some papers out of his briefcase. But he didn't look at them.

"We have some things to decide, Mr. Price," he said. "I've been talking to the Rodgers family as well as to the police about the ways in which we can proceed. Do you feel you're up to making some of these decisions today?"

Bill stared at the man's hands, which looked to be professionally manicured. Sunlight streamed through the window above the sink and shone off the lacquered finish on his nails.

When Bill didn't answer, Paige spoke up. "Bill? You said you wanted to talk about this now. And get it over with."

"Yeah," he said, the single word emerging with great effort. He sipped from his mug as Todd Winter nodded, happy to have been given the green light. Bill felt the irrational urge to laugh rising in his throat. He didn't know why. It seemed funny to be sitting at a table in his house, with his sister by his side, listening to a man young enough to be his own son talk about funerals and cemeteries.

"The first question has to do with Summer. Would you like her to remain in her present location, or is there another place where you'd like her to be buried? The Rodgers family is fine either way, so if you wanted her to stay where she is—"

"Sure, they're fine," Bill said. "Their daughter isn't dead."

Todd Winter kept going without acknowledging what Bill said. "And it's too early for there to be a tombstone." Todd cut his eyes to Hawkins.

The detective recognized his cue and said, "We'd already processed the body for any evidence relating to the crime, so as far as the investigation goes, we're finished."

"The reinterment would be an added expense," Todd said, "but given the nature of the situation, it seems only right that the City of Jakesville would handle that on your behalf. They informed me they want this to be as painless as possible for you, considering how difficult this time has been. Isn't that right, Detective?"

"Absolutely. We have that offer on the authority of the mayor's office."

"I should sue you," Bill said, speaking through clenched teeth. His hand formed into a fist, and he held back, resisting the urge to thump it against the table. "I should sue you and the hospital and anybody else I can find for what you've put us through."

"Bill," Paige said.

"And the Rodgers family should sue you as well." Some of the fog lifted from Bill's brain, only to be replaced by anger. He paused a moment to consider that anger was the one thing that chased his grief away. "We've all been through hell because you all fucked up. The hospital too. They have plenty of money."

"I understand that, Bill," Hawkins said. "I've apologized, and I'll keep on apologizing. To you and the Rodgers family."

"How did this happen?" Paige asked. "I'm not sure I understand."

Hawkins hesitated a moment before answering, his hand rubbing against the underside of his chin. "We were looking for two girls, and we found two girls. Badly beaten and unrecognizable. You saw her, Bill. You know the condition she was in. One girl, who we now know was Summer, was only partially clothed. In fact, the girl we originally thought was Summer was wearing Summer's jacket with Summer's ID inside."

"So Haley was wearing Summer's jacket," Paige said. "They must have switched or borrowed or something."

"All of this because one girl borrowed another girl's jacket," Bill said. "Candy didn't look at the clothes? She didn't notice?"

"She thought her daughter was dead," Hawkins said. "She didn't think about the clothes. You never saw them, did you? Haley's clothes were removed when she was brought into the emergency room. No one thought twice about it. And there's another curious thing about the clothes, something that we've been thinking a lot about as we investigate."

"What curious thing?" Paige asked.

Bill saw the intense interest on his sister's face. It showed on Todd Winter's face as well.

"We know these girls had to have been attacked somewhere else. We'd searched the park thoroughly, and they were found on a busy trail. So we have no idea where they were from the time they disappeared to the time they were found. The attack, the beating, appears to have happened on Saturday, given the severe condition of the injuries. We just don't know where those girls were for those thirty-six hours or so."

"You still didn't say what was so unusual about the clothes," Bill said, his voice flat.

"Right, right," Hawkins said, his index finger in the air. He cleared his throat. "The girl we now know was Summer died at the time of the attack, or shortly after. But Haley survived. So the attacker had these girls somewhere for all that time, with one of them alive. Clinging to life, but alive."

"Maybe they thought she was dead," Bill said.

"Maybe. But unlikely. You see, Haley wasn't just wearing Summer's jacket. She was wearing a lot of clothes, a hodgepodge of things. Much more clothing than Summer was wearing when they were found." Hawkins looked almost pleased with himself as he spun out the theory. "It seems possible the attacker knew Haley was alive and knew how cold it was the night they were taken to the park. Somebody put more clothes on her in order to keep her warm, to help ensure that she might survive the night. It says something about the attacker's mind-set."

"Attacker or attackers," Paige said, emphasizing the plural.

"Agreed," Hawkins said. "We don't know."

Bill's mind spun like a gyroscope. He summoned the energy to lift his shoulders.

"If one girl was wearing most of the clothes and you couldn't recognize either one, how on earth did you conclude which was which?" Paige asked. She sounded agitated, almost angry. Under normal circumstances, Bill would have stepped in and asserted his older-brother authority by telling her to calm down. But he didn't. He liked her flash of anger, her frustration with the absurdly heartbreaking situation they were all in.

Hawkins's face flushed. Not with anger, Bill thought, but with sheepish embarrassment. "Summer's ID was in the pocket of the coat Haley was wearing. Haley's coat, as it turned out. And Haley was found wearing a ring, but Candy Rodgers said it didn't belong to her daughter."

"Girls share jewelry," Paige said. "And clothes."

"Summer's bracelet," Bill said. "She wasn't wearing it."

"What bracelet?" Paige asked.

Bill's voice sounded raspy, tired. "Julia gave Summer a bracelet for her thirteenth birthday. She wore it every day since Julia died, but it wasn't on that girl in the hospital. I thought maybe it got stolen or lost when they were attacked, so I didn't say anything. It wasn't expensive, but it meant a lot to her."

"No one thought to check dental records or identifying marks. A lot of people assumed some pretty big things, but they did it because they were eager to get help for the girl we thought was Summer. And because they were focused on tending to the needs of the Rodgers family, who we thought had lost a daughter. We're a small community here. People get stretched thin. They don't deal with cases like this—"

Bill pounded his fist on the table, making the coffee mugs and spoons jump and rattle. "Enough with the bullshit excuses, Detective," Bill said. "You all fucked up. The biggest fuckup of all time."

Hawkins's face remained flushed but otherwise stoic. "I'm sorry, Bill. I've already offered to resign or be taken off the case. I'll take my lumps however they come."

Bill jumped up from the table, moving so fast he knocked his chair over. It clattered to the floor. His hand stung, and he had no idea what he'd even stood for. He wanted to walk. To walk away and just keep going, even though he knew he couldn't. He had nowhere else to go.

CHAPTER THIRTY-TWO

Bill stared out the window at the bleak backyard. The sky was overcast, the leaves long gone. "So Summer died right away," he said, his breath fogging the window glass. "She didn't suffer."

"That's safe to say, Bill," Hawkins said, trying to sound encouraging.

Encouraging. When the best hope you have is your dead child didn't suffer in the cold after being beaten to death.

Bill turned and looked at Paige, whose face was full of sympathy, and he knew exactly what she was thinking. She was remembering his revelation the day before about Julia's death, his guilt over ignoring her call so she died alone on the kitchen floor, leaving Summer instead of Bill to find her body. And he knew Paige conflated the two deaths, imagining that Bill's guilt over Julia's dying alone bled over to Summer's lonely death, her only companion unconscious and unable to help or comfort her.

Bill hated his sister's tendency toward psychoanalysis, even if her insights were correct. He couldn't shake the notion that the two people closest to him, the two people he cared about most in the world, died alone. And he wondered again why he ever let Summer leave the house that day.

Easy, he thought. *I had no reason not to. I had no reason to think* this *would happen.*

Todd Winter cleared his throat. "Would you like to discuss these other issues another time?" he asked. "Maybe everyone needs to process things further, and we're not working under any immediate time constraints."

"I think that sounds like a good idea," Paige said, sniffling. "Maybe we still need some time to process."

"No." Bill shook his head like an obstinate child refusing a vegetable. He walked back to the table and stood over the fallen chair. "No way. Let me ask you something. Whose clothes was Summer buried in?"

Todd Winter appeared unruffled by the question. "Clothes provided by Candy Rodgers. A dress that belonged to Haley."

"And the casket?"

"The Rodgers family chose it. It was really quite lovely."

"I want her out of there," Bill said, poking the table with the point of his index finger. "I want her buried next to her mother, on the other side of that cemetery. There's an empty plot." His voice caught, and he cleared his throat. "It's supposed to be for me, but I'd like Summer to be there, next to Julia. That's where she belongs. In her own clothes. Not Haley's. Not something Candy Rodgers picked out and prayed over."

Winter and Hawkins both nodded their heads slowly, doing their best imitations of wise sages who could handle anything. It made Bill even angrier to see them acting so calm in the face of what was going on. But, then again, how would a cop and a funeral director react to a tragedy? They saw it in some form nearly every day. If they couldn't handle it calmly, they wouldn't be in their lines of work. But the logical thought didn't ease Bill's anger at their stoic demeanors.

"That's all perfectly feasible," Winter said. "I can begin making the arrangements."

"And I want a new casket," Bill said.

Everyone remained silent for a moment.

Bill added, "One I pick out."

"I probably should have made this clear earlier," Winter said, "but the Rodgers family told me, told us, they're okay with Summer remaining in the casket she's already in. We could simply relocate it to the plot you're speaking of—"

Bill shook his head again. "One I choose." He pointed at Paige. "We choose. Paige will help me pick it out."

His sister looked surprised to be included in the task and probably even more surprised by Bill's insistence on paying for his own casket, but she wore a look of perfect support and understanding, even going so far as to reach over and squeeze Bill's hand.

Winter and Hawkins exchanged a look, but they held whatever objections they might want to make to themselves. Bill understood what they were doing. They were pacifying a difficult customer, indulging a man in the throes of grief.

Only Paige knew Bill well enough to know it wouldn't pass, that once he set his mind on a certain course of action, there was no turning back from it.

"I have some brochures. Or you can come by our office and look in person. We're operating on your schedule, Mr. Price."

"And I want one more thing," Bill said.

Winter maintained his practiced customer service façade, but something crossed Hawkins's face, a sliver of irritation at being held at the table so long while listening to Bill's expression of his desires.

But he waited patiently, along with Winter and Paige.

"I want to see her," Bill said. "Summer. I want to see her before she gets reburied."

"Bill." Paige's voice sounded edgy and panicked. For the first time that day, she revealed real concern about the things he was saying. "Why would you want to subject yourself to that? You don't want to remember her that way, do you? Do any of us?"

Bill ignored her. "She should still be okay to see, right? It's only been a day since the burial, and she's been embalmed." He turned and looked at Paige. "I've been looking at Haley for days. Her injuries. I can't imagine Summer's are any worse. And I'd like to really see my daughter one last time. I think it's the least you can do."

No one offered any further argument.

CHAPTER THIRTY-THREE

Just after seven that night, Bill grabbed his coat from the front closet and walked into the family room, where Paige was watching an HGTV marathon. A hunky guy with bulging muscles was taking a sledgehammer to the walls of somebody's kitchen, sending up a spray of dust and debris and laughing the whole time he did it. Bill paused, looking at the screen. They sure made the destruction of a home look joyous on that network.

"What's up?" Paige asked. She looked tired, and she yawned, lifting her hand to her mouth. "Excuse me. Long days."

"I have an errand to run."

Paige tried to mask her curiosity, and when she spoke, she managed to keep her voice cool and detached. "Anything I can help with?"

"No. No, it's cool."

"Okay," she said, eyeing him as if he were a dangerous animal.

"You know, you don't have to—"

Paige held up her hand. "Bill, stop. I'm staying. Please stop telling me I can go."

"But your family—"

"They're doing fine without me." She laughed. "I bet the kids haven't had a home-cooked meal all week. Kyle has the local pizza place on speed dial. His sister lives there too. She's helping. And Kyle and the kids are coming down for the funeral when it's time. I'm not going anywhere. Okay?"

"I'll try to stop asking."

"Good."

But he didn't move. He remained in front of her with his coat on. He imagined his face looked pretty lost.

"Did you want to say something else?" She shifted her body, moving her feet out from under her and placing them on the floor. She muted the TV. "Is this about the funeral?"

Bill nodded. "I have to decide if I want the church involved."

"Oh." Paige looked surprised by the statement, her eyebrows lifting. "Why wouldn't you? Did Summer not believe?"

"I don't know what she believed. She seemed kind of contemptuous of organized religion. She used to complain about the Bible-thumpers around here. She used to say that being out in nature or connecting with a friend was as good as being at Mass. She wasn't shy about sharing her opinions with me." Bill felt a little foolish standing and talking in front of his sister, like he was making a speech to the Rotary Club or something. But he made no move to sit down. "We haven't been going to church since Julia died. I guess I find it hard to go along with all of that after what happened. And now, I've lost my wife and daughter. Who would believe after that? None of it seems right."

Paige listened patiently, the glow from the TV reflected in her glasses. "I guess I wasn't sure," she said finally. "I didn't know how much you were going. But maybe this is the time for you to go back. It can be a great comfort."

"You still go?" Bill asked. "You hated it when we were kids."

"I like taking my children there. I like the community. And the school." She shrugged. "Have you been seeing someone?"

It took Bill a moment to understand his sister wasn't asking him about his romantic life. "You mean a shrink?"

"Yeah."

"No. I went with Summer a few times. Why?"

"It can help. Remember Mom and Dad sent me to one in high school. They said I was partying and drinking too much."

"You kind of were."

She ignored his comment. "It helped, even if I think they were wrong to send me. It's nice to talk to an objective party."

"I'll think about it." He turned to leave but looked back one more time. "You should lock the door behind me. You know, just in case . . ."

Paige stood up. "I've got it. And if there's trouble, I'll call your superhot neighbor."

Like Julia did the day she died, Bill thought. *She had to. . . .*

"God, I get tired of hearing how good-looking he is," he said, and went out into the cold night.

CHAPTER THIRTY-FOUR

Bill drove toward the cemetery. He knew it closed at seven o'clock, and every night, a Jakesville cop drove dutifully through the grounds, making a circuit to check for lingering mourners, bird-watchers, and teenagers rolling around in the grass, oblivious to the graves beneath them. Then the cop locked the gate, using a chain and padlock.

Bill saw the lights from the patrol car as he drove closer, its conical beams illuminating the trees and the headstones. Somewhere out there, across the flat expanse of grass, both Julia and Summer lay buried. He hated to think of the mumbo jumbo spoken over Summer's body, the syrupy praise and hand-raising, the muttered "amens" that accompanied her as she was placed into the cold, unforgiving ground. He remembered Candy Rodgers's smug certainty, her admonition that Summer could still benefit from having God in her life.

And Candy had emerged from Summer's bedside, claiming she had felt something, a statement that made Bill want to roll his eyes to the ceiling.

And yet, she'd been right. It was her daughter there, not his.

He pounded his hand against the steering wheel as he drove. He made a series of turns, navigating through the narrow streets of a small subdivision. Porch lights glowed and cars sat in driveways. Long days were ending for the families who lived there, and they gathered together in what, at least from the outside, looked like snug and comfortable certainty.

Bill found the correct street and eased to a stop across from the house he sought. The lights were on inside the boxy little structure. A blue glow from behind the curtains told him someone was watching TV. He imagined the two of them, mother and daughter, sitting on the no doubt out-of-date furniture. If asked, Bill couldn't say why he was sitting across the street or what he expected to learn. He knew if Hawkins found out about his presence there, he'd receive more than a lecture. There might be threats of legal action, some warning about the way he might have jeopardized the case.

But he couldn't just sit at home and do nothing but think about caskets, so he waited across the street from Teena Everett's house.

An hour passed, and the darkness grew deeper. A few stars peeked through the cloud cover. Bill watched the house and grew drowsy. He hadn't been sleeping enough, and the long days of roller-coaster emotions were catching up to him, making his every thought and gesture drag. He wondered if he'd be sitting across the street from the home of people he barely knew—people with at most a tenuous connection to whatever happened to Summer—if he were in full command of his faculties, if sleep deprivation and grief hadn't robbed his frontal lobe of some ability to decide between a good idea and a bad one.

Cars passed occasionally, their headlights making him squint in the glare. He wanted to know where people came from and went to, what it was like to be living a normal, settled life. Were they going to the grocery store? Coming home from work?

Bill thought of the thousands of small decisions he'd made concerning Summer's life. The times she insisted on riding her bike to soccer practice instead of getting a ride with him. The afternoons and evenings she spent alone after school while he finished working. The nights she said she was spending at a friend's house . . . and he never followed up. Summer had always been fiercely independent. One of the first words she learned to say was "self," and she said it whenever he or Julia tried to help her toddler body accomplish any task. Taking a drink, opening a door, putting on clothes. "Self, self," she'd say, and he and Julia would back off, taking the independence and high spirit as the best of signs.

Bill remembered meeting Summer's kindergarten teacher at a conference. The woman told them every time she asked for a volunteer to lead an activity—sports, painting, reading—Summer's hand went up first. "She might grow up to be president of the United States," the teacher said with a laugh. "At least a senator."

Had he backed off too much? Should he have struck a more favorable balance between losing his cool on Halloween and letting his daughter remain independent?

A car turned into the Everetts' driveway and cut its lights. From his vantage point and through the darkness, he saw it was a larger, light-colored car, something like an Impala or a LaCrosse. The vehicle looked too new, too high-end for Teena's mother to be driving it, and Bill watched a figure—a man—step out into the yard, his coat pulled up high on his neck against the cold, and walk to the front door, where he knocked. One of the porch lights was burned out, leaving the man in half shadow as he waited to be let in.

It took a moment for Bill to realize his heart was thudding. It seemed strange to have such a reaction. Wasn't Teena's mom like anybody else? Wasn't she likely to have a boyfriend or a friend, maybe a brother or a cousin, someone familiar enough to come by the house at an innocuous time in the evening?

Bill lifted his hand, reaching for the ignition key, intending to head home to Paige and the collection of awful decisions they faced the next day. But then the door opened, and the man shifted his weight, stepping back as Teena's mother greeted him with a lukewarm smile. When the man moved that way, the light from the functioning bulb caught the side of his face, and Bill realized it was his neighbor, Adam Fleetwood, walking into the Everetts' house.

CHAPTER THIRTY-FIVE

Bill moved across the yard, stepping gingerly.

As he walked, a series of thoughts tumbled through his brain. He thought of that last phone call Julia made, the one to Adam. The one Adam didn't answer. It made sense that she'd call their reliable neighbor if she was painting the kitchen. Adam was the guy who watched their house when they left town. He was the guy who came over to fix a leaky pipe under the sink when Bill grew frustrated.

But then Bill put the call together with the little comments Julia had made over the years, things she'd said about how attractive Adam was. And fresh in his mind were Paige's words on the same subject.

On the surface, Adam and Jillian Everett appeared to have nothing in common. In the past, Bill had occasionally met women Adam brought home, and he was always envious when he saw them. By and large they were younger and much prettier than Jillian Everett, earthy girls, comfortable in their own skin and every bit as willing as Adam to drink whiskey and hike in the woods. Bill could imagine all the things they were willing to do. Mousy, nervous Jillian Everett didn't fit the pattern at all.

Bill climbed the steps, his feet moving faster the closer he came to the door. He tried to peer through the curtains, but they were closed, obscuring anything going on inside. He knocked. The burned-out light hovered above his head like a dead star.

"Come on." He knocked again, longer and louder.

When the door swung open, Jillian Everett blinked a few times, a look of fearful worry etched on her face. And just behind her, standing, his broad shoulders seeming to fill the entire living room, was Adam.

"Mr. Price?" Jillian said. "Why are you here?"

Bill pushed past her, moving toward Adam. He didn't know what he was going to say. He fumbled for the right words.

"You can't just—"

"What are you doing here?" Bill asked Adam. "How do the two of you know each other?"

None of his normal, easygoing cool showed on Adam's face. Hands on hips, he stood, looking down on Bill, his lips slightly parted as though preparing to speak. But it took a long moment for something to come out.

"You seem upset, Bill," he said. "Maybe you should—"

"Just tell me why you're here," Bill said. He jerked his thumb over his shoulder toward Jillian. "Teena might know something about Summer's murder. They're all tied up in it."

"Calm down, Bill," Adam said, his face sterner. "You can't come in here like this."

"What are you doing here?" Bill shouted. His voice came from someplace inside him, someplace he didn't realize was taking over. And just as on the night he grabbed Summer by the arm and shook her to the floor, he momentarily stood outside himself, watching another version of his own body scream at Adam Fleetwood. "Tell me. Tell me right now."

"Did you follow me?" Adam asked.

"No."

"Then why are you here?"

"I came to . . ." Bill stopped. "I just . . ."

"You came to spy on me," Jillian said. "You think Teena knows something about Summer's death, so you were out there spying on us." She looked at Adam and then walked across the room, her shoes scuffing against the carpet. "I'm calling the police."

"Wait," Adam said.

"No, he can't just show up and harass us."

"Is that why you're here, Bill? Because you're checking up on Jillian and Teena?"

Bill saw nothing to gain by lying. "Yes, I guess so."

Something dark showed on Adam's face, something akin to the clouds passing across the stars outside. Adam's hands moved, searching for something to do, and for a moment Bill thought he was going to make a grab at him.

But he lifted his hands to his head and ran them through his thick hair.

"It's much more complicated than that, Bill," Adam said. He looked over at Jillian. "Don't make the call. I'll talk to Bill outside."

He placed his hand on Bill's arm, grabbing it as with a claw, and Bill could offer little resistance as Adam manhandled him through the door.

CHAPTER THIRTY-SIX

When they were out on the lawn, their breath puffing in the cool night air, Adam let go of Bill's arm. Bill wanted to reach up and rub the spot where he had gripped him, fully expecting a bruise to form there by the next day, but he resisted the urge. It somehow seemed unmanly to rub at the spot where his bigger and stronger friend had grabbed him.

"Now will you tell me what the hell's going on?" Bill said.

Adam placed his hands on his hips and craned his head around, looking back at the house. Jillian came to the door, pressing her face against the screen as she peered out into the night, but then she backed away, closing the inside door behind her.

Adam turned around to face Bill. High overhead, an airplane slipped by, its engines a soft roar in the quiet night, its lights blinking down on them like tiny red eyes.

"Are you okay?" Adam asked. "You were pretty wrecked last night. Grief and the booze. Do you even remember me coming by?"

"Vaguely."

"How do you feel?"

"Like my guts have been turned inside out," Bill said. "Like I'm being roasted over hot coals. I don't know how I'm doing or how I'm supposed to be doing."

Adam nodded, his face eagerly supportive. "I hear you. There's no right way."

"What are you doing here?" Bill asked.

"Okay. You know how I got that DUI last summer? The time you came and bailed me out?"

Bill remembered. Adam had called him about ten o'clock on a weeknight, informing Bill he'd been arrested for drunk driving and needed a ride home. Bill gladly did the favor, and the two men never really talked about it after that. Adam seemed embarrassed by the whole thing, admitting on the ride home with Bill that he'd had one too many. It was a simple favor on Bill's part. A drive to the police station and then back home. He never knew how Adam reclaimed his car from the impound lot.

"Sure," Bill said. He tried to find a comfortable position, first crossing and then uncrossing his arms.

"Well, they send you to alcohol school after that. It's just a series of weekend classes to keep your ass out of jail. Boring as hell, but everybody does it when it's their first offense. Well, I met Jillian there. She'd been busted too, right around the time I was. So that's how we met."

"You're dating?" Bill asked.

"No, no. Just friends." Adam switched to a hushed tone, even though the front door was closed and the house shut up tight. "But she has a problem with alcohol. Or she has in the past. She's been going to AA ever since her arrest, trying to stay on the straight path as her kid gets older. So I've just kind of helped her out. I'm a shoulder to cry on, a support system. I'm not in AA or anything, so I can't sponsor her, but I help however I can. Kind of a buddy system."

Adam's explanation made Bill feel like a world-class jerk. "I see," he said.

"She wanted to drink tonight," Adam said. "All this stuff with the police coming around and asking questions about her, about her daughter—it pushed her to the edge. Teena was at that house where that other girl was taken advantage of." Adam shifted his weight from one foot to the other. "She didn't know we knew each other, but when she found out, she said she wanted me to talk to you, to explain how tough this is on her. And Teena."

Bill pointed past Adam in the direction of the house. "That girl might know something. She needs to spill it all to the police."

Adam nodded, his face still eager. His eyes full of sympathy and concern. "I'm sorry, Bill. But I don't think this is the way you want to go about this. You need to head on out of here and leave this family alone."

Bill took a step forward. He pointed at Adam's chest with his index finger. "You need to find out for me. You know them, and she clearly trusts you. Do this for me."

"Bill—"

"Just do it. Just goddamn do it for me, Adam. Okay?"

Bill realized he was shouting, the sound of his voice echoing off the house behind Adam and coming back through the quiet night like a clap of thunder. Adam took a step back, as though the force of Bill's voice had struck him like a blow. He'd probably never seen Bill that way.

"That girl, Teena—she's naive, Bill. I don't think she'd hurt anybody. She needs a father figure, and I think I'm the closest thing she has." He leaned closer, and his voice took on a slightly emotional edge. "Maybe I see it as a chance to help another kid."

Bill understood what Adam meant—a chance to make up for the lost time with his son. "Good," Bill said. "That's good. All the better to find out if she knows anything else. If she looks up to you and . . . likes you or whatever, you can just find out what she knows. You know what the cops say—anything can help."

"Okay, Bill," he said, his voice slipping into a placating tone as though he were speaking to an unstable mental patient. "I'll do what I can."

Bill stood on the lawn, looking at the ground, his heart racing again. He wanted to say something else to Adam. Not an apology exactly, but an explanation, some sense of the jumbled chaos in his mind and heart. But nothing coherent formed. And nothing came out.

Adam simply started backing away, heading for the house. He left Bill out on the lawn alone, the cold wind shaking the trees and stinging Bill's cheeks.

Bill watched Adam go inside, a brief shaft of warm yellow light slicing across the lawn before the door cut it off.

Bill's phone vibrated in his pocket. He wished he could ignore it, but he didn't want to miss anything important.

Instead, he saw Paige's name on the ID screen. When he answered, turning and walking toward the car, his sister's voice sounded panicked. Shaky.

"Where are you?" she asked without offering any greeting.

"I'm coming home."

"Are you home yet? Like, in the driveway?"

"No, I'm not." A cold tension rose in Bill, a surging fear. "What's wrong?"

"There's a car in the driveway," Paige said. "It's just sitting there. It's been sitting there for a few minutes. It has its lights on."

"Are the doors locked?"

"Yes."

"I'll be there as soon as I can."

CHAPTER THIRTY-SEVEN

Bill drove down his street, expecting to see a car still in front of his house, but when he came close, he saw an empty driveway. Every light, inside and out, seemed to be blazing, making the house look festive, like a big party was just about to begin. He wondered what the neighbors would think of that, the man with the dead wife and the dead daughter pretending to be the Jay Gatsby of Jakesville, Kentucky.

Bill didn't bother to put the car in the garage. He stopped in the back of the house, his headlights momentarily sweeping across Adam's immaculate yard, and jumped out, rushing inside. Paige greeted him at the back door, undoing the lock as he approached and then locking the door behind him.

"Are you okay?" he asked. "Did you figure out who it was?"

"I probably overreacted," she said, although she didn't appear calm or at ease. "When you left the house, you told me to keep everything locked, and I did. I know whoever did this to Summer and Haley is still out there, and who knows what they intend to do to anybody else?"

"So, did someone come to the house?" Bill asked, looking around and taking in every detail of their surroundings in case the boogey-man was inside, ready to leap from behind a piece of furniture.

"No. Nothing happened." Paige walked into the kitchen. A glass of red wine sat on the counter, and next to the wine Bill saw a large carving knife, something Julia bought years earlier and which had not been used since she died. "But this car . . . I was sitting in the living room, trying to read. I've been watching so much TV lately, my mind is turning to mush, and you had those Louis L'Amour novels on the shelf out there, the ones that belonged to Dad."

"Sure."

"So I started reading, and I noticed a car going by the house really slowly. I thought maybe it was a cop, keeping an eye on things. But there were no lights on top or anything. And then I thought maybe it was you, coming home."

"Maybe it was a pizza guy looking for an address."

"I thought of that. But they went up the street that way, and then they came back down again." Paige pointed in each direction, and Bill saw her hand tremble as she did. "And then it came again and basically stopped in front of the house." She paused and caught her breath. She reached over and took a long gulp of wine. "This feels so good."

"So they stopped in front of the house," Bill said. "You know, Paige, you were always a little jumpy. Remember you used to come into my room whenever you heard a strange noise in the house or watched a scary movie. You slept with the lights on until you were twelve."

Paige made a disgusted sound deep in her throat. "Really, Bill? You want to bring that up?" She pointed to the front of the house. "The car sat there for a long time, its lights on. The engine running. And then it turned into the driveway. And it just sat there. I don't know how to describe it, but it felt like someone was in that car, and they were . . . I don't know . . . watching me. Aggressively. That's what it felt like."

Bill lifted his hand to his head and scratched. He believed his sister. Yes, he remembered her as the scared kid, the one who had a tendency to leave the bathroom door open while she sat on the toilet because she wanted the rest of the family to be able to reach her if a monster jumped out of the closet. But he still believed her. He just didn't know what it meant.

"Do you want me to call the police?" he asked. "I can."

"And tell them what? Your sister is afraid of a car?"

"It could be a gawker," Bill said. "Someone who heard about the story and just wants to see where a murder victim lived."

Paige's face scrunched with disgust. "Really, Bill? You think that?"

"What else can I think?" he said. He pulled the refrigerator door open and took out a bottle of beer, something cheap with a twist-off cap. "So many weird things are happening."

When he turned around from the refrigerator, the beer bottle lifted to his mouth, he saw Paige studying him. He knew what was coming next.

"Where exactly were you tonight, Bill?" she asked. "What 'errand' were you running?"

Bill carried the bottle to the kitchen table with him and sat down. He looked up at Paige, who remained standing, her body leaning back against the counter. "I don't know. I started out driving to the cemetery. It just bugs me that she's buried there, with flowers and things intended for someone else piled on top of the grave. I know it doesn't really matter. Anyway, it was closed." He swallowed some of the beer. "So I drove to the Everetts' house."

"Why did you do that?"

"It turned out to be a good thing." He told her about running into

Adam and his friendship with Jillian Everett. "It's a stroke of luck, and maybe it will help us understand what's going on."

For a brief moment, Bill felt satisfied with himself. Despite the stabbing, nearly continuous heartache he'd been feeling for the past day, he took comfort in the knowledge that he'd done something productive, something that might move them all a step closer to knowing what happened to Summer. And why.

But then he saw the look on Paige's face. Her hand held the stem of her wineglass, but she didn't lift it. She stared at him.

"What?" he asked.

"I just think you have to accept that this could all take a while," she said. "It's early, and I really believe the police will solve this and hold someone accountable. I think they usually do." She shook her head. "I'm sorry, Bill. I don't mean to be a downer, but we have to be patient."

Bill picked at the label on his beer bottle. It flaked beneath his touch, coming off in pieces that stuck to his finger rather than peeling away from the glass in one smooth, continuous sheet.

"That's very hard for me."

But when he looked up at his sister, he saw she was looking somewhere else. Her head was turned toward the front of the house, looking through the archway that led from the kitchen to the living room, her hand setting the wineglass on the counter and then lifting and pressing her palm against her chest.

"Bill?" she said. "Outside. It's the car again."

Bill didn't even think. He sprang up from the table and moved quickly through the archway and to the front door. As he moved, he caught a glimpse of the car through the window, headlights and taillights sliding past in the darkness. Bill fumbled with the locks and leaped out onto the stoop, running across the yard to the street.

He heard Paige call his name behind him but kept going. The car was new and silver, a four-door sedan with bright headlights.

Bill lifted his hand and shouted. "Hey!"

A figure sat behind the wheel, the gender indistinct in the darkness, and before Bill was anywhere close to the street, the vehicle accelerated, its engine revving like a deep-throated monster, and sped away, leaving Bill to watch it go, unable to catch even a piece of the license plate number.

CHAPTER THIRTY-EIGHT

Bill was surrounded by empty caskets.

The soft light and cloying piped-in organ music gave him the sense he'd walked onto the set of a foreign film, something surreal and absurd that wouldn't make sense to him even if it were in his own language.

Paige walked beside him, inspecting the caskets like she was picking out a new car. She touched the handles, felt the pillows, ran her hand over every surface, and inspected the interiors as though searching for the tiniest defect.

When Julia died, Bill rushed through this process. He felt pulled in more directions than he could count. He made certain that Summer's needs were his highest priority. He didn't know what else to do. So he came through the Winter and Sons showroom that day, his mind reeling like the survivor of a natural disaster, and pointed to and bought the first decent-looking thing he saw.

He didn't want to rush with Summer. He stopped next to a copper-colored casket, the lid heavy, the handles on the side like door knockers on a cathedral. It looked sturdy, eternal, the kind of object that spoke of permanence.

"This looks pretty good," he said.

Paige came up beside him. "Not very feminine."

"I'm not buying a pink one. Summer wasn't into ruffles and bows."

"Sure, you're right. It looks good." She then spoke out of the side of her mouth. "Are you going to be able to afford this? Remember Mom's and Dad's funerals? They were each close to ten grand."

"The City of Jakesville is paying for the burial."

"Sure. But what about everything else? You said work was putting the squeeze on you."

"I have some money saved. Life insurance money from Julia. It was supposed to pay for Summer to go to college."

"Well, if you need any help."

"Paige—"

"Kyle got promoted. I guess I didn't tell you with everything going on. So if you need for us to—"

"It's fine, Paige. I can pay for it."

She reached up and patted his arm, letting the conversation about money go.

Bill turned around. Todd Winter stood off to the side, his hands folded in front of his waist, his dark suit and youthful good looks making him seem more like a Hollywood leading man on the way to a premiere than an undertaker in a small Kentucky town.

"We'd like to take this one," Bill said.

Todd Winter glided over, his shiny black shoes making almost no noise against the carpet. He nodded his agreement with the choice and said, "It's one of our finest models. Airtight. Watertight. Guaranteed."

Bill hadn't eaten anything all day, and his stomach did a flip as he listened to Todd's litany of the casket's features. He didn't want to think of why a casket needed to be airtight or watertight. He didn't want to think about the pressure of the dirt and the rain and the years that would stretch out into infinity.

"Is there anything else we need to take care of?" Bill asked, hoping to be finished with the conversation.

Todd Winter looked suitably grim and serious. "Not right now. You brought the clothing over with you, and we've already been given the location of the plot. We could discuss headstone options today, if you're up to it, or we could address that another time."

The room seemed close and confining. They were in the basement, and as Bill looked around, he saw no windows or doors, no means of escape. The weather remained cool, and the heat in the funeral home suddenly felt oppressive, so much so that Bill removed his coat. A trickle of sweat ran down his side, from his armpit to his waist.

"I think that's all I want to do today," he said.

"I understand. I'll get the paperwork started," Todd said.

Paige examined Bill, her face moving closer to his, her eyes magnified by her glasses. "Are you sure you're okay? You're starting to look a little pale."

"Just warm," he said. "I'll feel better outside."

They all started toward the door together, toward the stairs that led back above ground and out to the living, breathing world. But before they exited, Bill stopped to ask Todd a last question.

"Do you know when they're going to take care of the . . . What did you call it?"

"Disinterment."

"Yeah, that. When is that happening?"

"Right now, I believe," Todd said. "This morning."

"Right now," Bill said, repeating the words. He wished he'd gone to the cemetery to watch. He would have if he'd known, even though he doubted they'd let him anywhere close to where the men were working. He just hated the thought of Summer being so alone, tended by strangers again. For one moment, he was thankful for the sealed, airtight casket. It would protect her from prying eyes the way Haley wasn't protected in the hospital. "And then what happens?"

"Summer will be brought back here," Todd said. "We'll handle the preparations. We've scheduled the visitation for two days from now, as you requested." He paused for a moment. "Do you still wish to see Summer before the casket is sealed? I know we're going to have it closed for the viewing when your friends and family are here."

Bill heard the sliver of doubt in Todd Winter's voice, the same sliver he'd been hearing from Paige over the previous twenty-four hours. No one was saying it directly to him, but the implied message was clear: *Are you sure you want to see your daughter this way? Are you sure you're up to it?*

"I do," Bill said. "You're going to see her, aren't you?"

"Yes, of course," Todd said. "I'll be here during the entire process."

"Then I'm going to see her too."

CHAPTER THIRTY-NINE

Bill wasn't hungry for lunch.

He sat at the table with Paige across from him, each of them with a steaming plate of baked ziti in front of them. Someone had dropped it off the day before, one of the neighbors whom Bill barely knew. He'd let Paige handle the meeting and greeting of well-wishers and casserole bakers, telling her to claim he simply wasn't up to talking to anyone.

As Bill pushed the food around on his plate, he wondered, in all seriousness, how long he could ride that excuse out. Did he ever have to go back to talking to people?

"I guess they're running the obituary for Summer in the paper tomorrow," Paige said.

Bill noticed that the grief, the stress, hadn't cooled his sister's appetite. She talked between bites, and he realized how very right his parents had been about her and her zest for life. For *everything* in life.

"Yes," he said. "For any one of Jakesville's twenty thousand citizens who've been living under a rock for the last few days."

"It will probably be as crowded as Haley's funeral."

"Maybe. Candy's lived here her whole life. She knows everybody.

People might be tired of hearing about it by now. Or maybe they'll be morbidly attracted to it. Who knows?"

Paige forked her food with precise movements, her face set in concentration. Bill could tell she had something else to say.

"What?" he asked.

"What do you mean?"

"Since when did you get shy? You want to ask me—or tell me—something else."

Paige set her fork down. "I was wondering if you'd given any more thought to the church. Or do you still want to just go from the funeral home to the cemetery and skip having a mass?"

"We're skipping it."

Paige opened her mouth to say more but stopped. Bill felt relief. He didn't want to argue with his sister. He didn't have the will to argue with anyone. His stomach roiled with nervous energy and the pain of grief, the feelings intensifying as the day went on. He checked the clock, expecting a call from Hawkins or the funeral home at any moment. It left him unable to think about eating or anything else.

"I'll go in with you," Paige said. "To see her. If you want."

Bill looked up.

"You're right. It can't be much worse than seeing . . . Haley in that condition. Can it?"

"No." Some of the tension eased out of Bill's gut. He made a small, tentative jab at his food. He lifted a bite and chewed. It felt rubbery and stiff, but he managed to swallow. "This isn't too bad."

"No, it isn't. Your coworkers sent over a twelve-pack of beer and a frozen pizza. They must know you well. It's nice to have people in your life who want to help when you need it."

"It is," Bill said. "Definitely."

He hadn't seen or heard from Adam since the night before when he ran into him at the Everetts' house. He thought about texting him that morning to check whether he'd learned anything. But he knew Adam. He'd want to move at his own pace, and if he learned something, he'd let Bill know in his own time.

Then the phone surprised Bill by ringing.

Bill fumbled putting his fork down and then scrambled to extract the phone from his pocket. "Yeah?" he said.

"Good afternoon, Bill."

Hawkins's voice, which sounded overly formal and stiff like a telemarketer reading from a script, set Bill on edge.

"What's wrong?"

"Are you busy right now?" Hawkins asked, his voice still off somehow.

"I'm home. Waiting for you to call."

"Say, can you meet me down at the station? I have some things to go over with you before we move forward with anything else."

"What things? Did something go wrong?"

"Is your sister still there?"

"Yes. Of course. She's staying for the funeral."

"Bring her along with you," Hawkins said. "I'll see you in about ten minutes. Okay?"

Before Bill answered, the detective hung up.

CHAPTER FORTY

The Jakesville police station had been built just six years earlier. It sat two blocks off the main square, efficient and cold, a modern redbrick and glass building, two stories high and fronted by a row of flagpoles. Bill had spent a lot of time there the day after Summer disappeared, answering questions about every aspect of his life, right down to his blood type and whether there was any history of mental illness in his family.

Inside, the building looked more like an office complex than it did a police station. The desks were neatly arranged, the carpet underfoot neutral and clean. Hawkins met them in the entryway, where the only visible concessions to security were the metal detector every one passed through on the way inside and several gunmetal cameras that kept their smoky eyes trained on everyone's movements.

Hawkins placed his hand on Bill's arm, his fingers landing in the same spot Adam's had at the Everetts' and reawakening the ache of the bruise there. Hawkins led Bill and Paige past security without stopping and through the door that led back to the officers' cubicles.

Bill had been there only in the midst of Summer's disappearance, so he couldn't say with any certainty whether the scene he and Paige passed through was normal, but to his eyes and ears there seemed to be a lot of men and women, both uniformed and plainclothes, rushing to and fro, phones pressed to their ears, papers and files clutched in their hands. A few glanced at them as they breezed by, their eyes touching Bill's and then sliding away.

"You caught him, didn't you?" Bill asked.

Hawkins didn't stop. And he didn't answer. He led Bill past the cubicles and ringing phones to a room at the back. He hustled them inside, where they found themselves standing around a conference table, the kind where Bill spent too many hours sitting during work meetings that droned on endlessly. He was struck by how antiseptic and mundane the room looked, and he could hardly imagine he was about to learn something about the investigation into his daughter's murder in such a bland place.

But he knew he was about to learn something. And while he settled into a chair with Paige sitting next to him, he realized how dry his mouth had become, and he eyed with some lust and envy the giant plastic watercooler near the door, its stack of white cups as inviting as manna.

"You're scaring me, Detective," Paige said as Hawkins sat in the chair at the head of the table, appearing patriarchal and firm.

He manipulated his bulky body, looking like a man trying to cram his large frame onto a child's bike. As he adjusted his coat and tie, Bill noticed for the first time that the detective's skin was pallid, the flesh around his mouth and jaw loose and saggy. Hawkins rested his hands on the tabletop, the skin around the edges of the nails jagged and scabbed as if the detective spent a fair amount of time picking or chewing at it.

Bill waited. He didn't know how he'd managed to go so long without saying—demanding—to know more. But a part of him feared every new revelation from the detective, and a part of him lacked the energy to speak up and argue.

Hawkins cleared his throat. "As you know, we went ahead with the disinterment of Summer's remains this morning."

For the first time that day, Bill's placid bewilderment turned to a slow-roiling irritation. He expected the weird euphemisms from the funeral director, but he wasn't sure he could handle hearing them from the detective. But he kept his mouth shut.

"She was transported back to the morgue before the funeral home."

"Is that normal?" Paige asked.

Bill almost told her to be quiet. He knew something was coming from Hawkins, and he didn't want it delayed.

"There is no normal here," Hawkins said, "but since this case has been so unusual, so complicated, we decided to take that step. You see, we thought it would be a good idea—*I* thought it would be a good idea—to confirm Summer's identity using the dental records we obtained when she disappeared."

"Confirm?" Paige asked.

Hawkins moved his hands around, placing first one and then the other on top. "With one mix-up already behind us, well, I wanted to make sure there weren't any more."

"A mix-up?" Bill asked, finally speaking. "Like what? Digging up the wrong grave?"

Hawkins ignored him and went on. "We took the body from Haley's grave back to the morgue at the hospital and checked the dental records against that body, expecting to find a match with Summer. Then we planned to release the body to Winter and Sons."

Bill's mouth suddenly felt drier, as if he'd swallowed broken glass.

"Expected?" he said. He found his own hand moving, sliding to the right where it found Paige's. He took hold of his sister's hand, which felt clammy and wet. "Expected?"

Bill repeated the word as though it meant something more than it did, as if it were a prayer that would ward off danger.

Hawkins stared directly at Bill. "It wasn't Summer in that grave, Bill," Hawkins said, his voice dropping lower. "To be perfectly honest, we don't know who that girl in there is. And we have no idea what happened to Summer."

CHAPTER FORTY-ONE

It took a moment for Bill to realize how hard he was squeezing Paige's hand.

Only when she gasped and tried to pull out of his grip did he understand the pressure he'd slowly been applying. He let go, his own hand slick from the contact with her skin.

"You don't know where her body is," Bill said.

"We don't know where *she* is," Hawkins said. "We can't assume at this point that she's alive or dead. This is a missing person case again. I would preach caution at this point. Given the condition of the two girls we found, it seems reasonable to think whoever did this wanted to hurt them. And hurt them badly. We're going to search the park again. In fact, it's being searched right now, but I can't imagine we'll find anything new."

Paige stood up. While she moved across the room toward the watercooler, Bill leaned forward and tried to rest his elbows on the tabletop. But he possessed less control of his body as everything started to quake. He felt like he was suspended over a pit, something the size of the Grand Canyon. If he moved, he'd fall inside, his body tumbling through the air like a skydiver with a malfunctioning parachute.

Paige came back with a paper cup of water and held it in front of Bill's face. He didn't see it. The object before his eyes meant nothing to him. Nor did the room or the people or the words the detective was saying.

"Drink this, Bill," Paige said.

His hand shook as he reached out for the cup. But he drank, and the cool water felt good, bringing him back to the room as the pit below him started to recede. He wasn't sure anything had felt that good in a long time.

"And if you're going to be sick, I can get the garbage can," she said, rubbing his back.

"I don't think I'm going to be sick," Bill said. "But I'm not sure."

Paige went and got the garbage can, a black plastic thing with a billowing liner. She set it at his feet and said, "More water?"

"Yes. Please."

She got it and then returned to her seat.

Bill drank again, and a dribble of water ran down his chin and under his shirt. "You don't know where she is. . . ."

"We don't."

"So Summer . . . She's alive? Or what?"

"We don't know."

Bill looked at his watch, at the date. His fuzzy mind managed to do the math. "Eight days," he said. "That's eight days she's been gone. Wherever she is . . ."

"We're certainly aware of that," Hawkins said. "We're going to do everything we can to find her. Everything. With the greatest urgency."

Bill concentrated hard and set the cup down on the table. He stared at the wood grain, the fine detail. "And who is this girl in the grave? This girl you exhumed?"

"We're in the process of trying to find that out," Hawkins said. "We'll certainly look into any missing persons cases in the area that might be a match, but none of them are recent. It's a big country with a lot of missing kids, so we're going to send out an alert into the national databases and hope someone comes forward. That could take time."

Paige looked composed, surprisingly so. Her brow was furrowed as she looked at the detective. "So we know that's Haley in the hospital, right?"

"Eight days," Bill said.

Hawkins nodded in response to Paige's question, the regret evident on his face as he was reminded of the initial mix-up. "We used the X-rays they took when she was admitted, and we compared them to her dental records. One hundred percent that's Haley Rodgers in the hospital."

"But they weren't with a third girl, were they?" Paige asked. "Bill, who were they with?"

"The only girls they hang out with are girls from school," he said, his voice raspy. "Are there any girls missing from school?"

Hawkins shook his head. "I'm not trying to raise any false hope here," Hawkins said. He stared at Bill and Paige as if they were schoolchildren he needed to keep in line. "Summer is still a missing person, and she is in grave danger. The gravest. And she's been gone for a week. But the door is cracked open. Just the tiniest bit."

Bill stared at the tabletop, the cup of water before his eyes. He felt the pit starting to open up again.

"Find her," he said. "Jesus. Find her. Why are you sitting in here talking to me?"

"We will," Hawkins said. "You saw the activity out there. It's a full-on search. We're bringing in resources from outside the jurisdiction." Hawkins stood up and came over to Bill, placing his hand on Bill's back. "We're on this."

"You should have been on it sooner," Bill said.

"What can we do, Detective?" Paige asked.

"I'm not sure there's anything you can do right now," he said. "I have to get ready to brief the media, and then this thing's really going to take off. Of course, if there's anything I can do for you, just reach out. I'll be in touch when I can."

His hand slid off Bill's back as he started to go.

Bill said, "There is something I'd like you to do for me."

"What's that?"

Bill took a deep breath, his shoulders rising and falling. "That girl, the one you just dug up. She's at the morgue?"

"Yes."

"I'd like to see her," Bill said.

CHAPTER FORTY-TWO

A security guard, a young guy with broad shoulders and a protruding gut, met Bill and Paige at the back of the hospital. Bill was surprised to learn that Jakesville didn't really have its own morgue and that autopsies weren't performed in the town. Hawkins explained all this as he—reluctantly—made a phone call on Bill's behalf, arranging for him to see the body of the unidentified girl from Haley's grave.

"You can look at her through the window," Hawkins said when he hung up. "You can't go in there and touch anything. The guard won't let you."

"Okay," Bill said. "That's fine. Okay."

When someone died in Jakesville under suspicious circumstances, the body would be temporarily stored in the hospital mortuary until the investigation was completed. If an autopsy was required, the body was shipped to Louisville. The unidentified girl, the Jane Doe as Hawkins called her on the phone, would remain at the hospital until she could be identified. Hawkins pointed out that some places had bodies that had remained unidentified for years.

"What happens then?" Paige asked.

"They get buried in potter's field. Not much else we can do."

The security guard didn't speak as he led them down a twisting warren of hallways. Bill tried to keep his bearings but lost them almost right away as they moved past walls all painted the same industrial yellow, the lights above dropping a harsh, fluorescent glare on all three of them.

Paige reached out and placed her hand on Bill's arm. She spoke in a low whisper. "Do you know what you're doing?"

"No."

"Do you want to stop and talk?"

"I want to find Summer."

"She's not here," Paige said.

"Just—" Bill pulled loose and kept walking.

The security guard gave them a suspicious sidelong glance.

They finally reached a room with a large KEEP OUT sign, and underneath that a red warning about hazardous materials in use. The man used a key from his belt to open the door, leading them inside. They passed a couple of empty desks, then went down another hallway until they stood before a large window facing the interior of the building. The guard slipped through a door to the right, and a moment later the blinds twisted open, offering Bill and Paige a clear view of the body of a young girl.

She lay on her back, a sheet covering the middle of her nude body. They'd removed the clothes that belonged to Haley—discarded them, Bill assumed. The very top of her head was bandaged, the face below bruised and battered beyond recognition like Haley's, and Bill understood why Candy Rodgers had never seen the face of the girl they thought was her daughter.

Bill also knew that the sight of the girl and the injuries to her body would have angered Summer. She declared herself a feminist when she was nine—thanks to the influence of her mother—and repeatedly spoke to him about the inequities that women faced in the world. Just a year earlier, when Summer was fourteen, she went with some of her friends—including Haley—to the campus of the local college in order to participate in a march protesting violence against women. Bill found the irony of her disappearance too bitter to comprehend.

The guard stood next to the window on the inside, his hands resting on his belt, his face turned away to give Bill and Paige privacy. But his posture spoke of boredom, of the dullness of standing around in a morgue surrounded by the dead. He'd likely seen other murder victims, as well as the aftereffects of car accidents and other sudden deaths.

Like Julia's.

Bill knew there'd been no autopsy on Julia. There was no need to cut her open and slice her up, given the fall she'd taken and the open bottle of wine on the kitchen counter.

"Bill?" Paige said.

Her voice brought him back to the present. He'd leaned in closer to the glass, studying the exposed portions of the girl's body. Feet and calves, arms, shoulders, and neck. He'd moved in so close, his breath fogged the glass.

"Are you seeing what you wanted to see?" Paige asked. "Did you just need to prove to yourself that isn't Summer?"

"She's so young, isn't she?"

"Yes. It's sad to think she's somebody's daughter. Bill, do you even know what you're doing here?"

"No, I don't." Bill suddenly felt like an intruder, a man who had stumbled into a place he had no business being. "I guess it goes back to what you just said."

"What did I just say?"

"She's somebody's daughter. Or sister or whatever. And she's here alone without a name. We know some of what she went through right before she died. The same thing as Haley, apparently. But who was she before that?"

Paige reached out and touched Bill on the arm. "They're going to find that out. I'm sure." She leaned in closer. "And they're going to find Summer."

Bill pointed to the glass. "What if Summer's somewhere like this? Alone? Unknown?"

"The police are once again sending her picture and information out everywhere. This is still a missing person case. Someone knows something."

"What if someone has her, Paige? Some freak . . ." Red spots appeared before his eyes. "He could be holding her. Hurting her. Do you know I sometimes think I can hear her screaming? It's just kids playing on the next block, but it sounds like Summer screaming."

His knees felt wobbly. He started to slide down, but Paige's hands held him up. He found some last measure of strength inside him and straightened.

"Let's get out of here, Bill."

"Yes."

Bill stared at the girl's still body for another moment. The red spots appeared before his eyes again. He brought his hand back and then forward, his fist clenched. His knuckles hit the glass with as much force as he could muster, and the excruciating pain did what the sight of the girl couldn't. It brought him to his knees where he wailed, clutching his limp hand.

"Bill? Shit. Did you break your hand?"

He squeezed his eyes tight, the red spots growing larger and exploding like fireworks against his closed lids. The pain rattled his body like an electric shock, searing every nerve ending and cell.

He didn't know how long he kneeled that way. Then someone was beside him, taking his hand gingerly.

Bill managed to open one eye. The security guard examined Bill's knuckles, gently turning the hand one way and then the other, pressing in some places.

"I was a medic in Iraq," the guard said, his voice flat. "Just keep breathing."

Bill tried to. He huffed and puffed, and the pain eased.

"I don't think you broke anything," the guard said, "but you sure tried to."

Paige started to help him up. "Let's go home and put some ice on it. Or do you think you need an X-ray?"

"No. No. No."

"No, what?"

"I'm not going home. Why the fuck would I? That's the one place I know Summer isn't."

CHAPTER FORTY-THREE

Bill flexed his hand as they went back out into the hall, the guard leading the way. Bill asked, "How can we get upstairs from here?"

"Upstairs?" the guard asked, the word seemingly unfamiliar to him.

"To patient rooms," Bill said. "The rehab wing. We want to visit someone."

"Are you talking about Haley?" Paige asked. "Is now the time?"

Bill ignored her. "Can you show us?"

The guard led them through the twisting, turning hallways until they ended up at an elevator. "Which floor?" he asked.

"We know," Bill said as he hit the up button.

On the elevator ride, Paige stood with her arms folded.

"What is it?" Bill asked. His hand felt limp and loose, his wrist sore. He kept flexing it.

"I figured you'd want to go home," she said. "If Summer is out there, alive, she could end up coming home at some point. What if she shows up and you're not there? Nobody's there?"

"You saw the condition of those other girls," Bill said. "You think she's coming home in any kind of decent shape? If she comes home.

What are the chances this animal beat those other two girls and left her alone?"

"You never know."

"I know," he said. "It's those kids. Probably obsessed with her. They probably spent every waking hour jacking off while looking at her picture."

Paige remained silent for a moment as the elevator dinged upward. "According to that chart, they didn't have to jack off."

Bill almost wanted to laugh, the comment was so crude and unexpected. His hand hurt so much, his anger was blunted. "Yeah, I'm learning a lot of things, I guess. I just want to find out if Haley is awake yet. She saw whoever did this to them. She can tell us. She's the one person we know who was there. It's time."

"If she remembers," Paige said.

Her words dampened Bill's spirits even as he knew she was right. He remembered the prognosis given when everyone thought this was Summer. *"Possible long-term damage."* But he hoped that wasn't true for Haley. She was a witness to the crime. She might even know where Summer was.

Bill hated the familiar smells and sounds of the hospital. The squeaking of the nurses' shoes, the calls over the PA system. The rattling of carts and bottles and equipment.

As they approached the rehab wing, Bill saw a man he didn't recognize standing outside Haley's room. His small head was shaven, making it look as sleek as a bullet. He wore a perfectly tailored suit that showed off his long, slender body. He looked like a runner, a guy who entered marathons with the intention of beating the previous year's time. He tapped his phone as they walked up, then started to go into the room.

"Excuse me," Bill said. "Where's the guard?"

When the man turned around, some recognition crossed his face. "Oh," he said.

Bill didn't recognize him, but he made a guess. "Are you Haley's father?"

"I am. And I know who you are."

The two men shook hands as Rich Rodgers offered Bill and Paige his sympathies. "You really didn't have to come by," Rich said. "I know you're going through a lot."

Bill and Paige exchanged a look. *He doesn't know. No one knows yet.* Or they were finding out right then if Hawkins was announcing it.

Bill let out a long sigh. He felt too tired to explain, too weary to go into it.

"Is something wrong?" Rich asked.

"Where's the guard?" Bill asked again.

"Oh, he's here," Rich said. "A couple of kids from school came by, hoping to visit Haley. The guard walked them out. Is something wrong?"

So Paige stepped up. "Yeah, there's been a new development there. . . ."

She told Rich about the discovery that Summer wasn't the girl buried in the grave, that she was once again a missing person. Rich listened, and the more Paige talked, the farther his chin dropped, until his mouth hung wide open, a tiny thread of spit linking his upper and lower lips.

When Paige was finished, the man was speechless. He didn't say anything. He just stared in disbelief.

"But we were wondering how Haley is doing," Bill said, trying to break the spell. "Did she wake up?"

Rich reached up, scratching at his bullet head. He still seemed unable to find any words. "Are you sure?" he asked.

"Yes," Paige said. "They're sure about this part."

"I don't know what to say. I'm sorry." He scratched his head again. "Or maybe this is good. Better, I guess. Right?"

"We hope so," Paige said.

"So," Bill said. "Haley?"

"Right, Haley. It's slow, her progress. I guess the two of you know that, since you spent a lot of time here. The progress is really slow." He sounded impatient, as though he thought Haley wasn't doing enough to recover, like she was sleeping in on a lazy Saturday morning. "They're working with her a lot, so we keep hoping for things to get better."

"So she's not able to speak yet?" Bill asked. "Maybe if we went in and, I don't know, tried a little harder. Tried something."

When he asked the question, Paige made a subtle noise with her mouth, something akin to "Tsk." But Bill ignored her.

"No," Rich said, looking behind him at the closed door to her room. "And I'd like to hear from her too. I really would." When he turned back around, he stared at Bill's face, considering him as though deciding whether he wanted to say the next thing. He must have decided yes, because he went on. "I'm just eager to hear from her mouth that the things being said about her, the things the police are telling us about these boys, aren't true."

"Yes, it's kind of hard to accept as a father. They're so young."

Rich didn't bother to lower his voice despite the ever-bustling presence of nurses and orderlies. "Haley has always had a certain gift for finding herself in over her head. Ever since she was a little girl. She's easily led, easily manipulated. She takes after her mom in that way."

Bill tried to think of something to say to stop the man from going on, but he couldn't.

"Not living here, I've worried about the kind of trouble she could be getting into, and now all of that has come true. When she wakes up, if she wakes up . . ." He stopped talking, and it looked as though he wasn't going to bother finishing the thought. But then he said, "She has a lot of explaining to do. To me. I don't care what she says to her mother, but I'm going to have some things to ask her and some things to tell her."

Paige forgot her tsking at Bill and decided to speak up herself. "You can't really think she was asking for this, can you? Someone attacked her. Look at the condition she's in. Nothing could merit that kind of violence. Another girl is dead and one is missing."

Rich stared at Paige like she was a rock that had suddenly started to speak. "I didn't say she deserved to be hurt. I didn't say that at all. But I think a firmer hand is needed sometimes. Especially with a teenager. And I don't think my ex-wife provides it."

"A firmer hand?" Paige said.

"Do you mind if I just take a peek in there?" Bill asked. "Maybe if I just—"

"What exactly is happening with the search for Summer, then?" Rich asked. "Where are they looking? It seems strange as hell they found two girls and not the third. What could have made that happen?"

Bill's hand felt like a water balloon. A little swollen, a little useless. He needed to ask a nurse for ice. "I don't know. I wish I did. I just know they're looking. And time is working against us in a big way."

"Do you think . . ." Rich stopped himself. His lips formed a tight line, a seam in his face. Then he said, "I understand Summer was kind of the leader among these girls. You know, I remember that shoplifting thing a few years back. Haley said Summer goaded her into it. Summer always seemed more assertive, more outgoing. God knows Haley wasn't that way. Summer was the leader, and now she can't be found. . . ." His voice trailed off, and then he shrugged, a helpless gesture, an attempt not to be fully responsible for the words he was saying, as though the shrug softened the blow. "Why would she be the only one they didn't find?"

The hallway grew quiet. Even the Muzak seemed to have stopped.

Bill shook his limp, bruised hand, and felt pins and needles in each of his fingertips.

"I wish I knew that, Rich," Bill said. "I really wish I did."

Rich's phone began to ring, and he didn't bother to excuse himself before he turned and answered it.

Then Paige took Bill by the arm, moving him back, pushing him toward the elevators. When they were almost there, Paige turned to Bill and said, "I feel even sorrier for Haley than I did before."

Once inside the elevator, Paige remained oddly quiet. Bill stared at the illuminated numbers, watching them light up one after another.

"What are you thinking?" Bill asked. "You're always thinking something."

"He was an asshole."

"Yes. But?"

"Nothing."

"Paige?"

She folded her arms across her chest and said in a low voice, "Do you know, Bill—do you really know—everything Summer was involved in? I mean . . . Let's talk about it in the car, okay?"

When the doors opened, Bill walked out while Paige tried to keep up. He saw the familiar figure of one of the security guards coming toward him through the lobby. The guy was middle-aged and paunchy, and his face changed when he saw Bill. It turned somber as he looked down, almost appearing to wish Bill wouldn't recognize him, but as they came up to each other, the man held out his hand.

"I'm sorry, Mr. Price," he said. "I'm just so sorry none of this is working out for you."

Bill shook the man's hand, which felt cold and clammy. "Thank you." He didn't know if the man had heard the latest, and he decided not to get into it. He accepted the sympathy however the man intended it. And the gesture brought some warmth to Bill's chest. "Thanks for all you did, keeping an eye on her."

"Of course. I'm happy to do it." He hitched up his pants a little. "I'm happy to help with Haley too."

"Sure." Bill started away, Paige at his side. He looked back and said, "I'm glad to hear kids from school are coming to visit. She'll be happy to see them when she can."

"Yeah. Sure."

Something about the man's tone stopped Bill. He came back and asked, "What's wrong?"

"Nothing," the man said, waving his hand in front of his face. "Kids. Some kid shows up here, and he looks surprised to see me, you know? He acts shocked that there's a guard on the floor where Haley is. And I tell him he has to go, that only immediate family and close friends can be up there now, and he, I don't know, he throws a little attitude at me."

"Attitude?" Paige asked. "He mouthed off?"

"Not so much," the guy said, shrugging. "Just . . . entitled or something. Smirky. That's why I walked him out. I thought maybe he needed to know he couldn't just show up anytime he wanted. That's a sick girl up there."

"Did he tell you his name?" Bill asked.

"Yeah. He had longer hair. Clinton, that's who he said he was."

"That's him," Bill said, turning to Paige. "Clinton Fields. Why was he here?" He turned back to the guard. "Did you tell the police? Detective Hawkins?"

"No. Why? This just happened."

"Tell Hawkins. Or I'll tell him. He shouldn't be here. Is he still outside?"

"He was leaving—"

Bill didn't hear him. He darted for the sliding glass doors, Paige right behind him.

"Bill?"

He ran out into the parking lot, the cold air hitting his face. He looked around, squinting. People came and went. An ambulance, its emergency beacons blinking, pulled out of the lot. But he saw no sign of Clinton.

"Bill, leave him alone."

"I can't."

"Let the cops do it. He'll tell the cops. Okay?"

"What was he doing here, Paige? What on earth was he doing here?"

"It's cold," she said. "Let's go home."

CHAPTER FORTY-FOUR

Bill tossed the keys to Paige. "You drive."

He climbed into the passenger seat of the Civic, using his left hand as much as he could, and reached across his body to pull the door shut.

"Where do you want to go?" Paige asked.

"What?"

"Where do you want to go? You said you didn't want to go home, so where do you want to go?"

Bill reached up, rubbing his hand across his chin. The windshield was dirty, the dashboard dusty. "What did you want to tell me?" he asked. "You have something on your mind."

"It's nothing, Bill."

"It's not nothing. It's never nothing with you. It wasn't nothing when you thought that wasn't Summer." Bill forced the next words out. "And you were right." He looked over at Paige, but she kept her gaze straight ahead. She must have felt his eyes boring into the side of her face. He wanted her to. Like lasers. As if his eyes were giving off heat.

"Don't do this to yourself, Bill. Just don't. I'm sorry I said it."

"Just tell me. I don't want to be treated with kid gloves." He reached up and brushed some dust off the dashboard. He didn't know why. He just wanted to do something useful. "I need to call Hawkins, okay? I'm not going to trust a rent-a-cop to do it. So hurry up."

"Okay." Paige turned to face him. Her face was drained of color, and Bill saw tiny red capillaries in her eyes, like infinitesimal rivers of blood. She bit her lower lip, then said, "Ever since you told me about that guidance counselor saying that Summer seemed upset lately, I've been thinking. And now they've found two girls, including Summer's best friend, the girl she's inseparable from, someone who is like a sister to her, but they can't find Summer. It breaks my heart to say it, Bill." Her voice was rising, growing thinner, more brittle. "Could she have run away? Could she just be involved in something we don't know about? Something we can't even guess at?"

Bill felt as though the air had been sucked out of the car. Something thumped deep inside his ear, a pulsing pressure. He formulated words, an angry, slashing response to his sister, but as he chewed them over, they felt empty and forced, a vain raging against something he couldn't comprehend. His shoulders slumped. He wasn't sure Paige could see it, but he felt it.

"Bill, I'm sorry. I'm likely wrong. She's in danger, and we—"

"Maybe," he said. "Maybe. She lost her mother. She and I butted heads. She never wanted to stay in Jakesville. Maybe she . . . I don't know. Maybe she did run off—I just can't bring myself to believe that."

Paige reached out, placing her hand on his. "Could she have gotten in over her head with something? Could she have just gotten in too deep?"

Bill turned and stared through the dirty windshield. He squinted against the weak, watery sunlight. "I just don't know, Paige. What on earth would it be? Is she pregnant? Is she mixed up in a crime?"

"Maybe she's mixed up in something, and those two girls got hurt as a result, but Summer is somewhere else?"

"You make her sound like a drug dealer. Or a mafioso. She's a kid. A teenage girl who's never been in any real trouble. She had everything going for her. She had a bright future. You should hear the way her teachers talk about her."

"Do you have a guess?"

"No, I don't. You know I don't. What do you think I lie awake at night thinking about? I think about what she could be involved in. Or whether she ran away. Or whether she's dead."

"Didn't that teacher or counselor say she was worried about Summer running away?"

"Counselor. Yes. She said Summer was talking about Julia a few weeks ago. And she was agitated about something."

"What?"

"I told you I don't know."

"Okay, okay. Where do you want to go now? To the park where they're searching? To . . . I don't know. The school? Where?"

Bill stared out the window as they started driving. He flipped through everything in his mind as they passed the other cars, the minivans and sedans, the delivery trucks. The normal business of a normal winter day for everyone but him. What could Summer have been thinking about?

Julia's birthday, maybe. Bill scanned through the dates, forward and back. Nothing had happened. And then—

"Oh, God," he said, lifting his hand to his forehead.

"What?"

"That's it." He turned to Paige. "That's it. Not Julia's birthday. Summer's. Next month she turns sixteen."

"And?"

"She and Julia talked about going on a trip. A spring break trip for her sixteenth birthday. For both of their birthdays. Just the two of them. Just the girls. Summer is turning sixteen next month. That's when they were going on the trip."

"Where were they going?" she asked.

"Nowhere. That's just it. They never planned it. Julia died. But they would have been planning it or getting ready for it now." He let out a groan of frustration. "I blew it. A while back I thought about planning something, a replacement for what she could have done with Julia. But I never followed through. I'm so stupid. She needed me to do that."

"And they never said where they wanted to go?" Paige asked.

"It was just fantasy. Hawaii. Paris. We couldn't afford that. But they could have gone somewhere, even just down to Nashville or something. Damn it. I blew it."

"Okay, maybe she was thinking of the trip."

"She was." He dug in his pocket for his phone. "I have to tell Hawkins. They can start searching in Europe. And I can tell him about Clinton being at the hospital."

"Do you want to go to the station?" Paige asked.

"Take me home," he said while Hawkins's line rang.

"Home? You just said you didn't want to go there."

"I do now. I want to talk to Adam."

When they arrived, Bill jumped out of the car and started toward Adam's house. Hawkins had listened calmly while Bill told him about Summer and Julia's planned trip. He told Bill he'd note it, but without a realistic destination in mind, how could they begin to use the information?

"Her computer," Bill said. "Maybe she searched for something."

"We'll check, Bill. Summer was curious. She looked at everything on there, but we'll look."

Then he told Hawkins about Clinton being at the hospital, about the security guard escorting him out. "What do you think he was doing there?" Bill asked.

Hawkins took a moment to answer. "I have no idea, but I don't like it."

"Exactly. Such an entitled little shit. Probably came here just to try to look like a decent guy."

"Let me call the head of security there right now. He's a former cop."

Bill hung up as he walked. The grass was springy and damp, the trees still bare. Adam kept a large compost pile, something he tended obsessively, churning the rich loam with a shovel or pitchfork on an almost-daily basis. Bill hated yard work and looked forward to winter only because it meant he didn't have to cut the grass for five months.

He walked around the stone fire pit and stepped onto the small back deck attached to Adam's house, knocking lightly on the door. A dog a couple of blocks away kept up an insistent barking, an unsuccessful attempt to let someone know he existed and needed attention. He thought of the body under that sheet at the hospital. How many unknown people were there in the country? Forgotten children or friends, discarded like unclaimed freight. And then he wondered if at that very moment Summer was on a similar slab in an unfamiliar city, her body tagged and ready to be put away until Bill could be found.

He shivered and brought his fingers together under his chin, tightening the opening of his coat. Adam still hadn't appeared, so Bill knocked again, hoping Adam wasn't asleep, taking a midday nap. Or in the bathroom. But before too long he saw Adam's figure emerge from the darkness inside the house and approach the back door, his face somewhat perplexed at seeing Bill there.

"Hey, man," Adam said as he pulled the door open.

"Hey."

Adam wore his usual nonwork clothes: jeans, work boots, flannel shirt with the sleeves rolled up past the elbows. He offered Bill a tentative half smile, his face surprised and expectant. He didn't make any other gesture—no handshake or support.

But why would he? Had Hawkins even announced the news yet?

"Is this a bad time?" Bill asked.

Adam remained in the doorway, not moving aside to let Bill in. "No, I was just packing. I guess I didn't hear you knock right away."

"That's okay. I should have called." Bill tried to see around Adam to get a sense of how much progress he had made on the move, but Adam's solid body filled the door frame. "Have you heard the news about Summer?"

Adam's eyebrows knitted together. "What news? What happened?"

Bill found it hard to believe anybody didn't know. But life went on around them. Everybody's lives went on. "I guess they're just announcing it now."

"Bill, what is it?" he asked, taking a step closer.

"Right." Bill swallowed, feeling a little strange making such an odd pronouncement to his friend. He flexed his hand, saw that his fingers were swollen. He could see that girl under the sheet, the lonely unidentified girl. The words stuck in Bill's throat. "Well, that girl they buried, the one we thought was Summer—she's not. I mean, she's not Summer."

Adam cocked his head but didn't say anything.

"It's a different girl," Bill said, trying to explain, to fill the silence with something that made sense, even though none of it did. "They don't know where Summer is. If she's alive or dead or who knows what. She's been gone eight days. Eight. She could be . . . Those boys or some maniac . . . I don't know what to think. She could be dead. Missing. Maybe she ran away somewhere. She might have wanted to just get away, to go somewhere different."

Concern deepened on Adam's face, as well as a touch of disbelief.

He tilted his head again, moving it back into its normal position and staring at Bill as he processed the information. "You're kidding," he said, his voice sharp in the quiet afternoon.

"No, I'm not. Fuck, would I kid about this?"

Adam reached up and scratched behind his ear, his head moving back and forth underneath his big hand. But he didn't say anything else. His eyes looked glassy, distant, as though the news had knocked him into stunned silence.

"I don't know what to say, Bill. I just don't. . . ."

"I need your help," Bill said. "Come out with me. Help me look. Help me do something. She's out there. Alive. Maybe. I don't know." He wiped his nose with his left hand. "Adam, I just want to find her. Damn it, you're the only one I can really get to help me with this."

"Slow down, Bill. Easy."

"Easy? No, not easy. Shit, she's out there. Look, you spend time outdoors. You know the woods. The parks, the campgrounds, the trails. You go out there all the time. You know out-of-the-way spots in the county. Help me look. Just—let's *do* something. Anything. We can find her. Let's get in our cars and drive down the highway. Maybe she's hitching somewhere. Or maybe she's in a motel or a shelter."

"You need to let the cops do these things," Adam said. "They don't want us blundering in their way. Besides, this is a big county. It's needle-in-a-haystack time out there. Come on."

"What am I supposed to do? Sit? Scratch my ass? Eat dinner and stare at the TV like all the other idiots in the world?"

"Come inside, okay?" Adam said. He stepped back and pushed the door open. "Let's talk. It's cold out here. You're cold. You're kind of a wreck."

"I can't stop, Adam. I can't take time to talk."

The usual brightness returned to Adam's face, like a switch had been flipped, animating him from the inside. "Come in," he said, moving farther back. "Of course we can talk. I was going to come over and tell you something once you were home. Something I think you're going to want to hear. Just listen a minute, and then we'll go from there."

CHAPTER FORTY-FIVE

Bill expected to find a house in chaos, but there was little evidence that Adam was about to move to Oklahoma. A few boxes were stacked in one corner, and a roll of packing tape sat on the kitchen counter, but the house was Spartan to begin with, light on wall hangings and decor, the furniture minimal and unmatched. The most personal details were some shot glasses and two baseball trophies on a shelf near the kitchen. Exactly what Bill expected a divorced guy's house to look like.

Bill sat on the couch while Adam went out to the kitchen. He reached into a cabinet and brought down a bottle of Jack Daniel's and then two glasses. He carried them over, set them on the coffee table, and poured Bill and himself a generous shot.

But neither of them reached for the glasses.

Adam sat with his hands on his knees and said, "So, what are they doing now? The cops?"

"Full-court press to find her," Bill said. He wanted to sound hopeful, to inject some positivity into his voice, but he lacked the energy. "Alive or dead, I guess." Bill let his weight settle into the couch, like sinking into quicksand. "I don't know what to think. I'm scared. I should be relieved. She could be alive instead of beaten to a pulp or dead and gone. But I've been getting jerked around like a fish on a line. I feel worse, Adam. My daughter may not be dead, but I feel more twisted up."

Adam lifted one of the glasses and leaned forward, presenting it to Bill.

"Thanks. I need this today." Bill slammed the shot, a trickle of it running out the side of his mouth and onto his cheek. He wiped it off with his sleeve while Adam drank his down. "That's good."

"I can't imagine what you're going through," Adam said. "If my son . . . If anything ever . . ."

Bill took a moment to place his head in his hands, rubbing his eyes with his palms. He rubbed until he saw red starbursts on the insides of his eyelids, and then he brought his hands down and looked at Adam. He held his slightly swollen right hand in the air. "Look at that," he said.

Adam examined the hand. "What happened?"

"I punched a window at the morgue. Hard. I saw that girl's body, the other one, the one they haven't identified." Bill burped. Some of the whiskey came up, a bitter taste he swallowed. "Someone could be torturing her, doing the worst to her. Or . . ."

"Let me get you some ice for that," Adam said. He went out to the kitchen again, and Bill heard the rattling of the cubes. Adam came back with a plastic bag full of ice, which he handed over to Bill, who gently placed it against the back of his right hand. He winced.

"Or she's . . . I don't know. What do you have to tell me?" Bill asked.

Adam shifted his head a little, as though the collar of his shirt fit too tight. "To be honest, I have to come clean with you about something. You may not like it very much. In fact, I guess I realize how stupid it was in retrospect." Adam's voice sounded softer. It steadily lost its usual heartiness as he spoke, as if his confidence was draining out of him. "But those boys from the high school, the ones they suspect, are having a press conference this afternoon. Jillian told me."

"They are? To say what?"

"I assume they're going to say they're innocent of anything that happened to Summer or Haley."

"And this other girl," Bill said. "The one who died."

Adam nodded. "But these kids . . . My name might come up in connection with all of it if they get pressed. And the cops might ask you about it, so I'm just going to tell you."

Bill's mind flipped through possibilities, but he couldn't imagine a scenario that seemed logical or plausible. So he just waited for Adam to go on, even though his friend seemed more nervous, more uncertain than Bill had ever seen him.

Adam cleared his throat. "I told you how I know Jillian. And how we've become friends—just friends—over the past year or so."

"Sure."

"And that Teena was looking up to me a little as well."

"You told me. What did you find out?"

"Well, look, Teena came to my house a few months ago. I didn't even know she knew where I lived. I didn't know the girl that well then. I would say hello to her when I went to their house, but she never really talked to me."

"Why did she come over here?" Bill asked.

"Pretty typical stuff." He smiled a little, a boys-will-be-boys gleam in his eye. "Kids. She wanted me to buy alcohol for her and her friends."

"And you did?" Bill asked, trying to keep the incredulity out of his voice.

Adam started scratching behind his ear again. "You remember what it was like to be a teenager and to just be looking for something to do. I figured those kids were going to find alcohol someway, and Teena promised me none of them were going to drive, so there wasn't that danger." He shrugged. "She and I went to a convenience store, the one over on High Street, and she sat in the car while I went in and bought them a twelve-pack. Then I drove her to her friend's house."

"Who was the friend?" Bill asked.

"I'm pretty sure it was Clinton Fields. She didn't tell me his name, and I didn't ask. But when that girl had to be taken out of his house in an ambulance, I recognized the house and the street." He reached out and poured another shot for himself but didn't drink it. "And the thing is, Bill, Summer was there. I saw her when I dropped Teena off."

Bill's hands started to tremble. "Why didn't you tell me?"

"The same reason I bought the beer in the first place." He sounded calm, matter-of-fact. "It's tough being a kid, and I didn't want to be the one to rain on their parade. They were having a good time, but they weren't hurting anything."

"But they were. Clearly. Look what happened. Just today he was slinking around the hospital, going up to the floor—"

"I agree, Bill. It looks bad for those boys. One of them has proven to be violent. A troublemaker. Hell, somebody ought to teach them a lesson. I wish we could."

"Forget that. You're supposed to be my friend." Bill hated the cloying sound of his voice, the wheedling tone he couldn't control as his anger rose. "That means you're supposed to look out for my daughter as well. Did you tell the police about this?"

Adam took a long time to answer. "I did. Yesterday. I called the detective in charge of the case, Hawkins, and I explained the whole thing. I even offered to go down and talk in person, but he said it wasn't necessary."

"Why did you wait so long?" Bill asked.

"I'd kind of forgotten about it until I saw that news story," he said. "And it didn't seem terribly relevant. Kids drink. It's no big deal."

"Are they charging you?"

"You mean for buying the beer?" Adam looked surprised by the question. "No, I think they have bigger items on their menu right now. Look, Bill, I realize I messed up. I betrayed your trust, even. I was just . . . You know, I didn't know all of this would end up happening."

"When was this?" Bill asked.

Adam shook his head. "I'm not sure. It was in the fall." He shook his head again. "I did it one other time for Teena. Bought her beer. That was later, in the winter, because I remember it was cold out. Maybe in December."

"Again?" Bill fidgeted. He wanted to get up. He needed to move around, but he stayed in place. "The same house?"

"Yes."

"Was Summer there?"

"I don't know. I didn't see any other kids."

Bill reached over and took the bottle, pouring himself a shot and drinking it down in one continuous motion. He hoped for some form of instant oblivion, something that would help him acquire a distance from everything going on right before him. But he felt nothing. It was as if he'd slammed a glass of amber-colored water.

"Everybody seems to know my daughter better than I do," he said.

"Kids keep secrets, Bill. It's what teenagers do."

"Gee, thanks. I didn't know that."

Adam let out a long sigh. "Bill, you need to be a little understanding about what it's like to be young. Teenagers kind of require that."

Bill stood up and started for the door. "This from a guy who barely sees his kid."

Adam's face went blank, a cold mask. "Yeah, nice shot. Easy too," Adam said as Bill reached the door. "Julia agreed with me. She saw it coming with you and Summer."

Bill froze. He turned around and looked back across the room to where Adam sat with his untouched second shot before him.

"Julia?" he asked. "You're invoking Julia?"

Adam shook his head, his face still expressionless. "Forget I said it."

"I won't. In fact, I need to know something." Bill saw his chance to push Adam further. "Something I've been meaning to ask you for the last year, and now seems like the perfect time."

CHAPTER FORTY-SIX

Bill came a few steps back into the room. He'd never taken his coat off, and he felt heat building up inside and under the wool. The two shots he'd slammed back swirled in his head, making it feel full of air.

"I know Julia called you on the day she died," he said. "At almost the exact moment she died. You told me that then. You told the police you didn't answer, right?"

Adam looked perplexed. "You're right. I was away from the phone when she called," he said. "You asked me about that when it happened, and I told you. And the cops. There's no secret there. I didn't even know I missed a call until . . . well, until I came home from work and saw the police and the paramedics over at your house. It was all too late then."

"Yeah, yeah." Bill reached up and touched his forehead, where he felt sweat forming. He wiped it away, lowering his hand to smear the moisture on his pant leg. "But that call isn't what I wanted to ask you about. Not really."

Adam leaned back in his seat, lifting his arms to rest along the back of his chair. He looked like a king, a king considering the supplications of one of his subjects, and that ease and lack of concern grated against Bill like sandpaper. He could imagine Adam in that posture, reclining on the bench between innings of a high school baseball game. Everybody's friend. Everybody's star.

"Was there more to it than that?" Bill asked. "Was there more to it than she just called you because you were the closest neighbor and she couldn't get ahold of me? I mean . . ." Bill looked around the room, his eyes landing anywhere but on Adam's supremely confident body. He didn't know what to do with his hands, so he stuffed them into his coat pockets. "The way she spoke about you sometimes. And things you've said about her. And now you're acting like the two of you would talk about me. Complain about me."

Bill hated that he sounded so weak, so pathetic. But he stayed there in the middle of Adam's living room, waiting for a response.

Again, Adam considered Bill for a long time. "You're asking me the kind of thing that a man really shouldn't ask another man. That's the kind of question that back in the old days would have resulted in two men going outside with dueling pistols. Or fists. You know?"

"That's not an answer."

"I think it is." Adam scooted forward and drank his shot. "Your wife was beautiful. And intelligent. Full of life and personality. And if something had happened between her and me over a year ago, what would it all matter now? Hmm?"

"Answer the question."

Adam stared Bill down and then shook his head. "You have nothing to worry about on that score. Julia called me because I'm your neighbor. That's it. And because you were . . . Where were you exactly when she called you?"

Bill turned away, starting back for the door.

Adam said, "Right. So neither one of us was able to do anything for her. But only one of us was required to."

Bill pulled the door open, felt the cool late-winter air rush across his face.

CHAPTER FORTY-SEVEN

The wind picked up as Bill trudged back across the lawn. Before he reached the back door, someone emerged from around the side of his house, a woman in a stylish raincoat, her long hair shiny even in the gray afternoon. She carried a microphone and was followed by a guy with a camera hoisted on his shoulder.

"Mr. Price?"

Bill recognized her from the local station. She'd talked to him the day Summer disappeared, her head bobbing along with everything Bill said to her. That interview had taken place inside his home, in the living room, the lights perfectly adjusted by the cameraman, the little details of the house—the framed photos, the books, the candles—shot in soft focus as what they called "B-roll."

Bill remembered her name: Rita Fitzgerald.

She had perfectly white, even teeth and prominent cheekbones. She came right up to him, the microphone in her hand like a relay baton. "Do you have a moment, Mr. Price?"

Bill understood. The news was out about the identity of the body in the grave. It was everywhere. They wanted a quick reaction, something emotional that the viewers could watch, a little catch in their throat while they shoveled potpie or frozen pizza into their mouths, and then they could flip the channel and watch a game show or info-mercial.

Bill stopped, his hands in his pockets. He knew how he looked on TV. How anyone looked on TV without makeup. The lights showed every flaw. The thinning hair, the winter pallor of his skin, the bags under the eyes. They probably wanted that. Authenticity. A regular guy with a regular kid who was missing again after being thought dead.

"I'll do anything to get the word out about Summer," Bill said.

That first weekend Summer was gone, he'd spent hours hiking through the woods with cops and firefighters and volunteers. His anxiety so high, his body so jacked with adrenaline that it felt like it was being fed to him through an IV. They all pounded through the woods together, calling the girls' names, looking for anything and everything that might be a clue. Bill had never realized how much detritus lay scattered around a town. Condoms and underwear, socks and razors. And what would it have been like if he'd come across Summer's body in a ditch somewhere? What if he'd found her bro-ken, battered body in some hole or a rotten barn?

Sort of like Summer finding Julia that day in the kitchen, he thought.

"Do you mind if we film you?" Rita asked.

"Of course not. Thanks for doing this."

"Okay," she said. She looked at the camera guy, who nodded as the blinding white light came on. "So, why don't you just tell us how you learned about the new situation with Summer."

"The police told me. At the station."

"And what are your feelings now?" Rita asked. "You've been through so much."

Bill knew his lines, the same lines the parent of every missing child said to a news media eager to get the footage on TV.

"I just want her to come home," he said, looking into the camera and trying not to squint. "I want her to come home safe. And for anyone who knows anything to share that information with the police. Summer might be in grave danger. She *is* in grave danger. She's been gone a long time, and I worry that she's hurt or sick or cold. Too much time has passed without any word."

"And do you have any message for the person or persons responsible for her disappearance?"

Bill blinked a few times. He felt the heat generated by the light, saw the uncaring, unfeeling eye of the camera taking him in. What good did any of it do? What good did it do to repeat the same clichéd bullshit for yet another reporter?

Bill started talking. "People do know things. These kids from the school, they know what happened to Summer. They do. Teena Everett. Clinton Fields. Todd Stone. Brandon Cooke. They know something about this, and they've been keeping secrets. And it's time we all got to the bottom of it. So I'd tell the parents to get their kids to speak up before it's too late for Summer. Everyone needs to know about the contest they were having, a contest involving sex. One that must have led to Summer being hurt. So ask them about that. They hurt another girl the other night. Gave her too much to drink and took pictures of her in that state."

Rita Fitzgerald's eyes opened wide. She looked comical, like a mugging silent-movie star. But she quickly recovered. "What contest are you talking about?"

"Ask Detective Hawkins. Or ask those boys. I'm sure everybody knew about it before I did."

Bill turned and started for the house.

"Wait," Rita said. "Did you know those boys are holding a press conference in the next hour? Do you have any comment on that?"

"Maybe they'll finally tell us all the truth," he said. "Clinton can explain why he was at the hospital today. Maybe trying to hurt Haley. It's time. It really is time."

CHAPTER FORTY-EIGHT

Bill came inside, welcoming the warmth of the house. Paige sat at the table, her eyes tracking him as he walked through the kitchen and down the hallway toward the bedrooms.

He stopped at the office and went in. He moved to the desk and sat, opening the laptop. He stared at the screen and the files, but didn't play them.

He didn't know who anybody was. Not his daughter, not his wife. He knew Paige only because they'd grown up together.

Had he really lost Summer that Halloween night when he grabbed her? Had she run into the arms of those boys because he didn't know how to be the father she needed?

"What are you doing?"

He jumped at the sound of Paige's voice.

She flipped the overhead light on. Bill sat there, still wearing his coat, not even able to formulate a story that would explain why he sat in the dark in his home office. The room Paige had been sleeping in since she arrived.

"Nothing," he said.

"Am I in your way in here?" she asked. "I . . . I didn't want to sleep in Summer's room."

"You're not in my way."

"What went on outside? I saw the reporters. There are more out front, if you want to talk to them."

"I'm fine. I'll talk to more soon."

"What did you say exactly?" she asked. "You looked kind of pissed."

"I wasn't pissed."

"Bill, I know when you're pissed. I've been on the receiving end of it."

"I just said my lines. My father-of-a-missing-child lines. It's fine. I want everyone to feel a sense of urgency. I want them moving."

Paige nodded toward the laptop. "What's up with that thing? Antiques collecting?"

"You know what—" He stopped himself. "It's nothing. Just an old computer I have."

"Okay. I guess you want to be alone."

"Paige?" he said.

"Yeah?"

"I want you to do me a favor." He hesitated a moment before going on. "If the worst happens with Summer, if the news is as bad as it could be—"

"Don't think that way, Bill."

"I am thinking that way," he said. "Everybody is. You are and the cops are and so are the reporters. How can we all not be thinking that way at this point? Just because there isn't a body . . . ?"

"Okay," Paige said.

"If the worst happens, just make sure I . . . pay attention during the funeral. I don't want to, you know, sleepwalk through it like I did with Julia's."

"You were grieving," she said.

"I just don't want to forget anything. You know?"

"I get it." She leaned against the doorway, arms crossed over her chest. "Is that why you still have all of Julia's clothes in the closet?"

Bill looked up at his sister. "What?"

"I was looking for something to wear the other night. A sweater or a sweatshirt. It was chilly. So I went into the closet in your bedroom."

"You could have asked."

"You were out. On your 'errand,' the one that brought you to that girl's house. Anyway, when I opened the closet, I saw all of Julia's things. Clothes and shoes and sweaters."

"So? It's only a year and a half."

"I think it's kind of sweet in a way." She reached up and ran her hand through her hair. "You can move on however you want. Okay? It's fine with me. And I'll help you however I can. Really. And you're right—we've all thought about the worst. That's true. But I'm holding out hope we don't have to think of that in any real way." She waited a moment, and when Bill said nothing else, she said, "I'll leave you alone."

Bill wanted to share the messages with her, but by the time he opened his mouth, she was gone.

He came out to the kitchen an hour later. Paige held a paper plate full of food and ate standing up at the counter.

"Want something?" she asked.

"I'm putting the TV on. Those boys, those idiotic boys, are having a press conference. They must have gone there after the hospital." He fumbled in the couch cushions, looking for the remote. "Why can't I find anything in here?"

"Take it easy," she said, coming over. "Here it is."

"Forget it. I'm just going to drive down there."

"Where?"

"Wherever it is."

"Were you drinking at Adam's house?" Paige asked.

"A couple."

"Stay here. They don't need you showing up and making a scene. And you don't need a DUI."

She flicked the TV on and found a local channel. A commercial played, something advertising senior independent living. Bill tuned it out. He hated to hear about the future, the notion that his life could stretch on and on after this. Without Summer. Without, ever knowing where she was or what really happened to her. How long could he live not knowing? The rest of his life?

The microwave dinged, and Paige came to the couch with a steaming plate of food. "Eat."

Bill looked at the plate. Some kind of chicken and pasta. The steam rose against his face, but he thought the food looked disgusting, like something already digested and regurgitated. "Put it down."

"You have to eat. You look like death on a cracker."

"Forget it. Who has time to eat?"

Three more commercials played, and then they had to watch a local anchorman, a middle-aged guy with badly dyed hair, recap all the details of Summer's disappearance. He seemed to take particular joy in the discovery that Summer wasn't the girl buried in the grave, giving special emphasis to words like "remains" and "identify" and "exhume." Then he switched to the live feed from the lawyer's office. Bill recognized the attorney, Ralph Bateman. He appeared in commercials all the time on local TV, despite his bad hair and sagging jowls. Bateman stood before some microphones in a conference room. Behind him, arrayed in a neat row, were the three boys. Each of them wore a coat and tie. Their hair was neatly combed, their faces suitably somber and downcast. They were trying their best to look like the victims, the innocent, put-upon victims. And their parents stood behind them, hands resting on shoulders, faces determined and resolute.

These are our boys, they said with their looks. *No one had better say anything bad about our boys.*

"Look at this, Paige," Bill said through clenched teeth. "Look at this fucking sideshow."

"Shhh."

Bateman nodded at the cameras. He introduced his clients, each of the three boys, and their parents, taking great care to point out that the families were all lifelong residents of Jakesville and that they had deep roots in the community. He bit down on his lower lip when he said how sorry they all were that Haley and the unidentified girl were injured so badly, and then he said the boys and their families were all praying for Summer's safe return.

"What manipulative bullshit," Bill said, pointing at the screen. "That one put a kid in the hospital."

But then Bateman shifted gears. His face hardened, and his tone became sharp enough to cut steel. "These boys have made some mistakes. Who doesn't when they're young? I know I did." He looked up, and the tiniest boys-will-be-boys glint appeared in his eye. "But these young men had nothing to do with any attack on those girls or with the tragic disappearance of Summer Price. Let me reiterate that— they had nothing to do with those crimes. They went to the hospital today to visit their injured classmate, to support her as she recovers."

Bill looked at Paige. Her eyes were fixed on the screen, her lips pressed together. The untouched plate of food steamed on the coffee table.

"In fact," Bateman said, "in light of some comments Mr. Price made to the media this afternoon, comments I was just informed of before we started here, I feel compelled to share some information these boys have now offered to the police." Bateman turned a page on the lectern, a theatrical gesture. "Apparently Summer Price was afraid of her father. His temper. Last fall, the Jakesville police responded to a nine-one-one call from Summer when Mr. Price became physically violent, shaking the girl and throwing her to the floor."

Bill's hand started to throb faster than the thrumming pulse in his ear.

"On more than one occasion, Summer expressed a desire to get away from her father, to get out from under his oppressive parenting. She missed her late mother very much." Bateman swallowed, his Adam's apple bobbing. "Like I said, these boys aren't perfect, and they're going to face some discipline from their school and their parents. *They've* never raised a hand against a girl. Thank you."

CHAPTER FORTY-NINE

Hawkins sent the department's media liaison officer over—a young woman with short hair and a disarmingly businesslike manner—to craft a statement from Bill. It reiterated what Bill thought of as his missing-child talking points. "Bring Summer home. . . . Somebody knows something. . . . We won't rest until we find her."

The officer distributed it to the media, the members of which took turns lingering at the end of the driveway. And she reminded Bill of how Hawkins wanted him to proceed. *Don't go off script. Better yet, don't talk to any reporters for a while. Let the statement speak for itself.* Bill paced inside the house, fearing that everyone would focus more on the boys or his comments and not so much on the desperate need to find Summer.

Bill distracted himself by finding a movie on TV. A Western, the kind of thing his dad would watch on a Saturday afternoon, it featured John Wayne—aging and paunchy—banding together with a ragtag group to save a town from a ruthless sheriff. The Duke wise-cracked, punched, and shot his way through the story, and Bill wished it were all so simple in real life. Couldn't Hawkins just take matters into his own hands and start roughing up the bad guys? Couldn't Bill?

Paige came in and sat next to him, her phone in her hand. She texted, barely looking at the TV. During a commercial, Bill said, "You remember our cousin Jimmy, right?"

Paige looked up. "Of course. Why?"

"Mom said something interesting when Jimmy was dying. You know, the cancer had come back and it was clear he wasn't going to make it. Mom said she was glad Aunt Denise wasn't alive to watch her son die. We were what, teenagers when Jimmy died? I'd never thought of being a parent that way. That the worst thing would be seeing your own child hurt. Or dying."

Paige remained silent, the phone held in front of her.

Tears pooled in his eyes, obscuring his view of the soft carpet, the coffee table with its scattered magazines. His uneaten food from earlier.

"I get it now. In a real way, I get it."

The movie came on again and Bill turned his attention to the screen. But the volume remained muted. John Wayne was punching a guy over and over, knocking him through doors and walls.

"Look, your family needs you," Bill said. "And there's no funeral here. Nothing." Bill pointed toward the front of the house. "You can come back if something changes."

"I'm staying. You're getting to the end of your rope. That's why you said all those things to the reporters today."

Bill stared at the screen, not fully paying attention to Paige. He was lost in his own thoughts. A spiral of horrific images played in his mind. Where could Summer be? Dumped in the woods? Locked in a basement? Stored in a morgue?

In a hostile place, dying alone?

He replayed what the lawyer said, what the counselor at school said. Even Paige's suspicions. Was something happening to Summer that would make her run away?

Was she starting a new life?

"She called him," Bill said.

"Who?"

"Julia. She called Adam when I didn't answer the phone that day."

That day. He was accumulating things that could simply be referred to as "that day." Julia's death. Summer's disappearance.

That day.

"She did?" Paige sounded surprised. "You mean she called him, looking for some kind of help?"

"I don't know. He didn't answer. He was in a meeting or something, so he didn't get the call." Bill lifted his hand to make a gesture, but he let it drop back onto the couch.

"What?" Paige asked.

"It's silly. But they were always kind of flirtatious, the two of them. Mildly flirtatious. She talked about how handsome he was, how strong he was, like he was a real man. I don't know. I told you I thought she might have been having an affair of some kind. Even one that was just emotional."

"He's good-looking," Paige said, then caught herself. "I mean, if you're into that kind of guy."

"The ruggedly handsome kind?" Bill said.

"I'm sure he has a small dick," Paige said. "All that digging and plowing in the yard must be compensating for something. Right?"

"Thanks, I think. Well. I was pissed he didn't tell me about buying the kids beer, and I was pissed Julia called him as she was dying. I just . . . All of this is bringing up a lot of old stuff."

"Sure. Of course." Paige reached out and squeezed Bill's arm. "I'll stay a few more days. Just in case. Okay?"

"Thanks."

"We can watch *Flying Leathernecks* or something like that if you want."

She went back to tapping at her phone, biting her lip in concentration. Bill turned the sound up again. A few minutes passed, and then Paige asked, "How do you know Adam didn't take the call from Julia?"

"What? He said he didn't."

"Did they check the phone records?" Paige asked. "The police?"

Bill had never thought about it. "Why would they? There was nothing suspicious about her death. It was an accident. They didn't check into anything like phone records."

Paige looked at Bill for a moment, seemingly on the brink of saying something else. But she didn't. She went back to pecking at her phone.

CHAPTER FIFTY

Before he could ask Paige exactly what she was talking about, the front doorbell rang. They both looked up.

"Expecting anybody?" Paige asked.

"Probably another reporter, some straggler with a late deadline."

Bill rehearsed a speech as he walked to the door, something intended to shame the journalist for bothering a distressed family at the worst possible time. Even as he played the scene in his head, he felt ridiculous. Yelling at someone for doing their job? Why?

And then he saw it wasn't a reporter at all. Anna Halstrom stood on the front stoop, a heavy coat bundled around her body, her long hair lifting in the wind. She smiled when she saw Bill, and he hustled to the door, pulling it open and stepping back so she could come in, out of the cold.

"Anna," he said. "Did you say you were coming by?"

"No. And I should have called." She stepped into the foyer, rubbing her hands together. "This is an impulsive visit. I'm on my way to a night class I take, and I realized I had to tell you something. I hope I'm not overstepping my bounds here."

"Why don't you sit?" Bill said.

"Okay. Just a moment."

Paige appeared, still holding her phone. Bill made the introductions, and Anna expressed her sympathies to Paige.

"We all love that girl," Anna said. She sat on the couch, tucking her long skirt beneath her body. She wore sandals despite the cold, and round, silver earrings the size of satellite dishes. Bill sat in a chair, and Paige remained in the doorway, twirling the string on her hooded sweatshirt while Anna started to talk.

"Is this about Summer?" Bill asked. "Did you remember something? I was thinking maybe she was upset because her sixteenth birthday was coming up. She was supposed to go on a trip with Julia. That would have happened next month. Did she mention that?"

Anna listened as though unsure what or whom Bill was talking about. "Oh, sure. Maybe that upset her, yes. But she never mentioned that to me specifically. I'm here to talk about Summer, but only tangentially."

"Oh," Bill said. He couldn't keep the disappointment out of his voice. He couldn't hide the anticipation he felt for every piece of information, the burning hope that it would finally be the key to unlock every closed door. "What is it, then?"

"It's about Clinton Fields." Anna pressed her lips together and turned from Bill to Paige and then back again, as though seeking their permission to keep talking. When no one said anything, Anna went on. "I think there's a misunderstanding about him, some confusion about his character. I thought about it because of what you said on the news and then what they said on the news."

"What do you know?" Bill asked.

Anna rubbed her hands together some more. The bracelets on her wrists jangled. "Everybody knows he broke that other boy's jaw at the bus stop a couple of years ago. But not everybody knows why." She held up her hands. "I have to ask for complete discretion here, from both of you. This cannot leave this house."

"Of course," Paige said.

"What is it?" Bill asked.

"Yes, Clinton broke that boy's jaw. And it's terrible. I abhor violence. I abhor the way we socialize our boys to solve problems that way. But . . . Clinton has a younger brother. About a year younger. He's at the junior high now. His name is Isaac. A really good kid, but Isaac is gay. He's been slowly coming out to his family and close friends. I know this because I've been consulted by my colleague at the junior high. It's a big issue to take on for a counselor, and we try to help each other out."

"I don't understand," Bill said. "What does his brother's sexual preference have to do with Summer?"

"Nothing," Anna said. "Except that when Clinton broke that other boy's jaw, it was because the other boy was saying horrible things about Isaac. Calling him . . . Well, you can imagine the names. Clinton overheard him and the fight started. Clinton was angry beyond belief. He beat the boy pretty good, but then again, who knows what any of us would do to protect or defend someone we love, right?"

She looked to both of them for support. Paige nodded. And Bill said, "Okay, so this kid said horrible things about his brother. Clinton must have told the police or the school that."

"He didn't. His family wouldn't let him, because they didn't want the secret about Isaac out to the whole community. To protect his brother, Clinton took the full punishment and let everyone think he's a thug. Do you see?"

Paige cleared her throat. "You're saying the situation is much more complicated than it appeared to be at first. That Clinton had a good reason for reacting as violently as he did."

"Basically. Again, I abhor the violence. But I also abhor that narrow-mindedness, the attack on a young boy's identity."

Bill didn't want to sound insensitive or obtuse, but he said, "Still, it was an attack."

"It was," Anna said. She looked at her watch. "I've taken too much of your time. I just wanted you to know. And . . . I know Clinton. There's sensitivity in that boy, despite his flippant exterior. I just don't know what to make of this whole situation, but I wanted you to have all the facts."

She stood up, her skirt flowing free as she walked to the door. She gave both Bill and Paige a hug and insisted that they call her anytime if they needed help or advice.

"I hope I didn't muddy the waters for you," Anna said as she went out the door, "but I believe in transparency. And now you know everything I know."

CHAPTER FIFTY-ONE

Later that night, Bill woke up on the couch. He'd sipped more whiskey and swallowed some kind of antianxiety pill Paige had handed him. When he opened his eyes, his head felt foggy, like a thin membrane of cobweb had been stretched over his gray matter.

The TV still played. Another movie, something black-and-white. The men wore their hair plastered back against their heads. The women all wore skirts and heels.

Bill looked around the room, squinting. His hand hurt, but he could move it. When he flexed it, some of the soreness eased. He saw a depression in the couch cushions where Paige had been sitting. For a moment, he felt like they were little kids again, falling asleep in front of the TV, waking up a little scared because Mom and Dad were already off to bed.

Bill straightened up, rubbing the back of his neck as he blinked to clear the cobwebs from his brain.

"Paige?" He whispered in case she'd gone off to bed and fallen asleep. "Paige?"

He looked at his watch: twelve fifteen. He reached for the remote and turned the TV off. He was about to stand, when Paige came hustling from the foyer at the front of the house.

"Bill?" she said, also whispering. Did she think he was asleep, sitting up with his eyes open? "Bill," she said again, her voice more insistent.

"You don't have to whisper. I can't believe I let you give me that pill. I need to be up and—"

"That car's back. The one I saw drive by."

Bill processed the news slowly through the fog of the pill and the booze, and then he remembered the car that had freaked her out the other night.

"Are you sure?"

"Yes. It's in the driveway. The end of the driveway."

"Maybe it's a reporter this time."

"This late?"

"They come around anytime they want," Bill said, remembering the morning after Summer disappeared, when the reporters seemingly lived on his lawn. "Just ignore them. Let's go out and—"

"No, Bill. Just get up and look. Please?"

Bill stood up, his lower back aching. He wished he hadn't fallen asleep in that position. He walked to the front of the house and looked through the window. He saw the headlights of a car glowing at the end of the driveway. They shone against the house, illuminating the back wall of the living room.

"I think they're just turning around," Bill said.

"No, they've been there for a few minutes. I waited before I woke you up. I thought they might just be turning around too, but they didn't leave. It's the same car. Look. It's a silver sedan. See?"

"It's a Camry or something like that." Bill patted his pockets, searching for his phone, but he didn't have it. "Call the police if anything happens."

"Anything like what?"

"I'm going out there," Bill said. A surging excitement grew in his chest, an upswing of energy he hadn't felt since he was a child, something close to giddiness.

"Don't go out there, Bill. You don't know who it is."

"Paige, my daughter's missing. For days, missing. I don't give a damn. Besides, what if this is it?"

"It's what?"

"Summer. This person. They have her, and they want to bring her home."

"Bill?"

But he was undoing the locks, pulling the door open, and running across the lawn toward the silver sedan as fast as his legs would carry him.

Bill wasn't wearing shoes. His socks slipped against the frosty grass, the cold seeping in and freezing the soles of his feet.

He didn't care.

The sedan's headlights still glowed, and Bill cut across them as his feet reached the driveway and then went around to the driver's side of the car. When he got there, the car shut off, the lights going out and leaving Bill alongside the vehicle beneath the cold glow of the distant stars.

A streetlight above provided some illumination. He looked through the window, trying to make out the figure behind the wheel, but he saw only a vague outline, a shape that didn't resolve into anything coherent.

Then the door came open. But no dome light shone.

"Bill?" Paige stood in the doorway. "Should I call the police?"

Bill waved her off, took a step toward the car, trying to see inside, into the backseat.

A woman stepped onto the driveway. She looked to be slightly older than Bill. Her professionally colored hair, a kind of reddish brown, hung loose to her shoulders. She wore no makeup, and dark skin, from lack of sleep or strain or illness, circled under her eyes.

Bill took her in quickly, but then resumed looking into the back of the car. He wanted to see Summer. He *hoped* he would.

"Mr. Price?" the woman said.

Bill ignored her, moving closer to the car on his cold, wet feet. But he saw nothing in the back except scattered fast food wrappers and crumpled cigarette packs. A liter bottle of Diet Mountain Dew, half-empty, sat in the cup holder in between the two front seats.

"Mr. Price?"

Bill turned to the woman. "Do you know where Summer is?"

The woman looked thin and bony, every part of her body a sharp angle. She wore a hooded sweatshirt with a Cincinnati Bengals logo stitched above her left breast. The sweatshirt looked new, but a greasy stain from spilled food stood out on one of the pockets.

"I wanted to talk to you, sir," she said.

"About Summer? Where is she? Why have you been driving by here?"

"Do you want to talk out here?" The woman shivered and looked down at Bill's shoeless feet. "Or could we maybe go inside?"

"Inside my house? At this hour?"

Bill looked back, and Paige still stood in the doorway, the phone in her hand. When she established eye contact with Bill, she made an exaggerated shrugging gesture as if to ask him, *What gives?*

"My sister wants to call the police," Bill said. "You're freaking her out."

"I don't mean any harm," she said. "I know it's late, but the media was around earlier. I would like to talk to you. Your sister can listen as well."

Bill studied the woman for a moment, and then he walked to the back of her car, stepping gingerly as small pebbles jabbed at the bottoms of his feet. He stopped at the trunk.

"Can you pop this?"

The woman looked puzzled. "Why?"

"Can you just do it?" Bill asked. "I'm sure the fob in your hand will do the job."

The woman shrugged. "If you insist."

"Please."

The woman reached into the car and brought out her key ring. She came alongside Bill, and he smelled cigarettes and a sour odor like spoiled food. The woman pressed the fob, and the car made a robotic chiming sound as the trunk unlatched. Bill threw the trunk open.

Bill peered inside. He saw scattered clothes, some papers, and a spare tire. He stuck his hand into the dark recesses where the streetlight didn't reach, and when he was satisfied that Summer wasn't inside, he nodded, and the woman closed the trunk again.

"I'm not a maniac or anything," she said.

"That's exactly what I'd say if I were trying to convince someone I wasn't a maniac and I really was."

The woman looked a little hurt. She ducked her head, her slightly greasy hair falling around her face. She looked like she needed a shower. "I lost my daughter too," she said. "And, I don't know, maybe we can help each other."

Bill shifted his weight from one foot to the other, trying to stay warm.

"You know something about Summer?" he asked. "That's all I really care about."

"I might. That's all I'm saying. I might."

The woman looked sincere. And somewhat pathetic.

And Bill was getting colder and colder.

"Okay," he said, nodding toward the house. "Let's go in."

CHAPTER FIFTY-TWO

P aige stood in the doorway as they approached, as if to say, *What the hell are you doing?*

But Bill waved Paige and her concerns aside, rushing into the house where the welcome warmth of the furnace greeted him. "It's cold, Paige. It's cold."

The woman followed Bill inside, and in the bright light of the foyer, Bill saw that she wore new jeans and expensive running shoes, but the pink polish on her nails was chipped, the skin nearby red as though it had been chewed on. Bill peeled off his socks and threw them aside, then rubbed his hands together to get warm.

"What's your name?" he asked.

"Taylor Kress," she said.

"This is my sister, Paige," Bill said. "She's staying with me."

Paige still looked uncertain about the whole thing, as if Bill had opened the door to some kind of wild animal or demonic force. Paige took the full measure of Taylor Kress, from head to toe, and clutched her phone like a life preserver.

"Why don't we sit at the kitchen table?" Bill said. "I'm going to get something warm to drink. And then Taylor can tell us what she knows."

"The police are patrolling the neighborhood," Paige said. "Maybe we should call them in."

"They don't go by as much as you'd think," Taylor said.

Bill and Paige looked at her, waiting for further explanation.

"I've been by the house before."

"We know," Paige said.

"I thought there'd be more cops around, given what you all are going through."

Bill felt unsettled by her statement, but not entirely surprised. He doubted the police in a town like Jakesville could devote their limited resources to babysitting his house full-time. And what proof was there that whoever had harmed Summer was likely to come along and injure him? Why would a person who preyed on young women want to hurt him?

Bill started coffee brewing while the two women settled around the table. Taylor pulled the sleeves of her sweatshirt down over her hands, and Bill again tried to determine her age. She looked older than him and, if possible, even more tired and worn.

"Her daughter's missing," Bill said.

"Oh." Paige straightened up a little, the information making her reassess. "I'm sorry to hear that."

The coffee started gurgling, emitting a rich odor that Bill happily inhaled. He wanted to get the stale scent coming off Taylor out of his nostrils.

"Her name is Emily," Taylor said. "My daughter. And I haven't seen her for a year or so. She ran away, I guess you could say. We had a falling-out, and she went to live with her stepfather after he and I split up. My ex-husband."

"In Jakesville?" Bill asked.

"No. We're from Ariel. Over in Sweetwater County."

Paige looked at Bill, seeking clarification.

Bill said, "About an hour east of here. Right, Taylor?"

She nodded. The woman started digging around in the pocket of her jeans, contorting her body in the chair so she could reach something. Paige moved back a little, as though she expected Taylor to pull out a gun or a live snake.

But the woman brought out a phone. She tapped it a few times and then sighed as she stared at something on the screen.

"This is her," she said. "My Emily."

She turned the phone around so Paige and Bill could see.

And then they understood why Taylor Kress was there.

CHAPTER FIFTY-THREE

Paige took the phone from Taylor's hand. Bill noticed a slight tremble as Paige moved closer to Bill, turning the screen so he could get a better look at the girl in the picture.

She stood outside a building, her weight leaning back against a brick wall, her arms crossed. She wore a short skirt and a black top, her right hand resting on her waist, her elbow at a forty-five-degree angle to her body. The way every young girl posed in every photo on social media.

She looked to be a little older than Summer. But she had blond hair the same shade and length. If Bill had seen Emily strolling into his house one day, trailing behind Summer and Haley, he wouldn't have batted an eye. He'd have simply assumed that the girls had added another look-alike to their group, another girl who to a stranger would be interchangeable with the other two.

"You think . . ." Bill didn't know how to go on. Here he was, sick and tired of people tiptoeing around difficult subject matter with him, but he couldn't bring himself to say the words he needed to say. "You think she's dead? That she's the girl they found in the park next to Haley?"

"I hope I'm wrong."

"But why would you think that?" Paige asked. "There are obviously a lot of young blond girls running around the world. The police have already mixed up two of them. Do you have reason to think someone hurt your daughter?"

"Hold on," Bill said, waving his hands in the air. "I'm calling the police. I don't care how late it is. I want Hawkins involved in this. We need to hurry up on all of this."

"Just wait a minute on that," Taylor said. She looked stricken. She held her hand out, gesturing to Bill to stop. Her fingers were bony, the knuckles pronounced. "I've dealt with them already."

"You mean here? Detective Hawkins?"

She shook her head. "I've spoken to the police in Ariel, trying to convince them something is wrong with Emily, that she's been hurt or taken." She pursed her lips and looked around the kitchen. "Do you think I could have some of that coffee?"

Bill filled three mugs. His hands shook as he poured, and he bit back on the impulse to spin around and scream at the woman, to get her to tell them everything she knew. The house was quiet, and he heard the soft, steady ticking of the kitchen clock above the sink. Time passing. Summer was somewhere and time was passing.

He handed the filled mugs to Paige and Taylor, then nodded at Taylor to go on.

She sipped tentatively from the mug and then drank some more.

"Do you want cream or something?" Paige asked, nodding at Bill, the gesture telling him to be a better host.

But Taylor shook her head. "Black is good for me. I've been living on a lot of fast food and soda the past few days. Microwaved burritos at the convenience store. This tastes really good. And warm. The heater doesn't do as much to keep the cold away."

"Were you sleeping in there?"

"No. I got a motel room. But still . . . it's cold to be driving around." She shivered. "I saw you on the news tonight. Boy, those kids fixed your wagon, didn't they? A guy roughs up his daughter and then she disappears. Nice."

"Is this what you came for? To remind me of my failures?" He took a seat between the two women at the round table, his hands cradling his mug. "So, you've tried to talk to the police?"

"Emily is nineteen. Older than your daughter, I know. But she's small. Petite. And she looks younger than she is. Since she's nineteen, the police don't quite take it as seriously. I mean, she's an adult. If she doesn't want to have anything to do with her mother, she doesn't have to." She looked at both of them, her eyes shiny with emotion. "Do you have children?" she asked Paige.

"Two boys."

"Maybe girls are worse. They fight with their mothers. Emily and I fought all the time." She looked over at Bill. "I guess girls fight with their dads too. We really fought. That's why Emily left me and went to live with my ex-husband. His name is Doug Hammond. My first husband, Emily's dad—we split up when she was five. He doesn't have much to do with her."

"Does this Doug live here?" Bill asked.

"No. But he has family here. He comes to Jakesville all the time." She put her mug down and stared into the dark liquid, as though an answer waited there. "I have a feeling about this. A bad one."

Paige lifted her hand to her face and wiped her eyes. Taylor continued to stare into her mug, and Bill saw hints of gray roots at the crown of her head. He tapped his index finger against the top of the table, counting in his head until what seemed like a reasonable and respectful amount of time to give Taylor to gather herself.

He asked, "Is your ex-husband violent? Do you think he might have hurt Emily? Or Summer?"

Taylor's hand shook as she spoke. "He's been in trouble with the law recently. He moved in when Emily was fourteen, so he didn't raise her or anything. He was a good guy when we met. Stable. He had a job. But he started behaving erratically a few years ago. He fought with people at work and got fired. He fought with me. He drank a lot. He just . . . went off the rails in a way I couldn't have foreseen."

"When's the last time you saw Emily?" Bill asked.

"Last year. Which wasn't odd. Like I said, we had a falling-out. But she always called me on my birthday. Every year, no matter what. Mother's Day, Christmas, all of it. I heard from her. Well, my birthday was last week, and I didn't get any call. And I'd heard all about this story. About the two girls being found beat-up, and then the one turning out not to be your daughter but another girl the police couldn't identify. I saw the pictures of Haley and Summer, and I saw the description of the other girl, the dead one, online. So I drove down here."

"Why did you drive by the house and not say anything?" Bill asked. "You've been driving by here, and no one even knows if your daughter's involved."

"I had a feeling. A bad feeling. I thought maybe whoever hurt your daughter and that other girl might have hurt Emily. I just wanted . . . I didn't know what else to do. I felt helpless. You understand that, right?"

Bill understood all too well. "Why didn't you talk to the police?" His voice rose, and he felt Paige's hand on his forearm, telling him to calm down. But the caffeine made his heart race, and he felt like he wanted to jump out of his own skin. "All this time. They could have been looking for this guy. For Summer."

"Easy, Bill."

"Why didn't you call?"

"Because nobody knew there was a third girl involved until now. I found out when everybody found out."

But he was up, reaching for his phone. "I'm calling Hawkins. Right now."

"Bill, it's late."

"I don't care." He hit the SEND button and listened as the distant, tinny ringing began. "What did this Doug Hammond do? You said he's off the rails? Is he violent?"

Hawkins answered, his voice groggy.

But Bill waited to speak because of the look on Taylor's face. She had something to say, but hesitated to say it.

"What is it?" Bill said to her.

"He's been arrested before. Domestic violence. He beat up his ex-wife before he and I got together."

CHAPTER FIFTY-FOUR

Bill couldn't sleep after the police left. He lay awake most of the night, staring at the ceiling and glancing at the slowly changing red numbers on the digital clock. The wind kicked up outside, rattling the windows and making a low keening sound that took up residence in Bill's head.

Screaming. He told himself it wasn't the sound of Summer screaming.

Hawkins had arrived thirty minutes after Bill's call, his hair more disheveled than usual, his shirt half-tucked into his pants. But he offered no complaints as he asked Taylor Kress a few preliminary questions while she remained sitting at Bill's kitchen table. And then Hawkins announced that it might be better if they finished their conversation at the station.

Bill saw a look of fear cross Taylor's face, her eyes shifting as though she wanted to find the nearest door she could run through. So Bill stepped in.

"Taylor," he said, "are you worried that Doug might hurt you if you talk to the police?"

"Not enough to stop me from talking," she said, "but Doug, you know, he's not really a bad guy. He's just . . . He can be sort of unpredictable."

Then she followed Hawkins out of the house.

Bill dressed quietly in the dark. It was five thirty, and in another hour the sun would be coming up. He walked softly past the office where Paige lay sprawled across the futon, her body wrapped in a tangle of sheets and blankets.

Light leaked in from the outside, and a sliver of it fell across Paige's face. She still looked like a little kid to Bill, even after the passage of so many years. He understood that the protective instincts he had for his daughter were simply an intensification of the feelings he had for his baby sister while they were growing up. Intensified to an exponential degree, but still with their origins in the same place. Even if he had hit her with a stick once and frequently tormented her, he would never, ever tolerate anyone else hurting her.

He went quietly out the back door into the cold night and started the car.

He'd looked up the address before leaving the house. He didn't have far to go, and he doubted his trip would pay dividends. It was a long shot.

He'd hoped meeting Taylor Kress and learning what she knew about her ex-husband would ease his mind, at least for a short time. But it hadn't. He felt more restless than ever, as if coming closer to an answer only made the not knowing more intense.

And what if Taylor Kress's information meant nothing? Just another suspicion and dead end?

Bill couldn't just wait and do nothing. He was tired of doing nothing.

He found the neighborhood about three miles from his own house. It was a subdivision built in the nineties, good-size houses but not mansions, the cars an assortment of minivans and sedans. Most of the windows were dark, the families sleeping another hour or so before alarms summoned them to rise for their Sunday.

Bill made two turns and then eyed the house numbers on the even side of the street. He stopped two doors away from his destination and cut the lights. And then he waited.

He yawned. His eyes felt like they'd been scrubbed with bleach. He felt the weariness of the whole ordeal in his joints and bones, like he'd aged twenty years over the course of one week. The heat blew out of the vents, the lights of the console casting a soft green glow against his body. Thirty minutes passed. Then forty. The sky started to lighten above the row of houses, the stars disappearing one by one like extinguished candles.

A light came on upstairs in the house he watched. Bill perked up, coming erect in the seat. He waited, his body tense. A few minutes passed before another light came on near the front of the house on the first floor. Then the porch light.

Bill turned the car off, reached for the door handle.

The door of the house swung inward, and a figure, tall and thin, wearing red shorts and a hooded sweatshirt, stepped out. He paused and did some cursory stretching in the front yard, then started running up the street. Toward Bill.

When he came even with the car, Bill opened the door.

"Brandon?" he said.

The boy stopped, his eyes squinting at Bill in the half-light of morning.

"Do you remember me?" Bill asked.

The boy took a step closer, and then uncomfortable recognition crossed his face. He looked like he wanted to back away, to retrace his steps and go back inside his nice, safe suburban house.

But he didn't move. He stood still while one hand played with the string attached to the hood of the sweatshirt.

"Mr. Price," he said.

"I'm sure you need to train," Bill said, "but I'd like to talk to you for a minute."

Brandon looked down the street toward his house and then up the other way, his eyes following the path he meant to take on his run.

"You're right. I do need to train. And I probably shouldn't talk to you. Mr. Bateman said—"

"Come on," Bill said, nodding toward the car. "Let's sit inside. It's warm."

Brandon looked like he might bolt, and if he did, Bill knew he'd never get another chance to talk to him.

"You seem like a nice kid, Brandon," Bill said. "You always did. Maybe nicer and more polite than your friends. That's why I wanted to talk to you. I'm sure you didn't do anything to hurt Summer."

"I wouldn't," he said quickly. "She was cool. A little bossy with the girls but cool."

Bill nodded. "Five minutes?"

Bill opened the driver's side door. For a moment, everything hung in the balance. Then Brandon walked around the front of the car and got in the other side.

CHAPTER FIFTY-FIVE

Brandon was taller than Bill. His head reached the ceiling of the car, and his long legs looked cramped in the front seat. But the boy also seemed painfully young. His chin was marked with acne, and his hands and feet appeared to be too big for his body. He twiddled his thumbs for a moment, and then he stopped and rested his hands on his knees as if he hoped to still them.

"I hear you might go to state," Bill said.

"It's looking that way. That's why I have to get out early and train."

"Of course. Dedication."

"The police also told me not to talk to anyone about this. And my parents."

"Detective Hawkins?" Bill asked. "He's a good man."

"He's all right." Brandon shifted in his seat, his eyes trailing toward the house again.

"You understand where I'm coming from, right? My daughter is missing. Summer. You're friends with her—I know that. You're friends with those other kids who know her. You know Haley."

Brandon nodded. "Yes. Summer liked to talk about stuff I didn't understand. She was smart, you know? About every subject. She was all into student council and other causes. Like when she arranged that fund-raiser for Syria. Remember? That bake sale? But she was cool."

"Think of what it's like for me not to know where she is. I thought she was hurt and in the hospital. Then I thought she was dead. Now I don't know anything." Bill sighed. "I'm going to level with you, kid. I can't sleep. I don't eat. I feel like a ninety-year-old man, you know? The worry, the grief, it just eats me up. She's out there somewhere, lost, maybe hurt. Maybe hurt bad. Maybe some maniac has her."

"You said all that stuff on TV," Brandon said. "You made it sound like we were guilty. My parents were really pissed about that. My dad was talking about suing you."

Bill laughed in what he hoped seemed like a friendly way. "I understand. I lost my cool. It's the stress. It's getting to me because I don't know where Summer is."

"I don't know where she is either," Brandon said.

His words disappointed Bill. They were such a flat statement of fact, such a clear denial that Bill worried it might effectively shut down the rest of the conversation. But then he regrouped.

"What about your friends? Clinton and Todd?"

Brandon stared out the window, remaining silent. Then he said, "I'm not as good friends with them as everybody thinks. I didn't have anything to do with that stuff with Alicia. I stayed away when they started taking pictures. I wouldn't do that."

"But you're going to get in trouble anyway?" Bill asked. "Right?"

"Maybe. The school is threatening to punish us all. Coach is mad, says I might not be able to practice with the team until it's all resolved."

"Right, I think I understand the problem you're having," Bill said. He adjusted his body in the seat so he faced Brandon more squarely. "You're kind of in a bind because of the cross-country team."

Brandon watched Bill, his eyes cautious, but he didn't speak.

"You get caught drinking or whatever, violating the team rules, you get kicked off no matter what. Right?"

Brandon still didn't answer.

"And I know about this contest at school. The one with the sex and counting the girls—"

"I didn't do that either," he said. "Not much."

"Sure. But you could get caught up in all of it and find yourself off the team. You know how these things go. Even guilt by association can get you into trouble at school or with the cops. And nobody will ever look at you the same if your friends did something awful, like hurting Alicia. Or Summer. Or Haley."

Brandon was shaking his head. "I didn't do anything."

"What were you three boys doing the day they disappeared? Did you see them?"

"We've talked to the cops. Plenty. There's nothing else to say."

"So you saw them?"

"No. I don't—I don't want to talk about this. Any of this." He pushed the door open, letting in the cool morning air. "I'm going to tell my parents you were harassing me. I don't have to listen to this. You're not a cop."

Bill reached out, placing his hand on Brandon's arm. Brandon pulled away.

"Look," Bill said, "if you talk first, you can get out of it. You can come out of it clean."

Brandon folded his long body and stood up from the car. For a moment, he hesitated on the sidewalk, his head turned toward his house, which now had more lights burning. Then he leaned down to the passenger window and said, "Those guys, Clinton and Todd—

they're intense. Clinton mostly. Todd does whatever Clinton wants. He'd be an okay guy, maybe, if he had better friends. Like I said, I'm not really close with them, okay? We hang out from time to time. I just want to run. That's it, okay? I didn't hurt anybody."

"Did somebody hurt them? Someone you know?"

Brandon looked away, back toward his house. "Everybody's acting weird. I don't know what to make of it all. Why don't you ask Teena? She was better friends with Summer."

"Did she say something?" Bill asked.

"I don't know. She came by and acted like she was moving away, like something final was happening. She gave me a big hug."

"Like she was moving? Did she say anything about Summer?"

He shook his head. "Teena's weird, you know. I don't need any of it, okay? I didn't hurt anybody."

He slammed the door shut and started back to the house.

As Bill was driving home, his phone rang. He managed to extract it from his pants pocket and keep the car on the road at the same time.

It was Paige.

"I know I left without saying anything—"

"Where are you?"

"I'm out. Maybe I'm going to look around. Okay?"

"No, not okay. Hawkins came by here looking for you. Did he call you?"

"No. What did he want? Did that woman give him something good?"

"No," Paige said. "Haley woke up."

CHAPTER FIFTY-SIX

Bill turned his car in the direction of the hospital. The sun was almost up, the sky awash in reds and oranges that promised a clear day. As he drove, a pulse thrummed in his neck. He took deep breaths, reminding himself he needed to be calm, to let the police do their work.

But how could he be calm when the only witness to the crime against Summer was finally awake?

He rushed through the familiar halls and impatiently rode the elevator. As the floors dinged off, he tried to will the machine to move faster, as though he were pedaling a bike and could control the speed. He jumped off at the rehab wing and headed toward Haley's room.

He saw Rich Rodgers standing in the hallway, wearing a pullover sweater with the collar of an oxford shirt peeking out. His hands were in his pockets as he waited. He looked like a tower of bottled energy. He glanced up as Bill approached, and he offered a faint smile.

"I guess we got some good news," he said.

"Yes," Bill said. Rich's words brought Bill up short. He needed the reminder that Haley being awake was good for more than his own selfish reasons. She had parents who cared. She was a young person who needed to recover. Bill felt some of the tension ease in his own body. "That is good."

He didn't know what else to do, so he reached out and shook Rich's hand. It was a strange gesture, making Bill think of the handshakes he received the day Summer was born. But it seemed like the only thing he could do short of hugging Rich, and he had no desire to do that.

"She's groggy, you know?" Rich said. "She'd been acting restless the last couple of days. Trying to form more words and things with her mouth while she lay there. We were hopeful things were going this way. Then early this morning, they called to say she's awake."

"That's fantastic." Bill wasn't exactly sure what he was doing there, intruding on a private family moment. When Hawkins called looking for him, he didn't say anything about going to the hospital. He just wanted to give Bill an update. But what else was Bill supposed to do? "I guess the police are in there now?"

"They are. Detective Hawkins and a doctor. Plus my ex-wife. I was in there for a while, but I've been out here calling relatives to let them know."

"Do you need anything?" he asked, trying to be helpful.

"Me? No. We're fine. The people from Candy's church have been coming every day and bringing food to her house. That's been our home base." He looked like he wanted to say more, so Bill waited. "Say, maybe I can ask you something." Rich tilted his head, so Bill followed him.

They walked down the hall and around a corner, putting them well out of earshot of Haley's room and the nurses' station. When they stopped walking, Rich looked around and then said to Bill, "Do you think they ever considered you a suspect in what happened to these girls?"

Bill suspected that Rich, like everyone else in town, had heard the story about him grabbing Summer on Halloween. "I think fathers are probably always suspected when something happens to their kids."

"Right," Rich said, looking thoughtful. The lights above shone off his freshly shaven head. The skin of his scalp looked pink and clean. "They made me give a DNA sample."

"Me too," Bill said. Rich looked relieved to hear that from Bill. "I want them to take DNA from those kids, but Hawkins says they need more evidence against them first."

"I guess they tread lightly with juveniles."

"Weren't you in Arizona when this happened?"

"I was. Yes." Rich leaned in closer. "See, I had bought a plane ticket to come out here, and the dates of my planned stay happened to coincide with the time of the attack. Candy didn't even know about it. Remember what I was saying the other day about using a firmer hand with these girls?"

Bill nodded, remembering it all too well.

"Well, I thought Haley needed that. So I bought a ticket. It was kind of an impulsive move on my part, and because I didn't tell anybody . . ."

"It looked suspicious."

"Exactly. But I'm glad to hear they treated you the same way."

Bill waited for a moment, expecting Rich to say more. When he didn't, Bill had to ask.

"So, did you come here? At the time of the attack?"

"No, I didn't," Rich said. "Something came up at work, and I couldn't. But they looked into all my records, and they saw that purchase, and it got them worked up for a while. You can understand that, right?"

"Yeah."

Rich clapped Bill on the shoulder as though they were coconspirators, a brotherhood of misunderstood fathers. Bill wasn't sure he wanted to be in the same club as Haley's dad.

Caleb, Candy's pastor, stuck his head around the corner of the hallway. He looked surprised to see Bill, but then smiled at him in a moderately friendly way. "The police are finishing now, if you want to come back," he said to Rich.

"Was she able to tell them anything?" Bill asked.

Caleb hesitated before answering, then said, "I think Detective Hawkins can fill you in on that."

CHAPTER FIFTY-SEVEN

Hawkins emerged from Haley's room and looked surprised to see Bill. The detective stopped in the hallway, still as disheveled as he had been the night before. Bill doubted the man had slept at all.

"You didn't have to come," Hawkins said. "There's nothing for you to do here."

"I was in the neighborhood." When Hawkins looked at him without saying anything else, Bill asked, "So, what happened in there? What did Haley tell you?"

Hawkins looked around at Rich and Caleb and then placed a meaty hand on Bill's shoulder. "Look, Bill, I'm sure you came here because you were hoping for something big, some kind of important revelation from Haley. But all along we weren't sure if she'd be able to remember anything."

Bill felt deflated before Hawkins even delivered the news he knew was coming.

"So you didn't get anything?" Bill asked.

Hawkins's tired eyes grew sympathetic. "She's groggy, Bill. Very groggy. She can barely hold her head up or open her eyes." He shook his head. "She's not ready yet. So, no, we didn't get anything."

Hawkins's hand was only resting on top of Bill's shoulder, but to Bill it felt like the detective was holding him up. Bill wanted to let his body go slack, to slide to the floor, his bones and muscles becoming a human puddle. He knew Hawkins was right in assessing the difficulty of getting anything out of Haley, but that didn't mean he hadn't been hoping for the past week. If she didn't see or remember anything, who would? Who would then hold the key to everything that had been happening?

"But all is not lost," Hawkins said. "The doctors have told us it's possible her memory will return as time goes by. We're early in the process here, so we have to give Haley time to get better. Waking up is a big step, but it's still an early step. They're going to do therapy and everything else they can think of."

Hawkins sounded more calm and reassuring than at any time since Summer's disappearance. Bill wondered if exhaustion hadn't added more syrup to his voice.

"Can I go in and see her?" Bill asked.

Hawkins shook his head again. "Her mother's in there now. And Haley needs to rest. I'm coming back later today."

"Just a minute, Detective. Just let me . . . Let me see her and find out what she knows. Let me do it. For God's sake, Hawkins, you know how precious every moment is right now."

Bill looked at the other faces arrayed around him: Rich, Caleb, a nurse. They all looked sympathetic. They all knew how much rode on Haley's fragile recovery.

But Hawkins was firm. "It's not a good idea, Bill. She can't even speak. And you're getting agitated. She needs calm right now."

"You know how long I've waited for this. It's all we've got right now."

"I do."

Bill went past him. He didn't think. He didn't weigh options. He brushed by Hawkins and pushed against the door of Haley's room, breezing inside.

But then he saw her.

Haley sat propped up against a stack of pillows, Candy by the side of the bed holding a cup of water. Haley's eyelids looked heavy, her facial muscles slack. Bill saw no sign of the beautiful girl he knew so well. He saw a tired, sick kid, someone who had been to hell and back.

"Haley." Bill managed just the one word. He felt like an intruder.

He'd come in so fast and so boldly that Candy just stared at him, her mouth open slightly.

Haley managed to move her head to the right, her eyes still not fully open. She seemed to be trying to place Bill, to figure out whether he was someone she should know.

As he stared at the girl, Bill remained frozen in place, realizing how long the road to her recovery might be.

Hawkins came through the door and stopped beside him. "Bill, let's go."

Bill turned and left without saying anything else.

CHAPTER FIFTY-EIGHT

Bill walked down the hall, heading for the elevator like a man in a daze. He couldn't shake the image of Haley in the bed, and he remembered again the words the doctor had told him on that first day in the hospital, back when he thought his daughter lay in the ICU unit, beaten and battered.

"Brain damage. Vision loss."

How badly was Haley hurt?

Bill played a ridiculous game of "What If" in his mind.

What if it really had been Summer in that hospital bed? She'd be awake now, perhaps on the road to a full recovery.

But then Haley? What would it mean for Haley? Could he, even in a mental exercise, trade his daughter's life for the life of another child?

And what if he had to care for a severely injured child the rest of his life as Haley's family might have to?

Bill didn't hear Caleb come up next to him. The pastor wore a neatly pressed button-down shirt and khaki pants. His cell phone was still clipped to his belt, and his neck bore the telltale signs of razor burn. Caleb must have been an early riser to be that cleaned up so early in the morning.

"Can I disturb you for a second, Mr. Price?"

Bill turned to the man and didn't feel like he could generate an answer. He nodded, barely moving his head.

Caleb pointed to two chairs near the elevator, and they sat side by side. Bill rested his hands on his knees and stared straight ahead. "You saw her, right?" Bill asked. "Haley?"

"Yes. She'd just woken up. She's very out of it." The man licked his lips and then looked over at Bill. "In fact, I was in the room when the police were first trying to talk to Haley. They didn't get anywhere, but Candy wanted me to be there, and since . . . well, since Rich's presence sometimes upsets Haley, we thought it was best that he wait outside. It was pretty crowded anyway. It was maybe more disturbing seeing her that way than unconscious."

Bill thought of the firmer hand and the plane ticket, Haley's bruised and battered face as she muttered, "*No no no no no,*" when Bill came close to her and said the word "Dad."

Caleb looked uncertain about going on, but he did. "She's been unconscious for more than a week, right? But when the detective was asking her the questions he asked her, trying to talk to her, I saw something else on her face and in her eyes, something I thought I'd bring to your attention."

"What was that?"

"She looked . . ." Caleb paused, choosing his words carefully. "She looked scared. But that's not quite the right way to put it. You could expect her to be scared after waking up in the hospital with those horrible injuries, a police detective standing over her and asking her all sorts of questions." Caleb winced a little bit. "What I'm saying is, we might have to go over what happened to Summer again. I'm not sure what we were saying really sank in. That she's still missing."

"For over a week now," Bill said, reminding himself of the awful march of time, the clock ticking against his daughter. "I guess that will be a shock. But not as bad as if you were telling her Summer was dead."

"That's true." Caleb patted Bill on the knee. "We do need to remember the positives, even if they're small victories."

Caleb didn't seem poised to say anything else, so Bill prompted him. "About this look on her face."

"Yes, right. Well, I'm going to continue to pray for her to remember more."

"She looked really awful when I saw her," Bill said.

"True."

"And the cops would probably scare her under the best of circumstances," Bill said. "Imagine waking up to that."

Caleb shook his head slowly, and the effort appeared to pain him. "I think she's also afraid of me. And her mother to some extent. I'm sure you know Candy can be . . . demanding. And so can I. Haley's been raised in a religious household over the last few years, ever since her father left. So there may be certain topics she wouldn't want to discuss with us nearby."

Somewhere up the hall a machine beeped rapidly. And then a nurse at the desk laughed, the sound echoing through the hallway. Bill looked over at her and saw she had her hand cupped over her mouth, another nurse nearby smiling and turning red about some private joke.

Caleb said, "Haley was acting differently in the weeks leading up to the disappearance. More secretive. Missing curfews. Candy was concerned to the point she made an appointment for Haley to come and meet with me at the church about a week before the girls disappeared. I think Candy wanted me to give Haley some kind of stern talking-to, you know, a warning about where her behavior could lead. But when Haley showed up, she didn't really talk about herself."

"What did she talk about, then?" Bill asked.

Caleb looked reluctant to speak, but he said, "She talked about Summer."

"Why?"

Caleb raised his hand, asking Bill to calm down. "You understand I'm betraying confidences here. And Haley didn't get specific. She just said she was concerned about her friend Summer, who I, of course, knew. She said something was bothering Summer, distracting her, but Haley didn't know what it was. None of it was specific, and I think Haley was just worried about her friend. I told her she could talk to you or to someone at the school if she thought Summer was in a real crisis, but then Haley walked it back. She said she might be overreacting."

"Did she think Summer wanted to run away?" Bill asked.

"She didn't say that specifically, no."

"And that was it?" Bill asked.

"Before you knew it, they had disappeared," Caleb said. "And now this." He made a helpless gesture in the direction of Haley's room. "I told the police, and now I'm telling you."

Bill leaned forward, resting his head in his hands. He felt the rough, chapped skin of his palms against his face. "Thank you," he said, the words muffled.

Caleb nodded, staring at the floor. "I was glad to hear the detective say they were going to talk to Haley again. Next time, maybe, if I have any influence over it, I'm going to make sure only certain people are in the room. Bill, I'm really praying there's more to the story with Haley."

CHAPTER FIFTY-NINE

Bill came home and found Paige sitting at the kitchen table. Her hair was piled on top of her head, and her glasses were down at the end of her nose. She stared at her laptop, a pad of paper and a pencil on the table beside her. When Bill came in, she slid the glasses off and looked up.

"Well? What happened? You've been gone for so long, and you didn't call. I almost went to the hospital."

Bill told her about barging into the room and seeing Haley's condition, how wiped out and damaged she looked. As he talked, Paige lifted her hand to her chest. Then he told her about Caleb and the concerns Haley had raised about Summer.

"It matches what Anna, the counselor at school, shared with me," Bill said. "Something was going on with Summer. Something she didn't want to tell me. Of course there's more to the story, but we don't know that Haley knows anything about it. Or if that part of her brain is even still functioning."

Bill went to the refrigerator and started poking around, but nothing looked good. The sight of anything—pasta, chicken, beef—made his stomach turn. His pants felt loose, and he guessed he'd lost five pounds or more. He gave up, shutting the refrigerator door louder than he intended.

"Do I get to know where you were in the middle of the night?" Paige asked.

Bill pulled a chair out and sat down across from her. He rested his head in his hands, his exhaustion catching up to him. "It was early in the morning, not the middle of the night. And I can't just sit here every night and do nothing."

"That's not an answer."

"I don't think I did any good," he said. He felt uncomfortable in the seat and squirmed around. "I may even have done some harm."

Paige waited, and when Bill didn't say more, she slipped her glasses back on. "Well, I've been productive even if you weren't."

"Doing what?"

She looked at him over the top of the glasses and leveled her index finger at him. "You know, I should have known you were a sentimental fool. Most men like you are."

"Men like me?"

"Hard and tough on the outside. Like Dad. Remember how he cried when I married Kyle? Out of the blue he's standing there crying as he gives me away. Could you believe that?"

Bill remembered the moment. He'd never seen his father cry, never seen the old man show much emotion about anything. But when he placed Paige's hand into Kyle's in front of all their friends and family on her wedding day, he started sobbing. Not just a little sobbing either, but great heaving sobs that seemed to come from the center of his body, rocking his shoulders and his limbs as the tears fell. Their mom handed him a wad of tissues, and he settled down only as the ceremony went on.

And he never cried again in front of his children, not even when he told them he'd been diagnosed with terminal cancer.

"I never asked him why he was so moved," Bill said.

"Of course you wouldn't. I didn't either. He's dead, and we never found out what he thought. Isn't it shitty that we do that? We let people die without knowing what they're really thinking."

Bill felt unease creeping up his spine. "What does this have to do with me? It's not going to be another round of 'You're Exactly Like Your Dad,' is it? Julia played that game with me all the time. I hated it."

Paige picked up the pencil and started tapping it against the table. "I got the clue when I saw Julia's clothes back there." She used the pencil to point toward the master bedroom. "Still."

Bill rolled his eyes. "I knew that would come up again. Tell Kyle I feel sorry for him." He stood, pushing the chair back with his knees. "I'm going to take a nap."

Paige acted like he hadn't moved, like he wasn't irritated with the course of the conversation. "When you told me Julia called you twice on the day she died and how much that affected you, it got me thinking. Maybe she left messages, and if she did, wouldn't my sentimental big brother save them?"

"Enough, Paige."

"I saw the phone plugged into the wall in the study back there. I was wondering what you were doing in there the other day with the laptop when I startled you. Now, look, I know most cell phones save a voice mail for only thirty days, so you had to have some other way to save the messages. But why keep the phone plugged in? Why keep it going? Is it the same reason you kept her clothes? Nostalgia? Romance?" Paige reached over and took out her phone. "I still have the old number in my contacts. I never delete anything." She pressed a button on the screen, and the faint sound of the phone ringing came from the other room. "You kept the line active. You're paying to have that phone on for sentimental reasons."

"Paige. Let it go."

"Isn't that expensive?"

"It's a family plan. Okay?"

Bill turned and started for the bedroom. He knew if he stayed, he'd say or do something he'd regret. He kind of wished they were young enough for him to whack her on the knuckles with a stick all over again.

"It doesn't matter why you did it. What matters is the account is still active. You said you didn't know if Adam answered the call that day," she said, making Bill stop at the end of the hall. He turned back to face her. "But I know. I have the answer right here."

She spun her laptop around so it faced Bill.

CHAPTER SIXTY

Bill stared at her and the smugly confident grin she wore. She looked like she always did when they were kids and she'd managed to outsmart or prove her older brother wrong on some matter. He wanted to resume walking away but couldn't.

So Bill started back across the room toward the kitchen table.

"What are you talking about?" he asked as he came closer. He stopped in front of the laptop and stared at the screen. It was a list. Dates and times on one side, locations down the middle. On the right were numbers in a minute-and-second format. "What is this?"

"It's your cell phone statement for the month Julia died."

Bill's eyes darted around the screen, trying to take in the information. "How did you get this on your computer?"

"I called the cell phone company."

"And?"

She swallowed her words a little. "It took some finagling. Don't be mad, but I told them I was Julia. I said I'd forgotten my password. All I needed was the last four digits of her social, which I found in your office back there. I knew the rest—her birthday and address. I had to talk to a supervisor. Normally it takes longer, but we struck up a rapport. We talked about being the mothers of boys. Anyway, she sent me a PDF."

Bill straightened up. He took two steps away from the table. "I don't want to know about this." He looked out the window in the direction of Adam's house. It sat quiet and dark, the yard empty. For all he knew, his friend had moved out already, leaving the house behind to be sold by his employer. "Nothing good can come of this."

"You've been beating yourself up over this for a year," Paige said. "You should know what was going on with Julia when she died." Paige reached around and tapped the screen. "Look there on the day she died. September nineteenth, in the afternoon. She did make the two phone calls to you. And then the one to Adam. See?"

Bill kept his distance for a moment, but then his curiosity, his intense, burning curiosity—and his guilt—compelled him forward. He leaned down and looked at the screen. It took a moment to find the correct date and time—a date he knew very well—and then he saw the calls. Two short ones in a row to his number.

And then one to Adam's number.

A longer call. One minute and twenty-seven seconds.

"Okay," Bill said. "I don't know what this means."

"Adam said he didn't take the call, right? But the call to him lasted almost a minute and a half. The ones to you, in which Julia left messages, lasted about twenty seconds."

Bill felt something burning in the back of his throat. Bile. The kind of sour taste that emerged just before vomiting. He pulled the chair out and sat back down. "Why are you doing this?" he asked, his voice slightly louder. "So she called Adam, and the call lasted longer. Maybe she didn't hang up right away. Maybe she fell as the voice mail picked up and so the line stayed engaged longer. It could be anything."

"I guess," Paige said. "But maybe not. Likely not. Look, Mr. Rough and Ready might be lying about this. You said yourself that things weren't great with you and Julia, that you thought she might have been . . . involved in some way with someone else. You said she talked about how dreamy he is. Shouldn't you know what was really going on with your wife when she died?"

Bill closed his eyes. They were sitting just a few feet away from where Julia had fallen. Like everything with Summer right then— yes, he wanted to know, but he wasn't sure he could handle it once he did.

He reached out, keeping his temper under control, and closed the lid of the laptop.

"I can't," he said.

"I thought about going over there myself, before you came home, but I thought that would be really weird."

"Forget it, Paige. Just forget it." He sat at the table, taking care to keep his voice steady and calm. And he did. "And I think it's best if you just go now."

Paige looked confused. "Go where?"

"Home," he said. "It's time. You've been here long enough, and your family needs you. Just go."

"Bill—"

"You've done a lot for me. And I appreciate it. But you're always digging into things and bringing things up that are better left alone. I just think it's time for everything to start getting back to normal around here. And I can't handle any more of your bullshit."

He stood up, turning his back on his sister as he walked toward the bedroom.

"That's it, Bill? You're just going to walk away from me? From knowing the truth about something you care about?"

Bill stopped once again at the entrance to the hallway, but he didn't bother to turn around. "Thanks, Paige. I mean it. Thanks."

As he started back toward the bedroom, Paige said, "You're turning your back on her again, you know. You're doing it again."

But Bill just kept on walking.

CHAPTER SIXTY-ONE

Bill managed to sleep for two hours that afternoon, and then wished he hadn't. He'd dreamed of Julia telling him that she and Adam had been having an affair since before she and Bill met. Even in the dream, Bill knew it was impossible for that to be true—he and Julia met before they ever knew Adam—but the pain of her words still pierced him, and he woke up with tears in his eyes.

He splashed water on his face in the bathroom. The house sounded quiet. Just the soft chirping of a few birds outside, and the staccato shots from a staple gun as a neighbor's new roof was installed.

Bill wandered down the hallway and out to the front of the house. He checked the second bathroom. The vanity was clear, no sign of Paige's toothbrush and lotions.

In the family room, the afghan she'd curled up with was neatly folded on the couch, the suitcase she'd been living out of gone. So was her car.

Bill felt as empty as a gutted fish. *Well,* he thought, *you drove her away too.*

Even before Summer disappeared, he worried about life without her. Would he be one of those lonely old men, the kind who spent his

final years shuffling around an empty house, unshaven, smelly? *Alone.*
Kids grew up and moved away. Summer hadn't shown any interest in
staying in Jakesville, not since she was a little girl. She already spoke of
college, already wanted to attend in another state. New York. Califor-
nia. And Bill hadn't felt any desire to meet anyone else or remarry. He
hadn't even thought of going on a date over the past year and a half.

He knew Paige would always be there for him, no matter how
many times he literally or metaphorically smacked her with a stick,
but she lived far away, with her own life and her own problems.

He walked over to the couch and ran his hand across the afghan
Paige had used. The kitchen was clean, the dishes washed and put away.

Bill was alone. And he couldn't stand it.

He went to the closet, pulling the door open so hard, he stumbled
back a little. He ignored—tried to ignore—Summer's coats, zeroing
in on his own. He yanked it off the hanger and pulled it on, the sleeve
sticking on his watch, forcing Bill to tug several times before the
sleeve slid up his arm.

He searched for his keys. He had no idea where to go or what to
do, but he refused to sit still. And wait. And wait.

He found the keys and went to the back door. A face stared back
at him. Bill cried out, a high, squeaking sound, and took a step back
before he saw who it was. He recognized the sad, slouched posture,
the stick-thin frame.

Taylor Kress.

She wore the same clothes as the night before and stood on the
porch with her arms folded across her chest, the Bengals sweatshirt
pulled tight around her body.

Bill let her in. Taylor smelled even more strongly of cigarette smoke
and maybe booze. She looked as fragile and frightened as a child, and
Bill wasn't certain what to do for her.

"I'm on my way out, Taylor," he said.

"Where are you headed?" she asked, her voice rough and low.

Bill felt compelled to be honest with her. "I don't know. Looking, I guess. Looking for Summer." He lifted his hands, the keys jangling. "Just driving around, maybe. She's out there, and I hate just sitting and waiting."

Taylor nodded. The lines on her face seemed more pronounced, the burden of years pressing down on her. "It's a helpless feeling," she said. Then she added, almost casually, "The cops keep calling me. They need Emily's dental records, I guess."

She stood just inside the door with her arms folded, a defensive posture that apparently had nothing to do with the cold outside. Bill reached out, placing his hand on her shoulder and giving it a light squeeze. Taylor nodded some more, her eyes cast at the floor, but she didn't say anything.

"So why don't you just give them the records?" Bill asked, having waited as long as he could stand.

Taylor's chin quivered. "I'm scared. I want to know, but then again . . ."

"You don't."

"You get it." She looked up, her eyes full of tears. "I came to town all full of piss and vinegar, ready to find out what happened to Emily. Ready to get after Doug. Now . . ."

"Now what?"

"It's hard. I was married to him. I loved him. Doug. He cared about Emily. He did."

"Would you like to come in?" Bill asked. "I have food people have been bringing me. Or coffee."

"Thank you," she said.

They walked to the kitchen, and Taylor slumped into a chair at the table. Paige would have known what to do. She would have embraced Taylor Kress, pulled her close, and let the woman cry on her shoulder for as long as she wanted. Bill looked around the kitchen, scrambling in his mind for something that would help.

"What would you like to eat? Macaroni and cheese? Ham? I think eating something can help us feel better."

"I'm not hungry."

"Coffee?"

Taylor looked around the room, her brown eyes large and slightly protruding. "Do you have something stronger? I could use something stronger."

Bill went to the cabinet and brought down the bottle of George Dickel and a glass. "Ice?"

Taylor shook her head, so he poured her a shot.

"None for you?" she asked.

"Not right now."

Taylor shrugged, a gesture that said, *Suit yourself.* She threw back the shot. She ran her arm across her mouth, using the sleeve of the sweatshirt to absorb the liquid on her lips.

"Is there someone I can call for you, Taylor?" Bill asked. "Do you have any family nearby? A friend?"

"No. I'm going to head home soon. I have a life back there." Her hand slid over to her glass. She picked it up and looked inside. "Can I get another of these?"

"Are you driving?"

"My daughter's missing. Maybe dead," she said, her voice devoid of emotion. "You understand. Another one? Please?"

Bill couldn't argue with that logic, so he tipped the bottle, realizing he might have replaced Paige's mostly easy company with that of a grief-stricken, confused mother.

After she'd drained the second shot, Bill found himself struggling for something to say. He asked, "Did the police have anything else helpful to say about the case? Do they know anything?"

Taylor shook her head with a sour look on her face. "Nothing. They're looking for Doug, my ex, because of what I told them about his record. The fact that he beat up another woman pretty bad and knew Emily."

Bill stared into the amber liquid in the bottle, wishing that some answer would magically materialize there, something he could hang on to and understand. "I don't want the police to forget about those boys from Summer's school."

"Please," Taylor said. She dug in her sweatshirt pocket and brought out a pack of cigarettes and a lighter. "Do you mind?"

"Yes."

She gave Bill a withering look but put the cigarettes down. "I guess I shouldn't. I haven't smoked since college." She stared at the pack for a long moment. "Do you really think kids could be that vicious?"

"They messed with that other girl when she passed out."

"I didn't say they're not creeps," Taylor said. "But from a creep to a killer is a long walk. I know that girl, Haley, was bundled up, like someone cared for her."

"Maybe someone wanted to protect her." But Bill's voice sounded unconvincing. He wasn't sure how much he believed what he was saying. "Did Doug ever hurt Emily?"

"Not that I know of. She went to live with him for a while when she fell out with me. I guess she thought he'd be looser with the rules." Something crossed her face, an almost wistful look. "He always had a soft touch with women."

Bill's stomach turned as she spoke, and he pushed the open bottle of whiskey farther away from him. "I guess we're all just waiting for answers right now. It's no fun."

"I've been waiting longer than you," she said with a trace of bitterness.

"But you won't hand over the dental records. Why?"

Taylor sipped her drink and remained quiet.

Bill didn't want to argue with her or get into a grieving contest, so he tried to steer the conversation toward something concrete. "Did you want something from me, Taylor? Or did you just want to talk?"

Taylor was nodding her head. "I do want something from you. I want to go to the spot where they found those girls, out there in that park. And I want you to go with me."

CHAPTER SIXTY-TWO

They pulled into the gravel lot near the small pond that sat in the center of Dunlap Park. To their left were picnic shelters and a playground. To their right were trails for hikers and bikers. One old man stood on the far side of the pond, bundled against the cool air, his fishing line and orange bobber gently moving in the light breeze. Bill didn't think the guy stood much chance of catching anything, given the cool, overcast conditions. But maybe he just wanted to kill some time out in nature.

Bill locked the car and looked around. He knew the girls were found on a trail, and as far as he knew, there was only one of those nearby, a nearly three-mile loop that ran through the park, along the river bottom, and then back up to the parking lot where they stood.

Taylor zipped her sweatshirt up and lifted the hood, covering most of her face. "Do you know how far it is?" she asked.

"No, I think we just have to walk. I haven't been out here either."

But he had wanted to come. He'd thought about it, known he would someday. Taylor just gave him the extra push to do it right then.

They started on their way, following the gravel path. During that short time when Bill believed—really believed—that Summer was dead, he'd felt the same desire as Taylor. He wanted to see the place where her body was found. He couldn't say exactly why, but he felt the spot must carry some significance to it, even if she'd actually died somewhere else.

He knew where Julia died. He walked over that spot every day in his own kitchen, a constant reminder.

He and Taylor walked mostly in silence, the only sound in the afternoon the crunch of their shoes over the gravel, the occasional cry of a bird. Taylor stumbled once, her sneaker catching on a rock. Bill reached out to steady her and felt the thinness of her arm.

"Thank you," she said as they continued walking. A few minutes later, she said, "The police tell me people have been coming out here. You know, leaving notes and candles and things."

"That's nice to hear," Bill said, although he didn't know why a stranger would want to come to the site where someone they didn't know had died or been hurt. But then—wasn't he doing the same thing with Taylor? He didn't know Emily, but he felt compelled to go along with her mother on this visit. When she suggested the trip and Bill visualized that sad, depressed woman walking through the park alone, the fumes of nicotine and booze wafting off her in the late-winter breeze, he felt something stab at his heart. She deserved some companionship, and he seemed to be the closest to understanding what she was going through.

The trees on either side of the path were bare. They jerked in the breeze and appeared to be clamoring for attention. The edges of the path were muddy from the winter rain and snowmelt. It looked like nothing would ever grow or bloom again.

When they came around a bend, Taylor pointed. "Look."

Ahead Bill saw a cluster of objects. Bouquets of flowers, a few stuffed animals, some votive candles, and pieces of paper with handwritten notes. Hundreds of items dedicated to the memories of the three girls whose lives had intersected at that place.

When they reached the spot, Taylor lowered her hood and lifted her hand to her mouth, her face dissolving into tears. She then clutched herself around her midsection, as if she'd taken a vicious blow, and went down on one knee, her hair blowing around and obscuring her face.

Bill remained standing. He looked at all the items, and from more than one, he saw Summer's face staring back at him. Her most recent school portrait, one in which her smile appeared so wholesome, she looked like the all-American girl. Some of the words jumped out at him from the notes: *We love you. . . . We miss you. . . . Our thoughts and prayers . . . Bring her home. . . .*

Bill felt the intensity of the violation all over again. Someone had taken his daughter. Someone had caused this to happen. It wasn't an accident. It wasn't caused by bad luck. Someone had entered the sphere of his life and made something unimaginably horrific happen. Someone had taken the most important person in his life. Again.

Bill stared at the items for a long moment, the wind whipping his jacket around his body. He bent down, putting his weight on one knee, feeling the moisture from the ground through his pant leg. He placed his arm around Taylor's back, the mingled scent of cigarettes and booze stronger up close.

"I'm sorry," he said. "Is this too much? Would you like to go?"

"Even if it's not her, I feel like she's lost. Like she's not mine anymore."

"I'm sorry."

It took a moment for Taylor to gather herself. She sniffled and wiped at her eyes before she spoke. "Isn't this beautiful?" she said, gesturing toward the makeshift shrine.

"It is." Bill wouldn't have chosen that word, but if it made Taylor feel better . . .

"Nobody here even knows Emily, but they put these things out for her. Isn't that just amazing?"

"I think people always care when a young person dies. It seems even more cruel, doesn't it?"

Taylor brushed her hair aside and over at Bill. She nodded. "Yes, it does. And if I've lost her when I wasn't on the best terms with her . . . If I could just have one more conversation with her . . ."

"I understand," Bill said. "I really do."

They sat side by side like that for a few more minutes, and then Bill stood up and said, "It's getting cold. Would you like to go now?"

Taylor nodded slowly. "Just a moment."

"You can come back whenever you want."

"Yeah. Maybe. I wanted to tell you something, kind of a follow-up to what we talked about the first night I came to your house."

Bill looked down at the crown of Taylor's head. Her face was turned away, obscured from Bill's vision. "What?"

"I'm not really sure about Doug, about his involvement."

"What do you mean?" Bill asked.

"Without the dental records, we're not even sure it is Emily. And if it's not Emily, then why would Doug be involved?"

"Where is this coming from?" Bill asked. He reached down and held his hand out to Taylor. He helped her to her feet, but she wore a distracted look on her face. She stared past Bill toward a spot behind him. Somewhere in the trees. In that direction, Bill heard a twig snap.

He turned his head.

Something moved there, a human figure, about thirty feet away. It took slow steps, moving softly through the woods, its red jacket a dead giveaway on the gray day.

Bill let go of Taylor. Waited. He remembered the stories, the perverts in the park. The cruising and the drugs. Or was it just a hiker? A nature lover?

One of the homeless who set up camp in the woods?

Bill took a step toward the person. "Who's there?" he asked. Then louder. "Who's there? This is private."

The figure came closer, resolving through the trees. Bill saw it was a man.

He heard Taylor breathing beside him. And then she gasped, a sudden, sharp intake of breath.

She shouted one word: "Doug!"

CHAPTER SIXTY-THREE

Bill ran after the man.

They weren't on a path, so they both ducked and dodged around tree trunks and low-hanging branches. Some of them whipped against Bill's face and arms, stinging as he went past. Bill kept his eyes on the red jacket, growing winded as he ran.

Bill's foot caught on a root, and the world turned upside down as he went sprawling. The impact knocked the breath out of him. He coughed as he pushed himself up, fearing that he'd lost the man.

Doug Hammond.

Bill saw him still ahead. And Doug appeared to be slowing too. He held his hand to his side, and he seemed to be limping. Bill forced himself to go on, to continue to push and pull air from his lungs. Every breath stung like a needle. But he gained on the man, the red jacket growing closer.

They emerged from the woods onto a flat area of land near the river. Doug made a lunge to his left, but his feet slipped in a patch of mud. For a moment he wheeled his arms around, trying to maintain his balance, but eventually he fell to the ground, face-first, his body making a small splash as it hit.

Bill saw his chance. He accelerated and dove when he came close enough, landing on Doug Hammond, the force of his body weight driving the air out of the man's lungs.

But Bill was nearly spent. His arms felt weak, his breath nearly gone. Doug squirmed beneath him, and Bill tried, like a cowboy on a bucking bronco, to bring the man under control. Desperation drove Bill to fight more intensely, even though his hand ached from when he'd punched the glass. Doug's body thrashed, and then his elbows flew as he swung his arms back. One caught Bill on the jaw, sending him backward and causing him to loosen his grip.

Doug seized the moment. He jerked free from Bill, slithering along the muddy ground like a snake. He kicked back with his foot, again making contact with Bill's jaw. Bill felt the grit from the bottom of the man's shoe, felt it scrape along his face.

In desperation, Bill lunged forward. He grabbed Doug around one shin, trying to yank him to the ground like a linebacker tackling a ball carrier. Doug thrashed and kicked his leg, each movement knocking against Bill's face and loosening his grip. Bill held on, but one last kick shook Doug free from Bill's arms and sent Bill tumbling back into the mud.

Doug started to run up a little rise ahead of them, looking back only once.

Bill scrambled to his feet. His entire body ached. And he had no energy, no wind left. Doug moved farther and farther away, and Bill fell to his knees in the river bottom, watching the man go.

"Where is she?" Bill called, his voice shrill. "Where is she?"

His voice sounded hollow and solitary in the empty woods.

Bill knelt there, his legs rubbery. Then he slumped back down to the ground, sitting in the mud. He didn't care. His clothes were a mess and his jaw ached. He felt a trickle of blood run from the corner of his mouth where one of Doug's kicks had connected with particular force.

When his breathing returned to normal—although his lungs and chest still ached—he felt around on his pants. He found his cell phone and brought it out with shaky hands. He could barely hold it steady, his arms were so weak, and when he went to dial the police, he saw there was no service.

"Shit," he said. He almost threw the phone toward the river but thought better of it. His mouth was parched. He hadn't exerted himself like that since . . . he couldn't remember when. A childhood race? A game of tag? The time in college a ferocious-looking dog chased him down an alley, and for just a moment he truly feared for his life?

He'd had the man in his grip. He'd held him.

And let him get away.

Where is she?

Bill silently cursed himself even more harshly than he'd cursed the phone. He pushed himself to his feet, his fingers sinking into the muddy ground. When he was standing, he wiped his hands against his ruined pants and started back in the direction he came from, toward the memorial and Taylor Kress.

He hoped he could find his way back absent any path.

He took his time. He couldn't do anything else.

As he walked, he stared at the trees, the gray sky and low clouds above. At some other point in his life, he would have moved through the woods filled with a sense of wonder and beauty. He would have strolled with Julia, or Summer when she was little, and everything they saw would have been worth commenting on. A stick, a log, a bird, or a butterfly.

But in the woods that day, Bill felt the death of hope. He'd come so close to having the man, and yet he'd wiggled free. Despair settled over him as heavy as the clouds above. At the base of his brain, a voice, one he'd managed to silence at every step of the way, now grew louder and louder, its tone insistent.

We may never know what happened. We may never really know.

Bill knew the stories of other families with a missing person. The parents who died never learning the fate of their child.

How had he come to be one of them? How had the world spun in such a way as to land on him?

No, he told himself. *Shut up. They'll find her,* he said back to the voice. *They'll know. Whatever it takes, they'll know.*

The words felt a little forced, a little uncertain, but it was the best he could do.

When he guessed he was about halfway back, he saw something off among the trees. It looked like a tent, but after staring for a few moments, he saw it was a sheet anchored with thin rope to several nearby trees. The cobbled-together structure must have housed one of the park's homeless population, and Bill eased closer, his shoes crunching over the leaves and twigs scattered on the ground.

When he came close enough to be heard, Bill said, "Hello?" When no response came, he called again, his voice louder and firmer, "Hello?"

Bill moved even closer, lightly walking to what seemed to be the front of the improvised tent, an opening that faced the direction of the memorial to the girls. Bill bent down, ducking his head and looking inside. He saw crumpled blankets, some scattered magazines, a thermos, and a foam cooler, the kind purchased in a convenience store for ninety-nine cents.

As Bill stared inside, he felt like an intruder. It might be an improvised space, but it was somebody's home, and he didn't need to be nosing into whatever they were doing in the woods.

And how did he know the person staying there wasn't dangerous? Or desperate?

Bill turned away and continued walking back. He quickly came in view of the memorial, expecting to see Taylor waiting, perhaps having called the police herself.

But she wasn't in sight.

Bill made the slow, lonely trudge to the parking lot as the sun faded, looking back only once at the memorial and reminding himself as he'd reminded Taylor—he could always return anytime he wanted. As long as the memorial stayed there. Eventually it would go away, though, time and tide erasing it.

But as long as it was there, he could go back.

When he reached the car, he looked around again. No sign of Taylor.

Nothing. Not a note, not a hint.

The old fisherman was in the lot, packing his gear into the trunk of his car. Bill asked him if he'd seen a woman leaving and gave a brief description of Taylor.

The man shook his head. "I didn't see anybody."

Bill looked around one more time. The man studied Bill's soiled clothes, his bloody face.

"You ever see homeless people out here? Or anything else?"

The old guy shook his head again. "I only come in the afternoons. And I keep my mind on fishing. The rest of it . . ." He made a dismissive wave. "Are you okay?"

"Yeah," Bill said, getting into the car. "I think I'm fine."

CHAPTER SIXTY-FOUR

As soon as he had service again, Bill called Hawkins from the car. It went to voice mail, and Bill called back three more times in a row before leaving a message. Bill was about to call 911 as he pulled into his driveway, but Hawkins called him right at that moment.

Bill limped a little as he walked, already feeling the soreness and strain in his arm muscles from grabbing onto Doug Hammond. But he told Hawkins what had happened in the park.

"Hold on," Hawkins said. Bill heard him giving directions to someone nearby. He instructed them to have cars sent to the area of Dunlap Park because Doug Hammond was spotted there. "You shouldn't have chased after him," the detective said when he came back on the line. "He's dangerous."

Bill went through the back door into the quiet house. He started unbuttoning his shirt, kicking his muddy shoes off before he ruined the carpet.

"And that's what you would have done, right?" Bill asked. "If you'd seen the man who might have harmed your daughter, you'd just let him run away?"

"I'm a police officer, Bill."

"And even if you weren't, you would have run after the guy. Come on." He slid his pants off and walked to the bedroom, intending to shower. "How close have you guys come to catching him? Have you even seen him yet?"

"We've had leads."

"Doesn't this look bad?" Bill asked. "He showed up at the scene of the crime. He was creeping around there, watching it. Couldn't that indicate guilt?"

"Evidence indicates guilt."

"That's such a cop answer. It's been days. Days and days. Something has to happen. You have to find her."

"I thought you thought the kids from school were guilty," Hawkins said.

Hawkins's question brought Bill up short for a moment. Then he said, "I'm just hoping for an answer. Of any kind. I want you to look into everybody until you have an answer."

"And you never saw Taylor Kress again? She just left?"

"Hell, I don't know where she went. I drove her out there. I already thought it might be some kind of setup, but for what? Why bring me out there and then just run away?"

Hawkins let out a slow breath. "I don't know. But his face is everywhere. We're getting tips. We'll find him."

"And Haley? Anything from her?"

"It's a fine line there. We want to hear from her as soon as possible, but I can't exactly go in there and ride herd over a girl who was beaten within an inch of her life. I've checked in with them several times today. Believe me, I'd love to go in and know everything she knows, but her brain and body are healing. We don't know what all happened to that girl. The trauma, emotional and physical."

Bill stood in his bedroom in just his boxers and a T-shirt. The house felt cool. "Taylor said something out there in the woods, something I haven't been able to stop thinking about. She said she was rethinking Doug's guilt, that maybe she'd jumped to a conclusion about him, and he's not guilty of hurting this Emily girl."

Hawkins hesitated for a moment. "Taylor's been . . . skittish. She hasn't produced the dental records we need."

"Yeah. She told me about that. She's scared she'll learn the truth, that it really is Emily."

"We can subpoena them, and we will. I understand her dread of finding out. But we have to get moving on this. It's no joke."

"I sometimes don't want to know the truth either," Bill said.

"I'm giving her the benefit of the doubt. For now."

The next morning, Bill showered and dressed in fresh clothes. He looked up a phone number. He knew the name of the church Haley's family belonged to, and he called, unsure if he was likely to find Pastor Caleb around the church office.

But the man came to the phone quickly, and after hearing Bill out, suggested they meet at the hospital in a little while.

"I think that will be the best opportunity for what you require," Caleb said, and he gave Bill a time.

But when Bill showed up, he saw Rich standing outside the door of the room. He wore tight-fitting workout clothes, as if he'd just taken a run, and his bald head glistened with sweat.

"Surprised to see me here?" he asked as Bill walked up.

"I was looking for Caleb."

Rich nodded toward the room. "He's inside already." Rich clapped Bill on the shoulder. "Look, I'm on your side here, okay? I'm not thrilled about talking to Haley this way, but if it helps with Summer . . . and the girl we haven't identified yet."

"Where is Candy?"

"Breakfast. With her mother. She slept in a chair in Haley's room all night."

Bill hesitated. When he'd first called Caleb, his plan seemed so reasonable, so practical. Just show up and talk to Haley when her mother was gone and the only thing resembling a cop was the security guard patrolling the hall. Maybe the calming presence of Caleb and the emotional appeal from Summer's father would jar something free in the girl's mind.

But Rich's presence made Bill uncomfortable. He worried about the man's firmer hand and how that would affect Haley's ability or willingness to speak about what she knew or remembered. Bill tried to think of a way to maneuver Rich out of the way but couldn't come up with anything, so when he went through the door of Haley's room, Rich followed right along behind him.

CHAPTER SIXTY-FIVE

Inside the room, Caleb stood next to Haley's bed. The girl looked much better. Her face was still bruised, and the rest of her skin looked pale and sallow, but her hair was clean and brushed. Her features seemed sharper. None of the slack-jawed bleariness showed.

A tray of food, mostly untouched, sat on the table, and more flowers and plants than Bill could count decorated the windowsill and the floor. It was a different kind of tribute than the one he saw out in the park.

"Hi, Haley," Bill said as he moved closer. He tried to keep his voice low and calm, his gestures restrained. She was still a sick girl, and he didn't want to overwhelm her in any way.

The girl's big eyes considered Bill, and then they filled with tears as he approached. "I'm sorry," she said.

Bill felt a quiver in his own chin. He stopped next to the bed and gently ran his hand down her upper arm. He was struck by the fact that he'd spent days in close proximity to this girl—touching her, speaking to her. Loving her, as though she were his own. In some ways, he felt like she had become his daughter as well, that some transference had taken place during those days he sat vigil at her bedside.

"I'm glad you're feeling better," Bill said. "You look better even than yesterday. It's good to see."

Haley smiled through her tears, lifting her hand to wipe them away. "Is it true they don't know anything yet? About Summer?"

"Not yet," Bill said. "But the police are trying. For a long time you weren't in such great shape."

"I know. Pastor Caleb has been telling me how much time you spent here. When you thought I was Summer." Some of the light went out of her face again. "I wish I was, Mr. Price. I wish I was Summer, and I was sitting here for you."

"No, no," Bill said. "Don't say that. We'll find . . . We'll figure things out with Summer when we can. You just take care and feel better."

"Actually, that's what Mr. Price is here to talk to you about," Rich said from behind Bill. "He wanted to ask you about something."

Haley's face immediately grew more guarded. She studied Bill from the corners of her eyes, looking small beneath the covers of the hospital bed. "Okay," she said, her voice as brittle as thin ice. "I still don't remember very much."

Bill wasn't sure what to say, so he looked to Caleb, who said, "Mr. Price just wants you to look at a photograph. A picture of a man."

Haley looked uneasy. "I'm still not seeing so well. Some things are blurry."

"Just do your best," Caleb said.

"Haley," Rich said, "this is serious, okay? You know Summer's in real danger. This isn't kids' stuff."

Some teenage defiance appeared. "I want to remember, Dad. I do. I want Summer to be found. When I woke up earlier, I'd kind of forgotten Summer was even gone. I thought it was a bad dream."

"Look at this picture, honey," Rich said. "Look at it long and hard."

Rich nudged Bill in the side, his cue. Bill took out his phone and called up the picture of Doug Hammond that the police had been circulating. It was a mug shot, and the man looked pissed off as he stared at the camera. His eyes were heavy-lidded, and his greasy hair hung over his forehead like a curtain. Bill stared at the face for a moment, and it seemed to be a pretty accurate representation of the man he'd chased in the park. The hair now possessed a little more gray, the face a little more puffiness. But if Haley had seen him, she'd recognize him from the photo on Bill's phone.

"Okay," Bill said, "just take your time."

He turned the phone around and held it in front of Haley's face. She didn't reach up to take the phone or move it any closer. Her lips parted slightly while she stared at the image on the small screen, her eyes squinting as though hit with a bright light.

"Have you seen that man anywhere?" Caleb asked, his voice calm.

It didn't take Haley long to start shaking her head. "No, I haven't," she said, her voice just above a whisper.

"Don't rush," Rich said, his heavy voice landing like a hammerblow. "Really look at it."

Reluctantly Haley reached out and took the phone from Bill's hands. She brought it closer to her face, her eyes narrowing as she studied it. She lifted her finger to her mouth and rested the tip there on her still-cracked lips. After a couple of moments, she started to slowly shake her head again.

"I don't know this man," she said.

"You're sure?" Bill asked.

"I'm sure."

Bill took the phone back. "It's okay. Do you mean you don't know him? Or you just don't remember him, maybe because he hurt you?"

Rich moved next to Bill, elbowing his way closer to the bed. He smelled like sweat. "That's the pertinent question."

Haley said, the defiance returning to her voice, "I don't know the man."

Bill sensed that everything hung in a precarious balance and that one good push could tip the moment into a place where none of them wanted it to go. Bill tucked the phone back into his pocket and gave Haley another reassuring pat on the arm.

"Thank you," he said, hoping to make a strategic exit. "Just take care of yourself."

But his path was blocked by Rich, who rather than getting out of the way, squeezed in closer to his daughter's bed. "Haley, we've all been talking about this, okay? We think you're hiding something from us. We know you went to Pastor Caleb to talk."

Haley looked around again, her eyes bouncing from one male face to another. "What does Mom think?"

"Your mom . . . Well, the less said about her, the better. But we know you might have been involved in something you shouldn't have been involved in. Or maybe Summer was. I'm not one of those guys who thinks a girl brings these things on herself, but sometimes people use poor judgment and get into a bad situation. Right?" Rich held his arms out, a gesture meant to say, *Hey, we're all being reasonable here.* "Or maybe somebody led you astray."

Bill wanted to object but bit his tongue. He hated to admit it, even to himself, but if Rich's methods worked, then so be it. He wanted to learn what Haley knew. If anything.

Haley's eyes bored in on her dad. Her chin quivered a bit, but she also thrust it out, stretching her neck. She looked like a fighter ready to step into the ring. When she spoke, her voice was calm but dripping with contempt. "I told you I don't know him. And I don't want to be harassed anymore by a man who is barely my father."

"Listen—," Rich said.

Both Bill and Caleb held their hands up, gesturing for silence.

And then Haley burst into tears. They shot out of her eyes and cascaded down her face while the girl's shoulders heaved beneath the blankets.

Bill took a step closer. He wanted to reach out, but he was partly to blame. The whole thing had been his idea.

"Easy now, Haley," Caleb said. "We'll go."

Haley let out a wet, heaving sob. She wiped at her face, sniffling, and then she said, "All I remember is the car. The car that picked us up. Don't you think I want to remember more?"

But the door of the room opened just then, and Candy walked in. She took in the three men and her daughter sobbing in the bed.

"What happened?" she asked, rushing to embrace Haley. "What is this? Was there bad news?"

Through her sobs and tears, Haley managed to collect herself enough to get a few words out. "They were asking me . . . That man . . . They wouldn't stop. . . ."

"She said something about a car," Bill said. "Candy, let her—"

Candy's eyes flashed with anger. She looked at each one of them as if she wanted to spring from her daughter's side and take care of them with her bare hands.

"Get out," she said. "She's a child, and she needs to rest. Get out."

Rich started to object, and Bill stepped closer to the bed. "Please, Candy—"

But Haley had collapsed against her mother, her body shaking with sobs. And when Bill saw the look on Candy's face, he felt he had no choice in that moment. The three of them left the room like scolded children.

CHAPTER SIXTY-SIX

Bill felt it was best to wait down in the hospital lobby instead of anywhere in the vicinity of Candy Rodgers.

While he waited for Hawkins to arrive, he replayed the events in the hospital room. Haley's tears. Her father's pushiness.

His own complicity. His own cowardice for not stopping it when he saw where it was going.

But if he'd stopped it, if none of them had pushed, would they have known about the car? The car Haley claimed picked the girls up on the day of the attack?

He called Hawkins and told him that piece of information. It might have been the big break they were looking for, the one that could only come with Haley awake and functioning.

Still, a burning sense of shame swept through his chest. He knew, firsthand, what it was like for that girl to sit in that hospital room. He'd seen the probes and cuts, the needles and sutures. It wasn't the best thing to push and push her the way they had until she crumpled in tears.

Bill wished he could erase it from his memory. But he knew from the way he'd ignored Julia's calls that those things never really went away. Everyone carried a bag of regrets around inside—from hitting a little sister with a stick to bullying a frightened and injured girl. He wanted his bag to stop growing.

Hawkins came through the door, a cell phone pressed to his ear. Bill stood up, dodged an elderly couple shuffling through the lobby, each using a cane, and approached the detective. He nodded, listening with lips pressed into a tight line as the person on the other end of the phone went on and on.

Finally he said, "Okay, bye," and hung up. He saw Bill. "Sorry about that."

"It's okay. I'm sure you're telling people about this car."

Hawkins looked confused for just a moment, and then he said, "Oh, no. That was my wife. I haven't been home much lately." The detective looked a little sad, his eyebrows lifted as though asking for sympathy. Bill had to admit he hadn't thought much about the detective having a home life. A spouse, maybe kids or grandkids, a dog, and a yard. "I'm going to go up and see what kind of shape Haley is in. You say her mom is madder than a hornet?"

"Yes. Not completely without reason."

"Then you'd better stay out of the way for a change."

"Why do you think I'm sitting down here on this uncomfortable seat?"

Hawkins started for the elevator, but Bill reached out and placed his hand on the detective's arm. He wore an overcoat, cool to the touch from the late-winter air outside. "This is something, isn't it?" Bill asked. "If you can find this car . . ."

"Of course. We've canvassed every possible route those girls could have taken. Like I told you, a couple of people saw them walking—"

"And someone saw Summer heading toward home. The old guy."

"Right. But no one saw them get into a car or talk to anybody. This might be the best we have."

He patted Bill on the shoulder and started away.

"Detective?"

Hawkins stopped again.

"When we were up there, talking to Haley . . . we might have—we did—push kind of hard."

Hawkins's brow creased, and his eyes clouded. "Yeah, you probably did."

"Could you tell her, tell them, I'm sorry?"

He nodded and boarded the elevator.

It struck Bill that he paced in the lobby like an expectant father in an old movie. The thought brought a twist of pain to his heart. He vividly remembered the day Summer was born—standing by Julia's side, her hand in his, the doctor giving instructions in a voice so calm he might have been reading a bedtime story. And then the blood-covered, gelatinous baby arrived, sliding out into the doctor's hands like a giant jelly bean.

How relieved Bill felt in that moment. How much he loved the two of them—Julia and Summer. How bright and full of possibility everything seemed.

He called Paige, just to hear a friendly voice. But the phone rang and rang, and then went to voice mail, Paige's cheery voice telling him he knew what to do if he wanted her to call back.

Bill hung up.

He went into the gift shop and tried to find magazines or books to distract himself. The covers of the magazines featured smiling celebrities without a care in the world. The covers of the novels were dark, with jagged fonts and running heroines looking back over their shoulders, pursued by some vicious killer.

Was there anything normal going on?

Bill turned away from the rack of reading material and saw Teena Everett walking into the hospital lobby. The girl looked around the open space, wide-eyed, as though not quite sure where to go. Bill walked out of the gift shop and headed toward her. When he was close enough, he said her name.

She jumped.

"Oh. Mr. Price. You scared me."

"I didn't mean to. You looked like you needed help."

"Oh . . . I came here to see Haley." She paused for a moment, playing with the zipper of her winter coat. She zipped it up and down with one hand, her eyes averted. "Kids are saying that she woke up. That she can talk now and everything."

"She's awake—that's true." Bill moved slightly to the right, trying to catch the girl's line of sight. "But she's still pretty weak. The police are up there now."

"Oh." Teena seemed disappointed. Her lips turned down in a pout. "Will they be done soon?"

"I don't know, but I'm not sure how many visitors Haley can have yet. Like I said, she's weak, and her memory isn't even really back. She's still piecing together everything that happened, and that could take a long time."

Bill knew he hadn't managed to keep the disappointment out of his voice, and Teena picked up on it.

"A long time?" she asked.

"Could be. Why?"

Teena shrugged, an exaggerated attempt at being casual. "I just wanted to talk to her. You know, tell her I hope she feels better."

"I think you'll have the chance soon," Bill said, trying to sound reassuring. "She's out of danger. It's just a matter of getting back to normal as best she can."

"How long?" Teena asked quickly.

"How long what?"

"How long until she's able to talk and remember stuff?"

"Nobody knows," Bill said. "I wish I could tell you. You should come back in a couple of days. She might be up for visitors then. I'm guessing, of course."

"A couple of days?" Teena looked skeptical, as if Bill had said a couple of years.

"Is something wrong, Teena?" he asked. "Do you need to tell her something now?"

"No, that's okay." She kept zipping the zipper, up and down, up and down. And she started backing away. "I just wanted to talk to my friend."

Then Bill remembered something. "Did you talk to Brandon Cooke the other day? He said you came by his house."

"I'll see you, Mr. Price," she said. "And I'm praying for Summer. Still."

Bill started to follow her, but he heard the elevator ding. He spun around as Hawkins stepped off, the phone to his ear again.

He wasn't talking to his wife. He was talking to someone in an official capacity, another cop or even one of his superiors.

"We're going to keep at it," he said. When he ended the call, he looked at Bill. "She's fuzzy, Bill, but she remembers getting into a car. And she's pretty sure the car was driven by a woman, but she couldn't identify her. That doesn't mean she doesn't know her. The doctor said her short-term memory is going to be affected the most, so the events surrounding the attack will come back more slowly."

"Did she describe this woman?" Bill asked.

"No. This may not even have anything to do with the attack. Maybe someone just gave them a ride. It was cold. . . ."

"Yeah."

"But we're sending this information out. If the person who drove them hears and comes forward, maybe we'll catch a big break."

"Right." Bill's mind raced, scrambling to think of possibilities. An awful one popped into his head. "Unless . . . unless the person who picked them up . . ."

"Is the dead girl," Hawkins said, on the same wavelength. "Or is involved somehow with the attack. We'll see, Bill. We'll see."

CHAPTER SIXTY-SEVEN

Bill returned home in the early-evening darkness.

He'd spent the afternoon at the police station, trying his best to feel useful as he watched a series of press conferences and phone calls and bulletins being issued. Bill spent time in a room with Hawkins and a handful of other officers, answering and then answering again every possible question they could think to ask about Taylor Kress. Bill felt like a kid who hadn't studied for a test. He knew very little about the woman, had spent only a short amount of time with her, and believed they were all spinning their wheels in mud while his daughter remained lost in the world.

But they hadn't been able to locate Taylor. Or Doug Hammond.

They located the dentist in Ariel and subpoenaed the dental records to see whether Emily Kress was the dead girl, the one who may have picked Summer and Haley up the day they disappeared.

When they were done with Bill, Hawkins warned him to stay out of their way, to head home while the police searched for Taylor and Doug.

"We're reaching out to the state bureau of investigation," Hawkins said. "We need more manpower to search, but you won't help any-body, least of all your daughter, if you interfere."

"How soon until the cavalry arrives?" Bill asked.

"Soon," Hawkins said. "Tomorrow, maybe. But you should go home."

But Bill didn't. He spent a couple of hours driving around Jakes-ville. He went out to the memorial again, hoping against hope he'd see Taylor again. But, of course, he didn't. He drove past the ceme-tery where the unidentified girl had once been buried. He drove around and around, growing increasingly frustrated, the news on the radio a constant reminder—as if he needed one—of how little any of them knew.

Returning home, he parked in the back, and his eyes trailed over the yard to Adam's house. A single light burned on the first floor. Bill had yet to see any sign of his neighbor moving out, but that didn't mean he wasn't gone. Adam had made the whole transfer sound urgent, so the light could be on a timer, and Adam's personal effects could be in the process of being packed to be shipped away when the house sold. Bill needed a whiskey, and for a moment, he wished for the lazy summer nights when he and Adam drank one together under the stars, a baseball game on the radio, Summer in the house with Haley watching a movie or playing a game. How far off the rails everything had gone. How very, very far.

Bill looked around the yard, his eyes straining into the shadows beneath the trees and behind the bushes. He felt like a target himself. If Doug Hammond showed up at the park to skulk around the scene of the crime, then what was to prevent him from finding Bill's house? His address was listed in the phone book and on every Internet site in the world. Yes, the police claimed to be keeping a closer eye on things, but how closely could they watch one house when they had other, more pressing matters on their hands? Bill remembered half joking with Paige about borrowing Adam's gun to go after Clinton Fields and his friends, but it didn't seem as funny now.

Bill stopped just inside the door. He flipped on the family room lights, and everything looked perfectly normal. He set the dead bolt behind him and wished for a chain. He decided to take a circuitous route through the house, turning on every light and checking every room. The kitchen and laundry room were clear. The living room as well. The only noises were the squeaks under Bill's feet as he walked, the clicks as he activated each light. He relaxed as he moved, his body settling down and his fears abating.

When he came out of the living room, preparing to turn down the hallway toward the bedroom, he saw a smear of something that looked like brown paint on the floor. It was about three inches long and shaped like a sickle.

Bill froze.

He knew the stain hadn't been there before. And it suddenly looked less like paint and more like dried blood.

His feet felt like they were no longer anchored to the floor. The lower half of his body tensed as it trembled, the shock waves moving up from his shoes to his chest.

He knew the door was locked—*dead-bolted*—when he came in. He'd felt the lock turn, felt the resistance as he stuck the key in and twisted it to the right.

Had he created the stain when he left the house earlier? Had he stepped in something? Had there still been mud on his shoes when he returned from the park?

But if so, why only in that one spot?

And hadn't he taken his muddy shoes off at the door?

"Hello," he said.

He fumbled in his jacket pocket, taking out his phone. He knew he couldn't stand there near the entrance to the hallway all night, like a scared little kid waiting for his parents to come home. Because there were no parents. He was the adult. He was on his own.

He made a quick move to the right, reaching with his free hand, and swiped at the light switch just inside the hallway.

The light popped on, and it took a moment for the sight before him to register.

A man was sprawled on the hardwood floor before him, a halo of sticky, drying blood around his head.

Bill couldn't see the face, but he recognized the clothes. The work boots. The flannel shirt. The jeans stained by days and days of yard work.

And, for some reason, Winnie the Pooh on the floor next to him, just far enough away to avoid being stained by the blood.

Adam Fleetwood. And he didn't appear to be breathing.

CHAPTER SIXTY-EIGHT

Bill waited outside in the dark while police officers and crime scene technicians and a woman from the coroner's office swarmed through his house. He'd gone outside as soon as he called the police. He knew from watching cop shows on TV that it was easy to contaminate a crime scene.

But more than anything—he didn't want to stand around in his house with a dead body cooling in the hallway. Was he supposed to pour himself a drink in the kitchen and wait?

And how many other people were going to die in his house?

Hawkins came out after an hour and approached Bill. The night wasn't as cool as he'd expected it to be, and he'd found an old sweatshirt in his car. He'd thought of calling someone, either just to talk or for moral support, but whom would he call? His closest friend lay dead in the house. His daughter was gone, his wife dead. He thought of calling Paige again, and at some point he would, but even that seemed strange. What would it be like to call his sister and interrupt her quiet family life with news of another murder?

On the patio, Hawkins sat down in the chair next to Bill. When his butt landed, he let out a tired sigh, and then he reached up and rubbed the back of his neck with his big right hand.

"I'm retiring in two years," he said. "Less than that really. Nineteen months."

"You're lucky."

"If the next nineteen months continue at this pace, I may not make it."

Bill nodded. He felt the same way. What else could go wrong?

"We'll have to send the body up to the medical examiner in Louisville, but it certainly looks like homicide. Some kind of blow to the head, although the object's gone. You didn't see anything missing? A lamp? A piece of art? Anything that could have been used as a weapon?"

"I didn't look closely."

"Of course." Hawkins rubbed his hands together. "Why was he in your house?"

"I don't know. He has a key. He's had a key for . . . years. He used to check on the place when we went away. We've always had a key to his house as well." Bill shrugged. "I wanted someone nearby to have a key in case we got locked out. He's the neighbor I know the best."

"So you hadn't asked him to come in and do something?"

Bill considered his response carefully. "No. He and I . . . We kind of had a falling-out. We argued about something, and I hadn't talked to him since."

"What did you argue about?"

Bill knew the detective's wheels were spinning. He knew they'd be spinning as soon as he heard about the body being found. After all, what were the police supposed to think when someone ended up dead in your house?

So Bill told him. About the discussion concerning the phone call, and then Paige's digging around into the phone bill. It all sounded ridiculous and petty in light of Adam's being dead, but Bill knew he had to reveal everything.

Hawkins said, "This last phone call Julia made . . . Even if Adam did answer it and spoke to her, that's not evidence of an affair."

"I know."

"I have to ask you where you were after you left the station this afternoon."

"I know you do." Bill told him about driving around and looking, even though Hawkins had told him not to. Hawkins didn't show any anger or say anything in response to Bill's confession. Maybe he had expected Bill to disobey. Maybe it was a tiny matter in the middle of a larger mess. "I came home from the hospital and found that."

A technician in a polo shirt came out of the house and whispered something in Hawkins's ear. The detective nodded and said, "That's fine." He looked over at Bill. "They're going to bring Adam's body out now. He'll be covered up, but if you don't want to see it . . ."

"It's fine." Bill pointed at the lit-up houses surrounding them. "Everyone else is watching us."

"When they're finally finished, you can go through and check again to see if anything is missing. Anything at all, even if it doesn't seem valuable. Just tell us. We're going to get into Adam's house when we leave here. Maybe something will jump out at us there."

"Look, this must have something to do with Summer. Right? Why else would someone be dead in my house this way?"

"Of course it's possible."

Bill's temper rose. "It's more than possible. That man, Doug Hammond, attacked me in the park."

"You chased him."

"Come on, Hawkins. His stepdaughter is missing, after he beat his ex-wife the same way. And then he's slinking around the crime scene and runs away from me. Fights me off. And now . . . this." Bill pointed back at the house where Adam lay dead. "Right? How do I know Hammond didn't come over here to hurt me, and Adam saw him? Adam kept an eye on things here." Bill felt horrible admitting it, since the two of them were on bad terms. But he had to consider it. "Maybe Adam saw this guy breaking in and wanted to protect me?"

"No forced entry. And you said the door was locked when you came home."

"He took the key from Adam after he killed him."

"He killed him outside and then dragged him in?" Hawkins used the arms of the chair to push himself up. "Look, do me a favor? Leave the investigating to us. Stay away from Haley too."

The back door opened and two technicians backed out, a stretcher on wheels between them. A long black bag, zipped and closed, sat on top of the stretcher, carrying the mortal remains of Adam Fleetwood. Bill watched while they loaded him into the back of a white coroner's van, the door slamming shut with finality.

Hawkins started to walk in the direction of Adam's house.

"Is that it?" Bill asked.

Hawkins looked back. "For now? That's it."

"Will you let me know if you find anything over there?"

Hawkins waved, but it seemed like a noncommittal, almost dismissive gesture.

When he was gone, Bill felt profoundly alone.

CHAPTER SIXTY-NINE

Almost three hours later, Hawkins came back to Bill's house, startling him with a firm knock on the back door. He'd locked the house and spent the time since the other cops left down on his knees in the hallway, scrubbing the floor with cleanser. Wiping up his friend's blood.

The act made him gag more than once. The smell of the cleanser and the sight of the blood caused Bill's head to pound, a pulsing that kept time with the hammering of his heart. The cleaning required multiple trips to the laundry room to dump out the bucket of foul water and wring out rags that had become sodden with blood.

He couldn't remember who had cleaned up Julia's blood after her fatal fall in the kitchen. He knew he hadn't. Not Summer; she had been too distraught. A merciful paramedic or cop? A friend?

Had it been Adam?

When Bill thought the hallway was clean, he went to the kitchen for a drink, pouring himself a healthy shot of Tennessee whiskey and then another. He had just thrown the second one down when the knock came against the back door. Bill's entire body jumped, and if the glass had still been full, he would have spilled it.

He was relieved to see Hawkins there. He worried it might be Doug Hammond, although it seemed unlikely the man would try to come back with such a police presence in the neighborhood. Bill let the detective in.

"I won't keep you long," he said, stepping inside. He took a couple of deep whiffs of the air.

"I've been cleaning," Bill said. "They just finished here an hour ago."

Hawkins nodded. "Yeah, they don't tell you on television that somebody has to clean up after these things. You know there are services that just do that? They clean up after suicides and homicides."

Bill shrugged. "You'll have to get me their business card."

Hawkins considered Bill for a moment, trying to determine whether he was joking. Then he said, "We made a thorough search of Adam Fleetwood's house. No sign of forced entry over there, but the place had been ransacked. It looks like someone went through the drawers and closets, probably trying to get their hands on something valuable they could sell. We can't say for sure whether the murder happened first or the ransacking, but we could presume it was the murder. Someone killed Fleetwood here and then went over there. You had a key. Did anyone else?"

"I don't know. And you think it's Doug Hammond?"

"I'm not jumping to any conclusions."

"So you're getting fingerprints and things over there? Other evidence? Just like you did here?"

Hawkins gave Bill a look that said, *I think I know how to do my job.*

Bill said, "Right. Of course."

"Have you had a chance to determine whether anything is missing here?" Hawkins asked.

"No, I haven't. I got caught up in the cleaning."

"Do you mind if we take a look?" Hawkins asked.

"I don't," Bill said.

The two men walked through the house as Bill tried to remember what he owned that someone would consider valuable. It was easy to show the detective that the appliances were there—the TV, the microwave, the DVD player. Bill checked the china cabinet in the dining room, and the silver candlesticks he and Julia received as a wedding present were still there, covered with dust.

They started down the hallway, the one filled with the scent of ammonia from Bill's cleaning.

"Computer's there," Bill said. "And the printer and fax machine."

They went on to the doorway of Summer's room.

"Anything in here?" Hawkins asked.

"You all took her computer and her e-reader. I don't think there was anything else."

"No jewelry?"

"Nothing really valuable."

"What about this open drawer?" the detective asked.

Bill took a step back into the hallway, seeming not to have heard Hawkins's question. He looked both ways, down toward his bedroom and then out to the family room.

"What is it, Bill?" Hawkins asked.

Bill straightened. "Remember that Winnie the Pooh I brought to the hospital? The one Summer sleeps with every night?"

"The one Haley didn't want at the hospital."

"When I came home earlier, and I saw Adam lying here on the floor, that Winnie the Pooh was right next to him. Where is it?"

"Probably tagged and taken away as possible evidence. What's your point?"

"Why was it right next to his body? Like he'd picked it up and carried it with him?"

CHAPTER SEVENTY

"What about that?" Hawkins asked.

Bill pointed into Summer's room. "It always sits right there, on top of her bed. Summer made her bed every day—she was good about that, almost anal—and she insisted on putting that bear right on top. And she slept with it every night even when she wanted to get rid of the other stuffed animals she owned. I made sure it looked like that."

"It's a stuffed bear. It probably fell on the floor during the struggle."

"It's not just that. . . . Summer loves that bear. She needs it to sleep and feel safe. That's always been the case."

"Okay," Hawkins said, looking around the room. "Is there anything else out of place? This drawer is open, and some clothes are scattered around."

Bill stepped into the room and looked at the dresser. He saw a jumble of underwear and socks on the floor, like someone had just dropped them there. He lifted his hands in confusion. "I don't know, Detective. Why would someone be going through her drawers this way and taking clothes out?"

"How about the closet?"

Bill pulled the door open and looked at the clothes on the rack, the neatly lined-up shoes and boots and sandals on the floor. Bill pawed through the clothes, but he didn't know what he was looking for. How many fathers had inventories of their teenage daughters' clothes?

"I don't know," Bill said. "I don't know."

"Did she keep clothes or personal items anywhere else in the house?"

Bill backed away from the closet. "No. Just her coats and things. But she was wearing her winter coat on the day she disappeared. Hell, I guess Haley was wearing her coat."

"Let's check your bedroom."

But Bill didn't move. He stood in the center of the room, the closet open before him. He questioned himself: Was he wrong about the bear? Did it matter that it was next to Adam's body, as though someone—either Adam or the person who killed him—had been carrying it?

He'd never moved it. Paige wouldn't, would she?

And he hadn't taken things out of Summer's drawers. So who had?

"Are you okay, Bill?"

His mind swirled. His thoughts were tornadic.

"Someone—Doug Hammond, perhaps—broke in here to get that bear and other stuff for Summer. Why would he do that? A souvenir?"

"I can't answer that, Bill. I can't even agree that it was Doug Hammond who did it. Why don't we check the last bedroom?"

Bill practically stumbled along behind the detective, his mind racing with every possibility relating to Doug Hammond and his presence in the house. He looked around the master bedroom, but things didn't really register in his head. Everything looked as it always did, but it was only when Hawkins prompted him that Bill remembered to look in the closets and drawers for any missing valuables. Again, they didn't have much. Julia's engagement ring and other jewelry were in a safety-deposit box at the bank, waiting for Summer to be old enough to use them. Or sell them, whatever she wanted to do. Beyond that, there just wasn't anything.

"It all looks fine," Bill said.

Hawkins nodded, but he didn't make a move to leave the room. He considered Bill, his blue-gray eyes showing pity more than anything else.

"I sense you're getting your hopes up, Bill," Hawkins said. "I don't want you to race ahead of the evidence. All we have are some displaced items, things that aren't valuable. . . ."

"No," Bill said. "No. That man came here to get things that would bring Summer comfort. That's why the bear was off the bed and on the floor. That's why the clothes were disturbed."

"You don't know that."

"I do," Bill said. "Summer's alive. She's still alive."

PART
THREE

PART
THREE

CHAPTER SEVENTY-ONE

Hawkins's phone rang, the sound even more shrill in the quiet house. The detective took the call and stepped away from Bill, turning his back and speaking in a lowered voice. So Bill moved closer, straining to hear.

"The Knotty Pine?" Hawkins said. "And they're sitting on her? Okay, okay. I can get there." Hawkins listened for what felt like a long time. "Oh, boy. Really? She said that? Why?"

Bill moved even closer, and Hawkins took a half step away. The detective let out a long sigh and rubbed his forehead with his left hand while his right gripped the phone. "Okay, okay. We'll get there as soon as we can."

He hung up and slipped the phone back into his coat pocket.

"What's that all about?" Bill asked. "Who's at the Knotty Pine?"

Hawkins seemed to be contemplating a professional answer, one with all the appropriate qualifiers and modifiers, but the late hour and long day combined to make him give in and speak directly to Bill.

"Taylor Kress," he said. "A couple of our officers found her at the Knotty Pine about twenty minutes ago."

The combination of excitement and relief Bill felt made him unable to speak. He tried to form words but couldn't.

It didn't matter. Hawkins said all that needed to be said.

"She's insisting on seeing you," he said. "It's not my favorite thing to have to do, but I'm going to try it. Get your coat and let's go."

They pulled into the gravel parking lot of the Knotty Pine, a cheap motel located on the bypass among a series of fast food restaurants, car dealerships, and, farther along, Jakesville's lone strip club. The Knotty Pine didn't seem to be the kind of place Taylor Kress would choose to stay given the more reputable chain hotels in the area, but maybe that was why she went there. To stay out of the way. The cops found her by searching the few hotels and motels in town, and when Hawkins stopped the car in the lot, two patrol cars were already parked near the open door to what Bill assumed was her room. Two uniformed cops stood outside, their arms crossed, their breath puffing in the cold air.

The motel's neon sign cast a green glow over the two men as they drove through the lot. Each room had a red door illuminated by a single, sickly yellow bulb. When the car stopped and Bill reached for the door handle, Hawkins told him to stop.

"Wait here a minute," he said.

"I thought she wanted to see me."

"She does. But I need to talk to her first. I'll leave the heat on, okay?"

Bill started to say something but stopped. He'd never seen quite the look of determination—or was it something else?—on Hawkins's face that he wore in the motel parking lot. His brows and chin seemed to jut forward, but his eyes were glassy and distant, almost sad.

So Bill kept his mouth shut and watched Hawkins approach the two cops, exchange a few words and a couple of nods, and then step inside the motel room.

Bill leaned back in his seat, watched the two cops tilt their heads toward the door of the motel room as though they were listening in on whatever Hawkins was saying to Taylor. Bill's hand crept toward the door again, but he stopped. He turned on the car radio, spinning the dials in search of a song or a show, anything that might take his mind off whatever was going on in that room. But he found nothing comforting, just a twangy minister spouting Bible verses, and loud, crass music he couldn't understand.

He tried to believe the moved stuffed animal and scattered clothes meant something good for Summer. Why else would someone break into the house and disturb Summer's things? Wouldn't they have to be trying to comfort Summer, to make her feel better, wherever they had her?

The voice in his head was frank: *Who would bring a stuffed animal to a dead girl?*

The heat in the car grew to be too much. Bill felt a trickle of sweat forming on the back of his neck. He dialed the heat down and then pressed a button to lower the window by an inch. The cool air brushed his face, easing his physical discomfort. He didn't want to be in the car. He didn't want Hawkins to be in the motel. He wanted the two cops in their dark uniforms to jump into their cars and go somewhere, anywhere they might find Summer.

More than ever.

It took fifteen minutes for Hawkins to emerge. He came through the doorway, his big body filling the frame, the bright light from inside the room outlining him. He looked to the car and made a waving gesture toward Bill, a summons to approach.

Bill hesitated, wondering if he really meant him, or one of the other cops. But then Hawkins waved again, his gesture more energetic, and Bill pushed the door open. His feet crunched against the gravel, his gloveless hands feeling the cold first.

Hawkins took a last look inside the room and nodded, and then he came out and met Bill about ten feet from the door, his big hand held out.

"I need to tell you something before you go in," Hawkins said. "It's the reason I had to go in there first."

Bill tried to look around the big cop, to see past him. "What is it?"

"We got those dental records from the other town, the ones for her daughter. Emily Kress is the girl found at the scene with Haley. And I just had to give her mother the official word." Hawkins stepped aside, his eyes downcast. "She's ready to talk to you now."

CHAPTER SEVENTY-TWO

Bill stepped through the doorway of Taylor's room. She lay on her side on the queen-size bed, her knees pulled up to her chest, a crumpled tissue held to her face. Her cheeks were red, her face contorted with grief.

Bill remained frozen in place, like an intruder. Even as his mind scrambled for a way to graciously back out the door and into the cold night, a more intense feeling, a stabbing and twisting of his own heart, compelled him to stay. He couldn't turn his back on this woman in her time of desperate need.

"I'm sorry, Taylor," he said.

He walked across the stained carpet and sat on the edge of the lumpy, uneven mattress. The bedspread was dark green and years out-of-date, covered with a variety of stains and cigarette burns. Taylor's shoes were off, revealing pink socks, and she still wore the Bengals sweatshirt. Bill placed his hand on her knee and gave her two pats he hoped were comforting. He was stuck for anything else to say, so he repeated himself.

"I'm really sorry."

Taylor sniffled. She made a shuddering sound from deep in her chest. "Thank you," she said.

Bill looked to the door, hoping Hawkins or one of the other cops had come back, but no one was in sight. "Do you need anything?" he asked. "Water or something?"

"The detective, the big one—he got me water." She sniffled again. "And another cop brought me tissues."

"Is there someone you want to call?" Bill asked. "I've got my phone right here. Maybe there's someone back home—"

"I'll call them soon," she said, her voice raw. "My brother and his wife will want to know. They'll help me with everything. I want to bury her back home, of course, close to where I live."

"Naturally."

Taylor lifted her head off the flat pillow and stared daggers at Bill. "There's nothing natural about it. Do you think it's natural you don't know where your daughter is? Is it natural mine's dead?"

"Of course not."

Her head dropped back to the pillow, and she let out a sigh. She seemed to be finished speaking, as though the small outburst had drained all her energy.

Bill shifted his weight, causing the mattress to squeak. He looked to the door again. No one. "Was there something you wanted to tell me?" he asked.

Taylor moved her head around, like a restless sleeper trying to get comfortable. She fluffed the pillow and then settled back in. "I was wrong," she said. "When I dragged you out to where they found my baby's body and let Doug come up to you, I was wrong."

"So you did set me up out there?"

"He wanted to meet you. He knew I had come to town, accusing him of hurting Emily, and he wanted to set the record straight. He knew the cops would be looking for him eventually, just as soon as I gave them those dental records and they identified Emily. He convinced me he hadn't done it, told me not to turn over the records. He tried to convince me Emily might still be alive. Or at least that he hadn't hurt her. When I stopped hearing from her, I flew off the handle. I wasn't rational. And I knew Doug had talked to her more recently than I had. He'd seen her. He'd spent time with her, but when I asked him, he was evasive. I couldn't get anything out of him. I thought he knew something. I *wanted* him to know something. He convinced me he hadn't harmed her."

"How?"

"He reminded me of how much he cared for her, of everything he did for her. He used to get up with her when she was sick or scared during the night. He's good at math. He used to help her with homework, stuff I didn't know." She sniffled. "We were a family, for a little while. We all had something. . . ."

"You said he beat his ex."

"Yes, he did. She ended up withdrawing those charges. Look, he gave me hope, just a little. And I needed that."

"You wanted to believe him that she might be alive."

"Of course I did," she said, her voice sharp. "Wouldn't you? Wouldn't you cling to any thread you could? That's why I didn't want them to have those dental X-rays. I wanted to stall and hope it was another girl instead of Emily. I feel like a fool now, hiding from the truth. Like a child."

Bill nodded. He knew all too well. "So you got me out there to talk to him, but he ran away. Why?"

"You ran after him, like a crazy person. You should have seen yourself. You looked like some kind of banshee."

Bill spotted a box of tissues on the floor a few feet from the bed.

He leaned down, picked it up, and held it out to Taylor. She pulled a few out, and then tossed the crumpled one from her hand in the direction of the trash can. "Thanks," she said.

"Okay, so what are you thinking about Doug now?" Bill asked. "Did he hurt Summer?"

"That detective told me something happened at your house tonight. Something awful?"

Bill could still see the blood smear, Adam's body facedown on the floor. The mess he cleaned up afterward. The bloody rags, the disgusting water. "Yes. My neighbor was killed. In my house."

"Doug was going there—"

"They don't know that it was Doug."

"I think it was him. He was desperate to talk to you, to clear his name. He felt like he owed you, like some kind of debt. It's a guy thing, a father thing. He actually understood what you were going through because we couldn't find Emily." She burrowed into the pillow, obscuring her face from Bill's view. Then she looked up again, her eyes glassy and red. "I'm sorry. If I'd behaved differently, if I'd been honest with you, then maybe you'd know what happened to your daughter by now."

Bill stared down at the woman, her body and heart crumpled by grief. She'd been right, and manipulation or not, he couldn't blame her or anyone else for reaching for a lifeline that said their child was alive. "It's okay, Taylor. I get it." He patted her leg again, letting his hand linger longer for a final squeeze of sympathy.

Then Hawkins was in the doorway, knocking lightly against the jamb. He looked sheepish, reluctant to interrupt. Or perhaps reluctant to go on with speaking to a broken, grieving mother.

"I have to talk to Taylor more, Bill," he said. "Are you finished?"

"We are," Taylor said.

Bill stood up and started for the door, and rather than stepping aside to let Bill go, Hawkins backed out, and he and Bill stood beneath the pathetic bulb, the cool night air swirling around them.

CHAPTER SEVENTY-THREE

Hawkins reached past Bill and pulled the door to Taylor's room shut. The detective's coat was unbuttoned, and he seemed unaffected by the cold temperature.

"She say anything interesting?" Hawkins asked.

"She apologized for jerking me around."

Hawkins just nodded. He didn't really seem focused on what Bill had told him.

Bill asked, "Do you think that Doug Hammond has Summer somewhere? That he beat the other two girls and then did something else with Summer?"

"Haley's saying a girl picked them up."

"Emily. She took them to Doug. Maybe Doug was in the car, and Haley doesn't remember."

Hawkins rubbed his thumb against his chin. "Maybe. So, he gets ahold of these three girls, he beats two of them, including his stepdaughter, dumps them out in the park after two days, but not before bundling Haley up because she's still alive. Meanwhile, where's Summer this whole time? Why keep her alive, if that's what you're arguing?"

"I don't know. . . ."

"Hammond doesn't have a house nearby. But then he comes to your house to get these items, to make Summer feel better, but he gets into it with Fleetwood and kills him."

"And leaves without what he came for."

Hawkins nodded his head slowly, and Bill could tell there was more on his mind, something else he needed to say.

"We're looking for Hammond," he said. "All over. We have officers sweeping Dunlap Park right now. But I don't want to fixate on him too much at the expense of everyone else. After all, no one saw him in your house. He didn't know Fleetwood, at least not as far as we can tell."

Bill waited for more, and when it didn't come, he asked, "What else are you thinking?"

"You said Fleetwood was moving, a job transfer. And that his ex-wife and kid live down there. He wanted to be closer to them. Right?"

"Sure."

"We'll be looking into all of that as well."

"He's the victim here, Detective."

Hawkins nodded. "Right. But when a crime is committed, we tend to get to know the victim first. Make sense?"

"It does."

"Do you know anything else about Adam Fleetwood? You told me about the phone call your wife made to him the day she died."

"I don't see how that phone call, or my wife, could somehow lead to his being dead in my house. Do you?"

"You told me you were out driving around before you went home and found the body in your house," Hawkins said. "Did you kill him?"

Bill stammered. "Of course not."

"But you suspected him of having something going on with your wife."

"I didn't kill him. He was my friend."

Hawkins's breath puffed in the night air, a cloud that floated away and disappeared. "Let's get you a ride back while I talk to Ms. Kress."

He clapped Bill on the shoulder, took a deep breath, and pushed open the motel room door.

CHAPTER SEVENTY-FOUR

Bill returned home and tried to sleep.

He undressed and lay in bed as the minutes turned into hours. He stared at the ceiling, watching the lights of passing cars flash across the walls of his bedroom. Every time a car passed, a stubborn and persistent hope rose in Bill's chest. He listened carefully, his ears tuned to the outside world like antennae, and wished one of the cars would stop, that Summer would jump out of it and run across the lawn and into the house.

He pictured the reunion. Yes, she'd look a little battered and worn, dirty and tired from the hell she'd been through. All the sweeter for them both as she came through the door and jumped into his arms . . .

The fantasy caused Bill to smile and cry at the same time. If only the world were so easy. If only it were all wish fulfillment . . .

He dozed for a short time, a restless sleep. Images rushed through his mind. He ran down a darkened alley, but his mind couldn't make it clear whether he was the pursuer or the one being pursued. It didn't matter. He felt panic either way, a sense that something was slipping through his grip.

Like Summer.

Or . . . like Doug Hammond.

He came out of the dream and sat up in bed.

It was just before four a.m. An insufferably cheerful bird sang outside the window, but no light came through. It was still too early for that.

"Shit," Bill said.

He scrambled in the dark, pulling on jeans and a long-underwear shirt. In the back of his closet, he found a pair of running shoes, a leftover from a brief flirtation with daily exercise the previous spring. But they had good tread and allowed him to move quickly if needed. He made a stop out in the hallway, pulling open the utility closet door. The hot-water heater ticked inside, but Bill reached around on the shelf until he found a flashlight with batteries in it. He tested the beam against the darkness of the closet. Satisfied, he grabbed his coat and left.

On his way, Bill made a call. Given the time, he wasn't surprised when it went straight to voice mail. He left a message.

"Look, I know you're still asleep. And you probably have the phone off so it doesn't wake you. But I'm about to do something either really brave or really stupid. Or both. But I want you to make me a promise, Paige, even if you just hear this on the recording. Promise that if something happens to me, now or at any other time, you'll keep searching for Summer. I know you have a family and you can't devote your life to it, but could you just do whatever you can to see the world doesn't forget about her?

"Thanks. And, you know, I love you. In case you didn't know."

CHAPTER SEVENTY-FIVE

Bill kept the flashlight off as he walked along the gravel path. He wanted to save the batteries until he needed them. And he didn't want to advertise his approach to everyone in the park.

He'd passed one police car, driving in the opposite direction as he came in. He expected—hoped, really—to see more, but there was no sign of any. If they'd already been through, as Hawkins said, maybe they'd be coming and going throughout the night. Bill hoped so. He thought about the police the way he thought about his night-light as a little kid—an amazing form of comfort in the dark.

Bill judged himself to be about halfway to the memorial when something rustled to the right of the path. He stopped. He held the flashlight in his right hand, and his left slipped into his coat pocket where he'd stashed a pepper spray canister he'd brought along. He didn't even know if it worked anymore. On an impulse, he'd bought it for Summer two years earlier, encouraging her to carry it with her when she walked to the bus stop or school or rode her bike to her friends' houses. He didn't think she'd ever picked it up; instead she'd chosen to leave it in a junk drawer in the kitchen.

Bill waited. The rustling came again, and he knew it was too loud to be a small animal. It was either something big—a deer, most likely—or else a person. And given how skittish deer could be, he bet it was a person.

Bill flicked the light on, shining it in the low brush on the side of the path. It took a moment, but two figures slowly emerged. First a man and then a woman. They both looked ragged and homeless, their clothes dirty, their hair matted and greasy where it spilled out from beneath wool caps. They squinted in the light, and Bill angled it away, giving them a break. The man zipped his pants, his face revealing no embarrassment.

They came toward him, Bill holding his ground with the pepper spray in his left hand inside the pocket.

When the man came abreast of Bill, he said, "Not a cop, for a change." And kept walking.

The woman looked Bill up and down, a sneer crossing her face. "Some creep," she said.

Bill waited while they continued down the path behind him and back toward the parking lot. He knew he'd locked the car and had made sure to leave no valuables exposed. When he was sure they were gone, he flicked the light off and kept going.

Bill turned the light back on when he reached the memorial. The beam played across the fading flowers and rain-streaked notes, illuminating the dead, marble eyes of stuffed animals that stared unseeingly into the night.

He shivered despite the warmth of his wool coat and long underwear. He turned away, orienting his body in the direction where he'd seen and then chased Doug Hammond. There was no path, so he could only approximate in the dark, but he felt as if he had a pretty solid sense of where he wanted to go. With the flashlight beam leading the way, he started off.

The woods were quiet. It was too early in the season for crickets and other bugs. Only the occasional call of a night bird and the light crunch of his shoes over the ground made any noise.

Every nerve ending in Bill's body jangled. He expected at any moment for other broken and haunted-looking figures to emerge from the darkened trees, the kind of people Bill never saw in his daily life, the kind he found himself bumping against only because someone had kidnapped his daughter.

And maybe she was out there as well. Would it make sense that whoever took Summer and left the other two girls in the park also lived there? Wouldn't it be likely that everything happened in close proximity? Bill knew the police had searched the park several times, but it covered a lot of acres. In Kentucky there were any number of rock formations and creeks, small caves and overhangs. Could the police and a load of volunteers really cover everything?

The beam from the flashlight cut through the trees. After a few minutes, Bill saw a blue tent and, next to it, a lean-to constructed of rough boards. He moved in that direction, his heartbeat thrumming in his ear. When he got closer, the beam played across the openings of the two structures. Bill saw legs and dirty sneakers trailing out the end of the wooden lean-to. The figure didn't move at all, and he moved the beam up the body until he saw a ragged gray beard and a bulbous red-veined nose. The man didn't flinch.

He angled the beam to the opening of the tent. The flap was closed, secured with a long piece of string. Bill hesitated, unsure of how to proceed, but before he needed to act, a hand came through the opening, pulling the string loose. The flaps parted, and a young guy with a tattoo on his neck stuck his head out, blinking against the light.

He and Bill just stared at each other, and Bill moved the light away from the man's eyes. A woman spoke from behind the man, inside the tent, and the guy, still looking at Bill, said, "I don't know if he's a cop or not. He doesn't look like one. He looks like a suburban dad playing like he's a hiker."

"Who's the girl in there?" Bill asked.

"He wants to see you," the guy said. "Are you making an offer?" the guy asked Bill.

It took a moment for Bill to understand, and then another to decide if the man was joking about pimping out his lady friend. But the man smirked, letting Bill know how little regard he had for him.

Some rustling came from inside the tent, and then a woman stuck her head through the flap. She had bleached blond hair and wore a large hoop in one of her nostrils. She smiled when she saw Bill, and her teeth looked perfect and white. "Are you a social worker or something?" she asked. "They used to come out all the time and give us condoms and shit."

"I'm not," Bill said. "I'm looking for a man named Doug."

The guy withdrew into the tent, and the girl stared at Bill a moment longer. "My boyfriend in kindergarten was named Doug. But I don't know where he is now."

"Is there a guy in this area named Doug?" Bill asked.

"I have to go back to sleep. The cops came through here twice tonight already. They're harassing us."

"They let you stay," Bill said.

"Fuck off," the girl said.

She went back in, and Bill wondered how far in over his head he really was.

Bill passed a couple more makeshift dwellings. Some of the people inside were awake and treated him with either indifference or outright hostility. The woods seemed to be a landing place for an eclectic collection of young and old, the broken and the defiant. He wondered about the parents of the young people. How many of them were lying awake at that very moment, wishing they knew the whereabouts of their sons and daughters?

Or, worse, how many of the parents simply didn't care?

Bill then saw a white square in the darkness. He took his time approaching, moving slowly through the night, but the closer he came, the more certain he felt that he was coming upon the makeshift tent he'd seen the day he chased Doug Hammond. It looked the same and appeared to be in about the same place.

Bill stopped about twenty feet away. He listened to the quiet of the night. He took a quick look above and saw fast-moving clouds passing over the moon and stars, pressing down like the lid on a pot.

Someone stirred inside the tent. Bill moved closer, the light shining on the opening.

"Hello?" he called. "Doug?"

A woman emerged, standing up and blinking as the light hit her in the face. Bill angled the light down, revealing dirty jeans and bare feet, the toes covered with mud.

"What the fuck?" she asked. "Cops again?"

"I'm looking for Doug Hammond. Do you know him?"

The woman crossed her arms. She looked to be about thirty, and the sweater she pulled around her body had an enormous hole in one elbow. Her hair was dyed pink, and she considered Bill with big eyes in a pale face.

"Who the fuck are you?" she asked.

"I'm looking for Doug. Does he stay around here? I'm supposed to talk to him."

"The fuck," she said. But she didn't go back inside. She studied Bill, shifting her weight so one dirty foot rested on top of the other, giving her the appearance of a flamingo. A pink-haired, very thin, and very dirty flamingo. "Are you *another* cop? Are you the guy who chased him? He told me some dickhead guy came and chased him."

"I might be. Is he around?"

"It's about that girl. Those girls, I should say. The ones they found up there." She gestured with her head in the direction from where Bill had just come. "The cops have been all over the place here. They chase us out, and we come back, and then they chase us out again. It's been terrible."

"Where's Doug?"

The girl shook her head. "He hasn't been here. We're all here, but no Doug. Just pushy cops and us. He doesn't live here. He doesn't live anywhere." She gestured with her head again, this time in the other direction, off in the woods. "Sometimes he stays with a bitch over there. Sometimes he meets a woman in a bar and goes to her house. He comes here every so often, I guess. He's been acting sketchy lately. Different."

"How?"

"I don't know. Nervous. Something went down, right? Something he's in trouble for?"

"When was he last here?"

She shrugged. "A day ago, I guess. Maybe less. He passed through."

Bill played the beam across the girl's dirty feet and through the tent opening. "Does he keep stuff here?"

"Some."

"Like what? Can I look?"

"It's nothing. Just some bullshit he brought back."

Bill was already moving forward, coming up next to the woman and approaching the opening to the tent. He shone the light inside. "Then if it's just bullshit, he won't care, right?"

"He's going to be pissed if you fuck with anything," she said.

"Did the cops look through this tent?" Bill asked.

"No, they just shone their lights in our eyes and hassled us. What the fuck, man?"

It was all fruitless, he thought. Everything he tried, every idea he had, every gesture he made. Fruitless.

Would he ever see Summer alive again?

The woman pulled the sleeves of her sweater higher and placed her hands on her hips in a defiant posture. "You need to go. Just go."

Bill wiped his nose. His eyes darted around, looking for something. Anything.

They landed on the woman's wrist.

His eyes opened wider. "Shit." He reached for her arm.

"What are you doing, jerk?"

Bill didn't explain. He tugged on the bracelet on her arm, working against the woman to get it off her wrist.

"That hurts," she said, trying to pull back. "What do you want?"

Bill gripped the bracelet. He managed to slide it over the woman's hand, yanking it past her fingers and pulling it free.

"My daughter's," he said, the words coming out in huffs and puffs. "This bracelet belongs to my daughter."

CHAPTER SEVENTY-SIX

Bill held the flashlight in one hand, the bracelet in the other.

The woman was saying something, going on and on about Doug bringing the bracelet back and letting her wear it. But Bill felt like he was underwater, all sound and external stimuli muffled and hazy.

"Have you seen her?" Bill asked. "The girl this bracelet belongs to."

The pink-haired woman squinted a little, staring at Bill. "I'll tell you what I told the cops. No. Never. They asked me like fifty times." She looked at his hand. "What's the big deal about this stupid bracelet?"

Then Bill understood something else. "Wait a minute. . . . He just took this earlier this evening. He was here, sometime recently. He was here. You said he hadn't been here for a day."

"Okay, I lied. Sue me. It was before midnight, I guess. Before the cops started swarming. Then he left again."

Bill dropped to the ground and started pawing through the other items on the bottom of the tent. The ground was covered by a dirty blanket, and he rummaged through the loose items scattered around the small space.

"What are you doing?" the woman asked. "That's my stuff."

"I don't know," Bill said. But he kept looking. He dug through a pile of clothes in the corner. He felt the woman's hand on his shoulder, pulling him back.

"Hey, pervert. That's mine. Get out of it."

Her nails dug in like a cat's, and Bill winced in pain. He shook loose from her grip. "Where is he?"

"I don't know." She took a menacing step forward, raising her hand as though to strike. "Get out of here."

"Okay, okay." Bill took the bracelet with him and stepped out of the tent, brushing past the woman and trying to give her as wide a berth as possible. He shone the flashlight into the area to his left, aiming the beam deeper into the trees. Something moved there, a flash of a red jacket coming toward him. Bill lifted the beam, aiming for the figure's face. But he'd already recognized the jacket. He knew who it was: Doug Hammond.

Facing him that way, directly, for the first time, Bill noticed Hammond's short, compact body. Like a wrestler's. The flashlight showed the dinginess of his clothes, a smear of mud across his right cheek. His fingernails were caked with dirt, and the red jacket had a large rip under the left armpit. But Hammond gave off a sense of power and menace, like a long coiled spring ready to be released.

Hammond held his hands out in front of him. He looked to be somewhere in between asking for peace and getting ready to fight.

"Where is she?" Bill asked. "Just tell me where she is so I can go there. Or the police can. I don't care. I don't even care if you go to jail at this point. She's alive, isn't she? Just tell me she's alive and where she is."

"I don't know where she is."

"You're lying. You came into my house. You said you wanted to talk to me, but you killed my friend."

"He doesn't know anything," the woman with the pink hair said.

Bill didn't look over at her. He refused to take his eyes off Hammond.

"I've been shacking up with him off and on," she said. "He doesn't know."

"You have to listen to me." Hammond moved his hands again, and now there was no doubting that he was trying to ask for peace. For calm. "You seem too agitated. There's a wild look in your eye. I don't trust it. And I'm trying to help you."

"I told you how to help me." Bill tightened his hold on the flashlight and felt a pulse in his palm where skin met the rubberized grip.

"I went to your house to talk to you. Taylor came to town, telling the whole world, even you, that I took your daughter and killed Emily. What was I supposed to do? I'm a guy with a record. I needed someone to listen, to hear what I had to say. I figure the father of one of the victims would want to hear it. I get it—I do. Emily was like a daughter to me."

Bill took a step closer. A hot energy coursed through his body, the kind of thing he might feel if he were laid up with an illness—a nasty flu or infection that needed to work its way through his system and out.

Hammond took a step back. "Easy. If you help me, I can help you. I can't tell you where your daughter is, but I can tell you what I know. Just help me with the police—"

"The cops are all over," Bill said. "They'll probably be back soon. Maybe they're pulling into the lot up there now. So spill it."

"He's right, Doug," the woman said. "They're way up our asses tonight. Did you do something?"

Hammond's body remained tense and alert. His voice sounded arrogant. "You wanted to come out here and take care of this yourself. You're sick of the police, sick of their inability to solve the crime. You came alone with your flashlight and your weekend-hiker clothes."

"Let's just take care of this right now. Tell me. Where is Summer? Is she out here somewhere? Just take me to her and you'll be off the hook for anything else you've done."

Hammond started backing up. "I killed a man."

Bill hadn't made the conscious choice to do so, but he realized he'd raised the flashlight like a weapon. The beam illuminated the bare branches of the trees, and Hammond's figure became less distinct in the darkness.

Then two hands clamped down on the arm that held the flashlight. The pink-haired woman took hold of Bill and used her body weight for leverage, trying to force his arm down and shake the flashlight loose. Bill made a quick twisting motion with his upper body and managed to throw the woman off him. She thudded against the ground, making a sound like the air had been forced from her.

When Bill looked up, orienting himself back to what lay ahead, he saw Doug Hammond moving forward, his body in a low crouch, his hands coming up in the direction of Bill's neck.

Bill swung. The flashlight made a sickening smack against the crown of Hammond's skull, the vibration from the blow traveling up Bill's arm and into his shoulder.

Hammond dropped to all fours. For a moment he stayed like that, shaking his head as though trying to clear the effect of the blow he'd taken.

The woman made a wailing noise. She pushed herself up from the dirt and scrambled to Hammond, cupping his face in her hands and cooing to him. "Oh, he's bleeding. Oh, Doug. Oh, baby."

Bill dropped to the ground next to Doug. He reached around and took the man by the front of his jacket, pulling him out of the woman's grip.

"Hey," she said. "He's hurt."

Bill pulled Hammond closer, brought his face closer. "Where is she?"

The man's eyes were half-lidded, and a trickle of blood ran down his forehead.

"Where?" Bill asked. "Where?"

Then a jolt rocked Bill, the sharpest pain he'd ever felt in his life. It traveled from the base of his skull down into his chest.

His vision swam, the dark woods growing darker. He felt control of his body slipping away.

He saw the pink-haired woman standing over him. She held something in her hands. A bag? A sock?

She looked like she was about to bring it down again, when everything went black.

CHAPTER SEVENTY-SEVEN

Bill saw Summer. She walked toward him across a darkened horizon. Her figure was indistinct, but he recognized her.

And then Julia joined her.

They both walked toward him, holding hands. Their faces obscured.

Bill wanted to cry out. To call their names.

But he could make no sounds. His voice was muted, his throat incapable of doing anything.

The figures stopped and turned. They started walking away, receding over a hill and out of sight. Bill still couldn't make a noise.

He ended up standing alone. In blackness. A world without light. No sun, no electricity.

For a moment, he thought he must be in some version of hell.

He felt tired. He wanted to sleep, to drift off into the blackness and be done with it all.

But he couldn't. He knew he couldn't.

Then something cold and wet hit his face.

He tried to open his eyes, but just like the struggle to make a sound, the struggle to open his eyes led to failure. He couldn't open them. He wanted to slide back into the part of the dream in which Julia and Summer walked toward him.

He wanted a chance to make a sound again. This time he would. This time they wouldn't slip away from him.

Then the cold wetness hit his face again. He smelled dirt. Decaying leaves and the rocky ground underneath him. He reached up, wiping the liquid off his face.

"Quit faking it," a voice said. "Open your eyes."

Bill tried harder. The lids peeled open, and the reality of where he was landed on him with the force of a hammerblow.

His head hurt. A sharp ache like his skull had been split apart. He worried that maybe it had. He recalled that snapshot in time—the pink-haired woman standing over him with something raised above her head. Was it an old-fashioned sap? A sock filled with ball bearings or quarters? He lifted his hand and gingerly touched the top of his head. He felt a sticky wetness there and, bringing his hand forward, saw the blood. But not too much. Not as much as he thought—*feared*—he might see.

But the pain. It made him wince, made him close his eyes again.

"Open them."

Bill did. It took a moment to focus, but he saw the man in front of him. Doug Hammond.

Bill jerked his body, attempting to stand up, but he couldn't quite move. Something bound his feet together. He looked down and saw the crude ropes around his ankles. His hands were free, but he couldn't rise or fight or run with his feet tied together. And Doug Hammond sat next to him, the flashlight in his hand, making sure Bill didn't. In his groggy state, Bill wasn't sure he could do anything even if he weren't bound.

"Take it easy now," Hammond said. "We had to put you down. You wouldn't listen, and you wanted to fight. And fighting isn't going to do you any good right now. You'll just lose. Trust me, you'll lose. It isn't your arena, is it?"

"Where is she? Summer? Just tell me."

"Are you going to listen?"

Bill blinked his eyes. The coldness from the ground had seeped through his clothes and into the center of his body. "Okay. What do you have to say?"

Hammond appeared to relax a little. He lifted a hand and touched his own head. "You smacked me pretty good with this." He hefted the flashlight in his hand. "When Karen hit you with that sap, she wanted to hit you again. And, I have to be honest, I kind of wanted her to. I wanted to do some of the damage myself to your thick skull."

"Why didn't you?" Bill asked. "You killed my neighbor. Hell, I think you kidnapped my daughter. You beat those other two girls. Why not just throw me into the mix?"

Hammond shook his head. "See? You don't listen. You've been going around telling everybody I beat those girls, that I kidnapped your daughter. You let my ignorant ex-wife infect your mind. And what has it gotten you?"

"The cops will be back soon. They're looking for you. They might be pulling in right now."

Hammond looked disappointed. He pursed his lips and shook his head again. "And then you'd never know why I killed your neighbor. You'd never know what happened to your daughter."

CHAPTER SEVENTY-EIGHT

Bill started to squirm. He tried to jerk his body up, lifting his torso and pushing off the ground so he could come to his feet. But Hammond was right there. He placed his hand on Bill's chest and shoved him back down. Then Hammond reached into his own pocket and brought out the canister of pepper spray. Bill saw the locking mechanism was open, so it would only take one push on Hammond's part to hit him in the face with a stream of the burning liquid.

"Where are you going to go?" Hammond asked. "Even if you got away from me and called the police . . . then what? I'd be gone. Just like Karen is gone. And you'd be sitting somewhere, holding your pecker in your hand. Why don't you sit for a minute? Take a load off. And listen to what I have to tell you."

Bill saw no other way. His head swam a little. The ground seemed to lurch like he'd just stepped off a Tilt-A-Whirl. If he did get to his feet, how fast could he move?

And he wouldn't know anything Doug Hammond knew.

Bill relaxed his body, and Doug Hammond removed his hand from his chest.

"You're cool?" Hammond asked.

Bill nodded. He wasn't sure he could say anything right then. He wasn't sure he wanted to.

"Good. Good boy." Hammond leaned back, his posture relaxing as well. "I wanted to talk to you out here that day, and I wanted to talk to you at your house earlier because I wanted you to know what was really going on. I had to talk to Taylor first, to remind her that I'd never hurt Emily. Shit, I was a better parent in some ways than Taylor. I watched out for that girl. Bought her a car, paid for her braces. I had to calm Taylor down after everything she'd been saying about me. And then I figured the cops might be likely to listen to you if you knew the whole story, straight from me. They weren't going to listen to anything I said. I have a record, and Taylor had already poisoned their minds about me." He leaned closer. "Hell, you're the most sympathetic guy in the whole town, maybe the whole country."

Bill made a grunting noise deep in his throat. "Why'd you kill my neighbor? In my house?"

"I came to your house, looking for you. I went to the back door so it was less likely I'd be seen. I knocked and knocked. No answer. So I tried the knob. What do you know? The door was open."

"I locked it when I left. I always lock it. Especially now."

"Makes sense. Hell, I wondered about it at the time. I thought it was odd that the door was unlocked if you weren't home."

"But you went in anyway. Why?"

Hammond looked surprised. "Have you ever been hunted? Do you know what that's like? I couldn't go anywhere. To eat, to get a drink, to get a motel room. Why do you think I'm spending time out here? I can't go anywhere without worrying some cop is going to grab me. And once I got in their hands, with my past record and the dead guy in your house and with Emily missing or whatever, I'd be finished. The only reason I stayed was to talk to you. That's why I thought I'd wait. You have a nice house—you really do. Taylor told me about it."

"I just saw her. The police told her Emily is dead."

Hammond looked stricken. His mouth opened but no sound came out, and some of the color drained from his face. "Dead?"

"Yeah." For a moment, just a single moment, Bill felt bad for blurting out the news so callously to Hammond. But Bill figured he already knew. Bill figured he'd killed her. "They used dental records."

Hammond's eyes lost focus, looking past Bill into the darkness. "Taylor must be crushed. She loves that girl. And, look, I wouldn't hurt Emily."

"Why did you kill my neighbor?"

Hammond's eyes snapped back into focus. "Because I went into your house. I needed to use the bathroom while I waited, and I wanted to look around in case you were in there and hadn't heard me knocking. I went down the hallway, and when I came to the door of your daughter's room, I saw your neighbor, the flannel-wearing guy, standing in there, right in the center of the room, holding a stuffed bear and going through your daughter's chest of drawers."

CHAPTER SEVENTY-NINE

Bill was shaking his head. Back and forth, back and forth, until it made him woozy, and he stopped.

"No," he said, the word almost a gasp.

Hammond was nodding his own head, certain of what he was saying. "He saw me standing there, and you could tell by the look on his face he didn't expect to get caught that way. I mean, how does a guy explain that? A teenage girl goes missing, and some middle-aged guy shows up in her house going through her bedroom drawers? At minimum, he's a really creepy perv, taking things from a girl who disappeared. But at the very worst . . . he looks like he's guilty, right? He had that stuffed bear in his hand, and some clothes that belonged to your daughter. Why was he in there taking those things? Why?"

The cold from the ground had spread throughout Bill's body. It was no longer a physical thing. It penetrated his mind and his heart, turning everything about him to ice. "What did he say to you?"

"He looked like a kid with his hand in the cookie jar. He told me some bullshit about how he was watching the house for you, that he needed to check on things, and he wanted to make sure no one had taken anything from Summer's room while you were gone. What fifteen-year-old has a lot of valuables?"

"But you killed him."

"He came after me. He tried to lull me into a false sense of security. He tried to play it cool and just casually mention that he was going to call the police because I shouldn't be in there." Hammond paused, the look in his eyes distant as he replayed the moments leading up to Adam's death. "I could tell he was about to make a play. I can always tell when that's going to happen. I could tell you were about to hit me tonight, but I didn't want to hurt you. It was a good thing I had my backup here. She took you down harder than I would have."

"So what did you do to him?" Bill asked.

"I'll give him credit—he was a strong son of a bitch. I didn't think I'd be able to take him once it started." Hammond pulled up the sleeve of his jacket, revealing an ugly bruise and several scratches on his arm. "There are more on my body from where he hit me. It was a good battle. But you Mister Suburbans don't understand what it really means to fight, do you? Well, I do. And I got the best of him." Hammond's tone turned almost gleeful, as if he were recounting a winning touchdown. He patted his pocket. "I used my trusty sap. And I used it more than once. And I aimed to hurt, not just to slow down." He almost looked regretful. "Sorry for the mess."

"You should have called the police and told them."

"Didn't you hear what I said?" His voice rose, and he leaned in, jabbing an index finger in the vicinity of Bill's nose. "They'd bury me. Under the jail. They'd stick his murder and the beatings of those girls and your daughter on me." Hammond reached out again, and this time he placed his hand around Bill's throat, squeezing and adding pressure until Bill saw red spots before his eyes. "Do you know what it's like to have the cops choke the life out of you? To want to bury you? I bet you don't."

Bill reached up, grabbing hold of Hammond's hand and trying to force it away. He couldn't make it budge. But Hammond released his grip, allowing Bill to breathe freely again.

"You think it's all so fucking simple, don't you?" Hammond rose to his feet, but he pointed at Bill before he moved and spoke to him as if addressing a dog. "Be still." He reached down and dug around in the dead leaves and mulchy ground. He came up with the bracelet Bill had found in the tent. "I found this in that asshole's house. I went all through it, digging in every drawer and closet. Look, I needed money. I had to find something to sell, and, to be honest, I couldn't bring myself to steal from you. That's how I found out who your neighbor was. I checked his wallet. No cash, but I saw he lived behind you. So this is all you need to know to understand what your neighbor was up to. And you can do with it what you want. I'm leaving town for good now. It belongs to your daughter, right? It has her name engraved on the inside. I saw her name engraved there, so I took it. Jackpot."

"One bracelet doesn't prove anything," Bill said. "Summer went to Adam's house sometimes. We were friends. Maybe it fell off there sometime. . . ."

"I found this at the bottom of his bedroom drawer. Why would he have it there? A souvenir?"

Bill sputtered. "I don't know."

"And then why was he going through Summer's bedroom drawers? Why was he taking things from your house? Like the bear and some clothes? It sounds to me like he knew where she was. Maybe he was taking those things to her, wherever she is. Or else he was just obsessed with her. Either way, it isn't good, is it?"

CHAPTER EIGHTY

The sun was starting to rise, the bright rays reflecting off the windows of the hospital so that the building gleamed. Bill parked and eased out of the car. His head still ached. His ankles were sore from where Doug Hammond had bound him. He felt as if he'd been through a war. Not just out in the woods the night before, but during the days of Summer's being gone. He felt an emotional and physical toll that slowly wore down every cell in his body, weakening them, battering them. What would he have left when it was all over?

If it was ever over.

He went through the automatic doors, carrying the bracelet Doug Hammond had given him. True to his word, Hammond let him go, cutting the ropes that held his feet. And then Hammond disappeared into the woods, heading in the direction of the river, the same direction he'd traveled the day Bill fought with him.

He knew Bill wouldn't follow. He knew Bill would go and do exactly what Bill was doing.

"Sir?"

Bill walked toward the elevators. He didn't realize anyone was talking to him.

The nurse called out to him two more times before he stopped.

"Sir? Are you okay?"

Bill stared at the woman for a moment, not sure what she wanted.

"Sir? You have blood on the back of your head and your jacket. Are you injured? Were you looking for the emergency room?"

"Oh." Bill reached up with one hand and touched the back of his head. It felt tender, the pain still throbbing with every beat of his heart. But he didn't care. "I'm good."

The nurse looked puzzled. And a little scared. He could see she was trying to figure out what to do about him. Bill used her moment of uncertainty to his advantage. He jabbed the elevator button a few times, and when the doors slid open, he stepped inside.

The nurse raised her hand as though she wanted to say something else to Bill, to stop him from going on.

But Bill just thanked her and hit the button for the correct floor.

The door to Haley's room was closed. A lone security guard stood outside. No sign of Rich or Pastor Caleb. One nurse gave Bill a quick glance as he walked by, but she put her head down and continued with her work.

"Sir, are you a family member?" the guard asked.

"I am. Kind of. You've seen me here before, right?"

"You need to leave now," the guard said. He was a young guy, in his twenties, but his face looked soft and doughy like he was an overgrown toddler. "Only immediate family. You need the family's permission or the permission of the police now. The family is insisting today."

"That's just it," Bill said. "The police are on their way. Detective Hawkins. You know him, right?"

"Sir, if you could wait—"

Bill brushed past the guard and gently pushed the door open. The room was muffled and dark. The curtains were closed against the rising sun. In a recliner across the room, Candy slept, covered by a blanket. Her mouth hung open, and her breath came easy and regular. She didn't stir as Bill came in. No doubt Haley had been hassled by countless nurses and technicians and cops. People drawing blood, people asking questions.

Haley slept with her mouth slightly open as well, making her appear to be the younger double of her mother. Her face was still slightly discolored and swollen, but it was a far cry from what it had looked like when she'd first been brought to the hospital more than a week ago. A monitor tracked her heart rate through a clip attached to the end of her index finger.

Bill moved alongside the bed. His right hand fingered the object in his pocket, and for a brief moment, he wasn't exactly sure how to proceed. He needed to wake the girl up. He needed to hear from her.

And he knew that as soon as he did, the clock would start to tick. It would only be a matter of time before Candy had him kicked out.

Bill decided to act and act fast.

"Haley?" He started out just above a whisper. When the girl didn't budge, he said in a louder voice, "Haley?"

The girl rolled her head to one side, moving in the direction of his voice. Bill cut his glance at Candy, who hadn't stirred. Haley's eyes slowly came open, as if she was expecting to see someone from the hospital standing there. When she saw Bill, she jumped a little, her body jerking as she moved away from him.

Bill raised his hand. "It's okay. It's Bill Price. I need to talk to you."

Then the guard came through the door, walking with a shuffling gait. "Sir? I called the police."

"Good," Bill said. "I told you they're on their way."

Haley looked at the guard and then at Bill, starting at the top of his head. Judging by the look on her face, she'd seen blood there. He knew his face and clothes were dirty from being on the ground in the woods. He looked like a crazy man.

"Where's my mom?" Haley asked.

Bill nodded across the room. "She's there. But she's still asleep."

"Mom? Mom, can you hear me?"

"Wait—"

"Sir?" the guard said. "You need to leave this room."

"Shhh," Bill said.

Candy stirred. With the highly developed alertness of a mother, she sprang from the seat, throwing the blanket aside and opening her eyes, ready for anything. When she saw Bill, her mouth fell open, and a flush of color rose in her cheeks. She looked disbelieving. She couldn't seem to comprehend the audacity of his coming back to the room.

"Get out," she said, each word like a driven nail.

"Candy, just listen."

"Get out." She looked at the doughy-faced kid in the neatly pressed uniform. "Are you going to do something? Are you?"

"I called the police, ma'am."

"That's it?"

"Candy, I just need a minute," Bill said. "I found something out. And Hawkins is coming. He should be here soon. Very soon."

"Bill, you've lost it," Candy said. "This is all too much for you, and you've lost it. Now get out."

"I want Hawkins to hear all of this," Bill said. "We need him to. It's time." Bill turned to Haley, who sat in the bed, her eyes wide and a look of fear on her face. "It's time to hear from Haley what she knows about Adam Fleetwood and what he had to do with taking Summer."

CHAPTER EIGHTY-ONE

Candy came closer to the bed. She moved her eyes between Bill and her daughter, her face uncertain.

"What is this?" she asked, and it wasn't clear whether she was directing the question at Bill or Haley.

Haley didn't say anything. She looked like she wanted to jump out the window.

Bill stared at the girl. "I don't know if she can't remember everything that happened that day yet, or if she doesn't want to tell us, but we need to know for sure. If Summer's still alive . . . there isn't much time."

Candy's voice became insistent. "Leave her alone. You've already been in here harassing her once. What kind of bully are you, coming in here and badgering a young girl who's been through a trauma? Are you a monster?"

"I'm not sure," Bill said.

"And are you really asking about your neighbor?" Candy asked. "The one they're saying was murdered?"

"Yes. Him."

Candy came around the foot of the bed. She sidled up next to Bill and placed her arm around his back, pulling him closer to her body so they stood only inches apart. She smelled like sleep, her clothes in need of a good washing. "I know how hard this is for you, Bill. I've been through it. Remember, I went through days when I thought my baby was dead. I get it."

"I know."

"I think at some point we have to . . . I don't know, have the grace and wisdom to accept what is happening to us. To know there are things beyond our control, and those things are in the hands of something bigger than all of us. Like when Julia died. You had to learn to accept that because it was beyond you." She rubbed Bill's back, a gentle, rhythmic motion. "Someone beat those girls. Beat them until one of them died, and, by the grace of God, Haley lived. I fear . . . I just don't know what happened to Summer. But I think we have to be ready for the worst."

Bill pulled away from her grip. "I'm not there yet, Candy. And I'm not planning on getting there any time soon."

Candy looked hurt by Bill's sudden jerking away from her, like he'd slapped her. She shrugged, adjusting the sweater she wore, and returned to the other side of the bed. As she went she said, "You don't have to listen to this, honey. You don't have to be bullied here in your hospital bed." She turned to the guard again. "Do they pay you just to stand around?"

The kid looked confused. "My boss told me to call the police if there was real trouble. This looks like real trouble to me."

"Adam Fleetwood," Bill said to Haley, ignoring her mom. "I know you know him. He was my neighbor. He's the one who hurt you. Who hurt Summer. Right?"

Candy held out her hand. "No, you don't have to say anything. Just because there's a crazy man in our room, bothering you."

"Adam Fleetwood," Bill said again.

Candy waved her hand in the air over Haley's bed. "No. You do not have to talk to him."

Something about the way Candy spoke struck Bill. He turned his attention away from Haley and toward her mother. He leaned over Haley's bed, moving closer to Candy. "Do you know about this? Have you talked about it?"

"This is family business," Candy said. "Private."

"Private?"

"Mom," Haley said. "Mom!"

Her voice froze the adults in the room. They stopped arguing and looked down at the girl in the bed. Her eyes were full of tears, but her chin jutted out. She looked determined.

"I'm going to tell him, Mom. I'm going to tell him all of it."

CHAPTER EIGHTY-TWO

"Tell me," Bill said. "Tell me now."

Before Haley could say anything, while she still sat there with her eyes wide and her lip quivering, Detective Hawkins came into the room. Hawkins was dressed in a suit and tie, and he looked as if he hadn't slept for days. He came through the door with his body alert, his hands hanging loose at his sides as though he expected to be attacked. It took him a moment to absorb the scene—Bill and Candy on either side of Haley's bed. Haley with her eyes wide and on the brink of tears. The security guard stood next to Bill, his face visibly relieved at the presence of the detective.

Candy said, "Detective, he's harassing my daughter."

"He forced his way past me," the guard said, his voice barely above a whisper.

"She knows something, Detective. It's Adam Fleetwood. I found Hammond out in the park. He told me he killed Fleetwood, and he told me everything else."

Hawkins looked at the top of Bill's head, then trailed his eyes down his back. "You're bleeding," he said, his voice flat.

"I'm fine." Bill reached into his pocket and brought out the object he found on the woman's arm in the woods. The plain silver bracelet Julia bought for Summer on her thirteenth birthday. "This was deep in a drawer in Adam Fleetwood's house. Hammond found it after he killed Adam. He went through Adam's house, looking for money or a gun, anything he could sell. Fleetwood's gun was gone, wasn't it?"

"We didn't find it."

"Hammond took it. He probably pawned it." Bill held the bracelet in the air. "But look at this. Isn't this Summer's, Haley?"

He handed it over to the detective. Hawkins studied the bracelet by holding it at arm's length. "Is it hers, Haley?" he asked.

"I don't know why you have that," she said.

Hawkins turned the bracelet over as though examining a fine diamond. "Sure, it has Summer's name engraved on it. But how do you know Hammond got it from Fleetwood? He could have just said that."

"She never took it off," Bill said. "Once Julia died, she never took it off. Right, Haley? Did she ever let you wear it?"

Haley shook her head. "Never. She always wore it."

"Why would it be in Adam's house?" Bill asked. "Was Summer involved with Adam in some way? Did she spend time over there?"

Candy was shaking her head. "No. No. You're going to twist this all around. It's going to be made to look like Haley committed a crime when the real criminal is the man who did these things."

"Mom."

"It's true." She was shaking her head still, her arms wrapped tight around her body. "What are you going to do, Detective? Have a field day with this story? Spread it all over the media? It will only reflect badly on my daughter."

"And on you, maybe?" Bill asked.

Candy opened her mouth. "What are you implying?"

"If Adam took Summer and hurt Haley and did all of this, then there has to be a reason," Bill said. "It's time we knew the reason."

"She doesn't remember all of it yet," Candy said. She moved closer to the bed, reaching out with one hand and gently stroking Haley's arm. "It takes time. Little pieces have been coming back to her. Like a dream she can only remember a little at a time. Right, honey? And when it was time . . . when everything was right, I thought Haley could tell. But she has to get well first. She's been through something awful. We all have."

"She has to tell it now," Hawkins said. He turned and told the security guard to stand outside the door of Haley's room. "Don't let anyone in."

When the guard was gone and the door swung shut, Haley took her mom's hand. She licked her still-cracked lips and offered a forced smile. "It's okay, Mom. It's time to get it out." Then she turned and looked at Bill. "I think I remember what happened that day. Most of the big pieces of it." She swallowed and wiped a tear away. "I'm just afraid of what it will make me look like. I know the whole town . . . the whole world is going to know."

CHAPTER EIGHTY-THREE

"Tell us now," Bill said.

Hawkins held his hand out toward Bill, a gesture that said, *Calm down. Easy.*

Bill swallowed hard, biting back on his anger. He knew Hawkins was right. He knew he had to restrain himself. Even if it felt like it was killing him.

Haley's chin quivered. Then she let out a long sigh before she spoke. "We were messing around. Adam and me. We did it for about six weeks, but it ended about two weeks before . . . before everything went wrong." She looked at Bill. "I came over to your house once, to meet Summer, but nobody was home. I texted her, and she was out. She forgot I was coming over or something." She looked down at her hands, which were folded on top of the bedclothes. She took in the plastic hospital bracelet around her wrist and the healing scratches and bruises on her hands from where she fought back. "I waited on your back porch because it was kind of warm out, and he came over and started talking to me. Eventually he asked me if I wanted to wait in his house. It started then."

Bill lifted his eyes and looked at Candy. She was looking away, a vein pulsing in her neck, her jaw set hard. He understood. He wouldn't have wanted to hear it either. He feared he might be in the same position soon enough.

"Why did the relationship end right before the attack?" Hawkins asked.

Haley said, "I got the feeling the whole time he and I were . . . dating or whatever that he really wasn't that into me. Not as much as I wanted him to be." She looked up at the detective, her eyes shiny. "He talked about Summer more than about me. More than anyone else, just about. I think he wished he were with her and not with me, that she had been the girl he had started something with."

"Did he say that to you?" Hawkins asked.

"No, but he just . . . Well, you can tell when a guy is really into someone else. Right?"

"So what happened the day Adam attacked you?" Hawkins asked.

Haley's face froze. Her mouth was slightly open, her eyebrows raised. "He didn't attack us. Not me. Adam didn't have anything to do with it."

"Who did, then?" Hawkins asked. "Have you remembered more?"

Haley closed her eyes. She reached up, the hospital bracelet sliding on her wrist, and placed her hand on her forehead as though something ached. She rubbed, the tips of her fingers pressing against the skin and moving it around.

"Do you know?" Bill asked.

"Give her a minute," Candy said, her voice a harsh whisper.

"We were going to see Clinton and Todd that day. We were going just to hang out with them." She winced as she seemed to be remembering something. "It was just supposed to be a normal day. Just hanging out. Drinking, for sure. I don't know."

They all stood there attentively, a roomful of adults, standing around the bed of a battered teenage girl, waiting for the next words to come falling out of her mouth.

If there were words to come. If the memories were there.

When Haley opened her eyes and spoke again, after what felt to Bill like an hour but was likely closer to ninety seconds, they all listened while she poured out her fractured memory of that day. Haley told them that she and Summer set out from Bill's house with every intention of meeting up with the boys from school. It was cold, and they wore heavy coats, but they were only walking two miles to a new subdivision being built. Todd's dad installed plumbing fixtures in the newly constructed houses, and the kids sometimes went there to drink and party where no one was likely to see them.

Haley claimed there was nothing unusual about the day. But she admitted that Summer had been acting somewhat unusual in the weeks leading up to the attack.

"Unusual how?" Hawkins asked.

"I knew it was her mom's birthday right around then," Haley said. "And she was just moody and distracted. She talked about the things they wouldn't get to do together."

"Like go on the sixteenth-birthday trip?" Bill asked.

"Oh, yeah," Haley said. "She mentioned that once. I didn't know what to do for her. I just tried to be around her, you know, just be a friend for her."

Haley went on to say that Summer seemed distracted again as they walked out to the new subdivision. She wasn't saying much. She walked with her head down, like some heavy weight was pressing on her shoulders. Haley almost asked her if she wanted to turn back or go somewhere else. She knew there would be drinking with the boys and maybe even the expectation of more than drinking. She told

Summer to just go to the mall or a movie or to just go sit at her house and do nothing if she wanted—

But Summer never had the chance to answer because a car pulled alongside of them as they walked.

"And they grabbed you?" Bill asked.

"No," Haley said. "Not that. Not that at all." Some of the energy and life drained out of Haley's face. Her eyes closed again, and Bill hated to see the finality of that gesture, as though the closing lids were extinguishing his view of his last glimmer of hope.

"She's fading," Candy said.

Bill moved closer. "Who was in the car?"

"Bill—"

Haley's eyes opened. Slowly. But they opened.

"It was a girl. That girl who sometimes hung out with some of the guys from school." She rubbed her forehead again, kneading her fingertips into the skin. It looked painful to Bill, like she was hurting herself. "She worked at . . . I can't remember. A restaurant like McDonald's or something. And they met her there. She's older, maybe."

"Emily Kress?" Bill asked.

Haley's eyes opened wide. "Emily. Yeah, that's her name. Emily. Blond and kind of short. She picked me up that day and took me to the house where the guys were."

"Why was she hanging around with high school kids?" Hawkins asked.

"They became friends wherever she worked. Clinton was really pushy, really confident. He'd talk to any girl. He wasn't afraid of anything. Emily partied with those guys. They drank together and everything. It made Clinton feel like a big man to have an older girl around."

"You said she picked you up?" Hawkins asked. "Or picked both of you up?"

Haley started shaking her head, her eyes distant as more of the memories came back. "Me. She picked *me* up."

"You said Summer was with you," Bill said. "You just told us that. Where was Summer?"

Haley continued to move her head, back and forth. Back and forth, her eyes seeing something only she could see. "She didn't get in the car. She decided not to go." She stopped moving her head and fixed her gaze on Bill. "She said she was heading toward home. To do something she had to do."

Every eye in the room turned toward Bill. It was like getting hit by a thousand spotlights. "What did she have to do?" he asked.

"I don't know," Haley said. "She didn't say. Or I don't remember."

Bill's skin prickled under the room's watchful eyes. He turned to Hawkins. "Maybe that elderly witness was right. Maybe that man did see her walking that way. Toward home."

"Did the two of you switch jackets that day?" Hawkins asked.

Haley's face scrunched. "Yeah, maybe." Her face remained frozen in an exaggerated mask of concentration. "Yeah. She was wearing that orange one, the one she didn't really like. And we switched because she liked mine better. The gray one. She always liked that jacket."

Hawkins nodded, then asked Haley, his voice gentle, "Did you see Summer again that day, Haley? Did she come to the house later? Did you maybe see her somewhere else?"

"Can I get some water, Mom?"

Candy lifted the plastic cup, angling the straw into the corner of Haley's mouth. She took several long pulls, her neck muscles contracting. She nodded at Candy, who took the straw away, reaching out with her other hand to wipe a drop of water off the corner of Haley's mouth. Candy looked around the room at the gathered men, her eyes nervously expectant.

"I don't think I saw her, no," Haley said. She wiped at her lips. "I really don't think I did."

Cold air blew on the back of Bill's neck, like the air-conditioning was running, even though it was only late February. He shivered.

Hawkins's voice remained low and calm as he asked, "So what happened to you that day? Who hurt you?"

Haley swallowed again, with the same force she'd used to take in the water. Bill waited with everyone else. Even though Summer was apparently not around for the attack, he still wanted to know. He needed to know something, some answer that completed one of these mysteries.

Haley told them she and Emily were at the unfinished house, a structure with walls and windows but no drywall, no plumbing. They were protected from the wind but not the cold, and the boys had a bottle of whiskey taken from somebody's parents. Yes, Haley said, she did a few shots with them as the bottle was passed around. The liquor felt warm in her body, even as the strong taste made her feel a little sick.

"I don't really know what went wrong," Haley said. "Everyone was having fun. I thought so, anyway. But then Clinton brought up that stupid contest they're having." She looked around the room, her eyes half-lidded. "Did you all know about that?"

Hawkins nodded on behalf of the adults. "We do."

Haley told them about an item on the checklist, one that Clinton and Todd kept bringing up that day: sex with a woman who was not a high school student. Haley could tell they had it in mind to check it off their list, and they kept trying to get everyone to drink more and more.

"Something went wrong. I can't really say what. It's like . . . It's like there's a black spot in my mind sometimes. But they did something to Emily she didn't want them to do. She told them no, that she was going to leave. She said no. I heard her. Maybe . . . Maybe she even called them something. She insulted them, said they were just little boys. I'm pretty sure she called Clinton a fag. It turned bad then. They started fighting."

"Who did?" Hawkins asked.

"Clinton. Todd. Emily. They tried to force her, you know. Clinton—it was like he wasn't normal, like he was possessed or something. He was so angry. I tried to talk to him, to calm him down, but he wouldn't. He scared me. He just started swinging."

"And you?" Candy asked. "Did they force you—"

"Clinton just kept swinging and swinging. I wanted to protect Emily—I know that. I think Todd might have . . . might have tried to stop him too. I think Clinton swung at Todd at one point. I wanted to help, but . . . I woke up here. I was really cold at some point. Really, really cold. I don't know how I got to the park. I don't know how I got here."

"Why was Summer's bracelet in Adam's house?" Hawkins asked, his voice carefully controlled. "Was there something going on between the two of them? Some reason it would be in there?"

"I don't know," she said, her voice weak. "Adam's house? I . . ."

"Why was it there?" Hawkins asked.

"I don't know. Summer left that day. She started toward home . . ."

"So maybe she was heading for Adam's," Bill said, his voice just above a whisper. "Why was she going there?"

Haley shook her head. "I don't know. I just thought she was going home."

Then everything was silent in the room. Candy came over and slid into the bed next to her daughter, pulling her close. Haley rested her head against her mother's body, her already-young face made instantly younger. Candy kissed the top of the girl's head, and Bill felt like an intruder on the intimate scene.

Hawkins apparently did as well. He cleared his throat. "Well . . ."

Haley perked up. "Do you really not know where Summer is?"

"Not yet," Hawkins said.

She turned to her mom. "I wish I hadn't let her leave that day. If I'd just gone with her, wherever she went. She just kept talking about her mom dying. She talked about it more right before that day than the whole year before. Mom, why didn't I go with her?"

"Shhh. You didn't know. You didn't do anything wrong."

Bill followed Hawkins to the door, but he stopped before he exited.

"Your mom's right, Haley. You didn't do anything wrong. In fact, you tried to save Emily. That's really something. Really."

Haley started crying, burying her face in Candy's chest.

Bill left the room.

CHAPTER EIGHTY-FOUR

"Do you believe that?" Bill asked in the hallway. He realized he'd shouted, so he lowered his voice when he said, "I mean it. Do you?"

"I'm not ruling it out," Hawkins said. "We've got one girl's fuzzy recollections. And you've got Hammond's story of going into your house, finding Adam, and then finding the bracelet at Fleetwood's. I'd like more, but it's a pretty good start."

An ache formed in Bill's chest. It grew into a stabbing pain. He looked at the hallway—the white walls, the bright lights—heard the incessant ringing of phones and beeping of monitors.

Bill took a step back and sank into a chair. Beads of sweat popped out on his head.

Hawkins said, "Are you okay, Bill? You look sick."

"I am sick." Bill wiped his forehead, the tips of his fingers coming away wet.

"I'll get a nurse."

"No, not that." Hawkins remained standing in front of Bill, looking down at him, hands on hips. "I was wrong about everything."

"We've all been trying to get it right."

"No. It's more than that. You're a cop. You went where the evidence took you. You did your best."

"I tried to."

"But me . . . I'm her father." He rubbed his forehead again. His skin felt hot and feverish. "I let that man into our lives. I befriended him. He had a key to our house. I trusted him . . . with everything. I didn't see any of this going on with Haley or Summer."

Hawkins bent down a little, his big face coming closer to Bill's. "You can't protect a child from everything. You just can't. And you're a single parent. So is Candy."

"But right in my backyard. Literally."

"Don't let your mind work too fast. Bill—"

"And Doug Hammond. I wanted to kill him, Detective. I did. I think I went out there to the woods tonight because I wanted to kill him. To hurt him. When I hit him with that flashlight . . . I wished I'd hit him harder. I wanted to hit him again and again." Bill could feel the blow, the shiver that went up his arm when the flashlight made contact with Doug Hammond's skull. It scared Bill, yes. But it satisfied him. He liked hurting the man he thought had hurt Summer. If Hammond hadn't got the better of him, if the girl with the pink hair hadn't disabled him with the sap, Bill couldn't say what he might have done. And not being certain about that made him feel sicker, sadder. "He was innocent of what I thought he'd done. If I'd hurt him, we wouldn't know what we know now. He really was helping. I think he cared about me because I'm a dad. Because he was distraught over what happened to Emily."

"He's not innocent, though," Hawkins said.

"How do you know that?"

"Because nobody is." Hawkins straightened up. "You're going to have time to beat yourself up soon enough. I hope you have a lot of years to do it. I really do. But right now we've got other things to think about. Okay?"

Bill shook his head. "Adam's dead. And if he did it, and if Summer is still alive somewhere . . ."

"Let's get going," Hawkins said.

CHAPTER EIGHTY-FIVE

Bill wasn't certain which way to go.

He asked Hawkins if the police intended to search Adam's house again, and to make sure to look in the attic and the crawl space and every nook and corner of the basement. And Hawkins promised they would, that a team was already on its way to Adam's house with the sole purpose of going over everything.

"We know what we're looking for now," Hawkins said. "We can hope for some DNA evidence, if Haley's story checks out all the way."

"And I suppose you'll be searching the park again?" Bill asked. "You know there are caves out there, hidden overhangs, and rock formations. If he wanted to hide someone . . . Adam was outdoorsy. He liked to camp and hike."

Hawkins was nodding. "We're going to hit the park again. We've been through there before, many times, but it can't hurt to do it again." He rubbed his chin. "We're going to have to call in other agencies. Firemen, paramedics. Maybe the National Guard can help. Or Fort Campbell. Volunteers." He shook his head, still rubbing his chin. "There's a lot of ground to cover."

"And not much time, right? Even if Adam took her and kept her alive, she'd be alone now."

"But we can't assume it was Adam Fleetwood," Hawkins said. "We're going to look into that, but we don't have a slam-dunk case against him, not by a long shot."

"Yeah, right. I'm having a hard time accepting all of this myself. Maybe she was walking toward home and maybe some other maniac took her."

"Right."

And both men understood the ticking clock they were dealing with. If Summer was alive somewhere, she was alone. Untended. Eventually the time would run out.

"Keep thinking the best," Hawkins said. "I'll stay in touch."

He left the hospital. And Bill felt very alone. Like a spectator to the events of his own life.

As Bill was walking through the lobby, intending to head home and clean himself up, his phone rang. When he read the name on the screen, a true feeling of warmth passed through him, the first really good feeling he'd had that day. He sat down on a couch in the lobby and took the call.

"Hey, Paige."

"Where the hell are you? Are you okay?"

"I'm at the hospital."

"Are you hurt? Bill, Mom and Dad are gone. And Summer . . . I don't want to lose you. I can't bear it. How are you? Just tell me."

"Whoa. I'm okay, Paige. I'm okay, I promise." People passed in front of Bill. Some of them carried bouquets of flowers, on their way to visit a sick relative or friend. Bill felt for them all, the uncertainty they might be facing. The fear of the unknown. That was worse than grief, worse than loss. He felt grateful for the sound of Paige's voice.

It tethered him to the world. A world of hope. "I'm not hurt. I came here to see Haley."

"Stay put."

"What do you mean?"

"I'm here. In Jakesville."

"What? Why?"

"Why do you think, dumbass? You left me that message. It sounded like a suicide note, like something Grandpa would have written to Grandma before he landed at Normandy. I got in the car and started driving. I told Kyle he had to handle the kids again. You needed me."

For a moment, Bill couldn't say anything. He watched more people go by, listened to the ding of the elevator. A couple emerged, the woman in a wheelchair being pushed by a nurse, the man carrying a car seat with a newborn in it. They looked happy. And scared. Bill remembered that day well.

"I didn't expect you to come, Paige."

"Well, I did. I'm just getting into town. I'm going right by the hospital. Where are you? Haley's room?"

"I'm in the lobby."

"Don't move." A silence fell over the line, and Bill thought the call was lost or Paige had hung up. But then she said, "I want to see you right away. I want to know your big, dumb, stupid, big-brother self is okay."

So Bill didn't move. He listened to his sister and stayed put.

CHAPTER EIGHTY-SIX

Paige gave Bill a hug. She sat down next to him on the small couch in the lobby and pulled him close to her. Bill gave in to the embrace, allowing himself to be wrapped in his sister's arms. He didn't care about the people walking by and looking, people who probably assumed that one of their loved ones had just died, leaving them to comfort each other in the public space of a hospital.

It felt good to have her there. When he'd called Paige, he hadn't intended for her to show up. Bill simply didn't want to have unresolved business with anybody else in his life. There'd been enough of that. Too many things left unsaid. Too many of the wrong things said at the wrong time. He didn't want anything bad with Paige.

When they finally let each other go, Paige looked him over. "You're filthy. You look like shit. And there's blood on your coat."

"I know. I was going home to get cleaned up."

"You said you weren't hurt, you jerk. What is this?"

Bill made a sound in his throat, something between a choke and a laugh. "There's so much to tell you."

"Do you want to go home now?" She reached over and ran her hand over the back of Bill's. "I can drive."

But Bill wasn't looking at his sister. He was staring up at a sign he'd noticed when he first came down from outside Haley's room. He'd seen the sign almost every time he'd come to the hospital, and in the darkest times of sitting vigil by what he thought was Summer's bedside, he'd found himself drawn to that place. But he always resisted.

Until right then, with Paige at his side.

"Would you go somewhere with me?" he asked.

The chapel was hushed and silent. It could seat about fifty people in two rows of pews separated by a center aisle, and multicolored stained glass windows decorated the back, behind the small altar. The place was empty.

Bill whispered anyway. "Let's sit down."

They sat near the aisle about halfway up. Bill recognized the look Paige was giving him. It said, *What the hell are you up to?* Except he suspected she didn't want to say anything out loud for fear of breaking the spell and driving Bill out of the chapel forever.

"Can we just sit for a minute?" Bill said. "It's kind of nice being somewhere quiet."

Paige nodded. As usual, she wore her hair piled on top of her head, and her Ohio State sweatshirt looked like she'd pulled it out of the dirty laundry. He checked his watch. Given the distance she'd had to drive, Bill knew she must have hit the road well before the sun came up, leaving everything behind to be with him. He couldn't have put his gratitude into words.

Bill stared forward, studying the multicolored window panels, the intricacy of the designs, and considered the patience and care that went into making them.

"I almost killed someone last night," he said.

Paige didn't ask any follow-up questions or press him. She sat still, her hands folded in her lap. Her quiet, settled posture encouraged him to go on. Bill had told her only the most cursory details of the night, focusing on the most important one as far as he was concerned—the boys had apparently killed Emily and had beaten Haley nearly to death.

"My God. I want to say I can't believe two high school boys would do that."

"But?"

"But I think they're capable of anything. You were right to call attention to Clinton breaking that kid's jaw. He sounds like a maniac."

"Yeah. And they're not our biggest concern."

Adam had possibly done something—something unknown—with Summer. "That man who I thought did it. Doug Hammond. I wanted to hurt him, Paige. I wanted to hurt him so bad. I wanted to beat him." He swallowed. "Can I make an absurd comparison?"

She nodded silently.

"It was like the time I hit you with the stick—it really was. I was so unreasonably angry over something being taken away from me that I didn't know any other way to solve the problem. I just wanted to lash out. I just wanted to hurt him. Like I wanted to hurt you that day."

"I'd say your daughter is more important than a bike. I'd say hitting that man was justified. He did kill someone."

"He *may* have killed the man who hurt Summer. He's the same as me. In fact, I'm worse. He was acting in self-defense."

"If he's telling the truth about Adam. We don't know for sure, do we?"

"Paige, if I'd killed that man tonight, if I'd killed Doug Hammond out there in the woods, then we'd have never known what happened to Summer. She'd be missing, and we'd all assume Hammond did it. I could have ruined any chance of ever really knowing the truth about Adam, whatever it might be. No, we're not sure about him, but how else do you explain all of these things? He seems to be in the middle of a lot."

"Oh, Bill." Paige scooted closer and took his hand in hers. "You're a father. You did what you thought was right. Don't beat yourself up over it now. It ended up working out, and that's what matters."

"What kind of father was I?" he asked. "I didn't pick up on what might have been going on with Adam. I didn't see it because he was my friend. I trusted one wrong man and wanted to hurt another one." He leaned forward, resting his elbows on his knees and placing his head in his hands. "My judgment was so wrong. So very, very wrong."

"You were taken in by him," she said. "You were taken in by his friendliness and his macho, hale-fellow-well-met bullshit." She shivered. "I was taken in by it, just seeing him out in the yard, lifting bags of mulch or digging with his shovel. Men and women are attracted to phony he-men like that."

"Yeah. I trusted him with my house. My wife. I would have trusted him to do right by Summer. Hell, we talked about going into business together. I fell for it all, and he could have hurt Summer. Even that possibility makes me crazy."

Paige let him sit like that for a long time. Staring ahead, focusing on nothing but his own guilt and misery. After a while, she placed her hand on his back, rubbing it gently. The gesture felt odd. All the physical contact between them felt awkward. They weren't an affectionate family. As a rule, they weren't huggers.

"Do you want to pray?" Paige asked.

"No."

"Do you mind if I pray? If you do, we can just leave. But I figure since we're here . . ."

Bill nodded. "Sure. Whatever you want."

Paige bowed her head and closed her eyes. Bill couldn't bring himself to do either, so he sat and waited. When Paige was finished, she crossed herself.

"Did you pray that we find Summer?" he asked.

"I did." She patted his knee. "And I prayed for you. That you find peace."

"You know who would think this scene was funny?" Bill asked.

"Who?"

"Mom and Dad. Here we are, the girl who hated church praying for her older brother."

"Who was always the favorite."

"So you say."

"I know." Paige stood up. "Come on, let's go home and get you cleaned off."

CHAPTER EIGHTY-SEVEN

When they arrived, they saw the police at Adam's house. Uniformed officers and technicians were out in the yard, prodding the grass and poking in the compost pile. Bill's stomach rolled when he understood what they were looking for.

A body.

All that digging Adam did in his yard. All the churning of compost, the spreading of mulch and dirt. Bill stood in the driveway for a moment, staring at Adam's property, but then he turned and headed inside. He didn't really want to know, didn't really want to see them pull something out of there.

Could it have all been going on right there?

Could Adam have been that ballsy? Could his daughter be buried so close?

Bill showered, gingerly washing the cut on the back of his head. It felt good to be clean, to wash the blood away. He dressed in fresh clothes and came out of the bedroom to find Paige making food. She'd pulled one of the casseroles out of the oven, something delivered to the house when the world thought Summer was dead. The sight of the steaming plate reminded Bill how hungry he was.

"Thanks," he said as they sat at the table.

But before they dug in, Paige stood up. She closed the blinds on the kitchen windows and the back door, anything that afforded a view of Adam's house. Then she sat down again.

"How long do you think that will go on?" Bill asked.

"They're leaving now. Haven't they already searched the place?"

"Yeah. But they weren't looking for . . . God, I can't even say it, Paige. I can't even think about what they're looking for back there."

"I'm sure there's nothing to be found back there. If he came to get that bear, like you said." She pointed at his plate. "Eat, Bill. You'll feel better."

So he ate. After a few minutes of silent chewing, Paige asked, "Did you see any signs that Adam was up to something? Maybe it seemed like his life was falling apart."

"We're dudes, Paige. We didn't bare our souls to each other."

She made a grunt of frustration. "Maybe it would have been better if you had."

"His life looked good to me, okay? Normal. A good-looking guy with a nice job. How did I know what might have been underneath it?"

Paige shuddered. "That's frightening." She laid her fork down and took a long drink of water. "I wanted to ask you about something you said at the hospital."

"Yeah? What about? My willingness to be in the chapel?"

"Not that." She shook her head. "You said something about going into business with Adam. What's that all about? You never mentioned it to me. Not that we talk all the time or are best friends or anything."

Bill pushed his plate away. "He had a friend who wanted to take over this self-storage place. It had gone bankrupt, a big mess, but they were trying to revive it and needed investors. . . ." Bill felt a tingling at the back of his neck. A chill ran up both arms, his skin contracting as it broke out in gooseflesh. "I guess some people still had stuff there. And some just . . ."

Paige leaned forward. "What's wrong? Your face just went gray. What is it?"

"They're searching Adam's house. They're searching in the woods where the girls were found. But they haven't said anything about the storage units. No one ever bought the place. It's just chained up and vacant."

"Bill?"

He was up off the couch. "I'm going."

"Bill? Call the police."

"I'll call on the way." He grabbed his keys and tugged on the back door, fumbling with the lock and yanking on the door until it pulled free. "You call."

"Wait." Paige grabbed her shoes and pulled them on, hopping as she moved across the room. "I'm coming."

Bill jumped into the car and started it as Paige climbed in the other side. He pulled away with the passenger door hanging wide open.

"Bill? Jesus."

"Call Hawkins."

"I don't have my phone."

He tossed her his. It landed in her lap.

"Call him. Tell him where we're going. Sure-Lock Self-Storage on Old High Springs Road. He'll know it."

Paige dialed as Bill drove.

He felt like every cell in his body was activated and his brain was burning. The car bounded out of the driveway, bottoming out as it turned onto the road, the momentum swinging Bill to the right and Paige against the passenger-side door.

"Ow," she said.

"Call him."

"I will if you don't kill us."

Bill accelerated up the street, ignoring the speed limit signs that said twenty-five miles per hour. He made two turns, emerging from the subdivision onto State Road Nine. He could go forty-five there and then fifty-five, so he sped up, faster and faster.

"It's voice mail," Paige said.

"Forget it. Call nine-one-one. They'll find him. Those cops are nearby"

Paige dialed. Bill watched the road. His body bounced in the seat. He tried to will the car to go faster, to use his mental and physical energy to make it move. He passed one car, crossing the double yellow line to do so.

"Come on, come on," he said.

And he tried not to think of what they might find there. He'd seen the cops in Adam's yard, looking for a body. It was a recovery effort as much as a search effort. And Bill understood the difference. Did he want to be the one to find his daughter's body?

But what if they found nothing? What if it was another dead end?

"It can't be," he said.

"What?"

"Did you call?"

"It's ringing."

It can't be, Bill thought. *If it's another dead end, I might break right there like glass shattered on rocks. It can't be another dead end.*

"This is about the Summer Price case. You need to send help to the Sure-Lock Self-Storage business on Old High Springs Road. It's an emergency." Pause. "Yes, someone might be hurt."

"They *are* hurt," Bill said.

"They *are* hurt. A girl is in danger. Summer Price. Tell Detective

Hawkins. He's running the case or whatever. Just send cops to that place. Summer Price might be there." Pause. "I'm her aunt. I'm with her father. Could you just do it? Please?"

Bill made the turn onto Old High Springs Road. The light was green. He cut the wheel, hard, tilting both of them to the left, making it feel like the car was going to go up on two wheels. A movie stunt.

"It's right up there," he said.

"Yes, please hurry," Paige said into the phone. "Send anyone you can find. Anyone."

Bill slowed a little when he saw the sign out front. He turned the car hard again, cutting across the oncoming traffic and drawing an angry honk from another driver.

"Jesus, Bill."

They pulled up the drive and found themselves face-to-face with an eight-foot-high chain-link fence. The fence was topped with razor wire, and the little box next to the entrance, the one a customer would use to enter the pass code, was hanging by some wires. It looked like a kid had taken a few good whacks at it with a baseball bat.

"No. No." Bill pounded the wheel. "No."

"The cops will be able to get in. They'll have bolt cutters or something. Or we could get out and look for a hole in the fence—"

"No." Bill threw the car into reverse. He backed up as far as the entrance from the road. "Hang on."

"Bill . . ."

"Just hang on."

Bill slammed his foot against the floor. The rear tires spun, and then the car shot forward.

CHAPTER EIGHTY-EIGHT

The car smashed through the gate.

The collision was louder than Bill imagined it would be. It sounded like he'd hit another car, the concussion filling the cabin and the impact rocking them in their seat belts. The gates flew back, ricocheting off the front and sides of the car. Paige let out a low gasp, and Bill shouted a triumphant yell. The moment the car hit the gates, something opened inside of him. He felt a release, a freedom he hadn't expected.

He felt like he was almost there.

When they were through, Bill hit the brakes, skidding to a stop. The storage units looked like garages with large doors that slid up on tracks. There appeared to be about one hundred of the units in total, five rows of twenty running back from the entrance Bill had just smashed through. Enough space existed between the rows of units to drive a car, but Bill decided driving wasn't the best way to search. They needed to be on foot. To be fast and loose. And able to hear.

"I'm getting out. You too. Start at the back and walk up and down the rows. Call her name and listen."

"But she might not be able to answer," Paige said.

"I'm well aware of that. Open the doors if you can. Look inside."

"But, Bill, what if . . ."

"I don't care, Paige. How could finally seeing her dead be worse than anything else we've already been through?"

Bill stepped out. The asphalt drive was cracked, weeds and long grass pushing through. The wind had blown litter against the fence and the doors of the units. Loose paper and plastic bags and soda bottles and cigarette packs. All the shit assholes threw out the window and never thought about again, what they let go out into the world so that someone else could worry about it or clean it up later.

Bill pointed to the first row. "These are back-to-back. I'll take this side, and you take the other. We'll keep doing that, okay?"

"Sure." Paige pulled her hood up, blocking the wind. "If you hear me scream, come running."

"I will."

Bill hustled down the row. Many of the units were still locked, but some had been thrown open. He pounded on the locked doors and called Summer's name, listening through the wind and the traffic noises for any sign of his daughter. He quickly came to a closed door without a lock. Bill bent down, grabbing the handle, but before he threw the door up, he closed his eyes for just a moment, bracing himself for what he might see.

But when the door was up and the fading light from the outside leaked in, he saw a mostly empty room. Only a stack of old newspapers and a TV with a smashed screen sat in the corner. He found three more doors he could open, and his trepidation lessened each time. But none of them contained anything noteworthy. Just junk and more junk, stuff people didn't even take the time to move out when the business went belly up.

He went around the end of the row and turned the corner into the next aisle. Paige was three-quarters of the way down. He watched her flip a door open and step back, peering into the darkened space. Bill walked toward her.

"Have you seen anything?" he asked.

"A lot of crap."

"Heard anything?"

"I heard you opening doors. I heard the wind." She reached up and wiped her nose. She threw open the door of another unit. "Nothing here."

"Someone was here," Bill said. "It smells like piss."

"Homeless people, maybe."

"Maybe," Bill said. "Do you want me to do this side while you go around?"

"Sure. I wish I'd brought my rape whistle. Or a gun."

"You saw that gate," Bill said. "Before we smashed it, no one could get in."

"Let's hope not." She went around the end of the row to the next aisle.

Bill went to work opening more doors, calling Summer's name.

Then he heard something. The tiniest little voice. The wind had picked up, so he had to tilt his head to hear, craning it in the direction he thought he'd heard the voice coming from.

Then he heard it again. His name being called by Paige.

He ran, following her path around the end of the unit and into the next driveway. Paige stood in the middle of the road, her arms down at her sides. Bill came up next to her, not seeing what had frozen her in place.

"That bike," she said.

Paige pointed forward where a red Cannondale road bike leaned against one of the unit doors.

"So?"

"It's pretty new. Look at it. A brand-new bike amid all this junk. And it's just leaning there, outside that door. Bill, why is it here?"

Bill's heart started to double-time. "Probably just kids."

"You just said it's tough to get in. Did they ride their bike over the fence?"

"Maybe there's a hole in back. Maybe it's been there for years."

But he knew that wasn't true. Paige was right. It was a brand-new bike. The kind of bike that spent its time in a garage at a nice, safe house.

He started toward the unit where the bike was parked. The wind swirled between the buildings, kicking up grit and paper and rattling some of the doors that weren't locked. Paige walked behind him, her presence comforting. He tried not to make any noise that would startle whoever was there. He trod lightly, but if someone was behind one of those doors with the wind blowing, he doubted they could hear him coming. Even the sound of the car crashing through the gate may have been distant and faint, chalked up to vehicle noise on the road.

When Bill reached the bike, he studied the door it leaned next to. No lock. He pressed his head against the fiberglass door and tried to listen. Nothing came through.

"Bill," Paige said, her voice low. "Be careful. You don't know who's in there."

"A kid with a nice bike," he said.

He grabbed the handle and threw the door up.

He stood face-to-face with Teena Everett.

CHAPTER EIGHTY-NINE

Teena's mouth fell open, and she took a step back.

When she did, Bill saw past her, into the interior of the storage unit.

In the corner, in the indistinct light, someone sat on a ragged mattress. Bill saw dirty blond hair and the familiar shape of the face that was so much like her mother's.

"Oh, my God."

Bill pushed Teena aside and darted toward the mattress. He dropped to his knees, reached out, and wrapped his arms around Summer.

"Oh, my God. Oh, Summer. Oh, baby. Are you hurt?"

Paige was there next to him, also reaching out for Summer. Paige was crying, and Bill felt the sting of his own tears. He saw his daughter through them, and he wiped them away to take her in.

Alive. She was alive.

"Dad," she said.

Her voice was faint, hoarse. Like she'd swallowed gravel. Her skin was pale, the circles under her eyes dark. She looked as though she'd lost weight, ten pounds at least. And she was dirty. Very dirty.

But she was alive. Alive.

Alive.

"Don't say anything," Bill said. "Shhh. We're here. It's okay. And the police are coming."

Summer moaned. She seemed out of it, a little delirious. Unable to focus her eyes. Bill looked around. He saw an empty water bottle, some bread.

"I'll get the car," Paige said.

"Yes, get the car." Bill took a quick glance at Teena, who had scooted back, her eyes wide.

Paige started moving away, then stopped. "The keys."

"Shit." Bill dug in his pockets and threw them to her. "Thanks."

Then he turned back to Summer. He eased onto the shitty mattress and moved next to Summer. Only then did he see that one of her arms was stretched out and away from her body in an unusual way. He saw the chain. A pair of handcuffs, one end around Summer's wrist, the skin red and raw beneath it, the other hooked through the chain, which was attached to a hook in the wall.

"Oh, God," Bill said. He tugged on the chain, feeling foolish once he did, but of course it didn't budge. "The police will get you out. They'll cut it off."

"I tried," Summer said. "I pulled and pulled until it hurt. Teena tried. . . ." She looked up at Bill, her eyes focusing for a moment. "He said he was coming back. That we were going away somewhere. He said he and I could start a new life somewhere else."

"He's crazy, honey. Just crazy."

"Did he get arrested? Did he . . . Is he . . ."

"He's dead," Bill said. "He's dead and gone. It's okay now."

"She said . . ." Summer made a vague gesture in Teena's direction, rattling the chain as she did so. "She talked about him. . . ."

Bill looked up. He'd forgotten about Teena. Forgotten her face at the door. Forgotten that she stood there, watching Bill reunite with Summer.

Teena shrank back a little, moving into the shadows by the far wall.

"Do you have the key, Teena?" Bill asked.

She shook her head.

"What are you doing here?" Bill asked. "Why didn't you tell anybody she was here?"

"I didn't know," Teena said. "I swear. I just found her a little while ago."

Bill heard the car approaching, the low rumble of the engine, the crunch of the tires over the grit and garbage in the driveway as Paige pulled up to the door. But as long as Summer was bolted to the wall, they couldn't take her anywhere.

Paige came to the open doorway, and Bill said, "There's a blanket in the trunk. Can you get it?"

Paige did, and Bill stood up and wrapped it around Summer's small, frail body.

He whispered in her ear. "They'll be here soon. It will be fine then. Just fine. Just a little while longer." He looked at Paige. "You've got the phone. Why don't you call them again? Hurry them up."

She took the phone out of her sweatshirt pocket, but before she dialed, Teena spoke up.

"No," she said, her voice echoing in the storage unit.

"What?"

"No. Don't call. Just wait." She stepped toward Bill and Summer. "I'm scared. You all are going to think the wrong thing. You're going to get me into trouble with the police. And I can't be away from my mom now. I just can't."

CHAPTER NINETY

Bill held his hand out, moved his body forward so it formed a barrier between Teena and Summer.

"What are you doing, Teena?" he asked.

"You can't . . . leave yet. I want to explain something."

"You will be in trouble if you knew about this and didn't do anything," Bill said. He shifted his tone, tried to sound placating. "But if Adam hurt you or threatened to hurt you, then maybe you won't get in trouble. Just tell the police what Adam did to you."

Teena's voice sounded hurt. "He didn't do anything to me. Nothing bad." She gestured with her hand. "He was like a father to me. He helped my mom. He really did. I thought he was . . . different than this. I didn't know."

"I know. We all thought that. But now we know he did a lot of awful things," Bill said. "Like putting Summer here. And being involved with Haley. Plain and simple. Did he hurt you too?"

Teena was shaking her head. She looked scared, nervous, like her circuits were overloading. Tears pooled in her eyes, and a vein pulsed in her neck. "He wasn't excluding me. He said he was going to help me too. Us. Me and my mom. I believed him. I wanted to believe him."

"What did he promise you?" Bill asked.

"Adam told me I was like a daughter to him. I was special. And when the time came, he and I could leave together. And my mom. We were going to start a new life."

"He was lying, honey," Paige said.

Teena's eyes were wide and the whites prominent in the half-light of the storage unit. "Yeah," she said. "Yeah. He did lie." Her voice faded. A sob caught in her throat, and she lifted her right hand to her chest. She quickly composed herself. "He said we would have left sooner, but he had to finish things at his job, to get paid more. He earned it. The day he died, we were going to leave. He was going to come to the house for Mom and me. He'd been getting ready to leave town. We were going to go that night."

"What was he going to do with Summer?" Bill asked. "Why was she here?"

"I don't know," Teena said. Her resolve appeared to be weakening. "I swear I didn't know about this until today. Tell them, Summer. I just found you an hour ago."

Bill looked at Summer, who nodded. It looked like it cost her a great effort just to move her head.

"How did you know Summer was here?" Bill asked. "Did he tell you?"

"Adam started acting weird around then. He didn't come by our house for a few days, right when the girls disappeared, and my mom cried and cried because she couldn't reach him. She was freaked out because my friends got hurt, and she thought it could have been me. She started to drink when she couldn't find Adam. It was terrible. I rode my bike to his house, to find him and ask him to come take care of Mom."

"Did you see something there?" Bill asked.

Teena looked reluctant to speak. Bill took a step forward, but Paige stepped in.

"Teena, it's okay to tell us. This is all over now. The police are coming."

The girl locked eyes with Paige, and her features relaxed. "I'm glad. I'm glad they're coming. I'm glad you're here."

"What happened, Teena?" Paige asked. "Why are you here?"

"He drove me back home. We put my bike in the trunk of his car, and we drove to our house. He went back to the bedroom and talked to my mom. He gave her coffee and sobered her up as best he could. And then when he left, he pulled me aside. He told me that he wanted to leave town with us, but he might not be able to. He didn't tell me why. But then he handed me something." She fumbled in her pocket and pulled out a piece of paper. "It was the address and the key, for this place. He told me if anything ever happened to him, anything bad, he needed me to come here, that there was something in this unit that he wanted me to know about."

"Did you come out here right away when he died?" Bill asked.

Teena shook her head, her eyes full of tears. "Not right away. I was sad, and my mom was sad. Devastated. She cried and cried. She started drinking again. I wanted to come out here and look, but I couldn't leave Mom alone. She's getting better, so I came out here. I had no idea what was out here—I didn't—but I thought it might be something meaningful. Something that would help me remember Adam. I had no idea. I mean . . . I was shocked when I saw her. I started crying." Her chin quivered. "She looked awful. And I couldn't get her loose."

"Really?" Bill said. "Did you really try to help her?"

"Tell them, Summer. I tried to help you. Tell them."

"We couldn't get the chain loose," Summer said, her voice a hoarse croak.

Bill heard the approaching cars just then, the whooping of the sirens.

Teena started shaking, her shoulders bouncing up and down as she sobbed. "He must have thought I was a fool. A stupid fool. I believed everything Adam told me, and it was all lies. He was someone terrible."

Bill turned to Summer, cradled her in his arms again.

"It's okay, honey," he said. "It's all over."

"Dad," she said.

"Yes, honey?"

"Thanks . . ."

"Thanks?"

"Thanks . . . thanks for not giving up on me."

Bill held her as close as he could.

CHAPTER NINETY-ONE

Bill entered Summer's room in the ICU.

After the doctors and nurses were finished, when an IV had been started to fight dehydration and a warming blanket placed on her body to combat hypothermia, when every part of her had been examined and investigated, Summer sent word that she wanted to speak to her father alone.

Paige and Hawkins stood with Bill in the hallway. Bill looked to the detective for approval, not that Hawkins could have kept him from his daughter if he'd even wanted to. But Hawkins nodded, content to wait his turn. And Paige smiled and winked, warming herself with a Styrofoam cup of coffee.

Bill stepped into the room. Summer sat beneath the covers, the very top of her light blue hospital gown peeking above the blankets. Winnie the Pooh sat in the crook of her arm, and already several bouquets of flowers decorated the windowsill across the way. Bill wondered how they'd appeared so quickly, whether the hospital staff brought them in just to cheer the place up.

Bill liked the sound of the door clicking shut behind him. It meant safety. Security. Protection for his daughter. He understood the long road that lay ahead, the mountains of schoolwork, the knowledge that the entire town knew what she'd been through. During the ambulance ride to the hospital, she told Bill she felt like a freak, like everywhere she would ever go in Jakesville, people would be staring at her, whispering about her, pointing at her.

Bill expected nightmares too, jumpiness and anxiety about being in public or being alone. Even with Doug Hammond arrested and Adam Fleetwood dead, she would struggle to feel normal.

A long road, indeed. But she was safe.

She was alive.

"Are you feeling any better, honey?"

"Yeah," she said. "I never thought I'd miss a bed so much. A bed, clean sheets, and warmth."

"I can imagine," he said, then shook his head. "No, I really can't. But I want you to know I'm going to try. I'm going to be right here with you the whole way. Whatever you need, I'm here. You know that, right?"

The corners of Summer's mouth curled up. "I know, Dad. You and Aunt Paige should join the army or something. You're like Navy SEALs."

Bill sat down by the side of her bed and took her hand in his. "I just did what any father would do. I wish I'd found you sooner."

But Summer shook her head. "Let's not do that. Let's just . . . Let's try to be happy."

"Okay," Bill said, squeezing her hand, the skin soft as a petal. "Let's do that."

But he could see something beneath her words and her smile. A distraction, an urgency to say something. Bill feared what his daughter might have to say, feared having to sit through a recitation of the hell she experienced, but he wouldn't look away. Only he could go through it with her, and he would. Every second of it, no matter how difficult.

"Did you want to say something, honey?" he asked. "Before the cops come in."

Summer didn't speak right away, and Bill rushed to fill the silence. "Haley's going to come down and see you soon, as soon as the police are finished. If you're up for it. That will lift your spirits."

"Good."

"Are you hungry?" Bill asked.

"Getting there."

"What do you want? We can get whatever you want."

"Dad?"

"Yeah?"

The hospital shrink, the one who would be seeing Summer more and more in the coming weeks, had told Bill to be patient. Above all, be patient. So Bill didn't want to press.

She was alive, he told himself. That's what mattered.

They had time to work everything else out. And it would take time.

"When I was out there . . . in that place . . . I had a lot of time to think."

Bill waited for her to say more, and when she didn't, he said, "Sure. I can imagine."

She took her time again. And Bill waited.

Finally she said, "I need to tell you something about Mom."

CHAPTER NINETY-TWO

Bill scooted closer to the bed, swallowing hard. His mind raced through possibilities, the thoughts tumbling like falling rocks.

"What about Mom?" Bill asked.

Summer lifted her hand to her mouth and started to chew on her fingernail. She just as quickly stopped, but she still didn't speak.

"Did you think about her a lot?" Bill asked. "Did she give you strength to keep going when you thought about her . . . out there?"

"Of course." She nodded. "The same thing happened when I thought of you. I felt stronger, more determined, knowing you were out there. And when you came through that door, I wasn't really surprised."

"I wish I'd gotten there sooner," he said. "I wish a lot of things had gone differently."

Summer shrugged. "The therapist lady I saw when Mom died always said not to beat myself up over the past. Or something like that. You shouldn't either."

"It's hard not to," he said. "Dads are supposed to protect their daughters." He looked at the floor for a moment. "Anyway, what about Mom?"

"Oh." Summer looked cagey, as if she wished she hadn't brought the subject up. "It's . . ."

"You can tell me," Bill said. "You can tell me anything."

"I know." She laughed a little, but the sound lacked joy. "But here we are, saying to let go of the past. Or not to beat ourselves up over it. And that's what I'm doing." She leaned forward, the Pooh bear remaining precariously balanced by her side. "You see, I know something about Mom. About the day she died. And I think . . . I *know* it led to everything that happened with me. It's why Adam locked me up out there."

Bill tried to be cool. He tried to stick to her therapist's mantra of being patient. But he couldn't. He couldn't stand on the brink of learning something about the last moments of Julia's life—those moments that had haunted him for more than a year—and just turn away without hearing everything there was to hear.

"What is it, honey? Tell me. I was trying to give you time to feel better. I knew we'd be talking about this sooner or later. I'd like to know why he put you out there. And whatever it is, we can handle it together."

She rubbed the bedspread, and then tugged gently on one of the bear's ears. "I saw something. When I came home from school the day Mom died, but before I went into the house, before I knew anything was wrong inside, I saw something." She looked down at the bear. "I came walking down the street, and I saw Adam leave our house. He looked like he was in a hurry. Like he was kind of nervous or something. At first, I didn't think anything of it. He came over sometimes, you know? To talk to you or whatever. And then when I . . . When I found Mom on the floor like she'd fallen, I forgot all about it for a few days. Maybe I was in shock or depressed or distracted. After her funeral, and we were both so upset, I just decided not to say anything. It didn't seem like a big deal, and I thought it would be weird if I just out of the blue said to you, *Oh, yeah, I saw Adam leaving the house the day Mom died.* Right?"

"I guess so."

"Besides, well, did you think Mom was acting weird before she died? Like something was wrong?"

"Like what?"

"Dad . . ." Summer took a moment, as though collecting her thoughts. But Bill could see she knew exactly what she wanted to say. She just didn't appear certain she could.

"Go ahead," he said.

"Dad, I wondered if maybe Mom and Adam were having an affair. There was one other time I came home from school and saw him leaving the house like that. I didn't think anything of it then either. And after Mom died . . . well, I wasn't sure about any of it." She paused, licking her lips. "I didn't want to hurt you when you were already so brokenhearted about Mom."

Bill took it all in, his heart beating faster and his skin prickling with energy. "Why are you thinking about all of this now? Did Adam say something to you out there?"

"I know what the police are going to want to know when they come in here," she said. She tugged on the bear's ear with more force, more urgency. "They're going to want to know why all this happened, why Adam did this to me."

"I thought he had a thing for Haley. For you, maybe."

Summer's mouth formed an "O," and she blinked her eyes a few times. "Yes, there's that. He and Haley were hooking up. And I don't know if he was really interested in me. He told me a couple of times how much I looked like Mom."

"What happened that day? Haley said Emily stopped to pick you guys up, but you didn't go. You let Haley and Emily go on to see those boys from school, but you said you had something to do. What did you do that day? Go see Adam?"

"I did. Do you remember right before . . . before the attack? Adam came over to our house. You and he were going to have a drink and watch some basketball game?"

Bill squinted. "Yeah. UK was playing Florida, I think."

"It was right after Mom's birthday. Remember?" Summer's voice gained an edge, a sharpness. "And Adam was in our house. I was doing homework in my room, ignoring the stupid basketball game. But I came out to go to the bathroom, and Adam was in the hallway. He was just standing there, looking at a picture of Mom. You know, that one from right after you got married? The one where she's standing alone in front of some lake, and she looks really natural and beautiful?"

"Of course. Kentucky Lake. I remember. She looks just like you in the picture. What about it?"

"When I came out, and he saw me, he seemed kind of embarrassed. But he said, 'Your mom was a special woman.'"

"Okay."

"It's the *way* he said it, Dad. It wasn't right. And I've never forgotten him being in the house those times, including the day Mom died. It pissed me off, him talking about Mom that way right after her birthday, right in our house. With you in the other room, supposedly his friend. It seemed creepy. Really creepy."

Bill swallowed. "So you went to see Adam the day of the attack. You just decided to do it that day?"

"I did. I'd been thinking about it and thinking about it. For a long time. And getting madder and more confused. I thought about running away. I thought about telling you. I guess I was kind of obsessed. And then I just thought . . . *Go ask him. Just get it over with.*" She shrugged, shaking Winnie the Pooh. "It was a Saturday. He'd be home. I didn't feel like being with my friends if I was thinking about Mom and all that stuff. I was driving myself crazy. What did I have to lose? What?"

Bill's mouth felt dry, his tongue swollen. "You should have told me."

"And crush you?" she asked. "You've been pretty down, Dad. Like, way down. You didn't need that if I was wrong. Hell, I wanted to be wrong. I did."

Bill waited before asking, "Were you?"

She said, "He and Mom, you know, didn't you ever get a weird vibe off the two of them? I mean . . . they could kind of act flirtatious when they were around each other. And Mom always talked about how handsome he was. I thought he was kind of gross, but Haley liked him." She cut her eyes at Bill, her features softening. "Dad, if this is going to bother you—"

"Go on," he said, fighting not to look away. "It's okay. Go on."

"I asked him. At first, he played it off, like I was joking, and he was joking. But I didn't let it go. I didn't just stop asking him because he wanted to act like it was no big deal. I said I really wanted to know why he was in our house that day. Was he there when Mom fell? Did he call nine-one-one?" She swallowed hard. "I just flat out asked if they were having an affair."

"I think they were because she—"

"He said they weren't." She rose up a little, moving her body toward Bill. "He said he wanted to, that they did have a flirtation and came close, but that Mom didn't want to. That day, the day she died, he went over there to close the deal, to be with her and convince her to leave you, and she told him no. Mom said she'd started to tell him with a note, but then she just decided to talk to him in person and called him over. And she let him down. She told him she loved you and me, and she wasn't going to risk everything she cared about."

Bill remembered the crumpled note. It was to Adam and not him.

She called me first that day, trying to patch things up, he told himself. *She called me first.*

For the second time in the span of hours, Bill experienced the most indescribable feeling of relief, a yearlong burden lifting from his shoulders. He raised his head, leaning back, his eyes taking in the bright white of the ceiling. He swore if he'd stepped on a scale at that moment, he would have weighed ten pounds less. He stayed in that position for longer than he realized, thinking that at any moment he'd float away, up to the ceiling and beyond. He felt so light.

"He was probably lying," Bill said.

"I don't think he was. I mean, it's just my gut, but he seemed to mean it when he denied it. He seemed, I don't know, hurt by the whole thing. Like Mom had broken his heart by turning him down." She reached out and placed her hand on top of Bill's. "Did you know all of this, Dad?" she asked. "Did you know that Adam was at the house that day? Did you know and just not tell me because . . . Well, I don't know why you wouldn't tell me."

"I didn't know he was there that day," Bill said, looking down. "I promise."

Summer's eyes were boring into Bill. There was still something else.

"Did you ask him something else that day?" Bill asked.

She nodded.

"Something that made everything escalate."

She nodded again. "I asked him if he hurt Mom. Physically hurt her."

CHAPTER NINETY-THREE

B ill's entire body trembled. He felt like a scared kitten, a small creature, overwhelmed by the circumstances around him.

"What possible reason did you have to ask such a question?" Bill asked. "Mom fell. It was an accident."

Tell me it was an accident, he thought.

"But, Dad, did Mom ever act that way? Did she ever drink in the middle of the day? And then climb on a ladder to paint after she'd been drinking? It just wasn't like her, was it? She wasn't clumsy. She didn't mess things up."

"No, she didn't. But she and I—"

"And if someone was innocent, how would they react to my accusing them? How?"

"They'd deny it. They'd probably deny it whether they were guilty or not."

Summer leaned back, sinking into the pillows. She closed her eyes for a moment.

"I should go," Bill said. "You're tired. This is too much." But he didn't mean it. He wanted—*needed*—to hear it to the end.

"No. Listen, Dad." She opened her eyes. "I accused him of having an affair with Mom, and he says he didn't have one with her. Fine. At that point, what's the harm? I'm a silly, upset teenager without a mom who made a crazy accusation. Right?"

"Right. I guess."

"He's not in any trouble for that if it isn't true. I could leave his house and no one would ever know we had that conversation."

"Okay." And then Bill understood the direction she was going. "So when you asked him if he—" Bill couldn't bring himself to say the word "murder." It felt so outlandish, so crazy and incomprehensible. Like a long word in a foreign language. "You asked him if he *hurt* Mom, and what did he do?"

"He wouldn't let me leave. He said that everything was complicated and no one was supposed to get hurt. And then he said again that I couldn't leave his house."

Bill looked down at Summer's hands where they rested on the mattress. He saw the red, raw skin on her right wrist, the bruises on her arm. "What did he do to you?"

"He asked me if I'd told anyone else about my suspicion that he killed Mom. I hadn't, Dad. Not you, not Haley. And I told him that I hadn't. I didn't want him to hurt anyone else. I told him that I didn't want to hurt anyone or cause any problems in case I was wrong."

"Why didn't you tell me?" Bill asked. "Summer, you could have come to me. We could have figured this out. You can always come to me."

"You were so unhappy, Dad. So, so unhappy. I couldn't add to it. I already had to look at you every day. The way you moped and thought about Mom. What if I was wrong and I brought that up for nothing?"

Bill blinked a few times, sniffed. "Okay, okay. And then what did Adam do?"

"He got up and came toward me." Her eyes were glassy, and Bill knew she was seeing the moment in her mind as she told him about it. "I thought he was going to, I don't know, try to comfort me. Or hug me." She shivered. "He overpowered me. He wrestled me to the floor and dragged me into the laundry room. He got out some ropes and stuff. I tried to fight back. . . . He might have hit me on the head or something. I think I was out for a minute." She reached up and touched the back of her head. "I woke up in the trunk of his car with my phone and wallet gone. He had the lid open and was standing over me. We were in his garage. He told me to be quiet, not to say anything or scream. I wanted to call for you—I did. I wanted to scream, but he said if I did, he'd close the lid and let me rot in there. No one would hear me."

"I'm sorry. I wish I'd heard. I wish I'd come running. . . . God, I'm sorry."

Her voice sounded flat. "He closed the lid on the trunk. Maybe half an hour later, he drove me to that storage unit."

Bill felt like the sun and the moon and the stars had landed on him. He could barely lift his head to look at his daughter. When he spoke, his voice was low and distant. "When you were out at that storage unit, did you ask him again?"

"Not really. I was too scared. I think . . . I think he didn't know what to do once I was out there. Like . . . he couldn't keep me around, because I'd tell everyone that he killed Mom, but he didn't know what else to do with me at that point. He couldn't kill me or anything. He wanted another way out, I think, but he didn't know what it was. He talked about going away and starting over. I was afraid he was going to leave me out there forever. That's why he told Teena where I was. I think he kept me out in that storage unit because he was stalling. Maybe he hoped someone else would get arrested. Or that he'd figure something out. He didn't hurt me. He didn't hit me . . . or anything else. He fed me and gave me water, until he died, I guess. He said he was going to bring me clothes. Even my bear . . ."

"He did try to do that," Bill said. "It cost him his life."

"He really seemed . . . confused. Nervous. I'd never seen him act that way. He was always Mr. Cool. I begged him to let me go, to let me go home. But he said that was impossible. He said I could never go home again because of what I'd accused him of."

Bill's jaw trembled. His tongue felt twice its natural size, but he managed to force words out through his mouth. "Did he tell you what he did to her? Did he say how this happened?"

"He only talked about . . . that once."

"You don't have to. . . ." Bill wished she wouldn't. He also wanted to know. He felt a hungry, gnawing desperation to know what happened to Julia.

Anything. Any detail. He wanted to know.

"After Mom shut him down, rejected him, he said he left. He went home to cool off. And then he said he felt bad about the way things ended, so he came back to the house. To apologize. And when he did that, he found Mom on the floor. Dead."

"But he didn't call anyone."

"I asked him about that. I *told* him that. 'Why didn't you call for help? Why didn't you call nine-one-one?' He never brought it up again. That must have been right before he died. When he stopped coming, I thought he was just going to let me starve in there. I thought that was my punishment for asking too many questions."

"Why didn't he call for help if that story is true?"

"Why did he act that way? Why else would he have done what he did to me?"

Bill stood up, knocking the chair askew with the backs of his legs.

When he came to his feet, his body wobbled. His head swam like he'd had too much to drink.

"Dad? You look pale."

He held out a hand to reassure her.

"Dad, I'm sorry. I wanted to tell you before anyone else heard."

Bill steadied himself. He came closer to the bed and bent down. He cupped his daughter's face in his hands and kissed her on the forehead. "You didn't do anything wrong. I wanted to know. I needed to know." He kissed her again. When he straightened up, he still felt shaky, and his steps toward the door of the hospital room were lurching, uneven. But he made it there. He pulled the door open and waved to Hawkins.

"Dad?" Summer's voice stopped him and he turned around. "I want to know what happened to Mom. I'm going to tell the police about it. I know . . . I know it might not be too late for them to examine Mom, to maybe look at her body again."

Bill stood in the doorway, his body on the threshold. "Are you sure?"

"Yes."

He went out into the hallway. "She's ready to talk to you," Bill said. Hawkins took in the look on Bill's face, concern showing on his own. But Bill shook his head, waving off the detective. "Go on," he said. "Before she's too tired. She has a lot to say."

When he was alone with Paige, she came to his side, sliding her arm around his back. "Are you okay?"

"I don't know."

"She's home, Bill. She's finally home. And you found her. Do you understand? She wouldn't be here without you."

He thought of the way he stormed out of the house the day Julia died. The ignored phone calls. The attack on his daughter that went unheard right behind his house.

And, yes, finding Summer. He had been late, but he found her.

And he would bring her all the way home as soon as she was ready.

"Thanks, Paige." He leaned against his sister, letting her take some of his weight. "I understand a lot of things now. Maybe more than I wanted to."

EPILOGUE

Bill held the door for Summer.

She stepped inside the house, wearing jeans and a sweatshirt Bill had brought to the hospital. She held Winnie the Pooh in one hand and a bouquet of flowers in the other, and when Bill closed the door behind them and turned the lock with a loud snap, he felt like they'd both taken an important step on the long road that still lay ahead.

The nightmares started in the hospital, so Bill slept in the room with her. He never left her side. But he couldn't stop the nightmares that were still bound to come, the jumpiness and anxiety about being in public or being alone.

A long road, indeed. But she was home.

She was alive.

"I'll get the rest of the flowers later," Bill said. "And the cards and everything. I can't believe so much came to the hospital in just five days."

"Yeah," she said. "It's nice to know people care."

She walked off to her bedroom while Bill filled the vase with water and placed the flowers on the kitchen table. He knew there was something else he should do to them. Was it aspirin that kept them fresher longer? He decided to text Paige to ask her. She had left the day before, after Bill insisted they were fine. And he told her she needed to get back to her own family.

"We'll visit this summer," she said as she got into her car. "We can't go so long without seeing each other."

"And we shouldn't only see each other when something awful happens," Bill said.

"Agreed."

They hugged. And Bill told his sister he loved her.

She looked surprised. "I love you too, Bill. See, there's a sensitive guy inside there somewhere."

"Don't tell anyone," Bill said.

He looked around the house. He felt hungry, and he assumed Summer would be as well. She'd eaten well at the hospital, and already some fullness was returning to her cheeks. He'd feed her whatever she wanted to make up for being dehydrated and starved in the storage unit.

He walked back to her bedroom, treading lightly. Her door was open, and when he peeked inside, she was sitting on the bed, running her hand over the smooth comforter and taking in the familiar surroundings, Winnie the Pooh in her lap.

"I asked Detective Hawkins about something," Bill said. "He said you could get the bracelet back soon. The one Mom gave you. The police need it for evidence, but they'll give it back eventually."

She offered a weak smile. "Good. It must have fallen off in Adam's house that day. The day he . . . you know. Took me or whatever."

"Are you hungry?" Bill asked.

"Getting there."

"What do you want? We can get whatever you want."

"Yeah, sure. Are you okay, Dad? Really okay with everything we found out?"

"I'm getting there," he said. "We're both getting there. It's not going away easily."

"I saw the news on TV," she said. "In the room before we left. I guess they think Clinton and Todd are going to plead guilty. Todd's saying he tried to stop Clinton, that he was afraid of him, so he wants to catch a break of some kind. And Brandon . . ."

"He's trying to get a better deal. His lawyer is saying he should get consideration for wrapping Haley in the extra clothes. And for making the anonymous call to the police. They all agree he wasn't there for the attack, but he helped them cover it up. I don't think he deserves much of a break."

"He wasn't as bad as the other two, but that's not saying much." Summer looked down, her lips pressed tight. "I can't believe Haley and I ever stayed friends with those guys. I kind of dated Todd, and he was involved with something so monstrous."

"Did he ever hurt you? Todd? Or Clinton?"

"No. We all knew Clinton was kind of crazy, but he'd always been that way. I should never have been close to someone like that."

Bill reached out and rubbed her knee. "It's okay, kiddo. Remember what the therapist said? Don't beat yourself up about the past. We've all made mistakes."

"Sure," she said, her voice low. She squeezed his hand. "Thanks. Is Teena in trouble too?"

"I think the police understand that she and her mom were vulnerable and fell for what Adam was peddling. And it helps her that you said she tried to get you out, that she tried to comfort you when she found you."

A bird called outside. The day was warmer, a hint of spring. Almost March, almost a time for abundant new life. Bill was ready.

"Pizza?" he asked. "I could go for that."

"Yeah. Sure. Mushrooms. Lots of mushrooms."

"I know how you like it."

"Dad? I know you know something."

Summer's blue eyes took him in, pinning him in place and refusing to let him slip away and off the hook. Just like her mother.

"I thought I'd let you get settled in first," he said.

"What did Detective Hawkins tell you?" she asked. "You promised to tell me as soon as you knew."

Bill couldn't argue. He couldn't dodge the question. He didn't want to. He didn't want to dodge anything in his life, no matter how difficult.

"Okay. Well, they got the results of the autopsy. It was pretty easy to figure out, really." He tried to make his voice gentle, to cushion the words he knew he had to speak. "They x-rayed Mom's head. The fracture was there. Not from a fall, but more like someone had hit her with something. Something like a wine bottle, maybe. That's pretty much it. They're going to change the cause of death to homicide. Officially. I'm sorry, but you were right. He must have lost his cool when Mom rejected him."

Summer stared straight ahead, her face stoic, her eyes clear.

"Are you okay?" Bill asked.

"I am."

"We can talk more," Bill said. "Anna Halstrom knows the name of a good therapist we can both talk to. I think we should."

"When will they rebury her or whatever?"

"Tomorrow. Maybe the next day. I'm not sure."

"I want to be there, okay? Both of us."

"Sure. Of course we'll be there." Bill studied his daughter. "Are you sure you're okay with this? Do you want to talk?"

"Are *you* okay with it?" she asked. "I knew about it sooner than you did."

"I'm getting used to the idea. I think." Bill looked around the room, trying to focus on the positive. "It's going to take a while." His voice sounded ragged. He felt ragged, like a tattered and torn garment. "A long, long while."

"We'll keep working on it."

"Okay." He leaned down and kissed the top of her head. "You should be proud for asking Adam what you did, for trying to find out what happened to Mom. And for surviving out there." When she didn't look up, he added, "I'm proud of you."

"Thanks, Dad."

Bill stood up. "You look tired. Do you want to take a little nap before we eat? It will take half an hour for the food to get here."

"Sure."

She kicked off her shoes and hugged the bear tightly as she slid farther up the bed.

Bill tucked her in, pulling the covers up. He started to close the door, but Summer stopped him.

"Just leave it cracked," she said. "A little. I like to see the hall light."

Bill did as she asked. Then he made an immediate stop in the office, the room right next to Summer's. He opened the ancient laptop and found the folder that held the two files he'd listened to more times than he could count over the previous year and a half.

He thought about listening to them one more time but decided against it.

Moving on. Really moving on.

He took the mouse, started to drag the two files to the trash. And then stopped.

What if Summer wants to hear them someday? Shouldn't she have that choice?

What if I want to hear Julia's voice?

He let go of the mouse, leaving the files in their place, closed the laptop's lid, and went to order food for his daughter.

ACKNOWLEDGMENTS

Thanks again to the bloggers, booksellers, librarians, and readers who borrow, buy, review, and talk about my books.

Thanks to Linda King for giving the book a thoughtful early read.

Thanks to Barry Pruitt for his insights on police procedures.

Thanks again to my amazing agent, Laney Katz Becker, for her never-ending work and support.

Thanks again to my wonderful publicist, Loren Jaggers, for getting the word out.

Thanks again to my dynamic editor, Danielle Perez, for her patience, care, and dedication.

Thanks again to everyone at Berkley for all of their hard work.

Thanks again to my family and friends.

And thanks again to Molly McCaffrey for everything else.

Bring Her Home

David Bell

QUESTIONS FOR DISCUSSION

1. Bill alludes to difficulties he had with Summer before she disappeared. Do you think this was typical teenage rebellion, or was it exacerbated by her mother's death?

2. The reader learns that Bill once grabbed Summer, leading her to call the police. Do you think the police made the right decision when they chose not to press charges? Did finding this out about Bill make you feel differently about him?

3. Bill thinks of Adam as one of his closest friends. Why do you think Bill was so drawn to Adam?

4. Bill turns to his sister, Paige, in times of crisis, even though their relationship is sometimes contentious. Do you think their sibling relationship is typical?

5. Taylor has a difficult time turning over her daughter's dental X-rays to the police. Do you understand why she hesitated to learn the truth?

6. Candy seems to imply that Summer was a bad influence on her daughter, Haley. Do you think this is true? Is it normal in a teenage friendship for one kid to be more of a leader than the other?

7. Bill and Julia were having difficulties in their marriage. Do you think their marriage would have survived had Julia lived?

8. Do you believe Doug when he says that he would never have hurt Emily and only wanted to help solve the crimes?

9. Were you surprised to learn that Adam had been in the house on the day Julia died? Do you understand why Summer kept that a secret from her dad?

10. Do you think Bill and Summer made the right choice, to have Julia's body exhumed for an autopsy? If it was your mother or spouse or sister, would you have wanted to know the truth?

11. Teena and Brandon, while not as deeply involved in the crimes as the other teenagers, still kept secrets and showed poor judgment. Would you want to see them prosecuted for their roles in the crimes?

12. At the end of the novel, Bill briefly contemplates destroying the recordings of Julia's voice from the day she died. Why do you think he thought about that? Do you think he made the right choice in keeping them?

CHAPTER ONE

Five police cars. Three news vans. And one coroner's wagon.

Jenna Barton saw them as she made the turn onto the last county lane. The vehicles were fanned out around the old weathered barn with one wall collapsing and the others hanging on for dear life.

The fields around her on either side, stretching away for miles to the edges of the county, were empty and barren, still marked by patches of snow from an uncharacteristically heavy storm for that part of Kentucky. The soil was dark and lumpy, the remnants of cornstalks sticking out like spikes.

As she came closer, the dirt and gravel on the narrow road pinging against the underside of her car, she saw the people as well. County sheriffs in their pale green uniforms and Smokey Bear hats. News reporters in their nice clothes, their hair perfect, were being followed by cameramen in flannel shirts and heavy boots. And a scattering of onlookers, the curious good old boys who heard the call on their scanners or read about it on Twitter, were standing around in their feed caps, hands thrust deep into pockets against the cold, hoping for a glimpse of something horrific. Something gory or gross, some story they could tell later that night in the Downtowner while they sipped beers or threw darts.

Yeah, they'd say, their bravado mostly covering their unease, *I saw them bring the body out. Wasn't hardly anything left. . . .*

Jenna parked next to a sheriff's cruiser, but she didn't get out. She sat in the car, hands clenching the wheel, and took a few deep breaths. She told herself this was probably nothing, another false alarm, one of many she had experienced over the past three months. Every time an unidentified woman's body was found in central Kentucky, along an interstate or in a culvert, an abandoned house or the woods, someone called her. Usually the media but sometimes the police, and Jenna would have to wait it out, wondering whether this would be the time they'd tell her they'd found Celia. As she sat in the car, her eyes closed, the heater making the cabin of her Civic feel even closer and more cramped than it already was, she wondered whether she wanted to know the truth or if she could keep her eyes shut and hide forever. Would she finally feel relief when they found her best friend's body?

The thoughts swirled through her brain like some twisted Zen koan:

I want to know.

I don't want to know.

A light tapping against the window brought her eyes open. Jenna blinked a few times, turned her head. She saw a smiling face, one wearing a pound of makeup. Becky McGee from Local 40 News. Becky gave a short wave, her shoulders rising in anticipation of Jenna's response.

Jenna turned the car off and stepped out. She'd been at work when Becky called and still wore her light blue scrubs. She'd rushed out of the office so fast she barely had time to grab her keys and purse. A damp winter chill hit Jenna as she straightened up, so she pulled her coat tighter, felt the light sting of the wind against her cheeks.

Becky placed her hand gently on Jenna's upper arm. "How are you?" she asked, her voice cooing as if she were talking to an invalid or a frightened child. "Tough day, huh?"

"Is it her?" Jenna asked.

"They don't know anything," Becky said. "Or they won't tell us anything. They've been poking around in there for the last thirty minutes. It's a potential crime scene, so they have to take their time. . . ."

Becky's voice trailed off as Jenna's eyes wandered to the old barn. Some cops stood at the opening where a door once hung, staring inside. One of them said something and then smiled, looking to the man next to him for a laugh as well. They were close to fifty feet away from Jenna, so she couldn't hear them, and she envied their ease at the scene, their lack of emotional involvement in the outcome of the search. She looked around. She was the only one truly invested, the only one who would buckle with pain if Celia's body was discovered in the shitty, run-down barn.

Jenna turned back to Becky. The camera guy, Stan, loomed behind her, the equipment in his hand but not shooting. Jenna had learned over the past few months what the red light meant. "What did they find?" she asked. "You said on the phone it was a body."

"Well, it's—" The cheer and lilt quickly went out of Becky's voice. She was a little older than Jenna, probably in her early forties, but her voice still sounded like the high school cheerleader she had once been. "Bones. I guess *a* bone to be more specific." Becky nodded, confirming the fact. "Yes, they found *a* bone. A surveying crew was out here, and they went inside the barn to get out of the cold or to take a smoke break, and they found a leg bone. Now they're digging around in there, looking for more." Becky made an exaggerated frown to show how awful she found the whole situation.

"Did someone call Ian?" Jenna asked.

"I did. He said he wasn't going to come. You know he never makes it out to anything like this." Becky lowered her voice. "I think he mistrusts any potential display of emotion. Plus, you know, a lot of people still think he's guilty."

"The police cleared him," Jenna said.

"Mostly," Becky said, her voice low.

Jenna wished she could be as strong as Ian, could so easily and readily draw lines and never cross them. It was easier for men. People accepted it if a man was cold and distant. "He's smarter than me, I guess. It's so cold out here."

Jenna saw the other reporters and their cameramen moving her way. They recognized her, of course, after all the stories and interviews, after all the features and updates on Celia's case. They knew she was good for a quote or two, knew the viewers loved to hear from her, even the ones who took to online forums and social media to criticize her. It was Jenna whom Celia was leaving the house to see that night back in November. It was Jenna who first called Ian when Celia didn't arrive at their designated meeting place. It was Jenna, Celia's best friend since high school, who could tell the viewers anything they wanted to know about Celia.

Jenna knew the reporters were using her, but she couldn't help herself. She felt obligated to speak to them out of loyalty to Celia, even though she always received crank calls—at work and at home— and hateful comments on Twitter and Facebook. People offered support too, plenty of people, she reminded herself. But the nasty ones stuck with her.

Becky nodded to Stan, easing toward Jenna, reaching out with one hand to brush something off her coat. "You know what would be great? We'd love to be able to get your reaction now, you know, and have it as part of the story tonight. And I've already heard from New York. Reena wants to do a live remote tonight, put it all over CNN. Of course she'd love to have you again. She thinks you're great." Becky tilted her head to one side, studying Jenna. "This is so cool that you wore your work uniform. It's so real. If you could slip your coat off and—"

"Please, Becky." She didn't want to be rude, didn't want to snap at the reporter, who Jenna knew was only doing her job and who had always been decent to her. Jenna tried to soften her words with a smile, but it felt forced, like squeezing toothpaste back into a tube. "It's cold out here."

"You want the coat on?" Becky asked. "That's fine. It's a little brisk, even for February."

"No, I don't want to talk right now," Jenna said, her voice friendly but firm. "Not *before*."

Becky was a professional, but that didn't mean she could hide all her emotions. One side of her mouth crinkled when Jenna told her no, and a glossy coldness passed over her eyes. "You don't want to talk now?" Becky's eyes darted around. She scooted closer, lowering her voice and adding a steely edge. "You're not going to talk to someone else, are you?"

"I'm not going to talk to another reporter, no. Of course not." Jenna sighed. "Whatever happens, I'll talk to you first."

"Good. Because you and I—" Becky's glance darted to the other reporters, who stood just out of earshot. She eyed them like a school of circling sharks, which in a way they were. "We've always had a rapport, ever since this happened. And with Reena in New York helping me—"

"After," Jenna said. "Okay? Let's just talk after."

"After what?" Becky asked.

"After we find out what's—*who's*—really in that barn."

"Are you sure?" Becky asked. She lowered her voice again. "You know it could take a while for them to identify anything. I mean, they have to use the dental records at this point. And you always have something interesting to say. And this whole town has been on edge for the past few months. Things like this don't happen here."

Jenna felt the heat rise in her cheeks, and as it did, the molars at the back of her mouth ground together like shifting tectonic plates. She didn't want to say the wrong thing. She had a tendency to do that, to blurt things out. The wrong things at the wrong times. Jokes at a funeral, curses in front of someone's grandmother. They never came out the way she intended, and sometimes she hurt people or offended them. She never seemed to know how her words would land, and she wished she could learn to keep her mouth shut.

But Becky read the look and nodded, reaching up to pat her hair. "You're right," she said, smiling, doing her best to set Jenna's mind at ease. "After will be better."

Better, Jenna thought. Better? Would any of this ever be better?

CHAPTER TWO

It was a first for Jared Barton: a beautiful girl in his bedroom.

Yes, he'd fooled around with girls before. At parties or in the park, fumbling in the dark, the sweet taste of some kind of flavored vodka on the girl's breath while they kissed, their tongues swirling like clothes in a dryer. And he remembered the ever-present fear of interruptions that hung over those encounters: other kids barging into the bedroom or, worst of all, police chasing them from the park, the flashlight blast in the eyes, the smug cops hustling them away with smirks on their faces. *Okay, Romeo, the park's closed now....*

But even though his mom worked full-time and his dad was long gone, Jared had never managed to bring a girl home. At fifteen, he felt a little behind. He had friends at school who boasted of blow jobs and even sex, and Jared listened to the stories in awe, not saying much for fear of betraying the fact that he'd never made it past second base, a private shame he kept to himself. But here she was, standing in his room after school on a Tuesday afternoon, the amazing Tabitha Burke.

Jared told himself to remain calm and to not—for the love of all that was holy—blow this chance.

Tabitha leaned over his desk, her long fingers picking up items and then placing them down, almost as though she was shopping in a store and didn't know what she wanted to buy. When they'd come in, Jared silently thanked whatever god dwelled above that his room was relatively clean, that there were no dirty boxer shorts on the floor, no stained socks or wet bath towels littering the carpet. For once he was glad his mom rode his ass about keeping things clean. He wanted to make the best impression possible, and he didn't think Tabitha would be the kind of girl who would leave dirty clothes on the floor or dirty dishes on her desk. Not that he'd ever been close to her house, let alone inside.

"Do you want a drink or something?" Jared asked. "I think we have some Cokes. Maybe my mom made iced tea."

"I'm fine," Tabitha said. She looked back at him, offering a smile that revealed a dimple on her left cheek.

Jared loved the smile—even though her teeth weren't perfectly straight—and he loved the dimple. He liked to caress her cheeks when they were close, making out and kissing her lips, her ears, her neck, running his fingers over her soft skin because he'd never felt anything like it. But that answer to his question about the drink. *I'm fine.* Tabitha said it all the time about almost everything. He thought of it as her motto, her catch-all response to most questions, and Jared couldn't help thinking of it as a line in the sand, something that always reminded him he'd know her some, but not as much as he wanted. He hoped—and kept hoping—that would change, that he'd hear that phrase less and less as time went by.

He'd only met her three weeks earlier on the icy January day she showed up at Brereton Jones High School in Hawks Mill, Kentucky. The semester had already started and, in homeroom that first day, Tabitha was escorted in by a guidance counselor. She carried no backpack or pens, no papers or books, and she looked tired, like someone who'd just come off a twelve-hour shift in a factory. Jared didn't care.

Tired or not, Tabitha was beautiful: almost as tall as he was, with fair freckled skin and green eyes. Her hair looked a little greasy that day, and she wore it back, but that only called more attention to her full lips, which Jared stared at while Tabitha explained to another girl that she'd just moved to Hawks Mill from Florida. They'd driven all night, she said, she and her dad. He'd just started a new job in town. . . .

But Jared didn't care about the details. He wanted to—*needed to*—meet her. He wasn't sure he'd ever wanted anything—*anyone*—so much in his life. It felt like hunger, a physical craving.

And he did meet her that very first day during sixth period. Jared went to the library instead of the cafeteria, where he normally spent his study halls, goofing around with his friends, drinking Cokes and watching stupid videos on their phones. But he knew he had a math quiz that day, and he knew if he went to the cafeteria he'd fail.

He hadn't stopped thinking about Tabitha since seeing her in homeroom. He'd spent the whole day hoping she'd end up in another one of his classes, and short of that, he hoped for a glimpse of her in the hallway. But those things didn't happen, so when he walked into the library and saw her sitting alone at a table, reading—of all things—a book by Dean Koontz, his heart raced like a motorboat.

She liked Dean Koontz. Jared loved Dean Koontz. And she just so happened to be reading one of Jared's favorites: *Whispers*.

Jared didn't stop. He didn't open his math book, and he didn't sit at another table. He went right up to Tabitha and complimented her on her taste in books. He knew he was taking a risk, approaching the new, very pretty girl and striking up a conversation. Jared felt the same that day in the library as the time he first went off the high dive at the community pool. He remembered the slow climb up the ladder, the terrifying view of the blue water on all sides. He knew kids were lined up behind him, and to turn away or back down meant instant humiliation.

So he jumped.

And how good it felt—the free fall through the air, the glorious splash into the water. The bubbles streaming from his mouth as he sank, and then the steady rise back to daylight. The terror and the glory.

He jumped with Tabitha too. He didn't think, didn't turn around and walk away.

He jumped.

She looked up from *Whispers* and smiled, the dimple catching his eye. "I read this before, a few years ago. And then I found it on the shelf here. It's one of my favorites, so I just started rereading it."

"It's one of my favorites too," Jared said, slipping into a chair across from her. She hadn't asked, and he didn't care. He acted, his body taken over by some force that allowed him to behave like a confident, mature human being. They talked about other books they liked. And movies. And food.

He never even opened the math book. He later failed the quiz.

He didn't care.

It all seemed to be leading to this moment in his room.

And so she stood before him, gently tucking a strand of hair behind her ear with one hand as she studied the books on the shelf next to his desk. "You really do like Dean Koontz," she said.

"He's the man who brought us together."

She turned and smiled again, then picked up the framed photograph on the top of the shelf. "Who's this?" she asked. "Is this your dad and your brothers?"

"Half brothers. Yes, that's them."

"Your dad looks like you. I can see it in the eyes."

"I guess so." Jared didn't want to talk about his dad. Not because his absence was particularly painful. It really wasn't anymore. His dad had left when he was five, and he remembered that pain very well. It felt as if he cried for weeks, stumbling around with his vision blurred by tears, asking if Dad was ever going to come back. His mom put on her best face for him, but even then he could see how much it hurt her. At night, after she put him to bed, he'd hear her crying through the thin walls of the apartment they lived in back then. Nothing ever scared him as much as the sound of an adult crying. "I can never see those things," he said to Tabitha.

"Didn't you say you don't really know your half brothers?" Tabitha tapped the glass with the end of her finger.

"I visited a couple of years ago. Dad paid for the plane ticket, so I went." Jared's first plane ride. He loved the window seat, looking out and watching the huge patches of nothingness beneath the wings. So much room in the country, so many places to go. "It was weird. It felt like I was staying with strangers. I mean, his new wife is okay. Shelly. And the kids are good kids. I guess. But how much can you get to know people in a week? Dad . . . I barely remember him, and he doesn't know me at all."

Tabitha nodded. She placed the frame back in the exact spot she found it, as though she were handling a precious work of art.

Jared waited, hoping she'd signal a willingness to talk more about her own family. He didn't want to press or push if she didn't offer any signs, even though he wanted to ask almost as much as he wanted to do anything else. *Almost.* There were other things he wanted to do with Tabitha more.

But he didn't know where Tabitha's mother was. On the few occasions the subject came up, Tabitha was evasive, suggesting only that her parents were separated, and her mother lived in another part of the country. Tabitha didn't seem to have much contact with her mother, if any. He wondered if her mother had problems, emotional or something else.

Jared knew only that Tabitha lived with her dad in Hawks Mill. Beyond that . . . not much. And most of his inquiries in those first few days they walked home from school together or hung out in study hall were met with some variation of the standard *I'm fine*. Since then, he'd kind of let the subject go, hoping that over time she'd open up more. But weren't relationships supposed to work the other way? Wasn't the guy supposed to be closed off and the girl the one who always wanted to talk about her feelings?

"I heard something about your mom today," Tabitha said. She still stared at the photo of Jared's dad and brothers, a photo Jared put out only because his mom said it would be a nice gesture. He didn't know who the gesture was for, since his dad was never coming back, but he did it to appease his mom.

"Oh." Jared tensed. The muscles in his stomach tightened as though bracing for a blow. She could mean only one thing. "People say a lot of stuff."

"Yeah, some kids at school told me something about her friend disappearing. Is that true? I didn't know if it was just some weird gossip or exaggeration."

Jared hesitated before answering. Okay, he had to admit, Tabitha wasn't the only one holding things back. He hadn't mentioned much to her about his mom at all, except to say she worked as a nurse and she was pretty easy to get along with. He left out the part about Celia, knowing he'd have to tell Tabitha someday but hoping they'd know each other better when they went down that rabbit hole. A shared love for Dean Koontz was a much better icebreaker than, *So, my mom's best friend disappeared without a trace and is probably dead. . . .*

"It's true, yeah."

Tabitha turned around to face him when he started speaking, leaning back against his desk and folding her arms under the gentle curve of her breasts. She didn't say anything but seemed to be listening with a particularly sharp focus, as though every word that came out of Jared's mouth mattered a great deal to her.

"It's kind of weird to talk about," he said. "Are you sure you want to hear about it?"

Tabitha nodded.

"Okay. My mom's been friends with Celia ever since they were in high school. I've known Celia my whole life. Back in early November, they were supposed to go out together. They were meeting near Caldwell Park. Do you know where that is?"

Tabitha looked confused. "I don't know where anything is yet."

"It's not far. They were meeting late at night, almost like they were sneaking out. I don't know why. I think they were trying to re-create some of the wild times they had in high school. But Celia didn't show up. At first Mom just assumed she'd changed her plans or something. Celia's married and has a kid." He snapped his fingers in the air. "Maybe you know her? Ursula Walters? She's in our grade."

"There's a girl named Ursula in a couple of my classes."

"She's kind of a pain in the ass," Jared said.

"She seems like a bully to me."

"Really? Why?"

Tabitha lifted one shoulder, a halfhearted shrug. "She just strikes me as the kind of person who thinks she should always get what she wants. I've known other people like that."

Jared waited for her to say more, but she didn't. "I've known Ursula since I was a kid. My mom thinks maybe Celia wasn't around for her enough. You know, Celia and Ursula's dad, Ian, were kind of wrapped up in their own thing too much instead of paying attention to Ursula. But that's another story. Anyway, Mom texted Celia and called her, never got an answer. She called Celia's husband. And then they called the cops, but they couldn't find her." Jared straightened up, scooting forward on the bed. "Wait a minute—have you really not heard about any of this? I mean, not until today?"

"No," she said. "I just moved to town. I don't know many people."

"But it's a national story. Or it was for a month or so, until they didn't find Celia and everybody decided to move on to some other kidnapping or plane crash or whatever. It was on CNN every night. That weird lady on the crime show? The one with the gray, poofy hair, Reena Huffman? She practically moved here." He almost smiled at the strangeness of the blank look on Tabitha's face. He didn't think it was possible not to have heard of Celia's case, given how much it played on the news. "Have you never heard of the Diamond Mom?"

"The what?"

"The Diamond Mom? That's what they call Celia." He looked around the room, trying to see if there was a clipping from the local paper he could show her, but he didn't see any. "Celia disappeared by the park, and the cops found this diamond earring at the scene. One of her earrings. Like it fell out when the maniac or serial killer grabbed her. Her husband and her mom identified it. They're worth a crap ton of money, I guess, the earrings. They're heirlooms, and Celia never went anywhere without them. She wouldn't just let them fall out and not notice. Celia's family is rich too. Anyway, that Reena Huffman lady started calling Celia the Diamond Mom. That popped up on the screen every night when she talked about Celia's disappearance. It's a play on some old song. 'Diamond Girl' or something. And I guess it makes Celia sound rich. The news shows love that stuff."

Tabitha's mouth hung open a little. Her eyes glistened, as though she might cry, as though the story about Celia had happened to someone she knew well. "So how's your mom?" she asked, her voice a little shaky.

"She's doing her best. The first couple of months after Celia disappeared were a disaster for her. She tried to act tough and cool and everything, but I knew it was killing her. You know how parents are. They feel like they have to be strong for us, but it really put her through hell. The media kept bugging her. People looked at her funny at work or the store, even though she didn't do anything. She blames herself, you know? She feels guilty about the whole thing." Jared felt a protective instinct swelling in his chest, some desire to shield his mom from the scorn and the pain and the attention. "It can't be her fault. After Celia disappeared, her husband told the cops she thought someone was following her."

"Really?"

"Some creep, I guess. But then, how do you prove that? I guess she just felt freaked out a few times when she went places, like a car was following her or something. But maybe she was imagining it. How can anyone know?" He shrugged. "The whole town's kind of gone crazy, you know? People have bought guns and security systems and dogs. They think a madman is on the loose. Maybe one is. It's been hard on Mom. I know she thinks about it all the time."

"That's terrible," Tabitha said, and her voice carried a weight that seemed heavier than her years. "Does everybody think she's dead?"

Jared noticed that Tabitha didn't pull any punches. So many people tiptoed around the topic of death. They said "passed away" or "deceased," but not Tabitha. She didn't play coy.

"I think everyone assumes that," Jared said. "Once someone has been gone that long, everyone thinks the worst. And maybe some creep was stalking her. . . . Sometimes I watch those cop shows on TV. After forty-eight hours, it's like impossible for them to find someone alive."

"I know," she said, again with the heavy weight in her voice.

Jared didn't want her to be sad, so he tried to say something hopeful. "People do think they've seen Celia. More than once someone in another town, sometimes way across the country, says they've seen Celia somewhere. The cops always try to check it out, but they haven't found her yet."

"And they haven't found her body?"

"No."

"I guess that's good. Kind of."

"You must live in some kind of cave, or a news media blackout, if you've never heard of the Diamond Mom," he said, trying to sound joking and casual.

Tabitha's cheeks flushed. Her lips, which had remained parted, clamped tight into a wire-thin line. The sympathetic emotion in her eyes grew hard and flat, almost like a light going out.

"That's not funny," she said.

"What's not?"

"That cave comment." Her words came out in rhythmic bursts, like steel banging against steel. "It's not funny."

"It's just an expression. Everybody says it."

"I should go." In one quick, fluid motion, she pushed herself away from the desk and grabbed her coat, moving to the door like someone rushing to catch a bus.

Jared barely had time to move. He walked a couple of steps behind her as she glided through the bedroom door, turning to the right and the front of the house. "Tabitha? Wait."

He followed her, hurrying. The denim from her jeans made a sharp brushing noise as she walked away from him, and Jared had to jog to reach her before she made it to the living room.

"Wait. Please."

She stopped. He started to reach out and touch her arm, but some instinct told him to back off, that no one as angry as Tabitha was wanted to be touched at a moment like this.

But she had stopped.

She kept her back to him, her shoulders moving as she breathed heavily with anger.

"I'm sorry," he said again. "I was just . . . I didn't mean anything."

She didn't respond. But she didn't leave. He took that as a good sign, one that meant he still had a chance to keep her in the house for a little while longer.

"I didn't mean to insult you or your dad. I don't care where you live. I was just being a smart-ass. I do that sometimes."

"It's not . . . That's not what I'm mad about."

"What, then?"

"Forget it," she said. "I should go."

"No, I want you to stay. Please?" Jared decided to pull out all the stops, open up the way he wanted her to. If he was going to lay it all on the line, he figured this was the time to do it. "I want to tell you something else. About Celia. And my mom. About what I had to do with her disappearing."

She turned to face him, her eyes open wide.

And she stayed.

David Bell is a bestselling and award-winning author whose work has been translated into multiple foreign languages. He's currently an associate professor of English at Western Kentucky University in Bowling Green, Kentucky, where he directs the MFA program. He received an MA in creative writing from Miami University in Oxford, Ohio, and a PhD in American literature and creative writing from the University of Cincinnati. His previous novels are *Since She Went Away*, *Somebody I Used to Know*, *The Forgotten Girl*, *Never Come Back*, *The Hiding Place*, and *Cemetery Girl*.

CONNECT ONLINE

davidbellnovels.com
facebook.com/davidbellnovels
twitter.com/davidbellnovels